You Were There Too

YOU WERE THERE TOO

COLLEEN OAKLEY

THORNDIKE PRESS
A part of Gale, a Cengage Company

Thorndike Press, a part of Gale, a Cengage Company.

ALL RIGHTS RESERVED
Thorndike Press® Large Print Women's Fiction.
The text of this Large Print edition is unabridged.
Other aspects of the book may vary from the original edition.
Set in 16 pt. Plantin.

LIBRARY OF CONGRESS CIP DATA ON FILE.
CATALOGUING IN PUBLICATION FOR THIS BOOK
IS AVAILABLE FROM THE LIBRARY OF CONGRESS

ISBN-13: 978-1-4328-7938-9 (hardcover alk. paper)

Published in 2020 by arrangement with Berkley, an imprint of Penguin Publishing Group, a division of Penguin Random House, LLC

Printed in Mexico
Print Number: 01   Print Year: 2020

For my husband, Fred

PROLOGUE

The sky is still blue.

That's what seems impossible to me. Not the fact that I'm somehow flat on my back, when just minutes earlier I was standing upright, both feet planted firmly on the ground.

Or that seconds before that, I was staring at the business end of a gun (a *gun!*), pointed directly at me (*me!*), as if I were on a movie set instead of in a throng of strangers milling about, oblivious that their lives would all soon be inextricably connected.

I blink, squinting against the electric cerulean of the sky, marveling at its continued beauty, its steadfast cheerfulness, somehow unmarred by what it just bore witness to. And then my other senses come screaming back one by one. And I'm aware of the heavy weight against my chest, a body pinning me to the asphalt, the drumbeat of my heart thudding in my ears.

Twisting my neck, I tear my eyes from the sky, and immediately wish I hadn't.

The blood is everywhere. Or maybe it's not, but like a piece of spinach wedged in a tooth, it draws the eye. It's the only thing I can see.

Panic grips me. I turn to the left, my eyes frantically searching. And that's when I see him. The top of his head, anyway.

It's still.

Like a fruit bowl in an amateur painting.

Like the sky.

Like my breath.

I try to inhale, to fill my lungs, but I can't, and it's got nothing to do with the weight on my chest.

Move, I think. Or maybe I say it out loud, but I don't know if I'm talking to myself or to the body trapping me to the ground.

Regardless, neither obeys me.

"Get off!" I shout, pushing with all my strength. And finally, I'm free. I inhale again, the thick metallic smell of blood filling my nostrils.

I don't think it's mine.

But I don't know anything for sure.

Or maybe, that's not true.

I knew this was coming, didn't I? The signs were always there, jumbled up like an

8

incomplete jigsaw puzzle, but there just the same.

I try to stand, go to him, but my knees buckle, as I realize the other thing I know for sure — and I can't believe I ever questioned it, even for a second.

It's him.

It's always been him.

CHAPTER 1

The office is cool and sparsely decorated. I count the plants (three), watch the second hand of the brass clock on the bookshelf make two full circles on its axis, stare at the large canvas on the wall, a lone red smear of paint in the center. I look anywhere but directly at Nora, the pristine, chignoned, straight-backed woman sitting in the executive chair across the desk from me — not because she's flipping through my portfolio and I've never quite gotten comfortable with witnessing the judgment of my work, but because she's wearing a neck scarf. Just seeing it, wrapped tightly like a noose, knotted right at her clavicle, makes my skin crawl with anxiety. How do people wear things wrapped around their throats? I've never understood it. Even as a kid, if my mom put me in a turtleneck, I would grasp at it, wheezing and crying and carrying on until she let me change.

I'm pretty sure I was strangled to death in a previous life.

Harrison says that's morbid, but I once heard one of those late-night television psychics say that a lot of the fears we're born with stem from events in our past lives. Like, if you are terrified of swimming in the ocean, maybe you drowned or were ravaged by a school of piranha or something.

Harrison also says I should stop watching so many of those late-night television psychic shows.

The room is silent, save the sharp machine-gun-fire rapping of Nora's pen against the desktop. A pattern has emerged. She pauses the pen when she turns a page and then resumes as she gazes — thoughtfully, I hope — at the photos of my paintings.

There are thirteen art galleries in Hope Springs, Pennsylvania (excessive for a town with two thousand inhabitants, if you ask me, and I'm an artist). Only three show contemporary work, this one, and two others who have already turned down my paintings. Translation? This is kind of my last shot. But I'm hopeful, because at least here, I actually have a third-degree personal connection — my old college professor Rick Haymond called in a favor to a friend, who

11

in turn called Nora, and now here I am.

"Mia?"

"Yes?" I say, meeting her eyes.

"Is this a portrait of . . . Keanu Reeves?"

I clear my throat. "Um . . . yes."

Her pen stills. She looks up at me, expectantly.

"That was part of my latest series."

She waits, and I clear my throat again.

"Have you ever watched *The $25,000 Pyramid?*" I ask.

"I'm sorry?"

"The game show."

"I — I believe so." She narrows her eyes, unsure of where this is going.

"You know how the celebrities start saying a bunch of random words, like 'wheels, buttons, beach balls,' and then the contestant has to guess what the category is — like, in this example: *Things That Are Round?*"

"OK."

"Well, I find that fascinating — the groupings of seemingly unrelated things that actually do have something in common. That's how I choose the themes for my series."

She continues to stare at me, and I can't decide if she's perplexed or bored. "And Keanu Reeves?"

"The theme was: *Things That Are Mediocre.*"

Her eyes remain locked on mine, but she doesn't respond. She reminds me of a detective on one of those cop shows, the patient one, willing to wait out the suspect. I cave. I would be a terrible criminal. "Also in that series is the orange Tootsie Pop."

"The orange Tootsie Pop," she repeats.

"Right, because orange isn't bad, but it's nobody's favorite, right? And then, let's see, Capri pants, store-bought tomatoes — that's why I painted them with the sticker still on — Easter . . ." She breaks eye contact as I'm speaking so I trail off.

She stares at the image for a beat and then looks back up, her face twisted. "You think *Keanu Reeves* is mediocre?" she says. "But he's so handsome and self-deprecating and . . . *respectful of women.*" The last phrase she emphasizes so forcefully her hand clenches into a fist.

"Yeah," I agree lamely. Because he *is* all of those things, and the way she's gushing tells me it wouldn't be prudent to explain that it's his lack of acting range I'm referring to and not him personally. "It was funnier when I painted it. Before . . ." I trail off again because I don't know how to finish that sentence. Before he became some kind

13

of *national treasure?*

"Hm," she says and flips through a few more pages non-committally. Then, more to the desk than to me, she says: "How . . . interesting." But the way Nora's voice goes down at the end and not up in praise is how I know she doesn't really think it is interesting. And how I know that I'm not going to get a showing at this gallery, either.

When I step back out into the midday June heat, I nearly run smack into two guys linked arm in arm. The one in man sandals and teal gingham shorts pulls the other back to let me pass. "I'm so sorry," I say, as my hand goes to my stomach, a protective mother's instinct for the fetus currently residing there, then I scoot around the men and out onto the street. Dodging in and out of other well-dressed tourists, I pass a chocolatier, an olive oil boutique and a store that sells nothing but spices. *Seventeen kinds of salt!* I whispered to Harrison when we, too, were another one of those tourist couples five months ago, and ducked in to look around. *I never knew there was more than one.* Having known me and my lack of culinary skills for the better part of eight years, this did not surprise him.

On Mechanic Street, the cell in my shoul-

14

der bag vibrates and I dig it out. A text from Harrison.

How'd it go?

I scroll through my gifs until I find a picture of an army tank and text it back.

That bad? Did you wear the lucky dress?

I hold the phone at arm's length, making sure my prize possession — a yellow wrap dress I scored at a thrift store and was wearing the night I met Harrison — is in the frame and press send. Not so lucky, I guess.

I slip the phone into the front pocket of my portfolio case, exchanging it for my car keys. Then I unlock the door to my Toyota, get in, turn the key and start the fifteen-minute trek home.

Five months ago, Harrison and I decided to move to this tiny town on a whim, which sounds like something I would do, but not Harrison. It was January, in Philadelphia, and it was snowing. Again. The kind of cold, wet snow that seeps into your clothes and your bones and makes you want to never leave your apartment, and if you do, makes you feel like you're never going to be warm again.

"Let's get out of here," Harrison said one Friday afternoon, when he got home from an extra-long shift at the hospital. He had had a tough few weeks, long hours on top of losing an eight-year-old boy during a routine emergency appendectomy. He didn't talk about it much — he never does — but I could tell it affected him.

"And go where?" I asked.

"Anywhere but here," he said.

Harrison is not the spontaneous type, so I immediately agreed. We drove north on 95 and ended up in Hope Springs, a tiny town west of the Delaware River. It was full of more antique stores and art galleries than any town needs, and I was drunk on its charm, and the way that the snow, for some mysterious reason, didn't quite feel so wet and cold and was piled up in pretty white mounds alongside the road instead of the gray, slushy heaps we were accustomed to. By Sunday, when we were packing up to leave, and dreading the drive back to the city, and I said, "I wish we could live here," which is what I say every time we go on vacation anywhere, Harrison said, "We can."

Then he said he'd been thinking about it for months — how the city hospital was so stressful and how maybe at a smaller hospital he could scale back, breathe a little — so why not now and why not in Hope Springs. And maybe it was because I had just had my second miscarriage and my first huge career failure and all of those things hap-

16

pened in Philadelphia and not in Hope Springs, or maybe because I really was convinced that the snow here was less cold and less wet and more beautiful, or maybe because the name of the town, *Hope Springs,* suddenly seemed significant, like an omen, but I said, "OK." And though it took a few months of interviews and tying up loose ends in Philadelphia, that's how we ended up moving from the apartment we'd lived in together for seven years and living here.

Two right angles of white picket fencing flank our driveway, which is the only way I know where to turn, since everything on the two-lane road that runs past our house looks exactly the same — green and tree-lined. I pull the car between them and roll slowly over the gravel until the stone house comes into view. It's a renovated three-bedroom farmhouse from the 1800s, so it has that great mix of old-world charm and a Sub-Zero fridge. The studio — a detached one-car garage behind the house — has windows on all four sides. Amazing light. That's what sold me on it. Or maybe it was simply the idea of having my own studio, instead of a one-hundred-square-foot den that also held a TV, a small bookcase and a futon, all flecked with hardened bits of acrylic paint, shellac, egg yolk (from an ill-advised DIY tempera phase) and various other substances from my artistic endeavors over the years.

The futon. Where, in my early twenties, I ate countless bowls of buttered noodles and slices of Nutella toast and watched reruns of *Family Feud* and then, in my late twenties, made furious love to Harrison on his all-too-short breaks home from his surgical residence shifts at Thomas Jefferson. Harrison convinced me to give the futon to charity when we moved — *It's starting to smell,* he said, gently, as if he were trying to talk me into euthanizing a beloved pet whose quality of life had deteriorated. And now instead of turning the car off and going into my studio to paint, which is what I *should* do, I have the sudden urge to turn my rusted Corolla around and drive to every single Goodwill store between here and Philadelphia until I find the futon and bring it home.

"Sorry I'm late," Harrison says when he walks through the front door that evening around nine, even though it's the third time that week he's gotten home past dark. Harrison's one of only four general surgeons on staff at the Fordham hospital, which serves not only the eight thousand residents

18

of Fordham, but many of the surrounding smaller towns, including Hope Springs. Though he said a smaller hospital would mean a slower pace, lately it's seemed like the opposite is true. He tosses his keys on top of an overturned cardboard box in the foyer that serves as our entry table, since I haven't gotten around to buying one.

Harrison leans over the back of the butter-yellow sofa I'm sitting on — one of the few new things I have managed to purchase for the house. I offer him my cheek and he kisses it, his full beard (also new since we moved here) scratching my face.

"Did your day get any better?" he asks.

"Not really."

He heads toward the kitchen, where I hear the fridge door open and then the muffled pop of a beer bottle being unscrewed. When he reappears in the doorframe, the beer's turned up at his lips. He takes three deep mouthfuls, pausing to swallow in between.

"I think I'm killing the tomatoes," I say. The house came with a large vegetable and herb garden that hadn't been tended to since the previous owner moved out. I planned to care for it, starting with weeding, but then realized I couldn't exactly tell what was a weed and what was a plant. And then the irrigation system stopped working.

And rabbits or rodents or bugs started having their share until each leaf (on plants *and* weeds) looked like Swiss cheese. And I realized that gardening actually takes a concerted effort and I have no idea what I'm doing.

"Well, I'm sure they deserve it," he says.

"Harrison. I'm serious. The leaves are yellow, which according to this website I've been reading means they're getting too much water or not enough or there's a lack of nitrogen in the soil or they're diseased."

"Huh," he says. "That narrows it down."

"Exactly."

I stare at his profile, taking in his black square-rimmed glasses; his undone bow tie, the ends hanging loose on either side of his unbuttoned collar like a disheveled groom; the ruffian beard that I'm still getting used to — and I get that fleeting inkling of wonder that I ended up with him. I had a type — and MD educated was not it. I preferred guys that had gigs to ones with real jobs, guys that missed rent payments. Abandonment issues were a bonus. But to be fair, Harrison was wearing a Skid Row T-shirt and standing in an art gallery when I met him, so it wasn't clear off the bat he was a functioning member of society.

I smile, remembering how it used to be,

in the beginning. The anticipation of seeing him. The pure thrill of reading his name on caller ID or hearing his knock at the door. It's unsustainable, of course, that level of elation and delight. Infatuation is like a rushing river that over time either dries up to a trickle and then nothing at all, or begins wearing its way into the earth, until one day it's a deep, yawning canyon.

Harrison and I are lucky.

We've got the canyon.

"You know — it's weird." He slides his beer onto the antique trunk that doubles as our coffee table and sinks into the couch cushion beside me. "They should have stores that sell gardening supplies and are staffed with people knowledgeable about plants that could help novices in situations just like this."

I jab my elbow to the side, connecting with his stomach. "Oof," he says, then grabs my hand, lacing his fingers through mine. He gently turns it over. Looks at it. Rubs his thumb over the red and blue splotches. "D'you paint today?"

"A little," I say. And by little, I mean forty-five minutes. Though it was Harrison's idea that I focus on my art when we moved here, I haven't had a serious session or painted anything decent in the five weeks since we pulled the yellow Ryder truck up to the front curb. At first, I told myself it was because we were getting settled. But at this point, I know it's something more . . . permanent. A zap to my confidence that started when that mustachioed Phillip Gaston typed, "an incohesive amateur display relying too heavily on an overly clever theme, without the talent to add depth and substance," regarding my first-ever solo exhibition in Philadelphia last year.

"Did you wear a mask?"

He's teasing me. I've been extra cautious with this pregnancy — to the point of asking Harrison if he thought the fumes of the acrylics I work with could be bad for a developing fetus. He said no, but even after he showed me proof online that they were safe to use while pregnant, I wondered aloud if I should wear a mask anyway.

"I didn't," I say. "Do you think I should have?"

"No," he says, and then pauses, a half grin on his lips. "But if our baby comes out with twelve toes, we'll know why."

"Harrison!"

We sit in silence for a minute, the words "our baby" hanging in the air. At least they are for me. I think of the two babies that we lost, and suck in a lungful of air to steady

22

myself. I had no idea how much I could grieve the loss of something I never really had. A person I never met. But I do. I am. And I wonder if the sadness will lessen with time — or if the fear of losing yet another will ever dissipate. I place my hand on my belly, silently willing this one to stay.

As if reading my mind, Harrison wraps his long arm around me, pulling me to his chest. They were out of his regular deodorant when I was at the store on Tuesday, so I picked out a new scent and the soapy pine forest tang of it tickles my nose. I burrow my head into him, as if I could tunnel a path and stay there for all of eternity. "You smell good."

"Really? I thought it was a little teenager-drenched-in-Dad's-cologne-ish."

"No," I say. And even though it's different, a new scent, it's still him. Still my Harrison. "It's you."

I'm on a ferry. At least, I assume it's a ferry — a large, slightly rocking barge of a boat filled with cars and people — but I don't know where it's going or why I'm on it. The sky is dull, the color of ashes from an abandoned campfire. A flock of gulls squawks overhead and I look up. When they've past, I drop my eyes back to the horizon.

That's when I see him. He's far away on the sandy shoreline, and though I can't quite make out his face, I know it's him. A strong wind flattens his shaggy hair, pasting the front of it to his forehead, the back flying up every which way like confetti at a parade.

And then suddenly he's on the boat. Standing in front of me. And the part of my brain that knows this is a dream wonders if it will be a kissing dream. Hopes it will be a kissing dream. The attraction I have for him is so intense, I have to will my dream knees to stay locked in place, my dream stomach to stop flopping over itself like a Raggedy Ann doll tumbling down the stairs.

"Hi," he says, his lips spreading into a grin that matches mine.

"Hi," I say.

He takes my hand. And though I know it should be chilly — he's wearing a coat and all I have on is some flimsy sundress — I feel warm.

And then we're in the middle of a museum, just like that. One setting morphing into another in the way only dreams can do. I'm staring at a sculpture, one that looks like Rodin's *Man with the Broken Nose,* but it's actually that awful Phillip Gaston's countenance and it starts talking. Shouting at me, really. I can't make out the words, but I'm both perfectly accepting that a sculpture is talking to me and equally embarrassed that it's happening in front of *him*. And then he moves so close to me, the smooth buttons of his coat press into my bare arm, his hot breath on my neck. He's saying something, too, but I can't focus. All the sounds meld together into a steady beeping that grows louder and louder until I wake up.

I open my eyes as Harrison sits up, sliding his glasses on and palming his cell in one fluid motion, silencing the offensive beeping.

"What time is it?" I ask, my voice hoarse. I try to swallow past my guilt — even as I feel silly feeling guilty. It was just a dream. *He's* just a dream.

It's only that — at times — he feels so real. And has for all the years that he's been starring in my nighttime reveries.

"Three thirty-five," Harrison says. He slides out of bed to call the hospital, shutting the bedroom door behind him, but I can still hear the low timbre of his voice in the hallway.

I lie there, trying to return to sleep, but it's gone.

25

When I was in high school and realized the same man was reappearing in my dreams time after time, it was exciting, a novelty. Some hot fantasy guy my hormone-riddled brain had conjured. I also thought it must be common, something most people experience, but when I mentioned it to my sister, Vivian, she hooted. "I wish a hot man would visit me every night in my dreams!"

"It's not like that," I said, embarrassed at how sexual she made it sound, even though sometimes it was exactly like that. "And it's not every night." And it wasn't. It was more like every couple weeks, or months even. I've noticed they only become frequent during big life changes: Graduating college. Getting married. Pregnancy. The dreams have been almost nightly the past week — more than in either of my previous pregnancies, and I wonder if it's because I'm further along. That this pregnancy is thriving. I take comfort in any signs I can get.

Anyway, after Vivian's response, I never mentioned it again. To anyone. Not even Harrison — but still I wonder if maybe he has his own fantasy girl. Some Camila Alves look-alike that he doesn't mention to spare my feelings. Then I think of the intensity of my interactions in my dreams, and a bud of jealousy sprouts in my stomach. On second thought, I hope Harrison doesn't have his own.

The bedroom door opens and Harrison reappears beside me. "I gotta go in," he whispers, leaning over to peck my cheek. I turn, so his lips land on mine, and reach up to hold his face steady, parting his lips with my tongue.

"Mmm," he says, pulling back an inch to look at me. "What's that for?"

I cheekily raise my eyebrows. His expression mirrors mine. "Three minutes," he says. "That's all I've got."

"I'll take it," I say. He grins and pounces in one quick motion and I laugh at his teenage-like eagerness. As his body so familiarly finds mine, his beard scrapes my cheek and his lips are against my ear. "Dios Mia," he whispers.

It's ours, this phrase, coined after we kissed for the first time huddled underneath the too-small awning of a dry cleaner's to escape a sudden downpour on our way from an art gallery to a dive bar. The night we met.

"Dios Mia," he murmured when our lips finally broke apart, both of us out of breath, his nose still millimeters from mine.

I cocked an eyebrow, not willing to risk breaking the spell by moving any other part

27

of my body. I only took high school Spanish, but I knew enough to know that the phrase *Oh my god* in Spanish was masculine: Dios Mío. I wondered if I'd misheard him, even as I said: "I thought it was Mío."

"What?" he asked, his lips curling up, as they grazed mine once again. And that was when I knew I'd heard him right. And that he was teasing me.

"You said Mia," I whispered against his mouth. "It's supposed to be Mío."

"And here you said you didn't know any Spanish," he said. And then his fingers were in my hair and his mouth was on mine and I didn't give a whit that water was bulleting in a direct line off the awning and right onto my shoulder, down into my purse, ruining everything I owned.

Now, with his words in my ear and the muscles of his back flexing beneath my palms, a wave of love and contentment floods through me, and whatever guilt I was feeling from my ridiculous dream melts away almost as easily as the night.

Almost.

CHAPTER 2

"Finley has lice," my sister, Vivian, says.

"Gross." I pull a face, and shift my cell between my ear and shoulder so I can scrape the last of the yogurt out of its container with my spoon.

"You have no idea. I had to leave work early to get her from school, pay a ridiculous amount of money for this special comb and lice-repellent shampoo, and then when we got home, the nanny left because she *doesn't do bugs.* That's what she said, verbatim. *I don't do bugs.* And now it feels like these things are crawling all over me and I basically want to burn everything in my house."

"GRIFFIN!" she yells and I pull the phone a few inches from my ear. I stare out the big picture window over the kitchen sink and eye the branches of the droopy tomato plants climbing out of the jungle of a garden as if they're trying to escape. Vivian is still yelling. "TOILET PAPER IS NOT FOR

EATING." Finally, her voice returns to its normal volume. "So, how are you? Have you finished unpacking yet?"

In a weak moment last week, I made the mistake of confessing to Vivian that maybe I'd been feeling a little aimless, that I wasn't sure the move had been the right thing for me, and of course she went full therapist on me, talking about adjustment periods and life stages and how I needed to finish unpacking — that it was a symbolic step of accepting where I am or some bullshit like that. Vivian's a psychologist at a private high school in Maryland, and sometimes she has trouble turning it off.

I consider how to respond, but before I can say anything, I feel a twinge in my stomach. I gasp, pressing a hand gently to it, but then it's gone as quickly as it came.

"Mia? You OK?"

"Yeah — it's nothing." I try to remind myself of the other thing Vivian told me last week — that I'm going to be sensitive to every little ache and pain because of what I've been through and I can't stress about it because pregnancy is full of aches and pains.

"FINLEY, STOP SPITTING ON YOUR BROTHER. So — unpacking?"

"I'm working on it," I say, even though I'm not. Not really. I keep meaning to

30

unpack. Buy the things we need, like an entry table, but the choices are so over-whelming. Or maybe it's the house that's overwhelming. We lived in a shoebox for so long, I don't know what to do with all this newfound space, or how to fill it. Ironic, considering I spent nearly my entire time in Philly working in an upscale furniture store, first in sales, then as a design consultant, helping clients pick out the perfect pieces and decide where to put them.

Deep down, though, I know it's not the space or the house that feels overwhelming, and suddenly I blurt out the one thing I've been terrified to admit — to myself, much less Harrison. "It doesn't feel like this is where I'm supposed to be."

"What do you mean?" she asks.

"I don't know — I can't explain it. But I keep thinking at any second we're going to drive back to Philly. That our apartment is still waiting for us. That we're going to go home."

"I think that's normal. You guys lived there for what — seven years? And honestly, Mia," she says, gently, "you've never han-dled change well." I know she's referring to Mom and Dad's divorce. How I cried myself to sleep for months. Started wetting the bed at age eleven. And then at Christ-

31

mas, convinced myself that Mom was coming back. That it was going to be our big gift that year. Needless to say, it was a disappointing holiday.

"NO, FINLEY! YOU JUST HAD A SQUEEZY YOGURT. NO MORE SNACKS. And remember — you've got all those pregnancy hormones rushing through your body. They can make you feel crazy. Hang in there. I'm sure once you get settled, and when the baby comes, everything will be different. Better. You'll see."

My gaze drifts back to the vegetable garden and the yellow-spotted tomato plants. I sigh. It's sensible advice, which is the only kind Vivian gives. And though I hate it when she's right, this time I really do hope she is.

There are only seven tomato plants at the True Value — six of them have little green orbs of fruit weighing down the stems and the seventh's leaves are yellowed and hangdog like the ones in my garden. I gently rub a leaf of the pitiful one between my finger and thumb, wondering if it has the same affliction.

"Epsom salt," says a gravelly voice behind me.

Instead of the man I expect to see, my eyes

32

meet those of a gray-bouffanted woman. She's tall and thin, with wrinkles of skin gathered at her jowls. Underneath her red apron is a flowery blouse open at the neck, where a thick necklace of shiny blue beads rests in her clavicle. Her name tag reads: *Jules.*

"Excuse me?" I ask, unsure if she was speaking to me, even though she's looking right at me.

She gestures to the plant I'm holding. "Soil's probably got a magnesium deficiency. Epsom salt can help. It's not a lack of water, because it's been getting the same amount as these others. And I don't think it's fungal — no black spots on the leaves."

She glances back at the cash register where a man with a thick neck and even thicker hands is counting change for a customer. Then she ducks her head closer to me, so close that I can smell the sourness of her breath. "Marty will probably give it to you for free, if you buy a couple of these others. It's past planting season and he wants to get rid of 'em."

"Oh, I already have tomato plants," I say. "But they all look like this one. I was hoping to get some advice."

"Mm," she grunts. "Epsom salt," she repeats. "We don't sell it here, though. You'll have to head over to the Giant."

"Thank you," I say.

She nods and turns to go.

"Wait," I say, wishing I could download all the information from her head into mine somehow. I was so naive in thinking that taking care of a garden would be simple — that the hard part of planting was already done and in a few months I would be harvesting waxy purple eggplants (if there are even eggplants in the garden — I can't tell what half of the vegetation is) and big plump tomatoes that Harrison could turn into spaghetti sauce or salsa or whatever else you can make with tomatoes.

She looks back at me, patient. "Yes?"

"Do you guys have a service — like people that will come out and do garden care or something? I'm new to all of this and not quite sure what I'm doing."

"You want a lawn service?"

"I mean, I don't need my lawn mowed or anything —" Although, on second thought that might be nice, too. Harrison can barely keep up with how fast the grass grows and it takes him two hours to do the back on the riding lawnmower he bought when we moved in. I offered to do it, but he cited *my delicate condition* and I didn't argue with him. Mostly because I didn't really want to mow the lawn.

"Well, we don't do that anyway," she says. "You'll have to call a landscape company. We do have garden classes, though, once a month. May was on crop rotation, but there's another this Saturday. I think it's summer annuals, but I'd have to check."

"Thanks," I say, and she leaves me alone with the pitiful plant. It's so dejected looking, I almost can't bear to leave it, knowing no one else will buy it in its condition. *Bleeding heart.* I can hear Harrison's voice in my ear and the way he makes fun of me every time I bring home something that's been abandoned — the futon was one such thing, left on the corner of my block; a cat I found on Sansom Street that turned out to be more feral than stray; a pink, child-size mitten left behind on a seat of a bus. I should have left that one — what if someone came looking for it, I wondered later with a pang — but in the moment, it looked so lonely, so vulnerable without its match, I couldn't bear it. Harrison just stared at me, eyebrows heavenward, for what felt like a full twenty-four hours after I explained it to him.

Fifteen minutes later, as I walk through the sliding glass doors of the Giant to buy

Epsom salt, I remember Harrison saying that morning we had one spoonful of coffee left.

I pick up a basket and hook it over my arm, then head to the coffee and cereal aisle, where I stand surveying the different flavors — medium roast, Colombian, hazelnut, French vanilla — even though I'll get the Folgers breakfast blend, like always. And then the yeasty smell of baking bread draws me to the bakery and I tuck a still-warm loaf of ciabatta into my basket. I stroll through the aisles and grocery shop the way that drives Harrison crazy — no list, just picking up things that appeal to me. Today, I choose a hunk of Gruyère, a tub of silky mozzarella rounds, tomatoes, a bag of Cheetos and a foam tray of triangled watermelon.

I walk toward the checkout and have that niggling feeling there's something I'm forgetting. And then like a flash it comes to me — Epsom salt. Of course. The actual reason I came to the Giant in the first place. It's from moments like this, I'm convinced "pregnancy brain" is a real affliction.

The salt isn't anywhere to be found near the table salt and seasonings and I have to ask two different stock boys before I finally find it lurking with the health and beauty products. The only size they carry is a twenty-five-pound bag and I heft it up into the crook of my arm.

At the checkout line, I become engrossed in a tabloid cover speculating on the number of babies Princess Kate is currently carrying in her royal womb. Even though she's probably not even pregnant, even though it's uncharitable, I can't help but think that she's greedy. Doesn't she already have three?

The clerk rings up each item and hands me my receipt. I step to the end of the lane to collect my two plastic bags of groceries from a balding older man in a black apron, when the automatic glass door twenty yards away slides open, drawing my attention. A man walks into the store.

I freeze. A cold electric current runs from the base of my skull down my spine. My heart thuds once and then stops.

Maybe forever.

It's *him.* And then, as if I've willed him to do it, he looks up, eyes locking with mine.

"Ma'am?"

I blink.

Turn my head toward the balding man, who is holding out my twenty-five-pound bag of Epsom salt. "Oh. Right," I say, before looking at the plastic bags of groceries I'm clutching in each hand. My mind a jumble, I futz about before finally shifting all the

37

bags to one hand, so I can heft the salt back into the crook of my right arm.

When I look back up at the door, no one is there.

He's gone.

Like an apparition.

A dream.

Loaded down with my purchases, I hurry toward the door and then stop where he was standing and look toward the produce section and the aisles where he may have gone. My eyes scan various shoppers, but none of them are him.

I've half a mind to take off into the store, going aisle by aisle until I find him, but then I give my head a firm shake. It couldn't have been *him*. Obviously. *He* is a figment of my imagination. It was only someone that looked like him. I hear Vivian in my mind: *All those pregnancy hormones can make you feel crazy.*

I have been out of sorts — forgetful, caught up in my thoughts. That must be what it is.

Still, I glance around the store one last time before exiting through the doors, into the full-blast heat of the day.

CHAPTER 3

I'm eating a wedge of watermelon when I hear the front door open and shut. It's not even five, too early for Harrison to be home, and I cock my head, my heart racing.

When I hear the familiar sound of his keys hitting cardboard, his footfalls crossing the hardwood, relief courses through me, but it's not until he actually appears at the doorway to the kitchen that I let out my breath.

"You scared me."

"Didn't you ask me to be home early?" he asks, shrugging out of his suit jacket and loosening the knot of his bow tie in one fluid motion.

I stare at him blankly. "Wait — is it Friday?" I really am losing it. Or maybe that's the problem with not having a job — all the days completely run together.

"Yeah," he says.

"Raya's coming!" I leap off the stool and

39

throw myself at Harrison.

He wraps his arms around me. "I'm gonna pretend all this enthusiasm is for me," he says. "And, I'm going to start cooking, because even though Raya said she's bringing dinner, we both know she's going to forget."

"No, she won't," I say, smacking him on the arm. He reaches for a slice of watermelon and bites into it, a pink stream of juice running down his chin. He swipes it with the back of his hand. "Is the mime coming with her?"

"Marcel's a performance artist," I say, chiding him.

"He's a mime."

I pause. "OK, he's a mime."

"I can't believe she's still with him," he says.

"Well, better him than Jesse, right?"

"True."

"And she really likes him, so you need to be nice."

"I'm always nice," he says.

"You are always nice," I agree.

"But I can't promise I'm not going to roll my eyes if he quotes David Bowie again. I swear it was at least three times."

"Fair enough," I say. "How was work? What was the middle-of-the-night emergency this time?"

"Appendectomy," he says, and his shoulders fall, as if he's only now allowing the weight of it to sink in.

I pause. Appendectomies are one of the most common — and easiest — surgeries Harrison does, next to gallbladders, but ever since he lost that eight-year-old boy in Philly during a routine appendectomy, they've been hard for him, emotionally. Not that he talks about it much. He tries to distance himself, to detach, as all doctors must if they are to survive the things they witness. But some patients, like Noah, inevitably get to him. He carries the weight of them around like rocks in his pockets. And I worry that one day he won't be able to stand from the burden.

"How'd it go?"

"It was . . . interesting, actually. When the nurse did the ultrasound to confirm the appendicitis, she also confirmed a pregnancy."

I raise my eyebrows. "The woman didn't know?"

"She does now. I think she was quite surprised. Almost made her forget how much pain she was in."

"But everything turned out OK? I didn't know a pregnant woman could have surgery."

"Yeah." He shrugs. "Went in laparoscopically. It's pretty low risk."

"Look at you. Saving two lives at once." I bat my eyelashes at him. "My hero."

He rolls his eyes. "Anything else interesting happen today?"

My mind flashes to the man I saw at the Giant. The man I thought was *him*. I consider telling Harrison. *I do have a funny story,* I would say, laughing. But is it funny? I think again about how I would feel if Harrison was having dreams about the same woman.

"Nope," I say. "I'm going to go change."

"I thought we'd never make it," Raya says as she sweeps past me into the foyer an hour later. "My cell reception was shit and we passed your driveway what — eight times?"

"Yeah, it's not marked well," I say as I hug her. She smells like Raya, a mix of acrid chemicals — from the bright red dye she douses her hair with every few weeks — and peppermint essential oil.

"Your hair's grown out," she says, fingering my black locks. I chopped it, my hair, on a whim after we lost the second baby. One morning I left the house with it swinging down to my midback, and by the time Harrison got home that night, it barely reached the bottom of my chin. A razor cut, the stylist called it, and I liked how raw it sounded. The edges jagged and sharp, like the way I felt.

Marcel follows and I offer my cheek for him to kiss. Though he's freshly showered, he still retains a faint metallic scent from the copper paint he coats himself with for his street performances. His tank top reveals arms covered in tattoos — a dragon breathing fire coils up his left side while M. C. Escher's famous hand-drawing-a-hand, various flowers, and a skull with a mustache decorate the other. His dark hair is slicked back on both sides with an impressive amount of pomade.

"Shit," Raya says, as she's embracing Harrison.

"What?" We all look at her.

"I was supposed to bring dinner, wasn't I?"

Harrison gives me a look over her head.

"Oh well, we'll order something," she says, pulling out her phone and inspecting it. "Finally — I have one bar. What delivery app do you guys use?"

I smirk. "Nothing delivers out here. Unless you want gas station pizza." We ordered it once in a moment of desperation, and a greasy-haired teenager came out on his

43

moped, delivering a cardboard box that contained what appeared to be a frozen grocery store pizza heated up under a hot lamp. Harrison thought it was hilarious, and I joined in laughing, but mostly to keep from crying.

Raya's face registers equal parts disgust and shock. "How are you surviving?"

"She's got me," Harrison says. "Don't worry, I'm sure I can find something to whip up."

Later, over grilled mozzarella and tomato sandwiches and red wine in the living room, Paul Simon sings about Graceland from the Bluetooth speaker as Raya regales us with stories from her day job as a tour bus guide in the city. I lean forward eagerly from my perch on the floor. Raya is funny and captivating and it's been so long since I've seen her, I feel the need to drink her in while she's here. When she's exhausted her crazy-tourist stories, she starts catching me up on our art school friends.

"Did you hear about Prisha?" Prisha Khanna was a year ahead of us, and by far the most commercially successful artist to come out of our time at Moore. A photographer, her provocative portraits of women have been part of a traveling exhibition in museums worldwide. I've never been partic-

44

ularly drawn to her work, but it was at the opening night of her first showcase at a small gallery in Center City that I met Harrison. For that alone, I'm happy for her success.

"The exhibit's coming to Philly."

"Really? Which museum?"

"*The* museum. Philadelphia."

"What? Wow," I say.

"I know! And some big celebrity bought one of her photos. I can't remember now — Taylor Swift, maybe? Anyway, she's big-time — that's why she's a finalist for Moore's Visionary Woman Awards."

"Really?"

"Yeah, it was in the newsletter. The gala's in September. I'll grab us tickets."

I make a noise that I hope sounds interested. Just because I'm happy for her doesn't mean I'm not also a little jealous. I try to swallow it down with a sip of water.

"Oh, and Fletcher. You know how she was always collecting those old lamps from flea markets, but wasn't sure what she was going to end up doing with them?"

"Yeah," I say.

"Well, they're an exhibit now — all fifty-six of them crammed into a room in a gallery on Arch Street."

"Like a light installation?"

"No, that's the thing — she put new bulbs in them, but didn't plug any of them in." She grins. "She's calling it: *Potential.*"

I laugh. "Sounds like Fletcher."

"Sounds more like Chris Burden, if you ask me," says Marcel. He's eaten around the edges of his sandwich like a bird, and he places it back on the plate in his lap.

"Who?" asks Harrison.

"The *Urban Light* guy?" Marcel says.

Harrison's face remains blank.

"Artist out in California," I say. "He installed, like, two hundred vintage street-lamps in rows in front of the Los Angeles County Museum of Art."

"At least those were turned on," Raya laughs. "And they're pretty at night."

Harrison leans forward to refill wine-glasses.

"Anyway, it's better than an exhibit of human skin." Raya eyes Marcel purposefully.

I slowly turn toward him; Harrison's head follows suit. "Um . . . explain?" I say.

"It's some article I read — there's a museum in London that has over three hundred tattoo specimens. Like, real pieces of human skin."

"Marcel's thinking of donating his," Raya chimes in. "After he's dead, of course."

"Ew," I say.

"Thank you," Raya says. "That's what I think, too."

"Why?" Marcel says. "It's art. Besides, how's it any different than preserving organs for scientific research? This is for posterity, too, in a different way." He turns to Harrison, no doubt looking for solidarity from the medical viewpoint, but Harrison holds up his hands.

"I don't know, man. It's a little too *Silence of the Lambs* for me."

"Yes!" Raya shrieks. "Put the lotion in the basket!"

We all laugh.

"So, what's the story with your tat, Mia?" Marcel asks. "I've never noticed it before."

I look down at the inside of my left wrist, at the three small Chinese characters, and smile. "It's nothing."

"Yes, please *tell us,*" Raya says. She's been trying to get it out of me for years.

"Nah. It's a long story." I feel Harrison's eyes on me, warming my skin.

"She lost a bet." Harrison pipes up. "To me."

"What bet?" she prods, but Harrison just smiles. Raya groans. "Whatever. Show them your new one, babe."

"His new what?" I ask. Marcel doesn't answer. He slides his plate off his lap onto

47

the coffee table and stands up, then turns, lifting his shirt up to reveal his skinny lower back — and a large full-color portrait of David Bowie.

"Oh!" I exclaim, before I can stop myself.

"I know, right?" he says, then quotes the words written beneath the image. *"There's a starman waiting in the sky. He'd like to come and meet us, but he thinks he'd blow our minds."*

"That is . . . something," Harrison says, catching my eye once again.

I hold my water glass up to my mouth and concentrate on not laughing, but it's no use.

That night I dream I'm back in the True Value. Jules is there in her apron and beads, but instead of sleeves her arms are covered in Marcel's tattoos, the dragon breathing fire onto her neck. She smiles and offers me a package. But her smile vanishes as I take a tinfoil-wrapped gift from her hands. I study the bundle, not understanding. When I look up, she's gone. And for some reason, a sense of dread fills my belly. I peel back a corner of the foil. A white downy feather peeks out. And then another. I quickly unwrap the rest with urgency, but it's too late.

The chicken in my hands is dead, and I

am gutted. Devastated. I'm grieving the life-less carcass of a helpless bird and I'm griev-ing it deeply, as if it were as precious to me as my sister or my dad or Harrison himself. Suddenly the chicken jerks in my hand, its big mouth gaping open, the large beak com-ing at me, a deafening squawk filling the air. Panicked, I open my mouth to scream, but nothing comes out. And then I wake up.

I open my eyes, taking in the darkness of my bedroom, my heart thudding double time in my chest. I take a deep breath.

It was a chicken. A nightmare about a chicken. I slowly release the air from my lungs.

Until I feel it. The heavy wetness, sticky between my thighs, and I forget all about the dream and the tinfoil and the chicken, and a wail escapes my lips, this time ringing out loud and clear into the air.

"Mia, what is it?" Harrison says, his voice groggy, his hand groping for my shoulder and gently squeezing.

The thin blanket on top of me is heavy, oppressive, so I throw it off and lay my hands gently on my cramping belly. "I'm losing it."

"What?" I hear the click of his bedside

lamp and light floods the room, temporarily blinds me. Harrison slides his glasses on and his gaze travels the length of me. His eyes widen, alarmed.

"Mia!" he shouts. I glance down and all I can see is the bright scarlet fanning out onto the sheets on either side of me. I know bleeding is part of the miscarriage process, but it's more — a lot more — than the spotting from the previous two losses.

"Oh my god — there's so much," Harrison says.

I jerk my head to him, even though he verbalized what I was thinking. "Seriously, Harrison?"

"What?" he says, standing up, but never taking his eyes off my body.

"You're a doctor. You're a *doctor!*"

"I know!" he says and rushes to the dresser. I let out a grunt of pain and clutch my stomach, feeling another gush of blood dampen the already saturated sheet beneath me.

"But Jesus," Harrison says as he reaches my side, gripping an old T-shirt in his fist. "You're my *wife!*"

The contraction passes and he puts his hand behind me, gently guiding me up, and then hands me the shirt. "Here, hold this down there. We're going to the hospital."

He scoops me up, and strangely, I flash to our wedding day when he spontaneously lifted me into his arms after the kiss, marching us back down the dirt-trodden path, grinning back like a fool at everyone cheering for us. Now, he rushes me to the car, grabbing his keys from the cardboard box in the foyer on his way, gently depositing me in the passenger side of his Infiniti, ignoring my shouts to take my car. "It's older — I'll ruin the leather in yours!"

The car is silent for the twenty-minute drive to Fordham, aside from my intervals of moaning brought on by a mix of the painful contractions and my overwhelming grief.

When we pull up in the emergency lane of the hospital, Harrison runs over to my side and lifts me back into his arms, hurriedly walking through the sliding glass doors into the fluorescent-bright waiting room. I turn away from the lights and bury my head into his neck.

I hear the exchange between him and the night nurse on duty as if I'm listening to a TV show.

"Dr. Graydon?" she says, recognizing him.

Harrison stops walking and without preamble announces: "My wife. She's having a miscarriage."

And at the word, I let out a sob against

his collarbone and press the hot wet of my
tears into his skin.

CHAPTER 4

Harrison doesn't cry.

I learned this a month after we moved in together, when he came home early from a shift at the hospital only to find me crossed-legged on the floor, my cheeks wet with tears.

"What's wrong?" he asked, rushing to my side.

"Nothing," I said, taking a deep breath and swiping under my eyes with my fingertips. "It's this song." I pointed at the air, filled with the sounds of Peter Cetera and Cher harmonizing: *"Two angels who've been rescued from the fall."*

He paused. "You're crying over a song?"

I shook my head no. "It's the movie!"

"What movie?"

"*Chances Are.* This is the song playing at the end when Cybill Shepherd walks down the aisle to Ryan O'Neal, and Robert Downey Jr. leans over and says, 'There's something I have to tell you. I'm in love with Miranda.' And Ryan looks at him and says —" I teared up again and couldn't finish.

Harrison looked at me warily. "Are you being serious right now?"

"What do you mean?"

"You're crying because a song reminded you of a scene in a movie that no one has heard of."

"*Chances Are* is a classic!"

"Is it?" He cocked an eyebrow, unable to wipe the grin off his face.

"Stop making fun of me. I'm an artist. I'm sensitive."

He laughed. "No, there's sensitive and then there's *this*. I don't even know what to call this."

"C'mon, don't you ever just need a good cry?"

"No," he said without hesitation. "I don't cry."

I would have thought he was being contrary but for the sincerity on his face. It stopped me short. "What do you mean? Like, ever?"

"Nope."

"That can't be true — not even when you lose a patient?"

"Nope."

"When's the last time you cried?"

He pondered the question. "Ita's funeral," he said, telling me he was eleven when his grandmother died. He remembered his mom fingering a rosary, muttering prayers in Spanish. His uncle walking a cartoonishly large ornate gold cross down the aisle of the church. And his dad tweaking his ear when, out of nowhere, a sob overcame him, shaking him to his core. "Be a man," his dad whispered, thumping his chest lightly with his fist.

"That's awful," I said, my heart breaking for eleven-year-old Harrison.

He shrugged. "No," he said. "What's awful is this song. Is that *Cher?* You hate Cher."

Dry-eyed, Harrison's currently sitting on a hard chair next to me, holding a Michael Crichton paperback open with his right hand, while his left gently rubs the inside of my wrist, absentmindedly tracing the small black tattoo with the pads of his fingers.

It's been four days since that night in the hospital. Since the nurse swiftly removed the blood-soaked disposable pads from beneath me, patted my knee and said, "The hard part's over," and I realized the "hard part" was our baby. Four days since Harrison assured me it wasn't my fault — "There's nothing we could have done" —

and I only half believed him.

And now, in the waiting room of an OB/GYN office for a postmiscarriage checkup, I feel like a soldier in a field of visual landmines. Nowhere is safe to look. Not the black-and-white photos of cherubic babies on every single wall, or the rounded bellies protruding from proud mothers-to-be, all glowing and puffed up with their success of carrying a baby nearly to term — I can't even look the receptionist in the eye, not wanting to see either her pity or judgment of my slack belly.

I keep my eyes trained to the floor, glancing up only when I hear a sharp peal of laughter that feels too loud for the hushed reverence of a waiting room. The woman is on her cell phone, her mouth wide and smiling, happy as can be, her stomach swollen and full. I stare at it sadistically, letting the raw jealousy, anger and grief course through me until I'm nearly vibrating with emotion.

She makes it all look so easy, this woman. I bet she was one of those who simply decided to become pregnant and whoopsie! Next thing you know, two darling little lines on the white stick. Part of me wants to jump up and grab her by the shoulders: *Why you? Why you and not me?* But I don't — not because that would be outrageous behavior

56

that would likely draw police officers to the scene, but because I'm secretly afraid she would whisper the answer, and it would sound something like: *You don't deserve them.*

The tears come quick, burning my eyes, stinging my nose, wetting my cheeks, and I brush them away with a practiced hand.

Dr. Okafor has a charming South African accent that set me at ease the first time I heard it. Today she's silent as she wands my belly, staring at the monitor. I bury my head in the crook of Harrison's arm, the grainy emptiness of the screen too much to bear.

After a few minutes of moving the baton back and forth and studying the screen, Dr. Okafor speaks. "OK," she says. "I don't see anything to cause concern here. How's the cramping?"

"Better," I admit. "But I'm still spotting."

"That's normal. Even for a few more weeks or so. If it gets worse, make sure you call," she says, echoing the ER doctor. She gives me a handful of tissues to wipe the goo off my belly. "Any questions for me?"

I clear my throat, hating to ask, but needing to know. "When can we . . . When is it OK . . ."

"To try again?" she supplies.

I nod and Harrison's bicep, which I'm still

holding on to, twitches.

"Physically, after your next normal cycle, you should be fine to start. Emotionally — it's up to you. Take all the time that you need. It's a difficult experience, I know."

Do you? I want to snarl. But I bite my lip. Maybe she does really know. I feel myself getting teary again and don't trust my voice, even to thank her for her kindness.

"I'd also like to recommend, if you do want to try again, that you see someone, a specialist, for testing. This being your third miscarriage, it's important to suss out any underlying factors that could be responsible, and if possible, hopefully correct them." I open my mouth to ask the obvious, but she holds up a hand. "I'm not saying it *is* anything. Plenty of couples after multiple miscarriages have gone on to have healthy, viable pregnancies. It's something to con-sider — that might help prevent you having to go through this again."

I nod. What she's saying makes sense, and I would do anything to keep from going through this again, but on the other hand, I'm scared . . . *What if something is wrong? What if we can't actually* . . . I can't even fin-ish the thought in my head, much less say it out loud.

I didn't always want to be a mother. In

fact, I think I was dead set against it for most of my life. My own mother left us when I was eleven and Vivian was fourteen. Ostensibly, she was leaving my dad because she didn't love him anymore. Apparently, she loved our neighbor Mr. Frank, who had been like an uncle to us most of our lives. But instead of her moving in with him, they decided it would be easier to pick up and move clear across the country to Seattle, and I remember thinking, *Easier for who?*

Vivian refused to go, but I went to visit every summer until college and it was like an alternate universe. Or a movie set where the role of my dad was being played by an understudy.

As I got older and realized that most mothers don't leave their children behind when they get divorced, I wondered if she was maybe missing some mother gene, some important basic instinct — and that maybe, that meant I was missing it, too.

While most people I know ooh and aah over babies, sniffing the tops of their heads like rabid dogs, I never understood the allure. Even when Vivian had Finley, who I did think was the most adorable baby on earth (until Griffin came along), I was terrified to be alone with her and I didn't know how to hold her or what it meant when she cried, and I certainly didn't feel any internal pull to have a baby of my own.

But then I met Harrison. And I don't know exactly when the switch flipped — before we got married, I had told him in no uncertain terms that I didn't think motherhood was in the cards for me, and later, as we were talking marriage, he said he didn't fully care one way or another as long as we were together. So no one was more surprised than me when, one morning over orange juice and waffles at the diner down the street from us, I looked into his eyes and said, "Let's do it."

"What?" he said.

"I want to have your baby."

Stunned, Harrison stared at me — one beat, two beats — and I got nervous. What if he thought that we had agreed not to, and he really didn't want them? And I — me! — started to panic at the idea of not having kids with him. Like I suddenly couldn't think of anything in the world that I wanted more. When I thought I couldn't take his silence anymore, and was ready to go into full offense mode about why I'd changed my mind and how it was absolutely the right thing for us to do, he opened his mouth and said: "Can I finish my bacon first?"

■ ■ ■ ■

Once I've arranged my clothing back in place and we leave the exam room, Harrison places his hand on the small of my back, guiding me through the waiting room. I keep my head down, not wanting to see any more pregnant women. We're almost to the glass door when a woman's voice calls from behind us: "Dr. Graydon?"

Harrison stops, turns his head toward the direction of the voice. "Hey there," he says, genially, and from the cadence of his voice, I know it's one of his patients. I clench my teeth, because all I want is to be out of there, to be in the car, at home, away from here. I consider forging ahead, through the doors. Harrison would understand, of course. But social conditioning commands me to stay put, to engage, to play the role of friendly doctor's wife. So I put on a small smile and pivot on my heel.

And that's when I gasp. Like punched-in-the-stomach, wind-knocked-out-of-me, loud-sucking-intake-of-air gasping.

It's not the woman Harrison is talking to that catches me off guard. It's the man that's next to her.

The man from the Giant.

The man from my dreams.

Fortunately, I've been crying on and off the past three days, so Harrison isn't too alarmed by this outburst. "Mia?" he asks, gently. Three pairs of eyes are suddenly trained on me, waiting for my response.

But all I see are *his* two familiar orbs, so brown they're almost black. And they're boring into me as intensely as they do in my dreams. I know it's because I'm gawking at him, transfixed, as if he has suddenly erupted in flames and I have never seen fire before.

I drop my eyes to the ground and try to recover, or cover up, because what could I possibly say? How could I explain?

"A cramp," I whisper, touching my stomach. "I'm OK."

Harrison pulls me toward him. "This is Caroline," he says. "One of my patients." I force my gaze to her, trying to ignore the thrumming of my heart, the bizarre, out-of-body fog I'm experiencing.

"Your husband saved my life last week." She smiles, and I focus on her teeth — Chiclet sized, off-white — simply because I have nowhere else to look.

I offer a weak smile back.

"Hardly," Harrison says, modestly. And then he goes into doctor mode: "Are you getting your rest? Not lifting heavy objects?"

"Yes. And here I am getting the baby checked out — doctor's orders and all." A memory is triggered — this is the emergency appendectomy Harrison performed last week. The woman who found out she was pregnant.

"Congratulations!" I exclaim, overenthusiastically, and Harrison squeezes my hip.

"Thanks," she says, putting her hand on her stomach. "It was quite the surprise." I nod, my gaze traveling back to the man beside her.

"Sorry," Caroline says. "This is Oliver."

Oliver.

I roll it over in my mind, my mouth. I get the sense that it should taste familiar. It doesn't.

But everything else about him is — from his relaxed posture, one hand tucked into the frayed front pocket of his jeans, the way the worn material of his burgundy T-shirt is taut and then loose in the swells and valleys of his arms, his chest. The longer top section of his shaggy, errant nut-brown mop falling into his eyes and the way he smooths it back at intervals, a habit he no longer notices. He's familiar in a way that doesn't make sense. Like a picture in a magazine that suddenly comes to life. Or like an ex-boyfriend you haven't seen in years. I know him, but I don't know this version of him.

He's talking to Harrison, but suddenly turns to me, and I'm busted for the second time, rudely ogling him. I know I should say something, make a lame excuse — a cliché *You look so familiar* — but when I open my mouth to speak, he beats me to it.

"I know you," he says, tilting his head. My heart thuds. My skin pricks with sweat. My eyes widen. But I also feel a small sense of relief. If he recognizes me, then I *must* know this man — and not just from my strange dreams. I must have met him before and don't remember it. It's the only thing that could explain . . . any of it. I lean forward slightly, but eagerly, waiting to hear how he knows me, waiting for it all to fall into place and make sense.

"Or I guess I don't *know* you — but I've seen you. At the Giant, I think? Last week?"

Oh.

"Sorry, that's probably weird," he says. His tone is friendly, but he doesn't smile. "But I have one of those photographic memories — never forget a face."

"Yeah," I manage, the word coming out squeaky. "I was there. On Friday?"

Oliver dips his head. Affirmative.

"Small world," Harrison says, amiably.

"Small town," Oliver quips.

And then Harrison is wrapping up the conversation and everyone is exchanging customary nice-to-meet-you pleasantries and I'm being ushered out the front door, bewildered at the bizarre normalcy of the encounter.

"Sorry," Harrison says in my ear as he opens my car door for me. "I know you wanted to get out of there."

"It's OK," I say, folding my body into the bucket seat, trying to sort out what's just happened and how it's possible and why I feel like I just rode the world's fastest roller coaster — exhilarated, terrified and like, at any second, I may throw up everywhere.

"Are you hungry?" Harrison asks, when we walk into the kitchen, my mind still a jumble of confusion and shock and grief.

I fixate on the lone barstool at the massive island in our kitchen. Its partner is in my studio, and it occurs to me now how cruel it was to separate them. It looks lost, like a child who's slipped away from his mother in the mall and ended up, bewildered, in a store he's never seen before. I need to buy more barstools. I add it to the list of things that feel impossible to accomplish.

"No," I say. My phone buzzes and I throw

65

it on the counter.

"Vivian?" he asks.

"Probably. Or my dad. Or Raya. I haven't called them back since —"

"I'll tell them," he says.

He picks up the no-longer-buzzing phone and starts tapping the screen with his thumb. I hear him say, "Hey, Vivian, it's Harrison," as he walks out of the kitchen.

I know I should go after him, that I'm copping out. That Vivian will call me anyway, and then Dad, and then Mom, and then my phone will keep obnoxiously and cheerfully ringing and dinging until the end of time. But if there's one thing I've learned, it's that miscarriages make people uncomfortable — even the people that love you the most. They never know what to say, so I somehow always end up being the one comforting them. *It's OK. I'm fine. We'll try again.* And I can't comfort anybody right now.

I need to be alone. I slip out the back door and walk toward the studio, so I don't have to overhear him say the words I've been avoiding.

Tubs of my paints and various art supplies litter the floor of the garage, canvases holding up the walls like middle school boys at a dance. Waiting. The garage still has the faint smell of wood chips. The previous owner used it as a woodworking studio to hand-carve his own boats, and a large canoe on two sawhorses greeted us when we first looked at the garage. I suddenly wish he had left it behind. I want to run my hands down its smooth edges, curl up in its curved basin.

Instead, I lie on the hard cement where the boat used to be.

And I think of Oliver.

Oliver.

It's as if learning his name has unlocked some treasure trove of stored dreams that I assumed had been lost forever, dissolved like sugar in water by the morning light.

They come rushing in like memories: Oliver sitting in a desk next to me in Mrs. Piergiovanni's class, loudly whispering while I'm trying to find the cosine in an isosceles triangle and hushing him, terrified I'll get in trouble. Oliver, my copilot in a biplane, laughing when I realize neither one of us knows how to fly and it starts falling from the sky, my stomach going with it. Oliver lying next to me in a cornfield, his hand hot between my legs, gripping the inside of my thigh —

I jerk my head. They're not memories. They're dreams. They're just dreams. It's not real.

He is real, though. He was standing there, mere inches away from me, as solid as the cement floor beneath me. The entire episode feels like a scene from a suspense flick. Like I was outside of it, watching it, breath bated, startled by each turn of events. And then it occurs to me that the most shocking thing of all was also the most mundane.

He's *married.*

It feels wrong. Like wearing a dress to swim in the ocean. Or a pair of too-tight shoes. It doesn't fit.

But there they were, two peas in a pod.

And they're going to have a baby.

A charcoal pencil is sticking out of an open bin near me, a silver *HB* etched into its side. I reach for it without moving my body, my fingertips barely touching the tip. I pluck it out and the sudden, familiar urge to create — to make something out of nothing — overcomes me, but there's no paper nearby. I start drawing on the floor. First one line that slowly morphs into a tiny finger, and then a hand, no bigger than a quarter.

I put down the pencil and cover the hand with mine. It fits perfectly beneath my palm.

Then somehow, I fall asleep.

■ ■ ■ ■

It's dark when Harrison comes in. But instead of telling me I need to get up, or even carrying me back to the house, he lies down beside me on the floor, his head next to mine, his dark eyes glistening in the moonlight. I turn on my side to face him, the tips of our noses almost touching.

"Dios Mia," he whispers.

I blink, long and slow. His cheek is resting on the hand I drew.

"Our baby," I whisper back. "You're lying on it."

His eyebrows rise above his glasses and he sits up a bit, then squints at the ground, until he can make out the slightly smudged, impossibly tiny charcoal fingers in the dark.

"Shit," he says. "I knew I would be a terrible dad." It's an awful joke. Too soon. But it makes me giggle. And I love him for it.

He lies back down, shifting his head this time so it's not on the drawing. And I love him for that, too.

"Can I tell you something crazy?" I whisper.

"Of course," he says.

"You know that guy today — in the waiting room? With your patient — with Caroline?"

"Yeah."

"I had this déjà vu feeling when I saw him. Like I recognized him."

"You mean from the Giant?"

"No. I mean, I do remember seeing him there. But only because I had the same feeling then, too."

Harrison waits for my explanation and I search for the words.

"I've seen him before."

"I'm sure you have — Hope Springs is a small town."

"No. I'm trying to say . . ." I pause, and then say it: "I've dreamt about him. Before." The second it comes out of my mouth, I realize how ridiculous it sounds.

Harrison squints. "What do you mean, like you've had a dream about someone that looks like him?"

"No. *Him.* I think. He was so familiar. Like I knew him, even though I've never met him."

"Because you've dreamt about him," Harrison repeats.

"Yeah."

"Huh." We sit in silence for a few beats.

"Do you think I'm crazy?" I ask.

"Yes," he says.

70

I tap his chest. "Hey."

His face softens. "But it's one of the things I love most about you."

I know he doesn't think it's a big deal, and I could try to explain it more, how long I've been dreaming about Oliver, how shocking it was to see him in the flesh, but suddenly I'm exhausted.

He puts his hand on my shoulder, gently cupping it, and rubs the pad of his thumb back and forth across my skin.

"I'm sorry," I say. "About the baby."

The sorrow in his eyes mirrors mine and I breathe deeply, feeling something loosen in my chest, as if his very presence is helping relieve the burden of my grief. I feel so connected to him in this moment.

Which is why I can't believe what he says next.

"Maybe," he whispers, "it really is for the best."

Stunned, I stare at him.

"I didn't mean . . ." he says, and then stops.

A tear slips out of my eye, down the slope of my nose and onto the floor between us.

"What *do* you mean?" I whisper.

He pauses, collecting his thoughts. "That we tried," he says. "That maybe it's not in the cards for us."

I snicker lightly, but without malice. "I thought you didn't believe in fate."

He repositions his head where it's lying on his elbow. "It's just, the other night — I don't know if I can watch you go through that again. That *I* can go through it again. You could have . . ." He doesn't finish the sentence.

I close my eyes. I know he means died. I could have died. But I don't know how to tell him part of me already did. Every baby that has left us has taken a piece of me with it. And while having a baby won't give me those pieces back, not having one might end me for good.

Finally, I open my eyes. "I want to go to the fertility specialist."

It's a statement, not a question, but still, I expect him to respond. To acquiesce as he usually does when we disagree. Or to argue, tell me he's not ready yet, that he needs more time.

But Harrison remains silent. And we stare at each other, our faces bathed in moonlight, the tiny hand of our baby lying between us.

CHAPTER 5
HARRISON

"What on God's green earth did you put your rook there for?" Foster asks, pouring the black liquid from the carafe into his mug and nodding toward the chess game set up on the table.

Harrison glances at the board, trying to remember his last move.

"I'm just gonna take it with my rook," Foster continues. Thirty years Harrison's senior, Foster Moretti is one of the founding partners of the Fordham Health surgeon group, and the only one still practicing. He's as old-school as they come, preferring physical exams — touch, look and listen — to technological devices. It's a common joke that he doesn't even know what floor the MRI is on. He only works two days each week, one day for patients in the clinic, one day for surgeries, but he just can't seem to stay away from the office.

Harrison remembers his strategy. "Yeah,

but then I'm going to take your rook with my bishop."

Foster gives his head a firm shake. "But you only have the one rook. I've got both of mine. A player with a single rook should never sacrifice it for one of his opponent's. Lev Alburt."

Harrison has no idea who Lev Alburt is, but assumes he must be some chess expert that Foster reads up on in his spare time. Foster takes Harrison's rook and Harrison take Foster's with his bishop and then they both study the board in silence for a minute.

"I was sorry to hear about Mia." Foster blows on his coffee. "How's she doing?"

Harrison thinks of Mia, lying on the studio floor last night. His heart clenches.

When they first met, he thought she was out of his league — too beautiful, of course, but also too everything else. Too witty. Too passionate. Too talented. Too interesting. Too *alive*. She was wearing that yellow dress. And two pink plastic barrettes, like the ones kids wear, secured the right side of her long black hair away from her face. It was obvious she put effort into how she looked, but equally obvious that she didn't care what anyone thought about it. It was so novel. Refreshing. He'd spent his whole life caring what other people thought, and throughout the night, found himself caring what she thought most of all. She could have had her choice of any man in the room. But she picked him, like one might choose a pastry from a bakery case. *I'll have that one.*

She chose him. And in that moment, he swore he'd spend his entire life making sure she wouldn't regret it. But how could he have known then how many things would be out of his control? He can't think of anything he hates worse than seeing his wife in pain and not being able to fix it. And even though it seems with each passing year he becomes more unsure of things he once knew positively (and often thinks it's an un-natural progression — shouldn't you be-come more steadfast in your beliefs about the world around you as you age?), he knows one thing for certain: Mia's sadness is his sadness and he'd carry it around with him like water in a bucket until the end of his days if it meant that she didn't have to.

To Foster, he lies. "She's OK."

Foster dips his head. "And you?"

Harrison lies again. "I'm OK, too."

And then his cell rings in his pocket, and because it's his on-call day, he knows it's the ER.

"It begins," he mutters.

■ ■ ■ ■

At four, when he finally has a minute to grab a sandwich from the doctors' lounge in the hospital, his cell rings again.

"Hey, Graydon, Leong. I've got another one I think you need to see — woman with a hundred-two fever, acute abdomen pain; she's tachycardic. From the free air in the X-rays, looks like a perforated viscus."

While Leong's talking, Harrison pulls up the patient's records on the computer. He tells Leong he'll be right down and takes one last monster bite of his sandwich, not knowing when he'll get to eat again.

The patient looks around Mia's age, early thirties (which is close to Harrison's age — thirty-five — but Mia often teases him that the few years' difference makes him ancient). Her blond hair's tied back in a messy bun, and she's lying flat on the gurney, her hands gripping the sides. Worry is etched on her face, but she's trying to hide it with a smile. Harrison quickly realizes it's not for his benefit — she's not even looking at him. There's a boy standing next to her, wide-eyed and trembling a little. He reminds Harrison so much of Noah that he goes cold, a torrent of memories flooding in.

76

Noah's lifeless face, his mouth an O around his endotracheal tube, as if he was just as surprised as Harrison was by what happened. The viscous blood that coated nearly every surface, as if a can of red paint had been carelessly upended. The monotone beep, a constant reminder of his failure.

Keeping his voice steady, Harrison smiles at the kid and grabs one of the lollipops that he keeps in his coat pocket just for situations like this. "Hey, bud," he says and offers it to him, but he turns his head away from it. Harrison can tell he's going to be a tough cookie. He sets it on the arm of the chair next to him and then looks from the boy back to his mom. "What seems to be the trouble?"

"My stomach," she says, through clenched teeth.

"And what's your name?"

"Whit—" Her breath catches. "—ney."

"Whitney, I'm Dr. Graydon. I'm just going to ask you a few questions, do a quick exam, and we'll figure out exactly what the problem is. Sound good?"

She nods.

Harrison quickly runs through the questions about her medical history, the quality and details of the pain she's experiencing and past symptoms. During the physical exam, when he gets to her belly, she shrieks at the contact, but then immediately cuts it off, glancing at her son. The boy glares with his Noah eyes. "Sorry, buddy," Harrison says, holding his hands up. "I'm all done." Her stomach is hard as a rock and hot to the touch. Leong's diagnosis was correct, which means Harrison needs to get her into surgery immediately.

"OK, Whitney, so basically what you have is called a perforated viscus, which means there's a hole somewhere along your digestive tract — anywhere from your esophagus all the way down to where it ends at your rectum. I'd like to do an exploratory laparotomy, which is just a fancy term for opening you up to find the hole and fix it."

As he runs through the details of the surgery, her eyes grow bigger, which is common — most people don't like the thought of being cut open. And then she asks the question most people ask, hoping to avoid being cut open. "What happens if I don't do anything?"

"Well," Harrison says. "We'll put you on antibiotics —" He glances at the boy and chooses his next words carefully. "But the prognosis would not be good."

"How not good?"

He clears his throat. "You would most

likely not make it."

"Whaaaaat?" the boy screams. Tears immediately spring to his eyes. "Noooo!"

"It's OK, Gabriel," Whitney says, putting her hand on her son's arm. "Sweetie, it's OK. I'm not going to die." She turns to Harrison, wincing again from the pain. "We'll do the surgery."

He nods curtly and then lays out all the risks of the surgery as quickly and quietly as possible, to not set the boy off again, then pats her hand. "We'll take good care of you, and in a few hours, you'll feel much better than this, I prom—"

He stops and clears his throat. It's the exact same words he said to Noah right before his surgery. And they were a lie. And he swears the boy, Gabriel, can see right through him, because he fixes him with another glare. "Don't you kill my mom," Gabriel says, his tiny hands in tight fists by his sides, as if he's planning to hit Harrison if all doesn't go well.

"Don't worry. I'm going to fix her right up," Harrison says in a soothing voice. And then, even though he knows he shouldn't, he looks him dead in the eyes and adds the words he couldn't finish earlier: "I promise."

Apparently, it's enough, because Gabriel reaches out with his stumpy fingers and grabs the Dum-Dum from the arm of the chair, unwrapping it in one quick motion and popping it in his mouth.

Noah wanted grape.

The memory hits Harrison like a line drive he didn't see coming. The way Noah spied his pocketful of suckers and secreted the purple out when he thought Harrison was distracted in talking to his mom. *Not till after your surgery, buddy,* Harrison said chidingly, plucking it from his hand. And now, as Harrison eyes Gabriel, the head of the lollipop creating a perfect ball under the skin of his right cheek, he thinks: *Noah never got his lollipop. Noah will never get another lollipop.*

He scrubs the morbid thought from his mind, steps out of the room and gives the orders to Sheila, the nurse assigned to Whitney. She has the consent form all ready to go, and Harrison signs it so she can take it in to the patient. "Oh, and Sheila?" he says. "See if there's someone we can call for the kid."

"Not my husband!" the woman yells from behind the curtain. "Do *not* call him."

Sheila raises an eyebrow and purses her lips. "Yes, we've been trying her sister, who apparently works at the movie theater and gets off in an hour. Haven't got a hold of

80

her yet, though."

He lowers his voice. "What's with the husband?"

"Separated, according to her," she whispers. "In the middle of some kind of custody battle."

He nods. "Send him down to the ped ward. Get him set up with some video games. That'll keep him until the sister gets here."

"Will do," she says.

He pokes his head back in the room. "Gabriel — you a Need for Speed guy? Minecraft?"

The boy's eyes get big.

"He loves Minecraft," Whitney says. "Don't you, buddy?" And then mouths, *Thank you.*

When Sheila slips into the room, Harrison calls up to the OR, relaying all the information needed in a steady, calm manner. Then he goes to the doctors' lounge and directly into the bathroom, which is thankfully empty. He puts a hand on either side of the sink and stares into the mirror.

Gabriel's plea echoes in his head: *Don't you kill my mom. Don't you kill my mom. Don't you kill my mom.* Heart thumping, he turns on the faucet and splashes water on his forehead, his cheeks, and then lifts his head, watching the liquid drip off his skin, beading up on his beard.

Then he leans to his right, grabs the trash can beneath the sink and throws up.

The first time Harrison lost a patient was two weeks into his residency. A car accident. An eighty-one-year-old woman, short of breath, was brought into the ER. She checked out OK and the attending said to keep an eye on her, to call out if he needed anything. Harrison sat at the side of her portable cot. The woman started talking about her husband, how he'd be worried she wasn't back in time for dinner. Harrison held her hand, assured her that her husband had been called. "I don't feel good," she said, then closed her eyes. Her head rolled back.

There's a look people get right before they die. Pale, yes. Weak. But it's something else. Intangible. A knowing. Harrison didn't have the experience to recognize it then, he just knew something wasn't right. He shouted for help. The attending came over, called a code, started chest compressions. Harrison looked on, helpless.

Time of death, 18:32.

Every doctor has their first death story, and every one handles it differently. Harrison was in shock. Everything was moving too slowly and too fast all at once. He stood in the corner, watching the nurses efficiently disconnect the IV, scribble notes in charts, pull the sheet over her face. He knew they were doing their jobs, but had this distinct feeling that he was waiting for something more, though he couldn't possibly think what that might be. The tolling of a bell? A reverent moment of silence? An acknowledgment of the life that was here and then — quick as a breath blowing out a candle flame — was gone.

The chief resident appeared, and Harrison thought for a second, *This must be it. What I've been waiting for.* The chief looked at the attending. "Salisbury steak in the cafeteria." He slapped the doorframe. "You ready for dinner?"

There's no class in medical school, no tips for dealing with death, mortality, grief. So you look to your elders and you learn, not *how* to detach, but that you must. Numb yourself. Some doctors pray, find consolation in believing that something or someone else is in control. Some drink. Some yell at their kids. Over time, Harrison found his comfort in the randomness of death. The fact that he can do everything exactly right, exactly as he's been trained, but it's not always enough. People die. And he can't save everybody.

But then, Noah.

And he learned there's a difference between people dying under your care and people dying *because* of your care. And the difference is as wide as an ocean. And he's not entirely sure he knows how to swim.

CHAPTER 6

I shuffle into the kitchen, my eyes swollen and bloodshot, my body weak and sore. I pour a cup of cold coffee from the pot Harrison made before he left, and then dig through the pockets of the jeans I wore yesterday for the number Dr. Okafor's nurse gave us for the reproductive endocrinologist. The first available appointment they have is nearly two and a half weeks out. I take it, hang up, and the too-tight corset that's been constricting my lungs, my heart, for the past five days loosens ever so slightly.

Gripping my mug, I wander aimlessly through the house, though my legs know exactly where I'm headed, taking me upstairs to the bedroom full of unpacked boxes. It's masochistic, this ritual I've adopted after each miscarriage, but I'm compelled to do it — that is, if I can find what I'm looking for. There are at least four boxes labeled *Misc.* where, while packing, I threw all the things taking up space on our shelves and in our drawers that didn't seem to have a specific home.

I sit on the floor, digging through box after box, sifting through old medical journals, photograph albums, random items I found while out and about in Philadelphia and brought home over the years — the pink child's mitten, a rusty hubcap, an old house key — but I don't find *it*. The desperation begins rising up my chest like a wave picking up steam as it pushes toward shore. What if it's gone? What if it got lost somewhere in the move or didn't make it into a box or it got accidentally tossed in the trash? But then finally there it is, in the third box, the knitted corner peeking out from beneath an old game of Boggle.

Relief courses through my veins as I tug it out, the tiny pink-and-blue-striped beanie, no bigger than a grapefruit. The first time we found out we were pregnant — the very first time — Harrison came home from his shift at the hospital the next day and knelt beside me where I was lying on the couch watching the Game Show Network. I don't remember what was on — *Family Feud* or *Wheel of Fortune* or *Supermarket Sweep* — but I remember the way he gently laid the hat across my flat belly.

"Where did you get that?" I asked.

"I stole it." He grinned. "From the nursery."

"Harrison!" I said, but I couldn't help but laugh.

"They won't miss it. All these sweet old ladies knit them for the newborns. I just — I didn't want to wait."

He placed his palm over the hat on my belly, his fingers spread, nearly concealing all the soft yarn. "It's your first hat," he whispered to his hand, to the hat, to our baby. "Second one will be an Eagles ball cap, of course. But this is your first one."

"What if it's a girl?" I said.

He paused, looking at me in mock shock. "Why can't a girl have an Eagles ball cap, too?" he said. "God, you're sexist."

I laughed again. "Touché."

I pick up the hat now, and hold it to my face, the yarn soft and scratchy against my nose. The tears come again, fast and furious, and I wrap one arm around my legs, pulling them up to my chest, and rock back and forth, mourning that very first baby that never got a chance to wear it. And the second one. And the third. And I wonder, not for the first or second or third time — where did they go? My babies. Where are they? I feel desperate to find them, like I've lost my keys and if I look hard enough, digging down in the cushions of the couch or underneath the coffee table or through the clutter on my dresser, I'll find them. They're there, waiting for me. Somewhere. I just have to find them.

My sobs turn primal, guttural, and I grieve in a way that I've never even let Harrison see. This is private, this bereavement, between me and my babies alone. And when I'm done, I'll tuck the hat back in the box along with my sorrow, hiding it away for safekeeping. And I'll do my best to set my sights on the next baby — the one that may actually get to wear it. Because what else can I do?

When I'm finally drained, my body left feeling like a sheet before it's hung on a line to dry — wrung out and beat, but somehow fresh and renewed at the same time — I gently place the hat back in the box. I inhale and exhale shakily and then take notice of the other things I disregarded when searching for the hat. The Boggle game, of course, an envelope full of old concert and movie ticket stubs, a loose picture of Raya from our first year at Moore — perched on her bed in overalls and a hat with a big flower on the brim. A stack of old sketchbooks I haven't looked at since college. I pull them all out and slowly flip through the pages of my work, renderings of Rodin sculptures that I would draw from every angle, nudes of classmates who modeled to make extra money, including Raya. One book is filled with hands — pages and pages of fingers and clasped palms and bony knuckles — one of the hardest body parts to reproduce with a pencil.

In the final book, papers falling loose, their corners sticking out the sides, I flip open the worn blue cover and my breath catches.

Oliver.

I don't even remember drawing the portrait, but there he is, fleshed out in shades of gray, his eyes the intense dark of Nitram B charcoal. My skin turns to gooseflesh as I stare at this likeness, knowing now that the man is not a figment of my imagination. That I was drawing someone who exists. How is that possible? I quickly close the cover and tuck the book back into the box, placing the other sketchbooks on top of it, as if I'm trying to bury the evidence.

But try as I might, as I drift through my morning, watering the garden, diligently distributing Epsom salt around the tomato plants, nibbling on a granola bar while watching *Let's Make a Deal* in the den — I can't put Oliver out of my mind.

On a commercial, I grab my phone from where it was plugged in on the kitchen counter and tap on the web browser. I stare at the blank search bar and consider what to type, before finally starting on something broad and generic: Dreams.

I read through some dry, perfunctory material about what dreams are (a series of images, events and emotions that occur involuntarily during sleep) and then scroll through the various sites that offer the meanings behind common symbols in dreams. It's mostly a lot of obvious psychobabble: to dream of throwing away garbage means you're ridding yourself of negative energy in your life.

Still, I click on S and scroll to Stranger.

A stranger in your dream signifies a part of yourself that is repressed and hidden. Alternatively, it symbolizes the archetypal dream helper who is offering you insight and advice.

Clutching the phone in my palm, I glance up at Wayne Brady talking to a woman covered from head to toe in a bacon costume and sigh. I click back to the search engine and try to narrow it down.

Dreaming of a stranger and then seeing him.

I hit enter and the results fill the screen. As I scan them, I realize I was hoping for some scientific study to pop up, a biological or psychological explanation of this phenomenon that would make perfect sense and clear everything up in one fell swoop. To my great disappointment, it's mostly links to forums and message boards. I click on the first one.

It's a question posted by DayDreamer06. I try not to cringe at the handle for what is most certainly a twelve-year-old girl who has Shawn Mendes posters papering her bedroom walls.

Have you ever dreamt of a person and then met that person in real life?

There are forty-seven responses. There are the expected No, that's not possible and a few that say they believe it could happen but it's never happened to them, but to my surprise, the great majority are personal anecdotes about their own experiences. From the very vague: About six years ago, I dreamt about a guy who I had a lot of feelings for but I couldn't really picture his face. He whispered his name to me right before I woke up: Matthew. When I met my now-husband Matthew, I knew I'd been dreaming about him. To the very specific: I once had a dream about a little girl with an orange-striped bow in her hair and a unicorn T-shirt standing next to a cash register and the very next day I saw her in the mall, standing next to a cash register exactly as it was in my dream.

I go back to the original search results and click on more links, all of which are filled with more stories like these. As I read through them one by one, what's most astounding to me isn't the details, it's the sheer volume of people who claim to have experienced this very thing. After an hour or so, the words and the stories start blurring together, but I keep reading anyway, taking comfort in the fact that I'm not alone, even as I know none of these anecdotes will be able to tell me the one thing I want to know: what in the world it could possibly mean.

In the middle of my sixth or seventh chain of stories — this one a Reddit board — the words disappear and the screen fills with Raya's face. She's calling me.

We typically communicate via text, so I slide my thumb quickly over the screen and put it to my ear. "What's wrong?" I say.

"Nothing," she says. "What makes you think something is wrong?"

"You're calling me. You never call."

"Oh. Well, we haven't talked since . . . you know. And I thought a text was kind of, I don't know. Flippant."

"I like flippant."

"How are you?"

"Fine."

"Really?"

"No." I sigh. "I'm terrible. I'm also fairly certain I'm going insane."

"Going?"

"Ha-ha."

"Why are you insane?"

I take a deep breath. I'm hesitant to tell her, not only because it sounded so ridiculous when I said it out loud, but because I got the sense Harrison didn't really believe me — or at least understand how shocking it was. I don't want the same thing to happen with Raya. But then, I realize, this is Raya. My friend who owns at least six different astrology books, burns sage with frequency and once buried quartz crystals in four pots of soil and placed them in the corners of our college apartment to "create a boundary of protection" when we thought she had a possible stalker. If anyone is going to believe this, it's her.

So I tell her.

Aside from a few well-timed and incredulous *what*s, Raya doesn't say anything until I've unloaded every single detail — from my first recollection of dreaming about Oliver when I was in college to seeing him in the Giant to meeting him in Dr. Okafor's waiting room. Even then, in the silence that follows, I have to prompt her. "Say something."

"You've been dreaming about this man for *years?*"

"Yeah."

"We lived together. How is this the first time that I'm hearing about this?"

"I don't know," I say. "The dreams always felt kind of meaningless — intense, but meaningless — until I saw him, anyway. It's weird, right? I mean, have you ever heard of anything like this before?"

"I don't know," she echoes, pausing to consider. "I mean, a few nights ago, I dreamt I went grocery shopping with Barack Obama. He kept trying to put this premade meat loaf from the deli section in my cart and I didn't want it. I was getting so angry, but he wouldn't leave it alone. He was all, 'Take the meat loaf. It's delicious.' So I started screaming at him. At Barack Obama!"

I wait a beat. "Was there a point hidden in there?"

"I'm saying — dreams *are* weird. Inexplicable."

"OK, sure. But after your dream, did you then meet our former president in an OB/

GYN waiting room?"

"What would Barack Obama be doing at an OB/GYN?"

"Raya."

She snickers at her own joke.

I press on. "I keep thinking I must know him somehow. Don't you think? I mean, I don't remember ever meeting him, but it's the only thing that could possibly make sense."

"Oh my god," Raya says.

"What?"

"I just remembered this documentary I saw once. It was about two girls who met as teenagers and completely recognized each other, even though they were strangers. It turned out they were twins separated at birth."

"Are you talking about *The Parent Trap*?"

"Was that it?"

"Not a documentary."

"Oh, well still, I've always heard that about twins — that they have this weird connection and dream about each other and stuff. Maybe this guy is your long-lost brother."

I think about some of the dreams. Oliver's hands. And clear my throat. "Ah . . . I don't think he and I are related."

"You never know. Your mom, she wasn't

exactly faithful."

I should be offended, but that part is actually true. "OK, my mom is . . . my mom. But I think I'd know if I had a half sibling running around."

"Yeah. I suppose."

"What else?" I wait a beat, but Raya appears out of outlandish guesses. "Don't you think it must mean something?" I say. "That I've been dreaming about this guy for years and then I actually see him? In real life?"

Raya pauses. "I don't know — do *you* think it means something?"

"Oh Jesus. Now you sound like Vivian."

"Really?" she says, clearly not offended by this comparison. "I always thought I'd make a good therapist. You know, one time, when I was fifteen, my grandparents took us to Salem, Massachusetts, for some family vacation, and I had this reading with a real, bona fide witch, and she actually told me I was going to be a psychologist when I grew up. She was obviously wrong, but —" She trails off, going silent. And then: "Oh my god. That's it — that's exactly what you need."

"A psychologist? Great — thank you so much."

"No, a *psychic.*"

"Uh, no." I love watching Warner McKay

96

at three a.m. talk to the dead relatives of his audience members as much as the next gal, but I don't know that I actually believe he's psychic. It's all so vague: *Who's got the J name? I'm sensing something in the leg . . . a J name, who was stabbed in the thigh, or fell off a cliff and broke it or maybe had their leg amputated?* It feels more like a really great guessing game.

"No, really. They understand all that stuff — dreams and what they mean and all that. And there are a ton of psychics all over Philadelphia. There's probably even one in little old Hope Springs."

"I don't know — I kind of think that's all a scam."

"Well, sure, probably some of them are. But some of them are truly legit."

"Hm." I was thinking more like a dream expert or a therapist might have more legitimate insight. "I'll think about it."

When we hang up, I consider calling Vivian, who is a therapist of sorts, if only to balance the scales of Raya's mystical approach with Vivian's logical one. But I can literally already hear what she'll say: *Mia, you've been under a lot of stress lately, what with the move, losing the baby — it can really do a number on your brain, make you sometimes think things that aren't necessarily true.*

I roll my eyes and stand up. Stretching my arms overhead, her pretend voice continues. *Do something! You have too much time on your hands, and you're sitting around obsessing. Unpack! Go for a walk! Take up knitting!*

God, fake Vivian is annoying. But I know she's also right. I do need something to occupy my mind. I walk into the kitchen, throw away my granola wrapper, and then I'm drawn out the back door, retracing my steps from the day before into the studio.

For a few seconds, I stare at the floor where Harrison and I were lying, at the charcoal hand, and then — there it is, again — finally. I'm struck with the same urge to create. The urge that's been eluding me since we moved to Hope Springs.

In practiced movements, I slip my simple gold wedding band off my finger and loop it on a chain around my neck. I pull fat tubes of acrylic out of boxes, a few brushes, and arrange them on the table next to the blank canvas. And then I sit down on the stool and an image comes to me as plainly as if I'm staring at a photograph. I begin to paint.

I stop once, to eat a bag of kettle-cooked potato chips and an apple, and then again to turn on the light when the sun fades from the windows and darkness creeps in. But

I'm still painting later that night when Harrison creaks open the door to the studio and stands beneath the transom, patiently watching as my fingertips sweep across the canvas with purpose, creating four trails of yellow and orange. I rarely use brushes when painting, preferring the control of my fingers to create lines, depth, texture, shadows. Satisfied with the markings, I pick my hand up off the canvas and glance over my shoulder at my husband.

"You're painting," he says.

"I am."

"It's a chicken."

"It is." The one from my nightmare, not dead and wrapped in tinfoil, but alive in brilliant chartreuse and carroty orange and robin's egg blue, squawking, its red beak gaping.

Harrison tilts his head, considering. "Things with feathers?"

I pause, my lip turning up on one side. "Maybe," I say.

Harrison steps into the studio and comes up behind me until he's close enough to clasp my shoulder. But he keeps his hands in his pockets.

"What time is it?" I ask.

"Late," he says. "Eleven."

I knew I had lost track of time, but I'm

still surprised to learn I've been painting for almost twelve hours. "Rough day?"

"Woman with perforated diverticulitis. Bad case. Tachycardic, acidotic. Had to get out before I could finish. I sent her up to the ICU for resuscitation."

I nod, even though I'm only vaguely familiar with the terms from overhearing Harrison use them on the phone.

"Didn't want to leave until I had checked on her a few times."

I nod again. We both stare at the chicken as if waiting for it to come alive at any second.

"I think I'm going to look for a job," I say, voicing the thought that's been swirling in my mind since conjuring fake Vivian's advice. For weeks really. But now, especially, I need something — more than my art — to keep my mind occupied.

"Furniture store?"

"Maybe." I notice the tail feather needs more detail. I dip my finger in the ochre, then a touch of dark brown.

"Have you eaten?" Harrison asks, but the words don't register, my focus fully back on my work. He used to take it personally when I would ignore him while working, or even when I wasn't working but was suddenly struck with something I wanted to try on a work in progress or a new idea altogether and my eyes would glaze over in midsentence. *I hate it when you do that,* he said one time, his voice low. It was quiet, but the new timbre — or maybe it was the seriousness with which he spoke — jerked me back to him. I looked at him, eyes wide.

I was talking. To you.

I'm sorry, I said, appropriately chagrined. *I just —*

He put up his hand to stop me, and I sucked in my breath, wondering if this was it. The proverbial straw. My eccentric artist ways were no longer charming to him and he had had enough. I thought of all the things I could have done to prevent it — I could have tried harder. To listen that first one hundred times he half joked about it bothering him. To be present. To put him first. To not get swept away in my work. But I also knew it was impossible, so I just held my breath.

He stared at me and then left the room. And I exhaled, feeling very much like I had dodged a bullet.

Now, he turns to leave, his shoes clunking on the cement in retreat. I jab my finger at the canvas in short, quick strokes, and then as the door creaks open, I remember. "I made an appointment," I say. "Thursday,

July fifth."

He doesn't speak and I wonder if maybe he didn't hear me. Or if he's already left, even though I didn't hear the door thunk closed. My hand hovers over the canvas, my ear straining.

And then, finally, he says, "OK," and slips out into the dark night.

Chapter 7

Though there's an antique store on nearly every corner in Hope Springs, there's only one furniture store: the Blue-Eyed Macaw. It's upscale, staged beautifully, and I can tell the owner handpicks every single item she sells. They're also not hiring.

I've spent two full weeks scouring job-opening websites, hoping something might become available that I'd be interested in — or at least not hate. The problem is Hope Springs is hopelessly tiny, and there were only two jobs that I even remotely qualified for: a waitress position at an Italian restaurant and a custodian for the elementary school. But they both required night hours, which wouldn't solve my need to have something to do during the day — and I also didn't love the idea of seeing Harrison even less. Expanding my search area to all of Bucks County didn't help, so I decided to take the old-fashioned approach. Show up to places in person and hope I could charm my way into a job, starting with the Blue-Eyed Macaw.

The manager, a tall woman with white-blond hair, a French-tipped manicure and a name tag that reads *Henley,* kindly lets me fill out an application anyway.

"You know, I think I heard Sorelli's has an opening for a waitress. Manager's name is Richard."

"Thanks," I say. "But I was really hoping for something in home décor or design. I used to be a consultant at Stanley Neal in Philly."

"That's a nice store," she says. "High-end."

I nod.

"Well, Nora, the owner, she does most of the consulting when our clients request design help." She holds up the paper I filled out. "But I'll give this to her."

"Nora?" My eyes widen. "As in, the woman who owns the art gallery on Mechanic?"

"Yeah, do you know her?"

I sigh. I hate small towns.

Back outside, I stand baking in the sun, the wind out of my sails. And I have to admit that I didn't really have a plan for where to go next in my job hunt. I had rather naively hoped my experience at Stanley Neal would be all the foot in the door I would need and the Blue-Eyed Macaw would hire me on the spot. I let out a groan as my hairline pricks with sweat and a drop starts trickling down the side of my face. I'm hot. My skin is sticky, my purple cotton sundress suddenly unbearably uncomfortable. I want to scream in frustration at the world.

The red letters of the True Value sign at the end of the block catch my eye and I think of my tomatoes and how the leaves have only gotten more yellow (a little on the brown side, to be honest) and have yet to bear one single orb of fruit. And suddenly I'm furious at Jules and her stupid Epsom salt advice that has done nothing to salvage the plants. I turn toward the storefront and all but stomp down the sidewalk to its jangly glass door.

After adjusting from the bright light of outside, my eyes scan the store until I spot Jules's helmet of gray curls over by a display of hammers. As I march toward her, my anger builds on itself, until I'm sure she's at fault not only for the tomatoes, but for the lack of any decent jobs in Hope Springs, the loss of *all* my babies and, quite possibly, global warming.

"Jules." I snarl her name, and she turns slowly, peering through her glasses at the UPC stuck on the handle of a hammer. She shifts her gaze to me, her eyes watery and wide behind the frames. Her face is a roadmap of deep wrinkles, her neck still jowly, and these trappings of age take the fight out of me as quick as air leaves a popped balloon. I'm deflated.

"Yes," she says in her throaty voice. "Can I help you?" She clearly doesn't remember me.

"My tomatoes are dying," I mumble.

"Oh." Her face brightens. "Have you tried Epsom salt? We don't sell it here. You'll have to go to the Giant."

I stare at her, mouth slightly open. I sigh. "I'll try that," I say. "Thanks."

She nods and begins humming as she hangs up the hammer she was holding and then ambles away from me, down an aisle, toward the back of the store.

Behind me, I hear the sharp intake of breath and then a low, deep voice: "Bad advice." Startled, I turn, and find myself inches from an all-too-familiar face.

A strangled-sounding hiccup of surprise emerges from my throat, and I take a step back.

He straightens his spine. "Sorry. It's Mia,

106

right?" His voice is friendly, warm, but the way he's looking at me is completely unnerving. Or maybe I'm just completely unnerved, his expression notwithstanding.

I will myself to respond — to say anything — but find I've lost all command of the English language. And I realize that these past few weeks, though I had not forgotten about him, I had somehow compartmentalized our interaction, like a museum curator handling a Dalí acquisition. File under *surreal.*

But now he's standing right in front of me, a melting clock come to life.

"Oliver," he says, gesturing to himself. "We met at Dr. Okafor's? Your husband saved my sister's life?"

I force myself to recover. "Yeah, yes, of course," I say, studying his familiar visage. His lopsided smile — a deep parenthetical line appears only on the right side, like a dimple that decided not to stay in one spot. His full, bushy eyebrows, his thin lips, the way after he pulls at the crown of his head, pieces of hair stay sticking straight up. Did I remember these details from my dreams? Or from seeing him in the waiting room? The difficulty in parsing dream and reality makes me heady.

And then I actually hear the sentence he

said, as it ricochets around in my brain like a pinball. "Wait — *sister?*"

"Yeah," he says. "Caroline?"

"I didn't . . . I assumed that you were . . ."

He stares at me for a beat. "That we were . . ." His eyes widen. "Oh! No." He chuckles. "I guess that makes sense, since we were at an OB/GYN together. But no — brotherly support. She's just kind of . . . freaked out by the whole thing."

"Oh."

Though I've been gaping at him like he's a wild tiger that suddenly appeared in the middle of the hardware store, I notice for the first time that he's holding a plunger. His other hand is stuffed in his pocket. It seems ludicrous — an accessory that doesn't fit the intensity of the situation — and I have to swallow back a bubble of laughter.

"Plumbing issues?" I say, for lack of anything else.

"Old house. If it's not one thing, it's another." He flicks his eyes in the direction Jules walked and cocks an eyebrow. "Problem with your tomatoes?"

I take a deep breath, trying to calm my still-racing heart, and stare at his ears. They stick out too far from his head, which would be an unfortunate flaw on someone else but on him it adds something — a charming vulnerability. "Yeah. Problem with the whole garden, really. I inherited it when we moved in. And I have no idea what I'm doing. Besides killing it."

"Well, whatever you do, don't use the Epsom salt."

And I remember his first two words to me: *Bad advice.* Embarrassed to admit it's too late, I shoot him a questioning look.

"It's kind of an old wives' tale — that Epsom salt will boost the magnesium in the soil; but most soil isn't deficient in magnesium, at least not so much that a regular fertilizer can't fix it. And Epsom salt can actually do more harm than good — causing leaf scorch. And if you have blossom end rot, it'll make that worse."

"Huh." My mind swirls with the information he's unloaded, as well as all my emotions: shock and confusion, of course, but also surprise at how easily we seem to have slipped into a somewhat normal conversation. If talking about Epsom salt can be considered normal. "So . . . are you a farmer?"

"Not exactly," he says slyly. "But I do have a little experience with agriculture." He runs his familiar hand through his familiar hair. The ends stick up.

"What do yellow spots on the leaves mean?"

He rocks back on his heels and makes a clicking noise with his cheek. "Any number of things, really. Overwatering. Underwatering. Nutrient deficiency. But it could have nothing to do with the soil at all — could be a fungal issue called blight or even a pest problem. Aphids, thrips, spider mites."

"Yeah, that's more or less what Google said, too. Was hoping someone might be able to narrow it down."

"Sorry to disappoint," he says, but the side of his mouth curls up and the familiarity of it once again takes my breath.

He glances at his watch — one of those techy exercise bands, causing me to wonder if he's a runner like Harrison — and I take a step back, clearly having held him longer than social etiquette allows. I open my mouth to say something benign, normal. Like how nice it was to run into him again. Good luck with the plumbing.

"I've actually got some time," he says, scratching his jawline with his free hand. It's covered in black pinpricks of day-old stubble. "Want me to come take a look?"

"What?"

"At your garden?" he says slowly.

"Oh, uh . . . no," I stutter, caught off

guard. "That's OK. It's fine. I'm sure you have a million other things you could be doing. Like plumbing."

"I really don't mind," he says. "I kind of owe you."

"You do?"

"Your husband saving Caroline and all." He pauses. "Harrison is your husband, yeah?"

"Yeah, yes. Right." I swallow, hoping I don't sound as idiotic as I think I do. And then I consider his offer — the thought of spending more time with him both appealing and daunting. I'm obviously a ball of bumbling nerves in his presence, but I'm also wildly curious to know more about him. Maybe I could uncover something — anything — that would explain the dreams. And really, what else am I going to do today? "OK, that would be great. I mean, if you really don't mind."

" 'Course not," he says. "Let me check out and then I can follow you."

I drive like a little old lady to my house, my hands gripping the steering wheel at ten and two, my eyes glancing in the rearview mirror every twenty seconds to check that Oliver is still there. That he is a real person, driving a real car (a gray Prius), coming to my real house. I even pinch myself. Hard.

On the skin of my wrist, leaving a red mark. It still stings as I pull onto the gravel driveway, Oliver right behind me.

"Wow. You've gotta lot of land out here," he says once we're out of our cars.

"Yeah. I've thought about getting chickens or something, you know, to make use of the space. And it is a farmhouse. I feel like it's a prerequisite."

Oliver doesn't reply and I will myself to stop talking as I lead him through the yard, but anxiety grips my belly, and I tend to ramble when I'm nervous. "I read this article a few years ago about the rise of suburban chicken farming, and it looked so quaint, so *This American Life.* And the chickens were kinda cute."

Oliver raises an eyebrow.

"I could totally see myself coming out here collecting the eggs every morning. I feel like I'd be a good chicken mom."

Oh my god — STOP TALKING ABOUT CHICKENS.

Thankfully, we get to the edge of the garden, affording me the opportunity to change the topic. "Here we are. Welcome to the jungle," I say, because that's what it looks like. A dead jungle, anyway. Most everything is brown and yellow and dry and withering, except for the weeds, which seem to be thriving.

"You know the thing no one tells you about chickens?" Oliver says.

I swivel toward him. "What?"

"They smell."

"They do?"

"Something awful."

I narrow my eyes at him. "How do you know that?"

"Worked on a poultry farm in Oregon once."

A poultry farm? I squint harder, as if trying to see him more clearly. These little unexpected tidbits of information remind me that I don't know this man at all. Even as I feel like I do. And it's frustrating, not least because it feels like he's being cryptic — offering small insights without any explanation. Maybe he's naturally a man of few words, but I want to know more — *need* to know — and it's starting to irk me.

"You know, it's funny — I worked on a poultry farm once, too."

His eyebrows shoot skyward. "Really?"

"No," I say. "Not really. That's a very uncommon thing."

His mouth breaks into its lopsided smile, deepening the groove in his cheek. He shifts his weight onto his other leg. "About seven

— maybe eight years ago, I stumbled across this organization called the Association of Global Organic Farm Opportunities, where you can get matched with a farm in the country of your choice and go work there for two, three months at a time. On a whim, I signed up. I've been all over — Peru, Alaska, Khartoum. I just got back from a vineyard in Australia."

He paces around the garden, studying it from all angles like someone buying a new car. "Wait — you get paid to travel the globe and . . . *farm?*" With his devil-may-care hair and hipsterish vibe I would have guessed Oliver did something creative — like a graphic designer or a drummer or a tattoo artist. I would not in a million years have guessed his actual job. Or that it was actually a job for anyone.

"Nah," he says. "It's volunteer. I only get room and board." Oliver bends his knees, fingers a few leaves, appraises plants.

"So . . . you're independently wealthy?"

His eyes flash in amusement. He jerks his head. "No."

I open my mouth to ask one of the string of new questions I have for him, but suddenly he stands, clapping his hands together, effectively cutting me off. "Right. Well, I have good news and bad news."

I tilt my head. "Bad news first."

"The tomatoes are past salvaging. We can harvest all of those jalapeños, and you might get a few more if we leave them in. The herbs are fine, they just need weeding. And I *might* be able to revive the Japanese eggplant, but everything else should probably come out."

I stare at him. "I have Japanese eggplant?"

His mouth turns up in a half grin. "You do."

"Oh." I scan the garden, wondering which one is the eggplant. "Well, what's the good news?"

"It should only take a few hours of hard manual labor to do it all?"

"Oh," I repeat. "That sounds like bad news and bad news."

He lifts his shoulders in apology. "I like to put an optimistic spin on things. Tiny character flaw."

Though I told him it wasn't necessary to help, I was grateful when he insisted, not only because it was an enormous job, but because I had more questions than answers and wanted more time with him. After grabbing the few garden tools left behind by the previous owner from my studio, we started working on opposite sides of the garden,

115

baking under the hot sun, the only sound the drone of bees and insects buzzing through the air. Now I pause, breathing heavily, and swipe at the beads of sweat on my forehead with my forearm. Oliver's on his knees, back curved, dark circles staining the armpits of his shirt. He's narrower than Harrison, wiry, but still, I can't help noticing his triceps flex and loosen with each grunting effort of uprooting the plants with his spade and hand.

"So," I begin. "Are you going to tell me what you do when you're not traveling the world, or do I have to guess?"

Oliver pauses in midtug and his onyx eyes land on mine. "I'm a writer."

"Oh." That fits him. This in-person Oliver and the man I feel like I know. When he doesn't elaborate, I prod. "Advertising? Playwright? Poet?"

"Ghost." He grunts and the roots of a plant come flying free, spraying dirt in an arc.

"Stories?" I ask. It earns me another half grin.

"No. It means I collaborate with other people — celebrity types that want to tell their life story but don't actually have the time or skill or whatever. Essentially, I write it for them."

116

"Anyone I know?"

"Maybe — you know Carson Flanagan?"

"That Food Network chef?" I ask excitedly. "Who doesn't know him? Who else?"

"Right now, I'm working with Penn Carro."

I scrunch my nose, vaguely remembering seeing some TED Talk that went viral where a guy was jumping around onstage like a jackrabbit on steroids, yelling at the crowd like some WWF wrestler. "Is that the guy with the ponytail and huge biceps that tells people how to get rich?"

"The one and only."

"God, is he as obnoxious as he seems in person?" I catch myself. "Sorry."

But he grins, a full-on wide smile, causing his lips to disappear and his face to completely open. "In person, he's worse."

I smile back and he holds my gaze for a beat before dropping his eyes.

"What about you?" he asks, attacking another plant. "What do you do?"

"Painter."

"House?" He cocks an eyebrow, teasing.

"No, but I may have to consider that soon to actually make money. The art galleries in Hope Springs haven't been receptive of my work so far. Although, to be honest, the ones in Philly weren't, either."

117

His head snaps up. "You lived in Philly?"

"Yeah." I try to understand his reaction.

"What part?"

"University. Cedar Park. Why?"

"I'm in Center City."

I freeze. "I thought you lived here."

"No," he says. "Just helping out Caroline, after her surgery and all. And then the pregnancy — she was shocked, to say the least, so I stuck around for a little bit."

I stare at him, wondering if maybe this is the puzzle piece I've been waiting for. University and Center City are so close — maybe we've passed each other on the street. In a restaurant? A coffee shop? A tingle travels up my spine at the possibility. But then reality sets in — it's a feeble explanation, at best. You see people all the time, but you don't *dream* about them. Over and over. Not to mention, when I first dreamt about him, I was in high school. In Silver Spring, Maryland.

"You miss it?" he asks.

I blink, coming out of my thoughts. "I do," I say, and I don't even realize how much until he's asked me. "I love the city — the energy, the people. It's so alive. Or maybe I just felt so alive when I lived there. Hope Springs is so . . ."

"Not that?" he offers.

"Exactly. Anyway, I miss all the restaurants. Indian food. Thai. *Delivery,*" I say, digging at the roots of the plant in front of me. "And the museums. The Rodin especially. God, I spent, like, half my life in that museum, it feels like."

"The Rodin? I don't think I've ever been to that one."

"What?" My voice rings loud and clear in the summer air.

"I know, right?" he says, not missing a beat. "I also strangle bunnies to death in their sleep."

"Sorry," I say, chagrined. "I thought everyone in Philly had been there at least once. It's like — cheering for the Eagles or getting cheesesteaks at Max's."

"Well, I do all *those* things. Can I have my Philly card back now?" He eyes me. I smile. "Honestly, I don't know all that much about art. I only have, like, one piece hanging in my apartment."

"Oh my god, let me guess. A rendering of the Eiffel Tower from IKEA."

"No."

"A canvas of horses running from IKEA."

"Nope."

"A black-and-white photograph of a bridge from IKEA."

"You're terrible at guessing," he says. "It

119

is a photograph, but it's not a bridge and it's not mass-produced, thank you very much. It's an original."

"Hm," I say, but I'm laughing. And it strikes me that I can't remember the last time I did.

We continue working, the conversation flowing more freely now. And as I learn more about him, I squirrel the facts away like I'm keeping a dossier:

He worked at a record store called Play It Again in his twenties.

He attended Fordham Community College but never graduated.

He has an energetic dog named Willy and takes him for runs often. His favorite route is along the Schuylkill River.

And though none of these facts explain why I may have dreamt about him, I realize that I'm thinking less about that, and more about the Oliver that's here and now. He's funny and — now that he's opened up a bit — easy to be around and I'm enjoying getting to know him. Or maybe I'm enjoying the respite from the reality of my life — the fruitless job hunt, the endless miscarriages, the way Harrison looks at me like I'm a glass that could shatter into a thousand pieces at any time. How I feel like I'm a glass that could shatter into a thousand pieces at any time.

Just when I'm starting to relax into the afternoon, I steal a glance at him. And something about the tilt of his head or the way he's clenching his jaw, struggling with a stubborn root, flattens me. I'm overcome with a feeling I can't name. Maybe it's only another flash of the déjà vu I've experienced on and off since seeing him.

Regardless, it triggers images of Oliver — recent dreams — to flood my mind. In some, we're standing, shoulder to shoulder, or across a room, a magnetic pull drawing me nearer. In others, he gives me things, weird things — an old rusted horseshoe; a file folder stuffed with diagrams of various animals; a brown paper bag that I thought was going to be a sandwich but instead contained teeth, hundreds of teeth, more than could fit in a paper bag. Even though the dreams are nonsensical, they still wake me up in heart-racing panics. Cold sweats.

And then there are the other dreams. The ones that need no explanation but result in my waking with a familiar throbbing between my legs, confusion and lust and guilt all roiling in my stomach.

"Mia," he says, his voice suddenly serious.

"Yeah?" Mine rises an octave with nerves; the fear that he could see exactly what I was thinking.

"That plant you're attacking?"

I look down.

"Yeah."

"That's the Japanese eggplant."

"Oh."

I glance back up at him in time to see him cover a smile with his wrist. I shake my head, trying to clear it. Stupid dreams.

Later, we stand sore and sweating and covered in dirt, admiring our hard work. Every inch of my exposed skin is on fire, and I realize belatedly that I should have slathered on sunscreen or at least worn a hat, as Harrison always likes to remind me.

"What now?" I ask.

Oliver slaps at a mosquito, scratches the back of his neck. "Well, you'll want to get some compost to replace the nutrients the soil has lost and then you could plant some fall vegetables in the empty areas if you want. July is perfect for starting kale, lettuce, spinach."

"OK." I nod, as he pauses to take a breath.

"And *then,* maybe pull weeds once a week? Water regularly? You know, the bare minimum garden upkeep." He's teasing me again.

"In my defense, the irrigation system

broke right after we moved in."

"Oh. You didn't say — I could probably fix that." He starts scanning the ground looking for the tubing.

"No, no," I say. "You've done enough. Truly. I don't know how I can repay you."

"We'll call it even," he says. "Although, if you're ever in Philly, let me know. You can take me to the Rodin. Let me get my Philly card back."

I laugh. "Deal."

"OK, then," he says, when we've reached the driveway. "I guess I'll see you."

And even though I know it's just something people say, I wonder if it's true. Though I suppose I could run into him again sometime, we have no reason to see each other on purpose, and I try to ignore the twinge of disappointment tugging my belly.

"Thanks again." He stands there for a moment, looks as if he's going to say something else. But then he turns and I wonder if I was imagining it. The hesitation.

I watch as he gets in the Prius, executes a perfect three-point turn in the driveway and waves as he drives off back toward the road. I lift a hand, and then his car is swallowed up by the trees, and he's gone — like a dream evaporating in the bright light of morning.

There are few things I find more obnoxious in life than those couples who gush in clichéd platitudes, reminiscing about the beginning of their relationships: *When I met him, I knew he was the one,* or *It was like I'd known her forever.*

Oh my gosh, how sweet, I always respond, smiling and nodding, while inside I'm thinking: *Please stop. You sound like a freakin' Nicholas Sparks novel.*

When I first met Harrison, he was standing by one of Prisha Khanna's life-size black-and-white canvas photographs: the one of two naked women loosely intertwined like an infinity scarf; a Celtic knot. He was impossibly handsome, in his black square glasses, his Skid Row T-shirt, holding a cotton-candy-pink martini in one hand and a navy sport coat in the other. When he smiled at me, part of me died a little, while part of me came completely alive.

But he felt brand-new — like a wrapped present, and I was a child on her birthday who couldn't wait to find out what was inside.

Which is why no one could have been more surprised than me when it occurs to me as I stand frozen alone at the edge of my driveway that that feeling I couldn't name earlier — when Oliver's profile triggered the flood of dreams — wasn't just a passing sense of familiarity. Or déjà vu.

It was that — even though I didn't even know any basic facts about him until today — I felt like *I'd known him forever.*

And all at once, I feel ridiculous and foolish.

I give my head a firm shake, shoot one last glance at the garden, the square patch of mostly brown soil waiting for whatever comes next, and turn and walk into my house.

CHAPTER 8

Later that night, Harrison is lying beside me, his skin still humid from the shower, his head propped up on three pillows. He's reading a worn copy of *The Hobbit*. Usually, his nose is stuck in one of his medical journals, which he keeps a stack of both beside the bed and on the back of the toilet, reading them cover to cover every month like most men devour ESPN or *Esquire*. But every now and then he picks up a real book — Stephen King, Michael Crichton or J. R. R. Tolkien, who was a favorite of his growing up. He rereads *The Hobbit* and *Lord of the Rings* every couple of years, and I've always found it endearing, the way I can picture him as a child, all legs and arms and big round eyes discovering the story for the first time. It's always made me feel closer to him, somehow, knowing specific details of his life before me like that. But tonight he feels distant — unreachable, even though my hand is inches away from his. And I know it's my guilt lying between us.

I know I didn't *do* anything wrong, technically. And I know it's perfectly normal to be attracted to other people, even when you're married. I'm only human. But is it normal to keep thinking about them, long after they're gone? I keep having flashbacks every time I try to put him out of my mind. Oliver, sweating in the garden. Oliver, his deep laugh ringing in the air. Oliver, nearly looking through me with those pools of ink he has for eyes. It's not that I've wanted to — but it's like that old adage when someone tells you not to think about an elephant and then that's the only thing you can think of.

And of course I told Harrison — not about the sweat and the triceps and the intense eyes — but about Oliver. Running into him and then him coming to help in the garden.

"Really? Wow — people in small towns really are nice," he said, and then stopped in his tracks at the sight of my lobster-red cheeks and nose. "Yikes, that looks painful." When he noticed the large mixing bowl on the counter filled with about thirty jalapeños, he said: "Is this your way of telling me you want a ten-gallon vat of salsa for dinner?"

He didn't mention my one-time confession of dreaming about Oliver, and I wondered if he even remembered. Maybe I should have said more — but to what end? *Remember how I told you I dream about him? Yep, still happening.*

Harrison turns a page now and it catches my attention, drawing my gaze to his hands. He has surgeon hands, his fingers long and capable, nails neatly trimmed. I'd know them anywhere. If there were a game show where you had to pick your husband's hands out of a lineup, I'd never lose.

"Do you want to have sex?" I say.

His eyes shift from the book to me, his studious eyebrows rising in surprise behind his square glasses. We haven't had sex since losing the baby, which is normal for us. I don't know about Harrison, but it takes time for me to be emotionally ready, and I never am, but eventually I just have to do it to get the first time over with. I hate that I know what's normal for us after a miscarriage.

"Yeah." He smiles and dog-ears the corner of the page he's on.

Though it was my idea, I have trouble getting into it. Harrison is going through all the right motions, the things I like, but when he tries to slip a finger inside me, I'm still dry. I know it's because I'm afraid to let go. He's being so sweet and attentive, and all I can think is this is the love we poured into making our baby — all three of our babies — and it wasn't enough to keep them here, and I'm holding the heartache in so tight, because if I don't, I'm afraid it will never stop pouring out of me.

But I want to have sex with my husband — I need to have sex with him. So I shut my eyes tight and try to clear my mind, while Harrison weaves his hand in my hair, kisses my neck, slowly makes his way down to my breasts.

Don't think of babies.

Don't think of Harrison.

Don't think of elephants.

I think of elephants.

I think of Oliver.

"Jesus," Harrison breathes in my ear. And suddenly we're having sex with wild abandon, like the early days of our relationship, with no agenda for baby making, all familiar routines put aside. "Whoa," he says after, when he's flat on his back, ruddy cheeked and sweating. The clock blinks 10:43 p.m. "What was that?"

I shrug, out of breath, a pang of guilt seizing my gut. "You didn't like it?"

"No, God no. I did. I just want to know

129

exactly what I did to cause that, so I can make it happen again," he says, grinning. I stare at my beautiful husband, his neatly trimmed beard, his kind eyes, and even though he didn't exactly cause it, all thoughts of Oliver are gone from my mind as quickly as they came.

I think of Harrison.

I think of babies.

And I feel myself splitting open like the seam of a too-tight dress. I burst into tears. Harrison gathers me in his arms and I lay my cheek against his warm, damp chest, my tears mixing with his sweat, creating a river of love and sorrow. The first time is done and I know the next time will be easier because this is what we do after we lose a baby.

The next morning, I'm eating a banana in the kitchen when Harrison bangs in the back door, breathing heavily, the top half of his shirt soaked through.

"Is it raining?" I ask, looking out the window to see for myself.

"Yeah," he says. "Started a few minutes ago." He strides to the refrigerator, grabbing a glass out of the cabinet to the right of it and filling it with water from the spout in the door. He gulps it down and fills it up again. "You're up early."

It's true — I'm rarely awake before Harrison leaves for work, but this morning my eyes popped open at 5:50 and I was up, not just because my skin was on fire from where the sun had broiled it, but because with each tiny movement of my body, it seemed as though every single muscle screamed out in rebellion. Gardening is apparently a full-body workout. But despite the soreness — or maybe partly because of it — I felt refreshed. Renewed in some way. And I realized, for the first time in at least four or five nights, I didn't dream of Oliver. I didn't dream at all.

"I had a good night's sleep," I say.

"Good," he says, kissing me on the end of my burnt nose and stealing a bite of my banana as he passes me by.

"You're running late, though," I say, noticing the time on the microwave: 6:13. Harrison's usually showered and out of the house by now.

"I know. I ran longer than I meant to."

"Really?" Harrison is a by-the-book kind of guy. He runs three miles, no more, no less, every Monday, Wednesday and Friday and has for as long as I've known him — even when he was a resident, he found a way to squeeze it in. It's unlike him to lose

131

track of time.

"I'm gonna grab a shower," he says.

"I'm gonna go to the studio," I say. And then: "Don't forget — our appointment is at two today."

He looks at me blankly.

"The fertility specialist?"

"Right," he says.

"Do you want to come pick me up or meet there?"

"Uh . . . meet, I guess." He closes the gap between us and kisses me on the lips. "Have a good day painting."

"Have a good day saving lives," I call after him. I finish my banana and run the short distance between the house and the studio, the rain pelting me like tiny pebbles all the way.

When I enter my studio, I'm greeted by my work in progress: a large panorama of a carnival at night — a carousel, a fishbowl game, a blur of flashing electric lights as the mechanical seats of a ride whip round and round in a frenzy. For all the weirdness of my life the past few weeks, the bright side is that I've been sketching and painting prolifically — faster and more than I ever have before. I've been re-creating the details from my dreams, like snippets from the set of a movie — first the chicken, then an apple tree in bloom, ducks in flight . . . I even sketched out that weird paper bag full of teeth. It's felt like important work, to capture these images that feel so real in the middle of the night and fade by the light of day. For some reason, I've felt compelled to make them tangible, to give them permanence.

Maybe it has nothing to do with the dreams and everything to do with the babies I keep losing. Maybe I just want to hold on to *something*. To prove that I actually can.

As I round out the wooden nostrils of a carousel horse, I think back to the dream, how weird it was. Like a nightmare, really. As if Oliver and I were stuck in a zombie apocalypse movie. The amusement park we were in felt desolate, but all the rides were moving, their bright lights blinking and spinning, nearly blinding against the dark sky. One of my hands clutched his; the other held a cloud of blue cotton candy. I ripped off tufts of it with my mouth, laughing at nothing. I turned away from him for a second, and when I turned back, there were suddenly floods of people everywhere. We were getting jostled by the influx of bodies surrounding us. Then my hand slipped from his and he was gone, swallowed by the crowd. But I could still hear him, shouting for me over and over until his throat was hoarse. I didn't understand — he was right there — why was he panicking? But it was contagious, in the way panic often is, and I woke up, fright filled, heart racing and confused.

I stand back from the large canvas and squint, taking in the painting as a whole, and then start contouring the edge of a Tilt-A-Whirl, trying to get the proper angle of it in midtwirl. I take it slow, really settling into the process and getting lost in my work in a way it doesn't feel like I've done since college.

I'm so absorbed that I don't even think about time, until a glance at my phone informs me it's 1:45. Shit. I'm going to be late to my appointment.

It's 2:13 when I fly into the waiting room of Dr. Hobbes's office in my paint-splattered T-shirt, my hands still covered in the colors of the amusement park. My eyes dart around the room, frantically searching for Harrison, an apology already formed in my mouth, ready to escape. But he's not there. I check in at the front desk and ask if my husband has come in — maybe he's in the bathroom. But a woman with braids and gold hoop earrings tells me she doesn't think she's seen him. I sit down and wait, thinking he must have gotten held up at work and will rush through the door any second.

But he doesn't. And halfway through the appointment — when my legs are up in stirrups and the nurse is firing a million questions at me about my lifestyle, family medical history, menstrual cycle — I realize he's not going to.

The downside of being a surgeon's wife isn't just the long hours, but that strangers' misfortunes can impact you so greatly. It's one of the things Vivian warned me about when I told her Harrison and I were getting married (well, right after she ribbed me for the many years I said I was never getting married). "It's a tough life, Mia. You have to accept that you are always going to come second." It's not that she didn't adore Harrison, it was just her pragmatic, big-sister way of making sure I had thought everything through.

"Of course I know that," I said, slightly annoyed. After all, I was the one who had been living with it already, through his first year of residency. What I didn't know was how the resentment would build up over time, along with the surprising added emotion of self-loathing. Because what kind of terrible person gets angry at her husband for missing a birthday party, an anniversary dinner — or a reproductive endocrinologist appointment — when he is literally saving someone else's life.

I'm folding laundry when Harrison walks in the front door, throwing his keys on the upturned cardboard box in the foyer, taking a deep breath as he slowly crosses the threshold into the den. "I'm sorry about the appointment," he says. I got his text when I was in the car on the way home, that a Mack truck had T-boned a church bus full of kids twenty miles north of Fordham and he had been pulled in to the ER to help with the influx of patients. I knew he couldn't help it — that this was his job — but that knowledge didn't keep me from pounding the steering wheel with the heel of my palm and primal grunting through my teeth in frustration.

"How did it go?" he asks.

"Fine," I say, picking up a pair of his boxer shorts and snapping them with my wrists to straighten them out. "I filled out a lot of forms, answered a bunch of questions. They took some blood. Should get the results back soon.

"What happened with the accident? Was everyone OK?"

"No," he says, rubbing a hand over his face. "Three fatalities. All at the scene, though. None at the hospital. So far." He knocks his knuckles gently on the back of the couch. "Craziest thing — these twin sisters, thirteen-year-olds, were sitting next to each other on the bus right in the middle of it where the truck rammed them. The one closest to the window had a punctured lung, diaphragmatic rupture, possible spinal injury, bleeding all over; I mean the works. But her sister was perfectly fine. Not a scratch on her. I checked her out myself."

It's something I've heard Harrison marvel at before — the mind-boggling randomness of life. Of death. But I don't feel like getting deep into some existential discussion right now.

"That is crazy." I feel another ping of guilt that here I was annoyed at Harrison missing a doctor appointment, while some parent was about to be dealt the worst news of their life. "Will the sister be OK? The one that got injured."

"I think so," he says. "They got her into surgery in time."

He walks around the couch and tugs at the sock that's currently in my hand. He lays it down on the cushion. Then he puts his hands on my shoulders and waits until I look at him. "Hey," he says.

"Hey," I say.

"I'm sorry about the appointment."

The way he's standing there, it's like he's holding me together, and forgiveness really does begin to pulse through my veins, melting the tension out of my muscles. "I know." I lean into him, laying my head on his chest. After a minute of listening to my husband's heart thud in my ear, I feel even better. "Good news is, the nurse said you can go by anytime this week to drop your sample. Dr. Hobbes says your swimmers are probably fine, since I keep getting pregnant, but it's protocol."

"*Drop my sample?* Doesn't that sound like fun," he deadpans.

"Could be," I say, lifting my head. "They might even give you a fresh magazine, if you ask nicely. Ooh! Or maybe a picture of Whoopi Goldberg." A few vodkas into a late night early in our relationship, Harrison confessed he had a high school fantasy involving her in the movie *Sister Act.*

He dips his chin and sighs a dramatic, tortured sigh. "For the thousandth time, it was the whole nun thing. Not her, specifically. And I'm never telling you anything ever again." Then he palms my face between his hands and kisses the top of my nose,

138

like he's done a thousand times, mostly in the early mornings, when he has to get out of bed and he thinks I'm still asleep.

"Come on," he says, wrapping an arm around my shoulders. "I'll scrounge us up something to eat."

Later, as I'm sitting on the lone barstool and he's standing across from me spearing a carrot from the chicken stir-fry with his fork, he says: "Two things."

I stuff a piece of soy-drenched broccoli in my mouth and watch his face, waiting.

"Foster mentioned something about one of those continuing education art classes his wife attends at the community college needing a teacher starting in August, I think. Current teacher is moving or retiring or something."

I raise my eyebrows.

"I know, I know. You think teaching is like giving up, but still, thought I'd pass it along."

"OK, thanks," I say. "Second thing?"

He grabs a glass from the cabinet and fills it with water at the sink. Takes a sip. "Caroline came in today for her follow-up."

I still. "Yeah? How is she?"

"Good. Incision's all healed. Everything's fine."

"Oh. OK." I'm wondering why on earth

he's brought her up. He rarely talks about his patients unless something unusual happened.

"Anyway, I was telling her how Oliver helped you with the garden and all of that, and one thing led to another, I guess, and she asked if we'd come for dinner."

"Oh. That was nice," I say, knowing Harrison said no. It's an occupational hazard — the doctor-patient relationship can feel so intimate at times that some patients mistake it for a real friendship, often inviting Harrison to bat mitzvahs or birthday parties or fiftieth anniversary celebrations. While he'll attend big celebrations, where he's one in a crowd of people, he eschews the smaller, more intimate ones — coffee, lunch, dinner. Those, he feels, are crossing a boundary of sorts, creating a more personal connection that could compromise future care.

"Did you turn her down kindly?" I ask.

He hesitates. "We're going over there a week from Saturday."

"What?" There's no way to hide my shock. "Why?"

He takes a deep breath and another sip of water. "Babe, it's just — we've been here what, two months? And you haven't really —" He pauses. "I think it would be good for us. To get out. Make friends. Feel more settled."

I stare at him, trying to excavate the subtext of what he's saying. "We have friends."

"In Philly. Hard to borrow a cup of sugar from someone an hour and a half away."

"What do I need sugar for? I don't bake."

He looks down his nose at me, pointedly. "You know what I mean. Anyway, you already know Oliver. And I think you'll like her. She's funny."

As I scrape up the last few bits of brown rice from my plate, I gnaw the inside of my cheek, to keep myself from telling my husband that it's not her I'm worried about.

CHAPTER 9

Sometimes, I'll work furiously on a painting, finish it in two days and be done — never to paint another stroke on it again. But then there are the ones that take me weeks, months even, and every time I look at it, I'll still see more I can add, angles or shadows to be tweaked, sections that need to be completely painted over and redone. The carnival painting is the latter. I'm not sure if it's because I keep remembering details from that dream — a man on stilts with red circles on his cheeks and striped pants, or the moon dangling in the sky like a slivered almond — or because I want to stay living in it, like an actor clinging to a favorite movie set, long after production has ceased. Or maybe I'm trying to get lost in something other than my thoughts.

Like how Harrison still hasn't gone to the fertility clinic, even though it's been a week since he missed the first appointment and the clinic is only ten minutes away from the hospital and he can't really be *that* busy. I reminded him about it on Monday evening and then asked once more on Tuesday and he snapped at me: *I said I'll go and I will, Mia. Give me a freakin' break.*

Or how I'm going to see Oliver again in two days, when I wasn't sure that I'd see him again ever. It feels a little dangerous. Not deadly dangerous, like swimming with sharks, but mildly dangerous, like touching a candle flame on a dare. Although, sometimes, I guess, it only takes a tiny flicker to burn an entire house straight to the ground.

On Saturday night, Harrison pulls into the driveway of a blue clapboard Colonial with white trim in downtown Hope Springs. I'm jittery, like I drank three cups of coffee in a row on an empty stomach, and I swallow, trying to calm my nerves. I considered begging off. If I had feigned illness or exhaustion, Harrison would have easily canceled. But honestly, Oliver's just a man. He has no idea that I've dreamt about him — or what we've done in those dreams.

Thank God.

Harrison and I follow the flagstone path and go up four cement steps onto the porch. He pulls the handle of the screen door, opening it to rap on the frame of the solid wood one behind it.

Three deep barks ring out from the bowels of the house, and when the door opens, a horse covered in black fur greets us, nearly knocking me over. Harrison grabs my arm to steady me. And Caroline comes flying out in a blur, reaching for its collar.

"Willy!" she says, while simultaneously apologizing to us and pulling him back in the house. "He gets excited about company." She calls over her shoulder, "Oliver! Come get your dog."

And then he's there, not ten yards away. Standing at the transom between the living room and the kitchen, hair wet from the shower, ears sticking out making him look boyish and manly at the same time, a kitchen towel slung over his shoulder.

The sight of him momentarily unsteadies me, that now-familiar out-of-body sensation taking hold, and I repeat my mantra.

He's just a man.

He's just a man.

He's just a man.

Oliver whistles. "C'mon, Willy." And the dog instantly stops struggling against Caroline and trots obediently to Oliver, sitting at his feet. Its tongue hangs out of the side of its mouth like a large piece of bologna.

Caroline straightens up, brushing back wisps of brown hair that fell loose from the knot at the back of her head. "Sorry about that," she repeats, her chest still heaving slightly from the effort. "Please come in."

Harrison gently places his hand at the small of my back and guides me in first.

"Stay," Oliver says, holding his palm up to the dog's snout, and then strides toward us. Everything about him is casual — from his bare feet to the plain white T-shirt beneath the draped kitchen towel to the open beer bottle loosely resting in his right fist, which he deftly transfers to his left to shake hands with Harrison.

Then he turns to me, his eyes friendly, warm. "Mia."

"Hi," I say, slipping my hand in Harrison's and squeezing.

"What kind of dog is that?" Harrison's still staring at the beast, his voice full of wonder.

"Willy's a Newfoundland. Gentle giant," Oliver says, his face nearly beaming with pride as he glances back in the dog's direction. He turns back to us. "Come on in. What can I get you — beer, wine?"

"Wine, please," I say. We both look at Harrison. He's still looking at the dog.

"Total beast," he's muttering in awe, and then, noticing the silence, he glances up.

"Oh, beer would be great. Thanks." Caroline directs us toward the sofa and chairs and Oliver retreats back into the kitchen, Willy following him obediently. Harrison and I sit on an old brown and orange flower-patterned couch staring at four taxidermied mallard ducks hanging in midflight on the dark-paneled wall above the fireplace mantel.

Harrison dives into the social courtesies — starting with the weather ("Can you believe this heat? Brutal"), asking Caroline how she's feeling, commenting on the delicious scents drifting in from the kitchen — while I murmur my agreement and look at the antique end tables, the guitar in the corner of the room, the worn patterned rugs, the dead ducks.

"They're dreadful, aren't they?" Oliver appears at my side gripping two beers by the neck in one hand and a stemless glass of wine in the other. I follow his gaze to the ducks I've been staring at as if they will come back to life if I concentrate hard enough. "Oh! I don't . . . they're kind of . . ."

"Morbid," he says, fixing Caroline with a look. He hands me the wineglass, then reaches his beer hand across me toward Harrison, who takes one, still engrossed in conversation with Caroline.

She stops in midsentence. "I heard that."

Oliver grins and lowers himself into the formal wingback chair next to me. "Well, I don't understand why you haven't gotten rid of them."

"I think they've kind of grown on me," Caroline says, then turns to us. "This was our great-aunt and -uncle's house. They took us in when our mom died. Kidney disease."

"Oh, I'm sorry." I glance from Caroline to Oliver.

He waves me off, but there's a sadness in his eyes. "It was a long time ago."

"So Mia tells me you live in Philly," Harrison says to Oliver.

"Yep. Headed back tomorrow actually."

I jerk my head up at this, and Oliver's eyes find mine briefly, then he glances away. My cheeks flush, and I train my gaze back on the ducks, trying to pretend my embarrassment is solely from my reaction at his news and not the way I felt when his eyes were locked on mine.

In the dining room, as we're all tucking into big bowlfuls of spaghetti carbonara, Caroline sighs with pleasure.

"Oh, it's nearly perfect, Ollie," she says, chewing with relish.

"Nearly?" he says.

"Well, nothing is as good as Sorelli's. Have you two eaten there yet?" Caroline asks. The name of the restaurant sounds familiar, but I can't place it — maybe I've passed by it while downtown. "Best Italian food ever," she continues. "It's a shame, since I can't ever step foot in the restaurant again."

"Why not?" I ask, reaching for my glass.

"While I worked there, I had sex with the manager."

I nearly spit out my wine.

"Turns out he's married."

"You knew he was married when you slept with him," Oliver says, monotone.

"I know, but it adds something to the story when you say 'turns out,' doesn't it? Anyway," she says to us, "now I'm pregnant with his baby! And done with the job at Sorelli's."

"You know, you don't have to share *everything.*"

And that's when I remember where I heard about Sorelli's. "Oh, right! This woman at the Blue-Eyed Macaw was telling me about the open waitress position there."

Oliver sweeps his hand out, palm up. "And there you have it — one of the many perks of a small town. Everyone knows everything."

"So, Caroline, are you currently looking for work?"

Caroline shakes her head as she swallows the bite she's chewing and wipes the corners of her mouth with her napkin. "Luckily I found something pretty quickly — I'm assistant to the manager of Parks and Rec."

"Oh, that's great," I say. "So what kind of stuff do you do?"

Oliver leans forward. "Yeah, what do you actually do, Care? You haven't really said."

"Well, I get coffee and answer phones and that kind of thing, but I also get to sit in on meetings and make suggestions." Caroline grins. "Like, you know how as a kid I always hated that Hope Springs didn't have a Christmas parade?"

"No," Oliver says.

"Yes, you do. I used to write letters to the mayor every November and I'd get that annoying form letter back about how they had plenty of wonderful celebrations like Shady Brook's Holiday Light Show and that stupid train ride turning into the North Pole Express, even though it doesn't even go anywhere. But what kind of small town doesn't have a Christmas parade?"

"Hope Springs," Oliver deadpans, and then he studies Caroline's face, which looks positively fit to burst with news. "Let me guess," he says. "They do now."

"They do now." Her lips curl into a smug smile. "I've already booked both the high school and middle school marching bands and a Santa to ride in a convertible tossing out candy at the end."

"Sounds like fun," I say.

"Thanks. So what do you do, Mia?"

"Oh." I buy time by resting my fork in the bowl. "I've actually kind of been job hunting myself recently. Something part-time."

"Mia's an artist," Harrison interjects. "A painter." I warm at the pride in his voice. But I know what's coming next — the subtle questions to determine if I'm a *serious* painter, if it's an actual career or a cute hobby — and I'm not eager to delve into my failures once again, so I change the subject.

"I saw the guitar in the den — do either of you play?" As soon as I ask it, I realize I'm hoping it's not —

"Oliver," Caroline says. A man with a guitar might be a cliché, but it's a cliché for a reason — it's really hot. I used to think a man playing *any* instrument was sexy, until I went to Harrison's parents' home in Buffalo for our first Thanksgiving together and learned he played the trumpet in his high school marching band.

150

"Oh my god. You *have* to play me a song," I said, late that night in his childhood bedroom.

"What? No. It's too loud. It'll wake my parents."

"They're not asleep yet."

After a lot more cajoling, he acquiesced. Pursing his lips to the mouthpiece, he started blowing, his fingers moving rustily, his eyes bulging from the effort, as I stared in wide wonder at this new side of Harrison.

Then his dad banged on the wall, startling us both. "What the hell is that noise? We're trying to sleep." And that's when I started laughing so hard, I couldn't stop.

"Was that even a song?" I asked, through the fits and starts.

"It was KC and the Sunshine Band," he said, half-wounded. " 'Get Down Tonight.' "

The fact that it sounded nothing like that only made me laugh harder.

"Meh. I used to," Oliver says now, countering Caroline. "I haven't played in a while."

The conversation continues over another bottle of wine — four people getting to know each other during dinner. And I'm really surprised to find that I'm enjoying myself. I mean, one would think it would be eternally awkward to sit at a dinner table

151

with your husband and the man you've been having less-than-platonic dreams about. And it was, at first. But the thing is — Oliver is so normal. I mean yes, he's dead sexy in his urban hipster way. Objectively speaking, of course. But he's also affable and self-deprecating and funny. Actually, weirdly, in that way, he reminds me a lot of Harrison. I steal a glance at my husband, feeling warm as he spins one of his tales from the ER. It's a classic — one I've heard him share a few times — from his first week on rotation as a surgical resident at Thomas Jefferson about three buddies who went out drinking together.

"Let's call them Moe, Curly and Larry," he's saying. "They get drunk as skunks. Larry decides he's going to drive home. Moe, realizing that's not safe, tries to stop him. Won't let him in his car. Larry, pissed, pulls out his gun — naturally — and shoots Moe."

"Oh no!" Caroline squeals.

"So Moe pulls out his gun and shoots back. Then — then! — wait for it. Curly, he's packing, too. Of course! So he pulls out his gun and shoots Larry, wanting to defend his buddy. Multiple gunshot wounds all show up at the ER at once." Harrison laughs, shakes his head. "Fortunately, liquored up as they were, not one of them could hit the broad side of a barn, only sustained flesh wounds, and they all pulled through."

Relaxed, I reach for a piece of bread out of the basket in front of me. A comfortable silence falls over the table, as everyone pushes back from their plates, the only sound the heavy panting from Willy lying in the corner, eyeing the floor for a crumb to drop. I rip off a hunk of sourdough and chew.

"Oh my god," Caroline announces, slapping her palms on the table. "I just had the weirdest sense of déjà vu. Like we've all been here before."

"Really?" My head whips toward her.

"Yes. Oh, never mind, it's gone."

"That's odd," Harrison says, slowly. Thoughtfully. "Mia got that, too. When we ran into you at Dr. Okafor's." I swivel toward him, and that's when I see it. His face is relaxed, open, and I know he's had one glass of wine too many. Oh God. No. Nonononononononononononono. This is not happening. I glare at him wildly, trying to catch his attention. He doesn't look at me. I clutch my fork, ready to — what? — launch it at him? Stab myself directly in the heart?

"Tell them, honey," he urges.

"No," I say. "It's nothing."

"No, it's funny," Harrison says, and I realize he thinks it really is. There's no malice in his voice. "She thought she knew Oliver." I stare at him with wide, desperate eyes and he looks at me. Really sees me. And then he shrugs. "Probably from the Giant or wherever you guys ran into each other."

Oh, thank God. I slump back in my chair.

"Or from her dreams."

"Harrison!" And suddenly I'm stone-cold sober, staring at my husband in disbelief.

"What?" Caroline says. "You had a dream about Ollie?"

"No," I say. I feel Oliver's eyes on me and I immediately start laughing to cover my embarrassment. "It was probably just someone that looked like him. Dreams are so weird, aren't they?"

"Oh my god, they are," Caroline says. "I have that one where I'm back in high school, but I've forgotten the combination to my locker, or where my classes are, or I've missed, like, forty-five days of school and they're not going to let me graduate. Do you have those?"

"I don't know." Harrison's forehead wrinkles. "I don't think I really dream."

"Everyone dreams," Caroline says, as if she's the foremost expert on the subject.

"Some are just better at remembering them than others." It's something I've told Harrison before and normally I would jump in, agreeing with her, but I'm currently too busy trying to decide if it's better to slink under the table and lie there until it's time to leave or fake a sudden illness and rush to the car.

Caroline stands up, clutching her stomach. "Ugh. Pregnancy indigestion is no joke. Anyway, I hope you all aren't too full. I made bread pudding for dessert."

"Oh, I'm stuffed," I say, a little too enthusiastically.

Harrison stands up, and I'm relieved he got the hint — since he so clearly missed all the others I'd been lobbing in his direction. I ball my napkin on the table and scoot my chair back, ready to thank Oliver and Caroline for the delicious meal and make our exit. Harrison stretches his arms overhead and then pats his taut belly. "Sounds great. I love bread pudding," he says. "Point me toward the bathroom?"

And then they're both gone, and I'm alone. With Oliver. I fiddle with the napkin on the side of my plate and try to pretend that everything is completely normal. In my peripheral, I see him lean forward, his eyes nearly boring a hole in the side of my face.

I glance up and offer what I hope is a small, normal smile. He doesn't return it.

"Is that true?"

"What?"

"You've dreamt about me?"

"Oh." I attempt a coquettish giggle, one meant to convey: *Yes. So silly how the mind works, right?* But it comes out sounding maniacal instead. More like: *I'm going to slit your throat tonight while you sleep.*

He tilts his head, his expression serious. "Was it before we met?"

My heart slams into my chest. My mouth turns to cotton. *What?* I try to say the word out loud, but it doesn't come. I swallow, my throat like sandpaper.

"How did you . . . ? Why would you . . . ?"

Something clatters in the kitchen. A crash, more like, but neither of us moves. "Because," he says, his black marble eyes penetrating mine, "I dream about you, too."

My mouth remains open; a breath comes out, and sounds a little like *Oh.* Or maybe it doesn't. Maybe I don't breathe at all. Maybe the earth collapses on itself. A meteor strikes. My body floats up into the sky as weightless as a balloon filled with helium. Anything is possible.

"Well!" Caroline breezes back into the room. "Thanks to your gentle giant" — she

tosses a glinty glare in Oliver's direction —
"the bread pudding is now all over the
kitchen floor. Which is fine, because I don't
think it was my best, anyway. But the good
news is, I found push-pops in the freezer."
She holds up a cardboard box and then
darts her eyes suspiciously between us,
either feeling the thick tension in the air or
just noticing the way Oliver and I are looking at everything but each other.

"What?" she says. "What did I miss?"

"I'm so sorry, babe," Harrison says when I
maneuver his Infiniti into the driveway later
that evening.

"Huh?" I look at him in the passenger seat
as if I've suddenly realized he's there. I've
spent the entire car ride home wavering
between good old-fashioned shock and trying to decide how exactly to tell Harrison
what Oliver said — because of course I'm
going to tell Harrison — and the best I've
come up with is: *The strangest thing just happened.*

But I haven't been able to push the words
out of my mouth. Fortunately, he's been
chatty, thanks to the wine, dissecting the
night the way couples do: *biggest goddamn
dog I've ever seen . . . . I knew you'd like
her . . . carbonara was a little too eggy.* Usu-

ally an active participant, tonight I mumbled affirmations and stared out the windshield into the long stretch of road in front of us.

"You've been so quiet, and it hit me," he says. "I didn't even think about Caroline being pregnant — how that might affect you." He's looking at me with such concern. Love.

"Oh — no, Harrison. I mean, yeah, it's hard, but —" I swallow. "You were right. I did like her."

"Still. It was stupid of me. Insensitive."

I want to explain. To tell him it's not that. *The strangest thing just happened.* I will myself to say it out loud.

But the words won't come.

Not when we step into the bright light of the foyer.

Not when we're pulling limbs out of shirtsleeves and pants.

Not when Harrison is methodically flossing each tooth.

In bed, Harrison presses his lips to my temple and says: "Forgot to tell you, I went to the fertility specialist today." And instead of the elation I should feel, guilt cuts deeper into my stomach. My sweet Harrison. Unaware of the secret lying between us. I want to tell him — but I just can't. Because *the* strangest *thing just happened,* and really, who on earth would believe it?

Besides Oliver.

CHAPTER 10

When I wake up Sunday morning, Harrison's side of the bed is empty, and by the silence in the house, I know he must be out running — even though it bucks his regular schedule. Maybe my husband is becoming unpredictable. I roll over, glancing at the digital clock on his nightstand: 9:36. And I sit straight up, every nerve in my body awake and alert.

I dream about you, too.

I throw off the covers and, still wearing the white tank I slept in, yank on a pair of Harrison's old boxer shorts. I go into the kitchen to make some coffee, chugging the first cup that I brew like it's vodka, the hot liquid scalding my throat. The second one I take into the living room.

I prop myself on the couch in the living room, my hands wrapped around the mug, and as I sit there in silence, the world comes sharply into focus. I notice the thin film of dust on our flat-screen, the twittering of birds fluttering right outside the window.

I dream about you, too.

Is that *really* what he said? It all happened so fast. Maybe I misheard him. Perhaps I had too much wine. Or the acoustics were bad. Or I had a ministroke that caused a hallucination, something I read about in one of Harrison's medical journals once.

Maybe he said: *I* think *about you, too.* Or maybe he didn't say anything at all.

Maybe I am completely losing my mind.

"Mia?"

I startle and jerk my head to see Harrison standing in the doorway between the kitchen and the den, sweaty and red-faced. "Sorry," he says. "I thought you heard me come in."

"No, lost in thought, I guess."

He tugs the hem of his shirt up to absorb the sweat from his chin, revealing his tan belly, a few dark curls framing his navel. "Hey — you wanna go paddleboarding today? Foster was telling me about this little outfit up the Delaware. It's only about thirty miles from here."

All I can do is stare at him. My husband. Who wants to go paddleboarding with me. And is standing in front of me, solid and real. And I think of Oliver and the dreams and the near out-of-body way I felt at times around him. And I don't know what's happening to me, but suddenly I'm cold, my limbs nearly convulsing with chill. I tug a blanket off the back of the couch and wrap it tightly around my shoulders.

"I don't think I'm up for that today. I have some errands to run."

Harrison shrugs. "OK. I might go into the office then, after I shower. I've got an abdominoperineal resection tomorrow, and I want to study up on the technique."

I nod. It's something I saw him do a hundred times as a resident before a big procedure — he'll spend hours poring over at least four different medical textbooks, refamiliarizing himself with all the anatomy, the techniques, going down every rabbit hole in his brain of what could go wrong and how to prevent it.

When I hear the squeak of the pipes and the rushing of water toward the shower in our bathroom, I pick up my coffee and take another swig. But it's lukewarm now, and bitter.

While I sit there, drinking it anyway, a million questions tumble through my brain. And I realize there's only one person who can answer them.

The instant I rap on the wooden door with

my knuckles, Willy's deep bellows answer from inside and it feels like a replay from the evening before, except this time Harrison isn't by my side. The street is quiet, the sun already burning the pavement.

A few minutes tick by and I'm about to knock again when the door opens to reveal Caroline shooing Willy, but he gallops onto the porch anyway. Smudges of mascara raccoon her eyes; loose wisps of hair frame her face. She squints at the daylight. "Mia," she says, surprised. "Hi."

"Hi." Willy's cold nose mixes with his hot breath on my hand. I rub his head without bending over. "Sorry to pop in unannounced, but I don't have . . . I didn't know —" I glance past her into the dimly lit house. "Is Oliver here?"

She stifles a yawn. "Uh, yeah — I think so." She eyes me, curious. I know I should say something — an excuse as to why I'm there; but since I don't have one to offer, I remain silent. "Do you want to come in?"

"No, thanks, I don't want to intrude."

"OK. Well, I'll go get him."

She steps back inside, leaving me on the porch with Willy. Heart racing, I crouch down until I'm face-to-face with the dog, so I can scratch him properly behind the ears. But as soon as I'm within range, his huge,

163

sandpapery tongue laps the side of my cheek. "Willy!" I shout, wiping the gooey saliva off my face with the back of my hand and then on my shorts.

"I should have warned you. He's a kisser."

Oliver. I look up into his eyes, and as soon as I see him peering back at me, I know. I did not mishear him. The intense way he's looking at me — the way I've felt him looking at me on and off since the very first time I saw him — suddenly makes perfect sense. Because it's the same way I've been looking at him. As if he's not real. Or I can't believe that he is. As if he could disappear at any second. I rise slowly, my legs unsteady.

"Hi," I say.

"Hi." He's in plaid pajama pants and a rumpled T-shirt advertising a liquor brand. He reaches down for Willy's collar, gently guiding him inside. He shuts the door, and we're alone.

"Do you want to sit?" He gestures to the porch swing.

"Sure." Though the few words we've said are conventional — social customs — the words we're not saying thicken the air between us and everything feels tense, high stakes. When we're both on either end of the slatted bench, looking out at the street instead of each other, I take a deep breath.

164

"What did you —" I start, at the exact moment that he says: "So about last night —"

We both pause. I chuckle nervously.

"You first," he says.

I swallow. "What did you mean last night when you asked, you know, if I had dreamt about you before we met?"

"I meant" — he speaks slowly, as if English isn't my first language — "did you dream about me before we met?"

I flush. "No, I know — but why would you ask that? Unless you . . ."

He studies my face. And then nods slowly. Once.

Even though it's what I expected, I'm struck dumb. I open my mouth to speak and then close it, because I have no idea what to say.

A pickup truck ambles down the road in front of us, bringing my attention back to earth. To Oliver.

"Do you hear that?"

"What?" I ask, pushing my head forward. The car's gone and the air is once again quiet.

"The *Twilight Zone* music."

I stare at him blankly.

"Sorry," he says. "I make bad jokes when I'm uncomfortable."

I lift an eyebrow. "Tiny character flaw?"

"Something like that."

The swing creaks beneath us, swaying slightly.

"So, what do you dream about?" I ask. "You know, when I'm . . . there."

Oliver pauses. "Different things."

"Like what?" I press.

He shifts his weight in the seat, jostling the chains on the swing, but won't meet my gaze. And I know. It's as if every sexual encounter we've had in my dreams is playing like a movie reel between us, and my cheeks flame red, the tension mounting. Why did I even ask?

"I don't know," he says finally. He clears his throat. "One of them, we were on a boat —"

"A ferry?"

"No, a rowboat. It was raining . . ." He trails off, and I understand. That's the trouble with dreams, isn't it? It's impossible to explain them to someone else. They sound so ridiculous, nonsensical in the light of day. "What about you? What do you dream?"

I shrug, while frantically searching my mind for a tame one. "Once you gave me a brown paper bag full of teeth."

"What?" His head jerks up. "Whose teeth

were they?"

"How should I know?"

"Let's see," he says. "We were in an elevator, but when we got to the top of the building, it kept going, and we were suspended in the sky and I was completely freaking out but you didn't care. Like you hung out in gravity-less elevators all the time."

I start giggling. "You tried to kill me in a biplane once."

"You pushed me down a waterslide even though I had all my clothes on and was holding a turkey sandwich. The bread was soaked."

This sends me spiraling further and we're both laughing now, more a side effect of the anxiety than it actually being funny, but once we start, the release feels good and it's difficult to stop.

When we finally do, the silence stretches between us, growing unwieldy in its awkwardness.

"What do you think it means?" I ask Oliver quietly.

His head lolls slowly from one side to the other, as if he's stretching out his neck. "I don't know." He pauses. "I just keep thinking of Occam's razor."

I wrack my brain, trying to recall the meaning of the familiar phrase, and it comes to me: "The best explanation is usually the simplest." And then: "So what's the simplest explanation?"

He shrugs, and though I'm desperate for answers, it helps somehow to know he's as mystified by the entire thing as I am. "That we know each other somehow? That we've met before?"

"Yes! I've thought so, too." I lean forward a bit. "We *must* know each other, right? I mean, I feel like I know you. Is that weird?"

He shakes his head. "No. I know what you mean."

I try to ignore the chill that runs up my spine. "OK. Well, then maybe as kids? Where did you grow up?"

"New Jersey," he says. "Freehold. Moved here when I was fourteen. You?"

"Silver Spring, Maryland. Philly for college."

"Right," he says. "Philly."

"You said you're in Center City, right? I used to be in that area a lot." I decide to float my lame theory. "Maybe we've seen each other — a bar? A coffee shop?"

"Maybe," he says, thoughtfully. He's silent for a beat and then: "Or what about traveling? You know, like what if your family was on vacation in New Jersey and we happened to be at the same McDonald's or hotel lobby or something?"

"Wait — who vacations in *New Jersey?*"

He cocks an eyebrow.

"OK, say we have met at some point — it clearly wasn't something that either of us remember. And I can't help but feel like it would have to be meaningful in some way — some kind of connection that would explain the dreaming."

He nods. The swing creaks again.

"I Googled it — right after I saw you in the waiting room."

He cracks a grin. "I did, too, actually. And then again last night — stayed up way too late."

"You did?"

"Yeah."

"What'd you find?"

"Not much, except if you believe the Internet, we're not alone. A lot of people say this has happened to them before — dreaming about someone and then meeting them."

"Yeah, they just don't say what it means."

"Right."

We sit in silence for a few more minutes. "I don't know — maybe there is no answer, no explanation."

"Maybe," he says, and then after a beat, he mutters: "I just feel like there has to be."

Even though it's more to himself than to me, I'm buoyed. In those words, I hear it — the hint of desperation, the bewilderment that has plagued me on different levels since first laying eyes on him. And it's validation — that I'm not crazy. Or if I am crazy, at least I'm not alone in my craziness.

Oliver opens his mouth to say something and then stops. Hesitates.

"What?"

"I did find one thing. There's this professor. At Columbia University." He digs his cell out of his pocket and taps the screen a few times, then hands it to me. It's a headshot of a stern-looking woman, her arms folded across her suit-jacketed chest. I skim the words beside it.

Carolyn Saltz, PhD, a professor of clinical psychology and director of the sleep lab at Columbia University, has coauthored more than twelve studies on sleep and dreams. She resides in New York with her wife, four birds and a shih tzu named Freud.

I look back up at Oliver.

"I read through some of her research," he says. "And it was a lot of basic dream stuff, theories on why we dream, what they mean, but there was this one study where she delved into the idea of something called mutual dreaming, where two people share the same dream world."

I cock my head. "Like *Inception?*"

"Yeah. Kind of. Minus the technology and stealing-corporate-secrets thing. Says it usually happens between people who know each other really well — siblings, best friends, husband and wife . . ." He clears his throat.

"And it's the same dream — it sounds like our dreams are different, right?"

"Yeah," he admits. He tugs his hair again, and that's when I notice something I've never seen before — in my dreams or real life. A scar, a thin jagged line a few inches above his left ear, right at his hairline. "God, I just wish I could sit someone down and say, 'This is what happened to us — what does it mean?' "

I glance back at the screen. "Well, why don't we?"

"What do you mean?"

"Why don't we contact her?"

He cocks his head, considering. And I press on, a dog with a bone. "What do we have to lose?"

I scroll down the page and click on the contact link.

Due to the volume of inquiries, Dr. Saltz is unable to respond to individual emails. For interviews and media requests, please email: jleibowitz@hunterpr.com.

I turn the screen to Oliver. "Never mind. She probably gets a hundred emails a month, kooks asking her what their dreams mean. I guess it was a stupid idea." I sigh and hand his phone back over.

"What if —" Oliver stops.

"What?"

"Well — what if we ask for an interview?"

"But we're not media."

"We could be," he says, slowly. "I used to be a journalist —"

"You did?"

"Yeah. I still have some contacts at a few magazines. I could pitch an idea about dreams, see if someone bites."

I stare at him, considering not just his plan but also this new crumb of information about who he is. *Journalist.* It's not that it's surprising, given his current career, but I find that each time I learn something about him it makes me want to know more. But instead of probing, I go with: "It's not the worst idea."

He shrugs. "What do we have to lose?"

CHAPTER 11

"Pop's probably going to need knee surgery sometime in the next couple months," Harrison tells me on Monday morning, when we're sitting side by side in identical wooden armchairs waiting for Dr. Hobbes to grace us with his presence. It's the first time I've seen him since yesterday morning, and I haven't had a chance to tell him about going to see Oliver.

Well, I suppose I could have texted. Met up with him at his office for dinner. I could have not pretended to be asleep when he got home last night. The truth is, I don't know how to explain what's happening to myself, much less anyone else.

"Wait — what happened to physical therapy being enough?" Harrison's dad tripped going up their front steps a few months earlier. A brick had come loose, causing him to come down the wrong way on his knee. He didn't go see a doctor for five days, not

173

until Harrison's mom called, describing the swelling as grapefruit sized, and Harrison talked him into going in.

"Turns out, you actually have to do what the therapist says. Pop's . . . struggling with that."

"Ah." Mr. Graydon is not known for his ability to take direction from others.

"If he does, I think I'll go out there to help Mom. Just for a few days. She's not strong enough to lift him."

"Yeah, of course," I say, staring at the files on Hobbes's desk, as if I can glean the information in them telepathically. I don't even know if they're our results or somebody else's. I glance down at my lucky yellow dress and pick imaginary lint off the shoulder. "Want me to come with you?"

Harrison's head snaps toward me. "Do you want to?" He cocks an eyebrow. "Sleep on that ancient mattress and listen to Mom and Pop argue about whether the television is too loud over and over again?"

I consider this. Those parts are pretty awful. "We also get to eat your mom's cooking, so — it's not all bad."

His mom's picadillo has been known to cause tears of happiness. And tears of frustration the one time she tried to teach me how to make it and — after I added twice the amount of cumin (or cinnamon or some c spice) as needed — kicked me out of the kitchen with a string of Cuban swear words.

I glance at the clock on the wall and Harrison notices. "I'm sure he'll be here soon," he says. I rub my sweaty palms over the hard edges of the chair's wooden arms and try to relax.

"So, there's something I've been meaning to tell you."

Harrison eyes me, no doubt noticing the gravity of my voice. "OK," he says.

I open my mouth — even though I still have no idea where to begin — but then the door opens and Dr. Keenan Hobbes breezes into the room, greeting us without so much as an apology for the wait. Deep lines carve his face, making him look more grave than necessary. Or maybe it's that I hope he looks more grave than necessary.

When he's finally settled at his desk, he leans forward, the light reflecting off his shiny dome, unconcealed by the few white hairs combed over it. He clasps his hands together, fingers interlocked. Looks at me. "Well, the good news is your eggs are fine," he says. "Healthy, and you've got a lot of them left. We like to see that."

I try to exhale, but the tightness in my

175

lungs remains. I eye him warily. "And the bad news?"

He waits a beat, glances down at the notes beneath his hands as if he needs to confirm the news he's about to deliver. "The genetic testing found an issue with the sperm." He looks at Harrison.

"Really," Harrison says, genuinely surprised. I am, too, considering Dr. Hobbes seemed pretty sure at my first visit that Harrison's "swimmers" weren't the problem.

"You have what's called balanced translocation."

Eyes wide, I sit back, having never heard that term before. I turn to Harrison, like I do every time I need something medical explained, but he looks as flummoxed as I am.

Dr. Hobbes shifts in his chair, causing the leather to squeak unpleasantly. "If you remember from your science lessons in school, we all have twenty-three pairs of chromosomes. When he was conceived, a couple of Harrison's chromosomes got mixed up, attaching in the wrong places. That happens to about one in five hundred of us, and most people don't even know. He's got all the genetic material he requires, so he developed normally. Problem occurs when people with balanced translocation go to reproduce."

"Wait . . . you're saying I have a chromosome disorder?" Harrison says, cutting him off.

"Yeah," Dr. Hobbes says. "Essentially."

"Huh."

I look from Dr. Hobbes to Harrison and back again. "So what does all of this mean?"

"In the most basic terms, you guys are experiencing a mismatch. The sperm carries the dad's half of the DNA for the baby, right? But if that particular sperm that makes it to the egg happens to have the mix-up, the DNA won't line up correctly with the chromosomes of the egg, causing either extra genetic material or not enough, which often leads to a miscarriage or, if carried to term, can cause pretty severe birth defects."

I pause, trying to comprehend it all, but I'm stuck on the first thing he said. "Harrison and I are a . . . mismatch?"

"Well, your egg and sperm, anyway," Dr. Hobbes clarifies.

I swallow past the wet cotton ball now lodged in my throat and blink. "So that's it — we can't have a baby?"

"No, that's not what I'm saying at all. A lot of couples that are balanced translocation carriers do go on to conceive and have perfectly healthy babies, in time. But your chance of having a miscarriage is greater than normal — as you've experienced — which can obviously be emotionally taxing."

"Mm," I say, glancing at Harrison. That's an understatement. I hear his phone vibrate and he digs it out of his pocket.

"Some couples prefer to go the IVF route, combined with PGD — preimplantation genetic diagnosis — which can spot an abnormality in the embryo before it's implanted, thereby only implanting healthy embryos."

"So — we have options," I say, the vise grip on my chest finally loosening.

"You have options," Dr. Hobbes agrees.

I reach for Harrison's hand and squeeze, but he doesn't squeeze back. He's looking at his phone. "I'm sorry, I've got to run," he says, dropping my hand and standing up. "I'm on call today."

"Of course," Dr. Hobbes says. He turns to me. "Mia, why don't we go through any questions you may have and then you and Harrison can talk things over later and come up with a plan for what you might want to do."

"OK." But when I look to Harrison for agreement, his eyes don't meet mine. He's turned toward the door, his thoughts already on whatever emergency is calling him to the hospital. He puts his hand on my shoulder, but before I can even cover it with mine, it's gone. And then so is my husband.

Later that evening, Harrison comes home to eat and change before he has to go back to the hospital. He's on call through the night and sometimes it's easier for him to stay there, rather than drive back and forth every time he gets summoned.

I spent the afternoon researching all of the terms and options Dr. Hobbes and I briefly went through that afternoon, and now I'm near bursting with thoughts about it all. While Harrison was heating up leftover chili and then eating it, I started running down all the pros and cons of IVF and genetic testing.

"I know it's expensive," I say, following him into our bathroom, where he starts brushing his teeth at the sink. "But I did get an interview today — for that job you mentioned at the community college. If I get it, maybe it could help offset the cost." I don't actually think I'll get it — I was pretty floored to have even gotten a response, considering I have no teaching experience — but it doesn't feel prudent to mention that now.

Harrison spits and hangs his toothbrush back up in its wall holder. Then he puts both hands on the counter and stares into the mirror.

"What are you thinking?" I ask. "You haven't said much."

"It's a lot to take in," he says, running some water into his hand. He swishes it around in his mouth and spits again.

"I know. It really is a lot of money."

He shakes his head. "I'm not worried about the cost."

Suddenly I feel foolish. "God, are you upset about the chromosome disorder? I mean, of course you are. That was a shock to me — I can't imagine how you must be feeling."

"Yeah," he says. "That was . . . unexpected. And I do feel bad — awful, really — that it's my fault this keeps happening."

"It's not your fault, though. How could we have known? But now that we do know . . ."

He shakes his head and then squeezes past me in the doorway and starts unbuttoning his shirt. I go sit on the bed, pulling my knees up to my chest. I scrutinize him. Sometimes talking with Harrison is like one big guessing game, analyzing every head tilt and grunt and then asking follow-up questions until I get to the heart of what's bugging him. This is one of those times. "Harrison, talk to me."

He dumps his button-up in the hamper and pulls his T-shirt off over his head. "I'm just not sure I can go through it all again."

"Another miscarriage?" I say. "I agree — that's why IVF is the best option. They'll only choose the healthy embryos."

"It's not a guarantee," he says. "IVF doesn't work every time."

"Well, no," I admit. "But it will significantly raise our chances, Dr. Hobbes said. And it'll work for us, I know it."

"Mia —"

"This is the only way."

"It's not," he says, his bare back to me. He's standing at the dresser, but he hasn't moved to get another shirt out of the drawer.

"What do you mean?" I wait for a response that doesn't come. "Do you want to adopt?" It's an option we haven't ever discussed before.

"No," he says. He opens the top drawer and picks up an undershirt.

"Then what? I don't understand."

His phone buzzes and he glances down at the screen clipped to his belt. It's one of the most annoying things about being a

181

surgeon's wife — no matter what you're do- ing, or how important it seems, the hospital always takes precedence. It has to.

"Work?" I ask, even though I know.

He nods. Pulls the shirt over his head and turns to look at me. "I'm just not sure if . . ." He stops. Collects his thoughts. "What I'm trying to say is, having a child is such a big responsibility. And maybe I'm not ready for it."

I laugh a little, relieved that it's simply cold feet. "Nobody's *ready* for it, Harrison. People just do it."

"But that's what I'm saying — we don't *have* to."

And that's when I look into his eyes and everything stills. They're not first-time- father nervous, his eyes; they're pained. Like he's been holding a world of hurt in and it's starting to overflow. And it makes my heart beat a little faster in my chest.

"Of course we don't have to," I say slowly. "But we want to, don't we?"

His gaze drops to the ground.

"Harrison?" I can't keep the tremble from my voice. "Don't you?"

His eyes once again find mine, and I know the answer before he even says a word. It's been there, right under the surface of every conversation we've had since the miscarriage, and I haven't wanted to see. Part of me wants to run, to clap my hands over my head and hum like a child, to rewind time and figure out where this conversation — where Harrison — went so off our charted course, but instead I sit there, waiting for the words that I feel certain are going to destroy me.

"I don't know," he says. "I don't know anymore."

I turn my head slowly, away from him, my gaze shifting to the dresser. The picture of us from Costa Rica. One of my bras slung across it. A blue one. A handful of loose change. I look back at him.

"I don't understand."

He opens his mouth. Closes it. Like a fish gasping for air. "I don't know how to explain it. It's just all been so . . . hard. And I don't know that it's supposed to be this hard to have a baby. Maybe it's not . . . meant to be."

My eyes fly wide, remembering the night on the cement floor of my studio when he said something similar, and my shock gives way to anger. "What is it with you and all this fate stuff? You've never believed in any of that! Things don't happen for a reason, they just *happen.*" I'm parroting one of his favorite phrases. Harrison doesn't ascribe to life having any big grand design. Everything is random — no rhyme or reason to any of it.

Harrison shrugs. "People change, Mia," he says, his voice low, steady. It's this annoying thing he does whenever I get worked up. He gets calmer, in inverse proportion to my anger. I'm sure it's his subconscious way of trying to bring me back down, but all it does is infuriate me further.

"Not this much!" I can't help thinking back to when we first found out we were pregnant. "You were so excited. You brought home that little hat, for Chrissake! How do you go from that to not even wanting a baby? I just don't — I can't — understand it."

He looks at me, incredulous. "It shouldn't be quite that difficult," he says, slowly. "For the longest time, you never even *wanted* kids."

My mouth falls open. I would be less stunned if he had slugged me directly in the gut. It feels a little like that's exactly what he did. And I wonder how it's possible that in that instant I could hate him with the same intensity I loved him moments before.

He stands up. "Look, I can't do this right now," he says. "I have to go." I'm too numb to say anything, to even look at him. He grabs his wallet, tucking it in his back pocket. His phone. He pauses. "Mia, I'm sorry," he says.

And then, for the second time that day, he's gone.

CHAPTER 12

"Do you have any teaching experience?" I'm sitting across from a man in an ill-fitting tweed jacket with elbow patches, acne scars mottling his clean-shaven cheeks. His voice lacks inflection and I wonder if he's as bored as he sounds, or if it's the way he always speaks — an unfortunate character trait. He introduced himself as "Ross, like the guy from *Friends*," as if Ross was a wholly unusual name and needed a reference point.

"Um . . . no," I say, and I try to muster up some enthusiasm. I know I should add an addendum, like, *But I did tutor my class-mates in calculus for extra money in high school,* or *I've always wanted to transition into the field.*

But mustering up enthusiasm is not something I'm currently capable of.

For the past week and a half, Harrison and I have tiptoed around each other. "Maybe I just need some time," he said, when I pressed him again about babies, and I didn't know if he meant it or if it was just to placate me. Regardless, that wasn't the sentence playing on an endless loop in my head.

You never even wanted *kids.*

He had apologized immediately, and then again by text later that evening, and though I did forgive him for saying it, I couldn't forget it — only because I was terrified he was right. I didn't always want to have a baby. And there are women, other women, who've known their entire lives they wanted to be mothers. I feel less than, undeserving. Maybe I can't have a baby because I haven't yearned for one long enough. Maybe this is my penance.

Ross's eyes are fixed on his computer screen, which is turned at an angle so I can't fully see it, and he keeps clicking the mouse. I wonder if he's searching for me while I'm sitting there. Scanning my website. Looking to unearth any scandalous secrets on Facebook.

He punches the keys on the keyboard with the side of his fist and grunts through clenched teeth. It's the most enthusiastic reaction I've seen from him in the past ten minutes and it's not even directed at me. I furrow my brow and edge forward ever so slightly so I can peek at the monitor. Bright, colorful shapes fill the screen and explode when he clicks the mouse. He's playing Candy Crush.

"Um . . . Ross?"

His eyes dart back to me and widen, as if he's surprised to see me still sitting there. "Right." He glances back down at my paper resume in front of him. "OK. It's yours if you want it."

"What?" I say. "Seriously?"

"Yeah." He shrugs. "To be honest, only three people applied, and you're the only one with an MFA. Sessions are eight weeks long. First one starts August sixteenth. Summer session was Beginner Acrylic. So this one will be Novice. They alternate."

"OK. Yeah. Great," I say. "Thank you. I'll be here then."

He shoves a piece of paper at me and I take it. "Go to this website, fill out the forms so you'll get paid." And then he turns back to the monitor and I stand up and slip out of his office before he can change his mind.

In the parking lot, my cell buzzes as I slip into the front seat of my car. I rev the engine and turn the air full blast before answering.

"How are you?" Vivian says, her voice dripping with concern. We texted a few days ago, but I've successfully avoided her phone calls since telling her about the fertility results and Harrison's change of heart, for this very reason. It's not that I don't want or appreciate her sympathy. I truly do. It just reminds me of how sad I am, when I've been trying so hard not to dwell on it.

"Good, in fact. I got a job. At the community college."

"You're going to teach? Art?"

"No. Parachute Jumping 101. Yes, art."

"Oh."

"What, Viv," I say, monotone.

"Nothing."

I wait.

"It's just that when we had that opening here, you balked when I suggested you apply for it."

"I didn't want to move back home after college. Plus, I don't have an education degree. They wouldn't have even interviewed me." Both excuses were true, but that wasn't all of it. Raya and I always joked that you could be successful at art or you could teach it. I wanted to be successful. Viv knows there was more to it, but she doesn't push it.

"Well, I'm really happy for you. Congratulations." My prickly edges soften then, because I know she means it. Viv might be

189

exasperating and sometimes judgmental and she literally never forgets anything — even the stuff I'd like her to forget — but she really does want me to be happy.

"So what else is new?" she asks. I hear a clacking sound on her end and realize she must be at work, which is why our conversation hasn't been interrupted by her yelling at Finley and Griffin. She's probably typing notes into a student's file or a recommendation letter or an email to a parent.

I consider telling her about Oliver, but it's been almost two weeks since that morning on Caroline's porch. He left with my phone number and a promise to call with news, but I haven't heard from him. I wonder if maybe he got busy with work, his life, and chalked it up to one of those weird things. Meanwhile, I've dreamt about him and that carnival twice in the past week. And I can't help but wonder, when I wake up in the mornings, if he's dreamt about me, too.

"Nothing," I say.

"Harrison?"

"Same."

"Hang in there. You guys have been through a lot. I'm sure he just needs time."

It's nearly word for word what Harrison said, and it doesn't sound any better coming from my sister. When we hang up, I ditch the phone in the console's cup holder and lean back against the headrest, focusing on the cool air from the vents hitting my face.

I can't bear the thought of not having a baby with Harrison, after wanting one for so long. After everything we've been through. After being so close, only to have it all come crashing down time and again. What would be the point of all that pain if there isn't something beautiful at the end of it? Pain for pain's sake doesn't make sense to me.

I pick the phone back up and text him about the job. He replies within seconds.

That's great, babe. Let's go out to celebrate.

It's so normal, so Harrison, that it clenches my heart. Vivian's right — Vivian's always right. Harrison will come around.

He has to.

On the way to dinner, I've promised myself I'm not going to talk about next steps; Harrison asked for time and I vow to give it to him. But after I ask how his day is and he says fine, I can't think of anything else to say, so I sit there with my hands folded neatly in my lap, looking out the window at the fields passing by. And though I try to move past it, I think about how I want a

191

baby so much, that if wanting was a drop of water, I'd be a goddamn ocean.

I bite my lip so hard, I'm surprised it doesn't start bleeding, and when we pull up in front of the restaurant, I'm relieved to finally have something to say.

"Let's make a bet — mustache or no mustache?"

Harrison looks from the lit-up sign that announces Sorelli's on the front of the brick storefront to me. I confessed to Harrison when he got home that I wanted to go here not because of the food, but because I was morbidly curious to see who Caroline had had an affair with. "There is something seriously wrong with you," he said. And the expression on his face now tells me his opinion has not changed.

But it's not until we're seated at a dark corner booth that I notice something else about his face — the droopy circles under his eyes. The sallow skin. He glances at the napkin on the table in front of him. It's invitingly twisted up into a point like a dollop of whipped cream, and for a moment, I think he may just lay his head down on it.

"Harrison? You alright?"

"Yeah," he responds.

I open my mouth to press him, but a woman's voice interrupts me.

"Dr. Graydon?" We both look up to find a dewy-faced blond woman walking toward our table, her eyes locked on my husband.

"Whitney Crossland," he says, smiling bright, the deep wrinkle permanently creasing his forehead a mere second ago completely erased. "Long time, no see."

He stands up when she reaches the table and gives her an awkward half hug. "Whitney, this is my wife, Mia. Mia, this is one of my patients, Whitney. Just discharged what —" He turns back to her. "Two days ago?"

"Yep, and feeling great, thanks to you."

"How's Gabriel?" Harrison asks.

"Really good," she says. "Just found out his band is playing in the Christmas parade. First one Hope Springs has ever had." Harrison slides his eyes to me and I smile, thinking of Caroline.

"Little drummer boy," Harrison quips, his attention back on Whitney.

"I'm sure he'd love if you'd come watch."

"Tell him I wouldn't miss it," he says.

I just sit, observing the exchange, struck again by how little I know of Harrison's work life. He shares bits and pieces, of course, stories of funny or crazy things that happen in the ER when he's on call, or really weird or tough cases he gets, but he sees upwards of fifteen patients a day — and

193

those are just the ones that come into his clinic — so the minutiae of each one I'm just not privy to.

A waitress drops off a basket of bread and asks for our drink order, prompting Whitney to bid us farewell. "I should get back to the bar. I'm waiting on someone."

"Only two glasses of wine," Harrison says to Whitney, with a parental glare. "And water in between each."

"Aye, aye, Doc," Whitney says. "Nice to meet you, Mia."

"You, too."

I order a bottle of Chianti from the waitress, and then Harrison and I are alone at our table again. His face has fallen and I know the energy that pulsed through him as he talked to Whitney was a put-on, a facade for her benefit. I eye him, waiting.

"Perforated diverticulitis," he says, nodding in Whitney's direction, his voice quiet.

"What?"

"I told you about her a few weeks ago. So bad, I had to send her up to ICU before I could finish."

It sounds vaguely familiar. "She bounced back quick."

"Yeah, she's got a colostomy bag, though."

"Really?" I surreptitiously glance to where Whitney now sits at the bar. I look for the

194

telltale bulge on her stomach, but her blouse is loose and I wouldn't know if Harrison hadn't told me. "Gabriel's her son?"

He bobs his head. "Middle schooler. Cute kid."

The waitress comes back with the wine bottle and opens it at the table, pouring a splash into Harrison's glass. He tosses back the red liquid and nods, and she fills both our glasses then asks if we're ready to order. I get the bucatini and close my menu.

"Spaghetti alle vongole," Harrison says.

I jerk my head toward him. "That's clams."

"I know." He hands his menu to the waitress and she walks off.

"I can't believe you'd order clams after what happened to me in Maine."

He grins, crinkling the skin around his eyes. "Mia."

"What?"

"For the thousandth time," he says, patiently, "that was not food poisoning."

"It was! I must have eaten, like, fifty of those clams oreganata —" I pull a face, still unable to even think of them without getting a little nauseous. We were at a fancy wedding in Maine — the daughter of one of Harrison's patients, a big-shot Philadelphia lawyer whose life Harrison saved with a

195

triple bypass when he was chief resident. The wedding was huge — more than four hundred people — and the swankiest one I had ever been to, with Dom Pérignon for the toast and, like, eight forks at every place setting. "And then, the next day . . ."

I don't have to finish because we both know — the next day, Harrison had to pull the car over at least seven times during the eight-hour drive home.

"You also had roughly fifty glasses of champagne."

I smirk at him. "Not *fifty.*"

"Well, enough for you to start a conga line with the waitstaff."

"It was not a conga line! It was the Macarena."

"It was a conga line."

I scrunch my face, trying to remember. I feel certain it was the Macarena. He cocks an eyebrow sternly, but he's smiling.

"What were their names? Bert and Annie?"

"Beau and Annie," he says. "Bert and Annie are *Sesame Street* characters."

"*Ernie.*"

"That's what I said."

I grin and study my husband's face, wondering at the curiosity and fallibility of memory — and not just the alcohol-induced fogs. Like most couples, Harrison and I have gotten in more than one disagreement about the way something did or did not happen in the past, our recollection of facts colliding rather than merging. But now I think maybe it's not always necessarily a weakness, but a strength. The fact that we each carry different bits of the same memory, like pieces of a puzzle, so that when we put them together, we can form something that's whole.

Later, when I'm reaching for the Parmesan cheese shaker on the table, I notice he's looking past me, eyes narrowed. I turn in time to see a man in a short-sleeved lavender button-up, cargo pants and silver-framed glasses glaring at Whitney.

"Who's that?" I ask, in a stage whisper.

"I don't know," Harrison says, slowly. "When we were evaluating her in the ER, she kept screaming that we couldn't call her ex-husband for Gabriel. I'm wondering if that's him."

"You're unbelievable," the man says, his voice carrying across the room. "You're on a fucking date?"

"My personal life isn't any concern of yours," Whitney hisses.

"Well, it might concern a judge — they don't tend to award custody to *whores.*"

197

"Whoa," Harrison says, taking the word out of my mouth, and then he's up, closing the twenty-foot gap between us and the bar.

"Everything OK over here?" he asks when he reaches Whitney.

The guy eyes Harrison, nostrils flared, anger flashing in his eyes. "You her date?"

Whitney puts a hand up to stop Harrison from responding. "This is my doctor," she says. "And you're making a fool of yourself. Please just leave."

"Or what?"

"Or I'm going to call the police."

The man scoffs, but then his eyes dart around the room, and that's when both he and I notice the bartender and a few other diners have stopped to watch the exchange. His cheeks flame red, and if not appropriately chagrined, it's clear he's embarrassed.

"C'mon, man," Harrison says, putting his hand out to guide him to the door. Harrison mouths something to the bartender and, to my surprise, the guy lets himself be escorted out. Harrison briefly checks back in with Whitney before returning to the table.

"What the hell was that?" I say, wide-eyed.

"That is what happens when you mix an ugly divorce with alcohol. Guy reeked of Jim Beam. Bartender called him a cab."

"Jesus," I say. "Let's not ever try that."

He fastens his gaze on mine, and even though he's worn-down and has had a shit day and he just had to rescue a patient from a drunk ex-husband, his entire focus rests squarely on me. "Not ever," he agrees. And in that moment, our eyes locked, I see my husband, and I remember all at once how much I love him. And I wonder how I could ever forget, even for a second.

My cell buzzes on the table next to my plate and I pick it up. It's a number I don't recognize.

Up for a day trip to New York? We've got an "interview" on Friday.

I stare at the pile of bucatini drowning in Bolognese in front of me.

"Who was that?" Harrison asks.

I look up into his tired eyes. "Oliver."

He pops a forkful of pasta in his mouth, chews and then says: "More gardening advice?"

"Not exactly." My throat suddenly dry, I take a sip of water. Swallow. "There's something I need to tell you."

"What?" When I've finished, Harrison's forehead is wrinkly and confused, his eyes sharp, focused. "Do you actually hear what you're saying? The words that are coming

199

out of your mouth."

"Yes," I say.

"Mia, come on. I wasn't going to say anything, but I saw the way he was looking at you over dinner — *of course* he said he was dreaming about you, too. That son of a bitch. And you — you *believe* him?"

"Well, yes. I do. I know — believe me, Harrison — I *know* this sounds crazy. But, he's telling the truth. He is."

"How? How do you know?"

"I just do."

He sighs and opens his mouth to say something else, but the waitress chooses that moment to drop off the check. Harrison pays it and we leave and he doesn't speak again until we're in our driveway, the silver moon hanging in the night sky above us.

"OK, so what now?" He turns to me. His two hands grip the steering wheel, but there's no fight left in him. "Why are you telling me this?"

I take a deep breath. "We're going to New York. On Friday." I tense, sure this will set him off again, but he just exhales.

"You and Oliver."

"Right."

"Together."

"Yes."

200

His jaw clenches. Releases. He exhales. "What's in New York?"

"A professor. She's done a lot of research on dreams and we thought maybe she could help us."

"We," he repeats, almost under his breath. He drums his thumb on the steering wheel. And then: "Help you what?"

"I don't know. Figure out what it means, maybe?"

He stares out the window, away from me, and scratches the side of his beard. The sound of the hairs bristling under the pads of his fingers fills the car.

"Mia." His voice is low, quiet. "Remember after the first . . . the first baby — when you started bringing home all those things? There was that mitten and a hubcap and what else — the shoe, a Converse, I think."

I stiffen. "That wasn't . . . It had nothing to do with losing the baby —"

"Mia," he says gently.

"It didn't."

"I'm just saying — I know you're grieving. And grief, it can do things. To your mind."

"This is real, Harrison." The words come out shaky. "I know how it sounds, I do. But I need you to believe me." And I don't re-

201

alize how much it's true until I say it out loud.

He searches my face. I hold my breath.

"OK," he says, finally. "OK."

"You believe me?"

"I don't know," he says. "But if you need to go to New York, you should go to New York."

I exhale. "Thank you."

He pulls the lever to open his door and steps out into the night, so I follow suit. I walk toward the front path, his footsteps crunching the gravel behind me. And then, suddenly, his arms encircle my waist and he's pulling me to him. I turn, leaning into his chest, tucking my head under his chin. "Dios Mia," he breathes into my hair. His hand drops and finds mine. His fingers fiddle with my wedding band, twisting it around.

"I trust you, Mia, I do. But I don't trust *him.* If that guy tries something —"

I tip my head back to look at him, a half grin on my face. "You'll what? Beat him up? Defend my honor?" Harrison isn't the jealous type, and he's even less violent than he is jealous.

"No," Harrison admits, his head down, eyes still on my ring finger. "I'd probably just glare at him really, really hard."

I smile into his chest. And we stand there like that, under the moon, until a bird squawks somewhere in the distance.

"Shit," I say, lifting my head.

"What?"

"I completely forgot to look for the manager! Now we'll never know if he has a mustache or not."

He looks down at me, eyebrow cocked, and shakes his head. "Dios Mia."

Whitney watches out of the corner of her eye as Dr. Graydon leaves the restaurant, holding the door for his naturally pretty wife, because of course his wife is naturally pretty and of course he would hold the door for her. She doesn't mean to be bitter — Dr. Graydon was so kind, and he saved her life — but if it wasn't for Gabriel, to be honest, she might rather have died. Of course she would get a *Grey's Anatomy*–level hot doctor when she had a perforated intestine. Where was the old balding guy that set her broken arm two years ago? Why couldn't she have him for the problems with her "rectum" and the hot one for her arm? She knew why. Because life was unspeakably unfair.

"Another?" the bartender asks, pointing at her empty wineglass. She shouldn't. Dr. Graydon said two, max. But Holly was watching Gabriel, and Eli had embarrassed her in front of an entire restaurant of people, and lest she forget how pathetic her life had become, her Bumble date had never showed. The worst part is, she didn't even want to go out, but she felt bad that the first date they were supposed to have got sidelined by her unexpected trip to the ER, and was trying to make it up to him. In retrospect, she probably shouldn't have mentioned the colostomy bag in their text exchange this afternoon, but she didn't think that was something to surprise some-one with.

"Please," she says, pushing her glass toward the bartender.

Emotional stress. After the surgery, that was what Dr. Graydon listed as one of the possible culprits that could have caused her condition. She nearly bit her tongue off to keep from maniacally laughing when he asked if she'd been under stress lately. Does the pope wear a funny hat?

When the bartender sets the wine in front of her, she pulls up Instagram, just in case her no-show Bumble date is checking it, and snaps a selfie with the full glass. It's terrible, so she does another, and then another. Finally, she gets one that's passable and tags it: #roseallday #winelife #momsnightout. She downs her wine, pays the bill with her

American Express — the one credit card that isn't completely maxed out — and walks out into the warm, idyllic night of Hope Springs. But when the door to the restaurant closes behind her, she freezes. The parking lot, though scattered with cars, is otherwise deserted. Still. Too still. A familiar fear creeps up her spine, raising the fine blond hairs on the back of her neck. She nearly turns back inside to ask the bartender to walk her to her car, but then gives her head a firm shake.

It's just the wine; her vivid imagination. Eli got in a cab. He left. He wouldn't come back. He might be temperamental — even violent at times, when his rage got the best of him — but he wasn't *crazy.*

Still, she hurries to her sister's pickup truck — one more thing she owes her sister for, since Eli kept the one car they owned and she can't afford a new one just yet — and unlocks it as quickly as she can, sliding in and starting the engine in one fluid motion. It occurs to her once she's on Mechanic that she probably shouldn't be driving, considering she drank her three glasses of wine on an empty stomach. Then again, there are a lot of things she probably shouldn't have done in her life, starting with marrying her ex-husband. But how was she to know?

How do you ever know who anyone really is before you marry them? And furthermore, how did anybody get it right? It seems to Whitney to be pure luck — or bad luck in her case. Of course, that's not to say there weren't signs. Like their fourth date, when he accused her of flirting with the tractor operator at a pumpkin patch and didn't speak to her the entire ride home. Then later, threw her favorite ceramic coffee mug so hard at the wall that it broke the handle clear off. But the next day, chagrined, he glued it back and apologized profusely, saying he had such strong feelings for her, it scared him. It scared Whitney, too, but also made her feel something else — prized, worshipped, treasured — things she'd always wanted to feel, but never had.

Besides, the pumpkin patch had been his idea, and what kind of guy suggests that for a date, she reasoned. A sensitive, kind one. The type of man she'd been looking for.

And he was, so much of the time. Except when he wasn't.

Whitney pulls the car up to the curb in front of her sister's duplex and sits there staring at the blue light glowing from the living room window. And she wonders for the hundredth time if she's doing the right thing. Uprooting Gabriel from the only home he's ever known, from his father (because, for all his faults, Eli truly was a good father).

Sighing, she opens the door and stands, placing her hand on her colostomy bag. It's secured to her stomach, but she's still not used to it yet and lives with the general anxiety it will fall off at any second. A colostomy bag! She sighs again and wonders how her life came to this.

She lets herself into the house with the key Holly made her and locks the door behind her. Holly has fallen asleep on the couch — and no wonder, Whitney thinks as she recognizes *Antiques Roadshow* on the screen.

Wearily she pads down the short hall and into the bedroom she's sharing with Gabriel. She gently sits on the double bed beside his tiny sleeping frame and puts a hand on his cheek, feeling her heartbeat slow, her entire body calm with the nearness of her son. Before becoming a mother, she didn't know it was possible to love anything the way she loves her son. And though she adores his snaggletoothed smile, the overenthusiasm with which he delivers poorly constructed knock-knock jokes, even the manic repetitive noise of him practicing

208

the drums, there's something about her sleeping boy that particularly tugs at her heartstrings.

And it's in this moment, she simultaneously knows that though it is right to leave Eli, it was also right to marry him. Because how could she possibly regret a decision that resulted in this most perfectly imperfect boy? She doesn't deserve Gabriel, she knows that much. But she'd do anything in the world necessary to keep him.

She carefully changes out of her silk blouse and designer jeans — an outfit wasted on her no-show date — and retreats to the bathroom to empty her bag, brush her teeth and scrub her face. Then she tugs on a loose T-shirt and pajama pants and goes back into the den to turn off the television and rouse her sister.

Holly yawns and sits up after Whitney softly jostles her shoulder. "How was your date?"

"Nonexistent. I got stood up."

"Oh. Sorry," Holly says, reaching for a Dorito from the open bag on the coffee table.

And then something occurs to Whitney and she's startled it's the first time she's thinking it. "Hey — did Eli call you? Did you tell him where I was tonight?"

"What? Of course not." Holly crunches the chip and then licks the powdered cheese off her fingers.

And that's when the fear from the parking lot grips her in earnest; the same fear she has felt in flashes over the years, when Eli's temper boils over. When he does things she never thought him capable of. And yet, he's proven her wrong, time and again.

And now, he's proven one more thing: He knows how to find her, even when she doesn't want to be found.

CHAPTER 14

The Jerome L. Greene Science Center looks like a Frank Lloyd Wright creation on steroids: all glass and metal and right angles. Oliver came to the city yesterday for some dinner meeting with Penn Carro, so I drove to Philly at the crack of dawn and took the train into Manhattan to meet him for our ten a.m. appointment. I'm fifteen minutes early. I slide onto a bench and watch the college students, laden with book bags, curved over their phones, amble by on their way to class. And even though the campus is like a completely different world — expansive bright walkways and vibrant green spaces separating the stately Gothic buildings — dropped in the middle of New York City, I revel in the bustle, the spark of energy absent in sleepy small towns like Hope Springs. I realize just how much I miss it. How isolated I've felt.

At ten o'clock on the dot, Oliver comes

rushing at me. "C'mon," he says. "We're gonna be late." I follow him through the glass door and we squeeze into the elevator behind two girls, one wearing black lipstick, the other in plaid pajama pants. When they get off at the third floor, Oliver and I ride in an awkward silence.

The doors slide open and I follow him to room 427. As he raps on the door, I finally think of something to say: "I can't believe the magazine liked your story idea."

"Um," he says. We hear a "Come in" from the other side. "They didn't."

"What?" I whisper. But he's turning the handle and then we're in the office, face-to-face with the woman from the photo, except she's in full color — wearing a light pink tunic and a smile that stretches her thin lips until they're nonexistent.

"Oliver, I presume?" she says, sticking out her hand over her desk.

"Yes." He fits his hand into hers. "Thank you so much for taking the time to speak with me."

"It's a pleasure," she says, turning to me. "This is Mia."

"Hi," Dr. Saltz says, staring from me to Oliver as if she's waiting for an explanation as to why I'm there. Oliver doesn't offer one. I wiggle my fingers at her as she lowers

212

herself into her desk chair. She sweeps a hand magnanimously at us to follow suit. "Well, like I told you," she says when we're seated across from her, "I've got this twenty-five-minute window before my next class, so fire away."

"Right," Oliver says. He rubs his palms on his jean-clad thighs.

"What magazine did you say you were from again?"

"Um . . . we're not. From one."

My head snaps toward him, eyes wide, and then up at Dr. Saltz.

She cocks her head like a questioning bird, eyes narrowed, then looks up toward the ceiling, as if searching for help. More to herself than us, she mutters: "I told Janine to vet these interview requests, but does she listen? No. No, she doesn't." She drops her eyes back in our direction. "Let me guess," she says, her voice steady, laced with a not-small hint of anger. "You're having strange dreams and want to know what they mean."

"Er . . . yes."

She rolls her eyes and starts shuffling papers on her desk. "Thank you so much for wasting my time — and yours. But there are therapy offices all over the city of New York and I'm sure one of them can help you decipher what being chased by a *Tyran-*

nosaurus rex or showing up naked to your family reunion means."

She stands up with such force, the leather chair rolls back, slamming into the cinder block wall behind her.

Oliver half stands, too, holding a palm up. *We come in peace.* "No, wait. Please," he says. "We don't know each other —" He gestures to me. "We just met a few weeks ago. But we've been dreaming about each other. For months."

"Years," I say.

"Years," he repeats, and then his head swivels. *"Years?"*

I nod, holding his gaze. His have only been for the past few months?

"Congratulations," she says under her breath, but she doesn't move to leave. "So you guys are obviously soul mates destined to be together. There. Is that what you wanted to hear? I have things to do now."

"What? No — *no!* I'm married!"

She fixes a look at me. A cocked eyebrow; and I feel all the shame she's directing toward me. The judgment and guilt dealt in one swift blow — *You're married, yet you're here? With another man?* I drop my head. "C'mon," I say to Oliver. "We should go."

"SHE KEEPS DYING," he says, the fervor in his voice jerking my head up. "She

214

dies. In my dreams — *nightmares*. And I can't go on like this — I have to know what it means. Or how to make it stop."

I blink slowly. And then blink again. The air-conditioning unit squeaks and rattles to life beneath the window, before growing into a steady hum. And then I flash back to the conversation on my porch — how I asked him what he dreamt and he got so uncomfortable. But then, what about the elevator one? Surely I don't die in all of them?

"Most of them," he says quietly to me, and I wonder if I asked the question out loud, or just with my expression. Harrison says I'm transparent. That it doesn't matter what I say, because what I think is always written right on my face. "The elevator, the waterslide. They end the same."

And suddenly I feel so foolish. Here I am harboring a borderline teenage-girl crush on this man I've been dreaming about, while I'm actually — *literally* — his worst nightmare. Harrison will be so relieved to know the reason Oliver looks at me so intently is because he's waiting for me to choke on a noodle, a spring pea, to drop dead of a sudden heart attack.

I become aware once again of Dr. Saltz still hovering behind her desk. Her eyes dart from me to Oliver and back to me again.

215

Realizing we have no intention of leaving —
I'm not sure I could stand up if I wanted to
— she takes a deep breath, exhaling slowly.
She pinches the bridge of her nose, directly
between her eyes. She licks her lips. She
mutters something that sounds like, "Jesus,
be a fence." Then she sits down.

"You've got five minutes," she says. "What
do you want to start with?"

"Um . . ." I say, slowly. "I think the dying
bit would be good?"

"Great." She places her hands together in
front of her. "Dreaming of death often
doesn't literally mean that someone is going
to die."

"Often? So sometimes it does."

She shrugs. "There are not really any
statistics I can point to here. But the general
consensus is that it's symbolic of the ending
of something — whether it's a job, a relationship . . ." She pauses, looks pointedly at
me. "A marriage."

"Hey," I say, but before I can defend
myself further, Oliver speaks.

"I did just break up with my girlfriend.
Around the time the dreams started."

In my peripheral, I see Dr. Saltz lift her
hands, palms to the sky, as if to say, *See? I
rest my case,* but I keep my eyes trained on
Oliver. *Girlfriend.* After learning he wasn't

actually married to Caroline, I didn't even think about him being in a relationship with anyone else — not that it's any of my business.

"OK, so what about this whole dreaming of each other before we met? That's not normal, right? I mean, is there any research where that's happened before?"

She turns to me, expression bored, her voice monotone. "In dream science we refer to that as psychic dreaming, the idea that some dreams have a predictive quality to them, or can tell the future."

"Like . . . a premonition?"

She dips her chin. "So, in your case, you dreamt about a man and then, allegedly" — she gestures to Oliver — "met that man. Other examples are people who had nightmares about the twin towers falling in the months and weeks leading up to 9/11. Or people dreaming of earthquakes only to experience one days later. It's even said that Lincoln dreamt of his own death, just weeks before he was assassinated."

"*What?* I thought you said death was symbolic."

"I said it's often symbolic."

I clench my jaw, inhaling deeply through my nose.

"Is that true?" Oliver asks. "Did people

really dream about 9/11 before it happened?"

"It depends on your definition of true, I suppose," she says. "Are these people lying? I don't think all of them are — there are just too many stories for that to be possible. But is their perception of what's occurred accurate?"

"What do you mean?"

"Well, don't get me wrong, I think these anecdotes are all very intriguing. But I also think coincidence and perception can play a big role. In other words, people can see what they want to see sometimes. Maybe they want to believe someone is their soul mate" — again, her hawk eyes dart back and forth between us — "and so in retrospect they think, say, that man with the gold medallion walking on the beach in their dream must be the exact same person they meet a year later with a gold medallion walking on the beach and are now falling in love with. But perhaps it's just a strange coincidence. I mean, there are a lot of men on the East Coast that wear gold medallions — especially near Jersey." She pauses, but doesn't crack a grin at her own joke. "Or, in the case of 9/11, maybe the nightmare was just of an explosion in a building, but again, in retrospect, it's very easy to think that it must have been the World Trade Center."

Oliver leans back, jabs his fingers into his hair. But I sit still, processing what Dr. Saltz is suggesting, which is similar to what Harrison said — that I didn't actually dream of Oliver, just someone who looked like him. And that upon seeing him, I made the connection, because I what — *want* it to mean something? The whole idea is preposterous and the irritation that has been building is now full-blown anger.

"This is bullshit."

Oliver turns to me, eyes wide.

"What? It is. You know this isn't just a weird coincidence. I dreamt of *you* — not someone who looked like you. It's not my mind playing some trick on me."

The air conditioner shuts off and a tinny silence fills the room.

The wheels of Dr. Saltz's chair squeak as she shifts in her seat. "Look," she says. And when I do, really look at her, her features have rearranged themselves into a softer kindness. "My grandmother used to have this friend, Harley Dean. And whenever anybody lost something, they called Ms. Harley Dean, because she would know how to find it. One time my grandmother moved houses, and lost a pair of crystal candlesticks that my grandfather had given her. She told

219

Harley Dean — who lived two full states away — and the next day Harley Dean called her and told her to look in a cabinet underneath the stairs in the basement. Sure enough, my grandmother found a box there, and in that box were the candlesticks. Now, mind you, Harley Dean had never been to my grandmother's new house."

My brow wrinkles. "So how did she —"

"Said she dreamt it. That's how she found other people's lost things — she would dream about them. Where they were."

I sit back, not understanding.

"What I'm trying to say is, I can't explain that. I believe that it happened — I know my grandmother wouldn't lie about it — but I have no explanation. I would love to sit here and tell you the how and why of it, but I deal in science. And from my research and the fifty years of research before me, the science backing up this type of predictive dreaming just isn't there." She holds my gaze for a beat, shifts her eyes to Oliver. "But that doesn't mean it's not real." She starts moving papers around on her desk and stands up. "Now if you'll excuse me."

Oliver stands up and holds the door open for her. "Thank you for your time, Dr. Saltz," he says as she passes. She grunts and then pauses.

"You know, I'm surprised you didn't call Denise Krynchenko."

"Who?" he asks.

"You don't know of Professor Krynchenko? She's Harvard. Studies *all* that psychic stuff. Look up her book. It's a doozy."

Oliver stretches away from the door, holding it open with his foot, and grabs a pen from Dr. Saltz's desk. Scribbles the name on his palm.

"Thanks," he repeats. And then Professor Saltz is gone and we're alone. "C'mon," he says to me.

"Where are we going?" I stand up, my knees a little wobbly. "To a library?"

"No. I need a drink."

Another thing I love about big cities: You can find a bar that's open and serving at literally any hour of the day. Back in the bright sunshine, the first restaurant we come to off campus swells with brunchers at sidewalk tables, laughing over their smoked salmon tartines and Bellinis. We pass it, as if in silent agreement that the atmosphere doesn't quite fit our mood, and Oliver reaches for the heavy wood door pull of the next establishment — no patio, no brunchers. No brunch, apparently, as one staffer is in the middle of pulling the chairs off the tabletops in preparation for the lunch service. Our eyes adjust to the dim light, we hop up on barstools and, seeing as we're the only patrons seated at the long, scuffed wood bar, the bartender gets our drink order right away.

"Dying?" I say to Oliver the second our cocktails (old-fashioned for him, vodka tonic, two limes, for me) are placed in front of us.

"Yeah," he says, twisting the highball glass slowly on the bar top.

"Why didn't you tell me?"

"I don't know. How do you tell somebody that?"

He has a point. He rubs his hands over his eyes and temples. "This is all so weird."

"So — how do I die?" I mean it as a joke to lighten the mood. But it hangs in the air, heavier than I intended.

"Different ways," Oliver says. "The two of us hiking in the woods and you willfully stepping off a cliff, your body colliding with the rocks below. Masked man eerily laughing while peppering your chest with copper-tipped bullets from his artillery of weapons. Walking across train tracks, not hearing the locomotive whistle as it barrels toward you, leaving your head bloody, neck half —"

222

He stops when he sees my face.

"I know you're a writer and all," I say, once I find words again. "But sometimes . . . less is more."

"Sorry," he mumbles. "You know that's not even the worst of it, though — it's that I can't ever get to you. That awful feeling in dreams when you're trying to run but your legs feel like they're stuck in mud or you scream and no sound comes out? That's how it is every time. I'm right there, but I can't help."

I suppress a shiver and take another sip of my drink through the tiny black straw, the strong taste of vodka flooding my mouth. Exhaustion creeps into my bones, weighing them down. And not just because I got up at the crack of dawn. I'm tired of the dreams. Of thinking about them, dissecting them, feeling no closer to finding out what in the world they could mean.

I pluck the straw out of my drink, flick it onto the bar top, pick up the glass and swallow a proper mouthful. "Enough about all that." I wave my hand in the air between us. "Tell me about this girlfriend."

"Who — Naomi?" He shrugs. Scratches his cheek. "Not much to tell."

"How long did you date for?"

"Five years."

"Five *years?*"

"Off and on."

"What happened? When you broke up?"

He sighs. Takes another sip of his drink. "I don't know. It was right before I left for Australia. She didn't want me to go. When we met I had just gotten back from my fourth trip with AGOFO — the poultry farm in Oregon — and she liked that I did it. Or said she did. Said it made me interesting. Unlike the cookie-cutter guys she'd been dating. But then it wore on her, I guess. Or she thought I would get tired of it, do it a few more times for the experience and then settle down. With her."

"But you didn't want to."

"I guess not. Or I wouldn't have gone to Australia."

We watch the bartender at the far end cut limes and toss them into a square translucent bucket.

"One time, in college, I wanted to break up with this guy, but we lived in the same dorm. Literally right next door. So I stayed with him until summer break."

He jiggles his glass; the ice clinks together. "And?"

"I'm just saying — never occurred to me to go to Australia."

He laughs and we order another round

and I ask him about his time there. He tells me about his hosts, Albert and Bettina, and their quaint cottage on the Margaret River; her Vegemite and chip sandwiches wrapped in brown paper; his catchy chants of their hippie motto: *Earth care, people fare, then share!*

As I listen to him talk, I'm a little in awe that this is his life — that he jumps from country to country experiencing the world the way others only idly talk about. Why do some people have that — the ability to grab life by the horns and ride it like a bull, hanging on for the pure exhilaration? I always wanted to be that person; I fantasized about backpacking in Europe, flitting from museum to museum, studying the greats, smoking hand-rolled cigarettes and drinking Chianti until the wee hours of the morning, dissecting art and existentialism with like-minded souls — the kinds of conversations you can only have in your twenties, when all your thoughts seem eternally fascinating and remarkable.

But I never did.

We fall into silence and I fiddle with the straw again. And my mind drifts back to Dr. Saltz's office. The dreams. Oliver.

"What next?"

"Finland, I think. Just sent in my application, actually."

"That's not really what I meant."

"I know."

We both stare into our drinks as if the remains of melted ice are tea leaves that could tell us our future.

He pulls out his phone and taps the screen a few times.

"What are you doing?"

"Looking up that Krynchenko book."

I chew my bottom lip, thinking. "Do you believe in all that — the psychic stuff she was talking about?"

"Damn. It's out of print." He turns his phone to me. I glance at it and then back at him, waiting. "Do I believe in all that psychic stuff," he repeats. "No. But I didn't believe you existed, either, when I started dreaming about you. And yet, here you are."

Dreaming about you. Something clicks in my brain. "What are the others about?"

"What do you mean?"

"In Dr. Saltz's office, you said 'most of them' are nightmares about me dying. What are the others?"

He doesn't look at me. "Not nightmares." He throws back the rest of his drink and bangs the glass back on the table.

"Like what?" I press.

He shifts in his seat, stares forward,

seconds ticking by, and just when I think he's not going to answer the question, he turns his face squarely toward mine. "Let's just say you're not married in any of them."

"Oh," I breathe. I want to look away from his eyes — everything in my body impels me to look away. But it's impossible.

"I should go," he says, standing abruptly. "I'm meeting Penn for one more interview before heading back." He digs for the wallet in his back pocket and then throws two twenties on the bar top. "Can I walk you to the train station?"

"No, no, I'm fine. I'll probably . . . walk around or something. Maybe go to a museum."

"OK," he says. We share an awkward goodbye — made even more so by the fact that we're both clearly making a point not to touch each other.

And then he's gone, and instead of going back outside or to a museum, I sit there, rolling his words over in my mind. But it's not so much the words that I can't stop thinking about. It's what I saw in his eyes when he said them. A flicker of something. So brief, if I had blinked I would have missed it. And I wasn't quite sure what it meant, but I knew how it felt — like the

beginning of something I couldn't name.
Like a match had been struck.

CHAPTER 15

The first day of August, I get my period.

I stare at the rust-colored stain in my underwear as I sit on the toilet, Harrison's stacks of medical journals jabbing into my shoulder blades. I think of all the times in my twenties that I prayed for it to come, especially after a few blurry one-night stands where I'd be hard-pressed to come up with the man's last name, if necessary — but even in the first couple years of my relationship with Harrison. And the relief at seeing those first streaks of red would be palpable. Like I had gotten away with something. Skated on thin ice, and just barely made it to the other side.

Then, everything changed one morning over bacon with Harrison. And suddenly, I didn't want my period anymore. But it came just the same. Stubbornly. Resolutely. As if my body was saying: *You asked for this, remember?* It took us seven months to get pregnant with our first baby, and every time my period came it was more than disappointing — it felt punitive.

Even now — six weeks postmiscarriage — when this blood should signify a fresh start, a time to try again, it's just a stark, ugly reminder of everything I have lost. And may never find.

Continuing my effort to give him time, I haven't brought up trying again with Harrison, not since our endless back-and-forth conversations the week we got the fertility results back. But it's there, rooted firmly between us, growing thick and unruly like one of the weeds in the garden. And I fear that one day, it will get so big, we won't be able to see our way around it.

I slide in a tampon, change my underwear and get dressed. It's not until I yank on a tank top that I realize I'm sweating from the effort. Why is it so freaking hot? I shuffle to the thermostat in the hallway. It reads eighty-one degrees. I punch the arrows with more force than necessary, wondering if Harrison accidentally bumped the temperature too high or turned it off altogether, and nothing happens.

And I know: The air-conditioning is broken.

As if the day cannot get any worse, I call

three repair services and they're all over-booked; the shortest wait time is five days. I make an appointment, text Harrison the news and slip out of the house, searching for relief. Though it's not even ten, the air outside is just as stiflingly hot as inside, unmoving, as I make my way to the studio. I shut the door behind me and crank up the window unit as high as it will go. It rattles to life and I stand in front of the air blasting out of it until it turns ice-cold. Then I stand there a bit longer.

When I'm finally more comfortable, I sink to the floor, the cement cool beneath my bare legs. I lean my back against the wall of unfinished Sheetrock and thumb through my phone to the IVF message boards I've recently become obsessed with. It started innocently enough — I was just trying to get more information, to know exactly what in vitro entailed, so when Harrison was ready we could dive right in. I took meticulous notes about each step of the procedure, the names of the various drugs used, the days of the cycle that are for follicle stimulation, egg maturation, retrieval, implantation. But when I ran across the statistic that only twenty-nine percent of first IVF rounds are successful, my heart caught in my throat. *Twenty-nine percent?*

And that was when I found the message boards. Women describing in excruciating detail their latest procedures — the pain and bloating of hormone injections, the cautious excitement of implantation, the agonizing two-week wait, the heartrending disappointment of a negative pregnancy test. I created a profile so I could get into the boards, but I hadn't posted anything yet. I was a lurker, glued to the daily trials of one woman in particular, as if watching a prime-time soap opera.

Today MissyK874 had her long-awaited doctor appointment for a pregnancy blood test. She had (of course) taken two drugstore tests, which had both been positive, but apparently with IVF, those results were unreliable thanks to the HCG hormone given for implantation. Her appointment had been at 9:15 this morning, and apparently I wasn't the only one waiting with bated breath for the results.

MissyK874, any news? Sending lots of baby dust!
Fingers crossed it's a sticky bean! We're here for you.
Praying for your rainbow baby.

A text message alert pops up on my

screen, blocking the message board from view. My heart revs when I see the name: Oliver. I click on it.

Where's my pic? You promised.

He texted me first — which feels important to note — two days after New York, when I wasn't sure how we left it or if I'd talk to him again or if I *should* talk to him again. Two days after Harrison looked at me when he got home from work and said, "Well?" and then listened patiently as I told him every single thing that had happened in New York — everything except that flicker in Oliver's eye. I had started to think maybe I'd imagined it. That it was just an awkward situation and I had read too much into it.

And then Oliver texted me. It was a link to a Wikipedia article and one sentence: The Lincoln thing — it's true. I clicked on it and scanned the page until I got to a section titled "Premonitions."

About ten days before he was assassinated, President Lincoln claimed to have a vivid dream in which he saw a corpse decked in funeral vestments — its face covered — in the East Room of the White House. People around him were mourning loudly, weeping and sobbing, and when

he asked "Who's dead?" a soldier responded: "The President. He was killed."

I reread it slowly. Once. Twice. And then
texted him back: Is this supposed to make
me feel better?

Oh, right. Guess not.

I bit off a smile, gnawing on my lip and
trying to decide what to write back, when
three dots appeared. And then: What about
this?

I clicked the link through to an article
about a man in the UK who had a dream
that he had read the name of the winner of
a big horse race in a newspaper. The next
day he bet on the horse — and won. And it
happened eight more times in the next year.

Now you think our dreams are somehow
predicting horse races? I typed.

Worth a shot? Maybe there's a horse named
Bag of Teeth.

I laughed out loud and then replied: Wet
Turkey Sandwich.

Him: Falling Off Cliff

Me: Masked Man

Him: Locomotive

Me: That's actually a good racehorse name.

Over the next couple of days, we kept
texting, sending weird links and tidbits we
each discovered about dreams, as if trying

to top each other with the strangest one.

Like a three-year-old American girl who would wake up some mornings asking where her lady's maid was and calling her closet a "wardrobe" and even telling her mother — who was convinced her daughter was remembering a past life as a royal princess — to ring for breakfast.

We swapped stories of murders being solved, a woman saved from drowning, a bank robbery prevented, all thanks to dreams.

We shared facts. Like how dream scientists are called oneirologists. Or how twelve percent of people dream only in black-and-white. Or how dreaming was the genesis for Mary Shelley's *Frankenstein* and Stephenie Meyer's *Twilight.* Turns out, not just the plots of famous novels are attributed to dreams: also the sewing machine, the periodic table, DNA's double-helix spiral — even Google.

Paul McCartney wrote "Yesterday" after hearing it in a dream.

God, I love the Beatles, I replied to that one.

Who doesn't? That's like saying you love pizza.

Not everyone likes pizza.

97 percent of the world population likes pizza.

Are you just making up facts now?

How dare you! I'm a journalist. And then: Only 5 percent of the facts I state are made up.

And that's how our texts devolved into something other than talking about dreams.

I blink at the screen now, and then scroll through my library of pictures and find the one I'm looking for. I hold my breath, hit send and wait.

The ellipses pop up and disappear at least four times.

And then: Is that Keanu Reeves?

I grin. Three days ago, out of curiosity, I downloaded the book Oliver ghostwrote for the celebrity chef Carson Flanagan and started reading it. When I told Oliver last night, he said it was only fair that I show him my work, too.

Yep.

I explain briefly about the mediocre theme and wait for the requisite male response — how *Point Break* or *The Matrix* is the Greatest Movie of All Time. It takes him three long minutes to type his reply and then:

I don't know — he was pretty amazing in The Lake House.

I bark with laughter and it echoes off the steel garage doors. My phone buzzes in my hand.

Send me another.

My eyes light on the carnival painting dwarfing the easel it sits on. I snap a picture of it, but then hesitate. It feels personal, somehow. Too intimate to share, even though it originated in a dream about him. Or maybe *because* it was a dream about him. Or maybe it has nothing to do with the picture and everything to do with the way I feel when we're texting: light, buzzy, eager. Eager to come up with the cleverest response. Eager for his reply. Slightly guilty for all the eagerness. It's not like I've been hiding it from Harrison. He knows we're still in touch. I even told him some of the bizarre dreams we'd uncovered in our online explorations.

Still, I stare at the picture, and instead of hitting send, I pull up the IVF message board up. MissyK874 still hasn't posted, so I start browsing the other threads, and get lost in the world of other women with empty bellies that long for them to be full.

"Wow," Harrison says, when he's leaning against the frame of the open studio door that night. "You've been busy."

After a few hours of sitting on the cement floor, I took note of my sore tailbone and it occurred to me that if the air wasn't going to be fixed for five days, I needed to make it a little more comfortable in here.

Now, I'm lying propped on my elbow on an inflated air mattress, surrounded by blankets and pillows, eyes glued to Vanna White turning letters on the flat-screen I lugged in from the den. The television casts its blue glow on everything in the dark room, including Harrison, and I study the shadows and highlights contouring his face, his square glasses, the black of his wiry beard. I teased him relentlessly when he started growing it out, so I can never admit that I like it. But I do — and not just because it evokes a certain manly ruggedness, but because it's novel, something unexpected on a face I've memorized after six years. It's not just the beard that's different, though. He's been running more — at least five days a week instead of three; working later. I think about our dinner at Sorelli's — how tired he looked. No, not tired. I was with him throughout his residency — I've seen Harrison look tired. It's like he has the weight of the world on his shoulders. And I get a flash of guilt in my belly. Have I become so absorbed in my own grief, my own needs — the *dreams,* even — that I haven't noticed what's going on with my own husband?

"Come here." I extend my hand to him.

He slips off his shoes and lies down beside me, fully clothed. He drapes an arm over my waist, pulling me closer to him. We watch as a contestant buys a vowel. An *e.*

"A watched pot never boils," Harrison says, his breath hot on my neck.

"Dang it — it was on the tip of my tongue."

"Sure it was." I can hear the grin in his voice. I roll toward it and press my lips on his, as if I'm trying to trap the happiness. When I pull back, I look into his eyes, unsure how to phrase the question I want to ask.

"Is everything OK with you?"

"What do you mean?"

"I don't know — you just seem different, lately."

I feel his body bristle. "How so?"

"Well, the beard, I guess, for starters. You're running more —"

"I like running."

"I know, but it's just, I don't know — it seems like . . . I mean, I know things have been tough lately, with the baby." My voice cracks.

"Oh, Mia," Harrison says, rolling onto his back, forcing the air in the mattress to shift and wobble beneath us, and pulling me with him, so that I'm splayed across his chest, making me think that it is the baby he's sad about. I wish he would just talk to me about it. That we could share in our grief together. And then come up with a plan. A way forward. His fingers gently and methodically smooth my hair. One of my ears listens to his heartbeat. The other to Pat Sajak as he moves on to the next puzzle: A Thing.

"I started today," I whisper. "My period."

He doesn't respond, just keeps running the pads of his fingers over my scalp.

"Harrison," I say, after a stretch of silence. His hand stills.

"I've been looking into IVF." His chest rises beneath my cheek and then falls as he exhales. "I know. I know you're not ready yet. But I just wanted more information. It's a pretty intense process."

"I've heard that."

"And it can take a couple of rounds — sometimes more. Only, like, twenty-nine percent are successful on the first try."

"Mia," he says. A warning.

I ignore it. "By the sixth attempt it increases to sixty-five percent. Of course the odds are a little better for us, because I'm under thirty-five and we'd be using my own eggs, but still it's lengthy, an involved process. And I thought that if we at least get started, make an appointment for more information or an evaluation so that —"

"Mia," he repeats. Sharper this time.

The ding of letters lighting up on the *Wheel of Fortune* board fills the room. "Three *I*'s," says Pat.

And then Harrison: "I just . . ." He lifts his hand to his face, and I know he's rubbing his eyes beneath his glasses. Something he does when he's tired or thinking or both. "I need —"

"Time." I finish for him, my voice flat. "Yeah, I know."

I turn away from him, back toward the television, and after a beat, he follows, the mattress wobbling beneath us once again. He drapes a long arm around me, casually cupping my breast, a position so common and comfortable, the intimacy of it doesn't even register.

"When did you say they're coming to fix the air again?"

"Monday," I say.

He grunts. And then: "We should get out of here. This weekend. Go to the Poconos or Cape May — or what about that place in Jersey with the huge artwork garden you've

241

been wanting to see?"

"Grounds for Sculpture."

"Grounds for Sculpture," he repeats. "We could stay in a third-rate hotel, swim in the overchlorinated pool, eat those rubbery just-add-water powdered eggs at the free breakfast in the morning."

"I love those rubbery just-add-water powdered eggs."

"I know." He nuzzles my ear. "What do you think?"

What do I *think*. I let his words roll around in my head: *We should get out of here.* I think about the last time he said that, when we were living in Philadelphia, just after our second miscarriage, and the weekend trip ended up with us moving here. I think about how spontaneous it was, so unlike Harrison, and how he's doing it again. I think my husband is changing right in front of my eyes. His beard, his spontaneity, how he needs *time*. I think about how time feels like the one thing I don't have to give him.

"I don't know. Maybe."

The Game Show Network moves on to its nightly lineup of five *Family Feud*s in a row. At some point, Harrison removes his glasses, unbuttons his shirt. And then his arm grows heavy over mine, his breathing deepens. I nudge him gently and he rolls off of me, to his side of the air mattress. I turn off the television and lie beside him, waiting for sleep to come. But it doesn't. I listen to the rattle of the air-conditioning unit in the window, and then the overwhelming silence it leaves behind when it suddenly clicks off. I stare up at the crisscross shadows of the exposed wood rafters holding up the roof.

Restless, I pick up my phone from where it lies on the ground beside the air mattress and click on my text messages. I reread the last few from Oliver, and without hesitating this time, I hit send on the picture I took of the carnival painting.

Then I navigate to the message board again. As I'm searching for an update from MissyK874 — she hadn't been on all afternoon — my phone comes alive in my hand, startling me.

It's loud, the buzzing, in this tiny room, and I slide my thumb on the screen to answer it quickly, simultaneously registering that the name on the screen is Oliver.

"Hello?" I whisper, heart racing. I glance at Harrison's sleeping form. It doesn't stir.

"Do you know that place?" Oliver's voice demands in my ear. There's an edge of panic to it that sends my heart galloping even faster.

"Wait — hold on." I roll off the air mattress as smoothly as I can. I tiptoe to the door, easing it open and then pulling it closed behind me, as I step out onto the gravel. The rocks dig into the bare soles of my feet.

"What are you asking?" I say, gingerly hopping over to the grass for relief.

"Your painting. The amusement park. Where is that? Have you been there?"

"No." I cross an arm over my stomach, to ward off a sudden chill, even though the night air is still thick with summer heat. "It was a dream. A dream I had. One about you. We're there, in that carnival at night. Alone at first, and then all these people are there, too . . ." I trail off. "Why?"

He doesn't say anything for what feels like hours and I grip the phone, waiting. Wondering. Is it a place he recognizes? Somewhere he's been before?

"Oliver? What is it?"

"It's just . . . I've had that dream, too."

Chapter 16

After two days of sleeping on the air mattress in the studio and taking showers in a house so hot, I feel like I need another one the second I step out of it, I'm near salivating at the idea of a hotel room.

That's how I find myself sitting in the passenger seat of Harrison's Infiniti Friday night, heading south on Route 29 toward Hamilton, New Jersey, home to the Grounds for Sculpture, a forty-two-acre art park and arboretum known for its oversize three-dimensional sculptures of famous paintings. Though it's a short trip — only forty-five minutes — my mood buoyed the second we hit the highway, remembering the many miles Harrison and I traversed during our first few years together; road trips home for holidays, to weekend weddings, short beach excursions. I often loved the ride more than the destination, even though Harrison's Jeep rattled like the frame was going to come completely off the wheels at any speed above forty-five. It just added to the exhilaration of having Harrison completely to myself for the stretch of time and highway in front of us.

The Infiniti is smooth, quiet as it barrels down Route 29. Too quiet. I roll down the window and hot air whooshes into the car. I stick my hand into it, let the wind dance through my fingers.

My cell vibrates in my pocket and I dig it out, peering at the screen through the hair that's whipping around my face. It's Oliver.

I think this might be it.

I cast a sideways glance at Harrison. The day after my phone conversation with Oliver, I drifted around in a kind of stunned fog. So we did have the same dream, at least once. But what did that *mean?* It was so maddening, getting these little puzzle pieces that didn't seem like they would ever add up to one big picture. I told Harrison that night, but he didn't say anything. Just stared at me like I had sprouted a third arm, and sighed — a long, controlled exhale of breath — making me feel even crazier than I already felt.

Meanwhile, Oliver has gone into a deep dive of amusement parks in the United States. He's convinced the one in our dream must actually exist and keeps sending me images he's found online. At first I thought he might be on to something. The problem, I've found, is that they're all so similar — carousel, wooden roller coaster, Ferris wheel, funnel cakes. And I've started to wonder if the details I'm painting are from my dreams — was the carousel horse *really* ivory with a gold and red saddle? — or from some collective memory of what a carousel is supposed to look like.

I enlarge the current image Oliver sent with his text. It's an ornate carousel, with intricate gold curlicues decorating the rafters of the ride. I squint at it. There is something vaguely familiar about it — but then, there was something familiar about the last eight.

Maybe, I type back.

He sends another picture: a Tilt-A-Whirl with royal blue domed seats on a mechanical track. I sit up.

Getting warmer.

Right? And on the park map, it's right next to the carousel, just like in your painting.

Where is it?

Elysburg, PA. Couple hours away. Think I might go check it out tomorrow. Want to come?

Another sideways glance at Harrison.

247

Can't. Headed out of town for the weekend.
Cool. Where to?
Jersey. Grounds for Sculpture.

I realize, a beat after I hit send, what I've just admitted to. And I have no doubt what his response will be.

WHAT? WHO VACATIONS IN NEW JERSEY??!

I grin.

"Mia." Harrison's voice grabs my attention.

"Huh?" I look up at him.

"I'm talking to you." His voice is loud, competing with the wind.

"Oh. Sorry." I tug at the button on my door panel and watch the window automatically close. My hair stills. "What's up?"

"I said I've got something for you."

"What?"

"Reach into my bag." He gestures to the backpack at my feet.

I look at him curiously and reach down to unzip the bag's front pouch.

"No, the big one."

I grip the other zipper and pull, revealing a manila folder stuffed with papers. Assuming it's Harrison's work stuff, I push it forward to look behind it, without any idea what I'm looking for.

"That's it. Pull it out."

"This folder?"

He nods.

"What is it?" I ask suspiciously, as I tug it onto my lap. It's thick, half my palm wide.

"Research."

I turn the flap, my eyes landing on the headline of the first page: *Why Do We Dream?* I stare at it and then slowly turn to him.

"I thought we could go through it together."

"What?" I ask, even though realization is dawning. I flip through the thick stack of papers and see bright-colored Post-it Notes sticking out the sides, Harrison's illegible scrawl ending in question marks. It's not just some web search results thrown together. It's been curated, annotated — it took effort. "When did you even have time to do all this?"

"Last night, when I was on call. It was a slow night."

I can't help but gape at him. And I think of the way he gaped at me Wednesday night. His long sigh. "But . . . I thought you didn't really believe me. That I was being crazy."

"I don't think you're crazy," he says quietly. "Not completely, anyway." He grins. I swat at his thigh with the back of my hand. "Look, I do think this is . . . unusual. And I did hope that it was just some phase — like those two months you were determined to make your own paint using eggs and there was dried yolk on every single surface of our apartment. But when you were telling me about the amusement park dream on Wednesday, I realized this is not going away. And I thought about when I have a patient who comes in presenting unusual symptoms that don't match up with anything I've seen before. I don't dismiss what they're saying out of hand; I research to fill in the gaps of what I know and hopefully come up with a diagnosis."

"And if you can't, then you dismiss the patient as a hypochondriac."

He laughs. "OK, so the metaphor isn't without its flaws."

My hand finds his, our fingers lacing together. I squeeze gently. "Thank you."

He shrugs, as if it's nothing.

But it's not. In that moment, it feels a little bit like everything.

In Hamilton, we stop at a drive-through and buy a sack of chicken soft tacos for dinner. We eat them in our room at the Howard Johnson, reveling in the air-conditioning that we cranked to full blast and drinking cold bottles of gas station beer.

And we go through the articles Harrison printed out, one by one. The first few are from *Psychology Today:* examinations and explanations of various dream studies; researchers trying to understand exactly why we dream. Some believe dreams are our brain's way of forming and processing memories, while others think it's how we sort through all the information our brains have collected throughout the day — random snaps of passing cars, snippets of conversations we overhear but aren't paying attention to. Another theory suggests dreaming is psychological — how we work through difficult emotions like fear and anxiety in our lives. And some scientists believe dreams serve no function at all — that they're just random and meaningless firings of the brain.

Harrison had highlighted that line, and I shoot him an amused look as soon as I notice it. "Let me guess, you're in the meaningless camp?"

He holds up his beer from the corner chair he's sitting in. His legs are propped on the bed, crossed at the ankles. "I think it's important to consider all possibilities," he says diplomatically. He bites into his taco, and a few errant shreds of cheese fall to his lap. "The next few pages delve into Jung

251

versus Freud dream analysis — it's interesting, but nothing that really pertains, so you can skip through those." I flip through until I get to the next Post-it.

"OK, so here we get into some of the more . . . er . . . out-there stuff you and Oliver found, particularly the psychic dreaming. There are apparently three kinds. Precognitive means it predicts the future, so seeing someone you're going to meet, or those people who thought they dreamt of the World Trade towers falling." I follow along on the pages in front of me. "Then there are clairvoyant dreams, which supposedly give real-time information, so I think that lady who found the — what was it you said — candlesticks? That's clairvoyant. And then telepathic is people who communicate to each other mentally."

"Dream telepathy. Yeah, Oliver said something about that." But I'm no longer looking at the papers in front of me. I'm staring at my husband, who not only listened to everything I've off-handedly told him these past few weeks, he *paid attention.* Even though I know he thinks it's a bunch of nonsense.

And for some reason, I think of my childhood television. Growing up, we only owned one, which was embarrassing enough in the nineties, when all of my friends had at least two or three, but even more so because it wasn't even a new one. It was one of those old huge wood console boxes from the seventies that we inherited from my grandmother. Worse still, sometimes the picture would get fuzzy or go out altogether, or the sound would just vanish and you had to bang on the top and side of it with your fist to rattle whatever was loose just enough to get it to work again.

As I stare at my husband, it occurs to me that marriage is a lot like that TV. The connection gets loose sometimes — even to the point where you think it might not work anymore — but then something jars it and the wires slip back into place, exactly where they belong, lighting up the screen and bringing back the sound; everything working as it should.

"Come here," I say. And he does. And that's how the papers end up a scattered mess on the floor.

At breakfast, we eat reconstituted eggs with toast off a conveyor belt and drink the burnt, watered-down coffee, dumping in extra plastic cups of creamer to try to cover the taste. We spend the morning sweating through the landscaped acres of Grounds for Sculpture; the afternoon, swimming in the motel pool, the cool water a balm to the hot day. And then, the chemical scent of chlorine still clinging to our skin and hair, we go to dinner. A local pizza joint.

"Oh my god." I'm savoring my first bite — the perfect blend of tomato sauce, chewy crust and warm, melty cheese. "I wish this place delivered to Hope Springs."

"Really? But we've got that amazing gas station pizza," he says solemnly, until he can't hold it anymore, and his face cracks. "God, I miss Philly."

My head snaps up. "You do?"

"Of course. The food, at least. Especially Paesano's. I would literally kill for one of their sandwiches right now."

I study him. "Do you think . . . would you ever want to move back?"

His face clouds over. "No. I couldn't."

I'm about to counter, ask why, when my cell buzzes. It's Oliver. "Sorry," I say lamely to Harrison, before checking the message.

I AM THAT GUY.

What do you mean?

Grown man. In amusement park. Alone. Might as well be driving a white van and offering candy to children.

I grin.

Also, not sure what I was expecting to find,

but feeling a little stupid about my theory now.

Not the same park, then?

Not the same park.

"Is that Oliver?" Harrison asks and I look up at him.

"Yeah." I put my cell back down next to my plate, and he clears his throat.

"So, don't you want to hear my theory about your dreams?"

"You have one?"

"It's toward the end of that stack of research. We just didn't quite get to it last night."

I hold his gaze for a beat, a half grin on my lips. "Hit me with it."

He sets his pizza down on the plate, wipes his hands with a napkin. "So one of the things I kept finding and coming back to over and over is this fact that our brains don't make up faces. Experts seem pretty unified in believing that people who appear in our dreams are only those we've seen before — even if it's just someone you've passed on the street or subway that you didn't even necessarily take note of, but your brain did."

"Right." I'd come across that fact as well. "And we've discussed that. I mean it's not out of the question that I've seen him

255

somewhere before — we did both live in Philly."

"Right."

"But then, why —"

"Hold on, I'm not done yet. A lot of psychotherapists also agree that it's the emotions in your dream that are important — not who's in them or what's happening, but the way you feel. So, simply put, if you're scared or anxious in a dream, then there's something in your life that's making you feel scared or anxious. So I think that maybe you've seen Oliver in passing and your brain just locked onto his face for whatever reason. And instead of focusing on him, you should focus on how you feel in your dreams and what insights you might gain from that in your life."

He sits back, and I take it as the cue that he's finished. It's so very logical, so banal, so Harrison, that I almost laugh. "So . . . basically you don't think it means anything."

"I didn't say that."

"And you're completely dismissing the fact that he dreams about me, too — that we've had the same dream, even. Or what, you think it's just a weird coincidence? That he saw me in passing as well, and that his brain happened to lock onto my face to use in his dreams to teach him what . . . lessons

256

about himself or whatever?"

He sighs and his eyes won't meet mine. And I know.

"You still don't believe it. You don't think he's telling the truth."

He glances at me and then back down at the half-eaten slice of pizza, the grease collecting in the shallow cups of pepperoni. "It's not that." He hesitates. "Or maybe it is. I mean, come on — if the tables were turned, wouldn't you be suspect?"

I study Harrison's face. Consider this. And I know he's right at least on that point. I would be more than suspect. But this is not something that's happening to him. It's happening to me.

"I'm just saying," he continues, "the only thing connecting you to this guy is these supposed dreams. He isn't really part of your life — or doesn't have to be."

"But maybe he's supposed to be."

Harrison's head jerks up; a wild look flashes in his eyes. "What does that mean?"

"I don't know." I drop my gaze, realizing what it sounded like. And I don't know what I meant, really. I didn't even know I was going to say it — I only know that it felt like I hit on the truth, somehow. And that it's impossible to explain it to my husband, when I can't even explain it to myself.

I feel Harrison's eyes on me. Finally, he takes a long pull of his beer and then a deep breath. "Listen, I understand that this has been — tough for you, confusing, I don't know what to call it. But you haven't been yourself since this all started. You've been distracted, almost to the point of obsession —"

"Yeah," I say emphatically, all the muscles in my body tensing as if to underline the point. "I have been obsessing over it. It's only the most bizarre, inexplicable thing that's ever happened to me in my entire life."

"I know, I know." Harrison holds up a hand in deference. "I just feel like it's holding you back or something."

"What do you mean?"

"Well, like the house. You were so excited when we moved in. You had all these plans to decorate and wouldn't let me so much as pick out a coatrack, so I didn't mess up your — what did you call it — *design vision*. And all you've really done is buy a new couch."

He's right, of course. I was excited all the way up until the moving truck pulled into the driveway, and then, I don't know if it was my feelings of failure about my art, or just the shock of the change from our bustling city life — but I was struck with the deepest sense of ennui. And then: "We lost a *baby*, Harrison. Sorry if I'm not painting rooms and buying rugs."

"I *know* . . . I'm not —" he says. He takes a deep breath. Starts again. "I just think that maybe if you felt a little more settled, you wouldn't miss Philadelphia as much. We could move forward."

"What do I have to move forward to?" It shoots out of my mouth like a bullet from a gun I didn't even know was loaded. But then again, I've been storing up the ammunition ever since the night we stared at each other on the cement floor in my studio, our baby's hand and Harrison's words hanging between us: *Maybe it's for the best.*

He looks at me, his eyes sad, tired, but he doesn't respond.

And even though I know I should leave it alone, not push it — that he *needs time* — I can't stop myself. I give voice to the sentence that's been on loop in my head for weeks — the truth that I haven't wanted to admit. "It's not time you need, is it?" I say it calmly, quietly. Resigned. "You're never going to be ready."

He doesn't answer for so long, I begin to wonder if I even said the words out loud. But then, he takes a deep breath, exhales and levels me with the look in his eyes. A

259

look that tells me the answer, before he even says: "No. I don't think I will."

I wait for the water to fill my eyes, spill down my cheeks. Crying is as familiar a function to me as breathing at this point. But the tears don't come. Instead, something else wells up inside me. Something hot and caustic and out of control, like a vat of acid threatening to burn me alive if I don't let it out. So I open my mouth.

"Then what are we fucking doing?" I throw my napkin on the table and walk out of the restaurant alone.

Breakfast the next morning is markedly different from the one twenty-four hours previous. And not just because they're out of powdered eggs and we have to settle for make-your-own waffles. Harrison and I aren't speaking. When we got back to the hotel the night before, I got right into bed, turning my back to Harrison's side. "Mia," he said later, when he slipped in beside me, and I ignored him, pretending to be asleep. I know it's childish, that I should talk to him, to beg him to tell me what's *really* going on with him, but I also understand we'd just go in circles again. And I'm too hurt, too exhausted to try.

By the time we're driving back to Hope

Springs that afternoon, I can't wait to be out of the car. Away from him. But then, I realize, we'll just be in our house together. And as big as it is, it suddenly feels too small. I need to leave, to get out, and I know exactly where I'm going to go. I punch out a text to Raya, even though I know she'll say yes.

"I'm gonna go to Philadelphia tomorrow," I say, as Harrison pulls the car into the driveway.

He doesn't respond. Just turns the key, shutting off the ignition, and then gets out of the car, popping the trunk and hefting our suitcase from it. I follow him to the front door.

He sticks the key in the door, pauses and then turns to me, his eyes meeting mine for the first time that day. They're blazing, his jaw a tight line, and he says, "To see Raya or Oliver?"

"What?" I'm caught off guard by his anger and then put off by the audacity — *he's* mad at *me?* Doesn't he realize I'm also mad at him? "Raya, of course."

He pushes the door in and steps over the threshold. He throws his keys on the cardboard box with a touch more force than necessary, and it collapses under the weight, his keys scattering to the floor.

He stalks over, bends down to pick them up and then, realizing there's nowhere else to put them, sends them hurtling back to the ground. "We need a goddamn entry table," he growls.

And as if it's contagious, his irritation rips through me, and my fury from last night comes bursting back, as if it never left. "So buy a goddamn entry table," I say. We stare at each other for a beat, eyes blazing, the thick air between us crackling.

"Maybe I will," he says, finally, but there's no fight in it. He slips past me into the den, into the kitchen. And I hear the door of the fridge open, the clink of glass on glass as he fishes out a beer.

I pad silently to the bedroom, where I hang my sundress in our closet, scrub my face and my teeth and then stride out to the studio, where I crank on the window air-conditioning unit and crawl under the blankets of the half-deflated air mattress and pretend to sleep.

And that's when I remember that old console TV — and the day that no amount of banging could rattle those wires back together. And Dad finally put it out on the curb to be picked up with the trash.

CHAPTER 17

Raya's apartment is across the street from an Express Oil Change shop and a kebab restaurant. She specifically chose it for its proximity to the garage, where she sweet-talked the owner into letting her store her welding equipment and do her metal sculpture work on off-hours in exchange for janitorial services twice a week.

From the front, her building is redbrick and stately, four aged and dingy cement columns holding up a useless ornate balcony. From the side, a mosaic of artistic graffiti covers every square inch of the exterior eastern wall — a mishmash of turquoise vines, pink florals, orange paisleys. Today, the sky above it hangs gray and heavy, fit to burst with clouds.

After Raya buzzes me in, I take the stairs two at a time up to the fifth floor and am breathing hard by the time I reach her, standing in the open door to her apartment.

She's decked in khakis and a blue polo shirt, her vibrant red hair smoothed to the side, ending in a braid over her left shoulder.

"Why are you in your work clothes? I thought you had the day off."

"Sorry," she says, pulling me into a hug. I inhale her peppermint scent. "Antwon didn't show up this morning and they called me in."

"No! I hate Antwon," I say, though I've never met him in my life.

"I know. He's a bitch." Then she takes in my red-rimmed eyes and her face softens. I started crying as soon as I called her last night — the weight of everything that happened with Harrison the past twenty-four hours finally hitting me — and it doesn't feel like I've stopped since. "How are you?"

I shrug, biting my lip. "I've been better."

"I know," she says, squeezing my hand. "I hate to leave you. Maybe you could go check out Prisha's exhibit? It started last week."

"Maybe," I say.

" 'K. Well, I left you a spare key on the table. And there's a loaf of raisin bread in the freezer." I walk past her, dropping my bag in the middle of her living room.

"Is Peter here?" I ask, glancing toward her roommate's shut bedroom door, a vintage

264

Velvet Underground concert poster affixed to the center of it.

"I don't think he came home last night," she says, and then grabs her keys and turns to the door. She glances back at me one last time. "There's wine in the fridge. But try not to drink it all before I get back." And then she's gone, the door closing behind her, and I marvel at how easily we fell right back into roommate mode, even though it's been nearly ten years since we last lived together.

As I stand at the counter finishing my last bite of raisin toast, I glance at the clock on the microwave. It's not quite noon and the afternoon stretches out ahead of me, long and unrelenting. I know I can't stay here, with just my thoughts for company, so I head back outside, grabbing a bus in front of the kebab restaurant. When I slide into my seat, the rain starts, pounding the roof like a thousand bullets hurtling down at once, and I stare out the window at all the pedestrians caught wholly unprepared in the storm, holding their bags over their heads or whipping out umbrellas or hurrying for cover.

It's a long journey — a series of various bus stops where, between connections, I huddle beneath tiny Plexiglas bus stop shelters along with other riders, trying to stay dry — and when I finally get to the Philadelphia museum, the rain has let up. I meander over to the base of the Rocky statue, looking up at Sylvester Stallone as if he's an old friend I've happened to run into.

And I think of Harrison.

He brought me here on our fourth date. Made a big production out of it, telling me I had to wear sneakers and pull my hair back, that he was taking me somewhere special. And we ended up here. At the Rocky statue.

"You realize I've lived here for six years, right?" I said. "I've seen this statue. Walked by it at least a hundred times."

"Yes," he said. "But have you ever run up the stairs?"

I looked at him, deadpan. "Of course not. I don't run." A fact I had relayed to him on our second date.

"Exactly," he said, as if that explained it all. "It's like a crime against humanity to live here and never have run the stairs."

I narrowed my eyes. "Why?"

"Because it's a bucket list thing."

"Why?" I repeated. It was something I had certainly heard of, peripherally, people running the stairs. I knew it was a thing. But I never did know the reason behind it.

"What do you mean *why?* Because of the movie."

"The *Rocky* movie?"

He looked at me, bewildered. "Yeah."

That explained it. I confessed: "I've never seen it."

And that was when he became nearly apoplectic. "You, the biggest eighties movie buff I've ever met, have never seen *Rocky?*"

I shrugged. "Never saw the appeal. All that testosterone."

When he recovered from the shock, he grabbed my hand and we took off, his long legs easily traversing each step, my short ones going double time to keep up. By the time we got to the top, my lungs and thighs were burning so much I thought I was going to die. And then when he lifted me up effortlessly as though I were nothing but a paperclip and affixed his mouth to mine, I was sure of it.

That's when I knew I was in love. Because I ran up seventy-two stairs at the behest of a man who then made me spend the weekend watching all six *Rocky* movies back-to-back and I didn't mind.

Now I sit on those stairs, replaying that day, and the days, weeks, months, years that have passed since. How did we get here? I hate fighting with Harrison. Being at odds, squared against each other like boxers in a ring instead of spectators cheering for the same side. I think of all the stupid arguments we've had over the years — all the typical miscommunications and growing pains, when you grind your heels in and are willing to fight to the death over who did the laundry last, only to laugh about it a week later.

But this is different. It's not just a stupid argument. It's an impasse. As if a boulder fell from the sky onto our path and I can't see a way around it or over it or through it. Harrison no longer wants the thing that I want most in the world. What am I supposed to do with that?

My cell vibrates against my hip. I pull it out of my back pocket.

It's Oliver, and despite everything going on with Harrison, I still get the now-familiar buzz of seeing his name. And then the familiar wave of guilt at that buzz.

Guess what I found.

I chew on the inside of my cheek and hear Harrison's words in my head. *You've been distracted.* Maybe I have been, but isn't that preferable to wallowing in grief? Obsessing over why my husband suddenly doesn't want to be a father any longer? And it occurs to me that maybe this crazy situation with Oliver is the only thing keeping me sane.

What?

It's a link to an eBay listing. A book. *Psychic Psychology: The Science Behind the Supernatural* by Denise Krynchenko.

Nice work, detective. Did you buy it?

Of course. It'll be here by the end of the week. Still in Jersey?

I consider my reply. I have options, of course. I could just simply answer, *No, I got back yesterday,* and then pocket my phone and walk up the steps and into the museum, stewing about Harrison while looking at Prisha's wild success. Or I could . . . My fingers start typing before my brain has fully made up its mind.

Actually I'm in Philly. And I'm pretty sure I owe you a tour of the Rodin.

He doesn't text back right away, so I wait, while Harrison's other words fill my head. *To see Raya or Oliver?* But it's not like I planned it. I didn't come here with any intention of seeing him. Besides, maybe he'll say no. My right knee jiggles as I look up at the sky, still heavy with gray clouds. I study the people passing by on the sidewalk — the tourists consulting their phones for the directions to the Liberty Bell or the Reading Terminal Market, the people in suits rushing past them, a homeless man pushing his worldly belongings in a busted-up wheelchair. Just when I think he's not going to respond, that he got busy or that he might not remember our conversation or that what I've written is foolish, three dots pop up. And then words.

Be there in twenty.

The inside of the Rodin is cool and dry, a respite from the thick humidity of the day. I hover by the entrance, pretending to study the floor — a series of huge stone tiles each bisected by thick white lines to create four equal triangles — but I'm really wondering what the hell I'm doing here.

And then the door opens, and Oliver appears. In a faded black T-shirt and tight jeans that end in high-top Converses. Leather bands circle his right wrist below his exercise watch and a knit beanie slouches off the crown of his head. When he sees me, his face melts into its lopsided smile. We walk toward each other and then both stop short. And it's only then that I consider how I must look — my bloodshot eyes, red nose, sallow cheeks. Like I've been crying for the past twenty-four hours. I wait for him to say something, but he doesn't, and I wonder if we're both thinking the same thing — this

270

was a bad idea. I search for something to say, my eyes drawn to the beanie once again. This time I scrunch my nose.

"Why are you wearing that?"

"What — my hat? You don't like it?"

I do actually. Though it would look ridiculous on any other person, he, of course, somehow pulls it off. "It's ninety degrees outside."

He shrugs. "It's raining." As if that explains it all. As if the yarn his hat is made of would not get drenched instantly in a downpour.

Then he grins at me, and suddenly all my anxiety and worries feel a hundred miles away. Maybe because they are. They're back in Hope Springs.

"Right, well." He claps his hands together and the sound echoes in the cavernous room. "Where do we start?"

I stare at him for a beat, and realize how instantly at ease I feel, like I know him, really *know* him, and my lips slowly spread into a smile. "God, this is so weird."

"The hat?!" he says. "Jesus, I can take it off if it's making you that uncomfortable."

A laugh bursts out of my mouth, and just like that, I'm glad I came.

I lead him through the busts first — *Mask*

271

of Crying Girl, Head of Sorrow, Man with the Broken Nose — telling him all the facts I know, some I memorized from the placards, others from various art history classes and books.

"This piece was rejected twice from the Paris Salon, because of its departure from the notion of classic beauty.

"Rodin liked this one so much, he replicated it in stone.

"It's actually a monument to Joan of Arc."

He pauses at that. "What is Joan of Arc's favorite coffee?"

I narrow my eyes. "What?"

"French roast."

I groan. "Oh my god. That's terrible."

He laughs, and we start walking to the next bust.

"So, do you sculpt, too, or just paint?" he asks.

"I dabbled in all different mediums in college, but painting is what I love most. My best friend, Raya, is an incredible sculptor, though. She welds metal. What about you?"

"Me? No, I'm terrible at welding." He grins.

"I meant your writing. Is it just celebrity books or do you also write, I don't know — novels?"

"Oh God, am I that much of a cliché?"

Before I can respond, he answers his own question: "Yes, yes, I am. I have written a novel. Unfortunately, no one else wanted to read it. Thirty-seven rejections later . . ."

"Ouch."

" 'Pedantic' and 'tedious' were some of the flattering descriptors. And those were the nice ones."

"Ooh! I can play this game," I say. " 'An incohesive amateur display, without the talent to add depth and substance.' "

He raises his eyebrows. "One of your paintings?"

"A collection of them. My first — and not surprisingly last — exhibition."

"A big success, then?"

"Rousing." I grin.

He pauses, his eyes growing serious. "Is that why you're sad?"

I hesitate. "How could you tell?"

He shrugs. "I'm not a makeup expert, but I think the mascara is supposed to stay on your lashes?"

"Oh geez," I mutter, quickly rubbing beneath my eyes with my index fingers.

"You know," he says, tilting his chin down as if sharing a secret. "Someone once told me that the first sculpture Rodin ever submitted to the Paris Salon was rejected twice."

"Is that right?" I say, mock wide-eyed.

"I don't really know — she might have been making it all up. But the point is, what the hell do critics know?"

"What the hell do critics know," I repeat, a grin spreading across my face. And I realize Harrison was wrong. Dreams are not the only thing Oliver and I have in common.

We walk slowly, stopping in front of sculptures, but not really seeing them. Not anymore. We're deep in conversation. Trading bits of information about each other like kids swapping Halloween candy.

Finally, we reach the last sculpture — a large, solid piece of white marble. It's one of Rodin's more vibrant and overtly sensual works: *Eternal Springtime.* A couple embracing, the woman arched back while the man bends over her, clutching her in his arm.

"Well?" Oliver asks, arching an eyebrow.

I clear my throat, reassuming my position as tour guide. "So this is one of his more famous pieces. It, too, was originally supposed to be a part of *The Gates of Hell,* but was deemed too cheerful and, therefore, antithetical to the theme. The model was a woman named Adele Abruzzesi, but most historians believe he consciously or subconsciously included features of Camille Claudel as well."

"Who?"

I hesitate. "His lover." And maybe it's my imagination, but when I say *lover,* his eyes meet mine and I swear to God he can see what I'm thinking. The two of us in a very *Eternal Springtime* situation from my dreams. But then, just as quickly, his eyes flick back to the sculpture. As heat creeps up my neck, I start rambling about Camille and how she was arguably an even better artist than Rodin, but doesn't receive as much credit.

"Why not?" he asks.

"Because, patriarchy. Obviously."

"Obviously," he says, grinning.

I get a chill and start rubbing my bare arms. "God, it's frigid in here."

"Huh," he says, a half grin on his face. "Guess you should have worn a hat."

When we've made it through every sculpture and find ourselves back at the entrance, I glance outside. The sky is still doomsday, but the rain has held off.

"Come on, there are a couple more pieces out here."

Oliver holds the door open and then follows me out. I walk down the stairs and then turn around, pointing out *The Gates of*

Hell. And then we meander past the reflection pool, taking in the various plots of flowers and manicured bushes on the opposite side, still colorful even when drenched.

"How's your latest book coming? The Penn Carro thing?"

He grunts. "Not well. The guy talks in circles, basically reiterating his one main point ad nauseam."

"Which is?"

Oliver puffs out his chest and his voice comes out deep and full and energetic: "You know who succeeds in life? It's the people who *act.* Who *do* something. Who make *decisions.* That's the difference between CEOs on Wall Street and janitors that clean the floors and empty the wastebaskets on Wall Street. Are you decisive? Or do you leave things up to fate? You have to *create* your fate."

"Oh my god," I say. "You sound just like him!"

"Yeah, I just wish writing this book was as easy as imitating him."

"Sorry. What are you going to do?"

"I don't know, but I've got to figure it out by the end of September."

"Is that your deadline?"

"Yeah, self-imposed, anyway. I leave for Finland."

"Oh. You already heard back?" I don't realize I've stopped walking until he does, too.

He nods. Our eyes lock and I don't know what I'm feeling or why — only that it seems too soon. I clear my throat. "I think it's so cool that you do that. I always thought my life would be more adventurous, more jet-setting, more, I don't know — living in the moment." I shrug. "Maybe everybody does. But you're actually living it."

"Or maybe I'm just running away from it."

I peer at him. "What?"

"That's what Caroline says. That it's my way to avoid getting too close to anybody. To keep from getting hurt."

"What do you think?"

"I don't know, she's probably right." He wets his lips. "But I've never told that to anybody before — so maybe I'm cured."

I know it's a joke, but he doesn't smile, just holds my gaze. I feel my mouth going dry.

A crack of thunder startles us, and then a fat raindrop hits me square in the nose. I blink, and look up in time to see hundreds more falling around us and on us, pelting the tops of our heads, our shoulders, making pinging sounds as they hit their targets

— the cement pathway, the reflection pool. And before I can react, Oliver has grabbed my hand and is running, tugging me toward a tree with large weepy branches. We reach it just as the clouds bellow with another burst of thunder and a flash of lightning illuminates the air around us.

I'm about to make a joke — something about being under a tree during a lightning storm and safety — but my brain short-circuits when I realize Oliver's still holding my hand.

I jerk my hand out of his and take a step back, my heart hammering harder now than when I was running. I look at the ground, the bark of the thick trunk beside us, anywhere but at him.

He clears his throat. "I can't believe you were so scared of a little thunder." He teases, but something in his voice sounds off, artificial. And I fake grin at his joke, but we both know it's not the thunder I'm scared of.

CHAPTER 18

Raya is sleeping, curled up like a cat on her sofa, when I let myself back into her apartment later that evening, soaked to the bone, my hair matted to my face. I walked back to her place, meandering down side streets, popping into stores when the rain got too bad. I was lost in my head, replaying the afternoon in my mind — the spark in the air between us, the easy way we bantered, the thrill I got when something I said caused him to bark with laughter. And I reveled in it, the little thrill, that buzz of excitement that courses through your veins at the beginning of a relationship that, after years with someone, is impossible to replicate. But I'd been telling myself this entire time that it was harmless. An innocent flirtation.

But then under the tree, my hand clasped firmly in his, I knew he felt it, too. And it was more than thrilling. It was formidable. As big as the storm clouds hanging in the sky. And just as threatening.

"Hey, Mia."

"Jesus," I say, clutching my chest and turning toward Peter's voice. He's standing in the doorway to his room, his bird-like pale torso bare from the waist up, the left side of which is covered in a large tattoo of a man, presumably Jesus, nailed to a cross. I asked him about it once, and he shrugged. "I was Southern Baptist. For, like, a year." I remember Marcel's tats, and how he is going to donate them to a museum when he dies. And I decide it's definitely something Peter would do, too.

"I didn't know you were home."

"Yep," he says, grabbing a T-shirt off his doorknob and pulling it on over his head. "Headed out now, though." He walks toward me and bends over to scoop up an army green messenger bag from the floor at my feet. I step to the side. "Catch you later."

"Later," I say, as he walks past me and out the door. The sound of it slamming shut behind him wakes Raya. She pushes herself up to sitting.

I point at the closed door Peter just exited with my thumb. "Does he still deal drugs?"

"Yeah. He tried to get out of it for a while, but working for FedEx doesn't pay quite as well." She eyes me. "Forget your umbrella?"

"Something like that."

I pad to her room, and as I'm changing into a dry shirt and pants from her drawer, I spy a pair that looks familiar, and I realize I must have left them here at some point.

"Oh my god," I say, tugging them on and walking back out to the den. "I've been looking for these."

She eyes them, squinting. "Sweatpants?"

"Harrison gave them to me for our anniversary and I haven't been able to find them."

"Your husband bought you sweatpants for your anniversary. How romantic," she deadpans. I settle next to her on the couch. "Do you want to order something?" she asks. "I'm starving."

I realize I haven't eaten a thing since the raisin toast that morning. "Yeah, me, too."

I grab the wine as she calls for Indian takeout, and then when I settle in on the opposite end of the sofa from her, I ask, "How's Marcel?" before she can ask about Harrison, because I'm too tired to even think about him right now, much less talk about it all.

"Oh, we broke up."

I jerk my head toward her. "What?"

She sighs. "We got in a fight over carrots."

I stare at her, but she doesn't elaborate.

"I'm sorry — I'm gonna need a little bit more."

"We were making salad, for dinner," she says. "And he julienned them."

"The carrots," I say, trying to understand.

"Yeah. Everyone knows you cut carrots for salad into coins," she says. "But when I said something, it turned into this huge argument over what was the most aesthetically pleasing and then it kind of devolved into essentially an all-out war about artistic expression and talent and commitment to craft."

"As these things do," I say.

"Then he called me a David Smith wannabe and I called him a sidewalk mime and he stormed out."

"Ugh. You are *not* a David Smith wannabe."

She shrugs. "He apologized. But I broke up with him anyway."

"Why? I thought you really liked him."

She shifts her eyes.

"Raya?"

"Jesse called."

"No. Oh my god. What the hell, Raya?" I think of Jesse, her androgynous concave frame, the ball cap she always wore over her floppy Justin Bieber hair, the lip ring. Raya met her at a friend's birthday party, and the two of them didn't come up for air for eight months. Raya had slept with women before, but never had a relationship like this. They were inseparable, like trying to distinguish fire from its flame. But Jesse was also insecure and manipulative and wildly co-dependent and it took Raya years to extricate herself from their relationship. They'd break up in these dramatically angry displays of emotion, but Raya always seemed to get pulled back into Jesse's orbit — until finally, the last time they broke up and Jesse moved to Portland.

"Did she move back?"

"No. She's still in Portland. Said she misses me. That she's my twin flame."

"What the hell is that?"

"It's like soul mates on crack. It's your soul's perfect mirror. And in all the reincarnations, you're drawn to each other, but you're so alike that the relationship is superintense and typically can't sustain itself."

I roll my eyes. "Well, I agree with the her-being-on-crack part."

"Mia."

"Raya." I hold her gaze until she sighs.

"I know, I know. I think I just need to swear off creative types."

I hold up a finger. "Um . . . first of all, Jesse's a bartender — is that technically a creative type?"

"She's a *mixologist,*" Raya says defensively. "Anyway, I've just started to think, maybe there isn't room in a relationship for two artists. We're all moody and narcissistic and self-loathing as fuck. There's no balance."

I stare at her, dumbfounded, recalling the one doubt she voiced when I was dating Harrison: *Doesn't it bother you that he doesn't really* get *you, artistically?* Her words cut me, because the truth was, it did, a little. He respected my work — he never trivialized it like some guys I had dated — but he didn't share my interest in it. We would never have long, in-depth conversations late into the night, say, debating the ethical evaluation of art or the merits of a famous sculptor's latest work — an exhibition of various windows that he did not create, but just purchased in flea markets and home goods stores and hung in a gallery in Bushwick. But I told her then, and I still believe now, that I didn't think your partner had to — or that it was even possible for them to — fulfill you in every way. "That's what I have you for," I said to Raya, and I meant it. But that didn't mean it didn't cross my mind every now and then — like today, when Oliver so fully understood what having your art rejected felt like, and I didn't have to say more than a couple of words. Not that I was comparing him with my husband.

"Maybe I need someone who has a real job," Raya continues. "A retirement plan. Health insurance."

"OK, now you're just scaring me." I force myself back to the present. "Have you been spending time with Harrison?"

"No," she says. "But that's my point! Maybe I need to. Be with somebody like Harrison. You guys don't fight about carrots."

"No, we fight about big stuff — like whether we should have a child."

"Sorry," she says.

I wave her off. "Look, every couple fights about stupid stuff," I say, thinking about the entry table. The buzzer sounds.

"Food's here," she says.

Once we're settled back on the couch with chicken saag and have refilled our glasses with Syrah, she turns to me, her face filled with sympathy: "So . . . what are you gonna do?"

I sigh. "I have no idea. I suppose we should go to counseling or something. That's what Vivian says, anyway. That's what she always says."

"Well, maybe she's right. It sounds like an

impartial person might help you find common ground."

"Common ground? It's not like you can meet in the middle when it comes to having a baby, though, can you? You can't have half a kid."

"I know. But still, it might help. At least understand why he's changed his mind."

"Yeah." I wait a beat. "I think I'm just scared, to be honest. What if we go to counseling, but it doesn't help? What if he doesn't change his mind? If this is just who he is — forever? Then I have to *do* something. Make a decision between Harrison and a baby. And as much as I want a baby, I don't know if I'm ready to do that."

Raya grunts with empathy. "Well," she says. "You don't have to do anything right now." She picks up the bottle and fills my glass. "Except drink more wine."

I look at her gratefully and take a sip. "Can we talk about something else now?"

"Sure. What'd you do today? Did you make it to Prisha's exhibit?"

Maybe a change of subject was a bad idea. "Not exactly." I sigh, and with just one look Raya knows something happened. I tell her about meeting up with Oliver.

"Oh my god!" she says, as if she's just had

a serious epiphany. "What if he's your twin flame?"

I stare at her a beat. "You think Oliver is my soul mate on crack."

"Maybe!"

"You *do* realize that I'm married, right?" Which is awfully hypocritical since I was the one all heart-thumpy over touching his hand mere hours ago, but still.

She waves me off. "You know I don't believe in long-term monogamy."

"Yes, you only believe in sane things like past lives and twin flames and clearing a room of negative energy with smudged sage."

"Exactly." Raya grins. We sip our wine in silence for a few minutes and then she stands up. "OK, come on."

I don't move. "Come on where?"

"We're going to a psychic."

"What? No. I'm not going to a psychic."

"Why not? Look, when you dream about someone and then meet that someone in person, and it turns out that person has been dreaming about you . . . it means the universe is trying to tell you something. And you need to listen. Besides, no one else has helped you so far."

I try to construct a rebuttal, but can't think of one. She smiles, knowing she's won.

"I know the perfect place. It's near this corner Marcel used to work."

I look up at her. "You *do* hear how that sounds, don't you?"

She considers what she said. "Oh my god — see?" she says. "Jesse or no Jesse, I can't be with someone who works corners for a living."

It's dark when the Lyft drops us off in Center City in front of a sushi place and a glass entrance to an old apartment building. To the right of that door, a red neon Palm Reader sign shines bright against the cinder block wall, the outline of a hand flickering, as if the bulb is on its last legs.

"This place looks sketchy as hell," I say, downing the last sip of Syrah from my red Solo cup.

"It is," says Raya, nudging me, then walking over to the metal door. "That's how you know it's legit." She tries the handle, but it's locked. She knocks.

As we're waiting for someone to answer, Raya keeps talking. "I used to walk right by here when I'd come see Marcel do his thing on my days off. And this lady would stand outside smoking cigarettes. She always asked if I wanted to see my future."

"Did you ever do it?"

"No. I wanted to, but it was way too expensive."

"Raya! How much is it?"

"Like, a hundred dollars."

"Uh, no." I turn around. "Where's the Lyft?"

Just then, the door opens and a woman fills the frame. "Can I help you?" she says, with a muddled Caribbean accent that sounds put-on.

"Yes," Raya says, grabbing my arm and turning me back around. "We're here to have a reading. Well, she is. I'm here to watch."

The woman flicks her eyes, framed by fake long lashes, from Raya to me. "Come on, then," she says and starts walking back down what looks like a very dark hallway. Raya catches the door and starts to follow.

"Raya — no. It's pitch-black in there. If this were a movie, this is the part where the eerie music starts and we'd be yelling at the two stupid women on-screen to turn around and go home. And we don't even know who that woman is. She could be anybody." Suddenly we hear a click and light fills the hallway. And then a voice follows the light: "I'm Rita."

Raya smiles at me.

At the end of the hallway is a set of stairs

that goes down. We end up in a small room with a beaded curtain separating us from the other half of it, but I can make out a card table and chairs and a cheap floor lamp. On our side of the room is a desk littered with papers and an old-school desktop computer.

"Fancy," I mutter to Raya.

The woman is holding out her hand to me. "I think you're supposed to pay her," Raya says in my ear.

"Uh, I don't have any cash."

"We take Visa, Mastercard, Discover," the woman says. "No American Express."

I sigh and dig in my wallet and produce a credit card. She takes it, disappearing through a wooden door that I didn't notice when we first came in. "Remind me to freeze that account," I say to Raya. "And never listen to you again."

After what seems like hours, but is probably only fifteen minutes, the door opens and I straighten up, ready to get this ridiculous charade over with. I've seen Whoopi Goldberg's fake reading in *Ghost* and I have a fairly good idea of what this woman is about to do. When it hits me that Whoopi's character's name was Rita Mae, I nearly laugh out loud. I don't think it's a coincidence.

This Rita enters the room and then steps aside, leaving the door open. She stands there, not speaking, and just when I'm about to ask if we can get started, an old man lopes in behind her. He's astonishingly tall and thin, brittle looking, and it's hard to tell if he's hunched over due to his age or because the ceiling is too low for him to extend to his full height. I glance at Raya, but she's just staring.

Rita takes his hand and leads him through the beaded curtain, the movement causing an array of clacking sounds. He sits down in one of the folding chairs, and when he's settled, Rita stands beside him, head up, hands folded at her groin, like a sentry on guard. Raya and I just watch them, until it becomes apparent that we're supposed to follow. We scoot through the beaded curtain and I slide down into the chair opposite the man at the table. Raya stands behind me.

There's a long stretch of silence and then the man finally speaks. It's a harsh language. I would have assumed Russian, if not for Raya whispering in my ear: "Slovenian." I'm about to ask how in the world she knew that, until I remember the glass blower from Slovenia that she dated when he was a visiting professor at Moore.

"I am Isak Vidmar," the woman says, not

291

looking at us.

I'm about to say I thought her name was Rita when the man speaks again and then holds out his hands on the table, palms up. "Give me your hands," Rita says, still not looking at us, and I realize she's merely the translator for this man, Isak, who is apparently the psychic. I turn my head and shoot Raya a look. I have so many questions, starting with: Is there a big Slovenian population in Philly, and I had no idea? She nudges me and I pull my hands out of my lap and place them gently in Isak's. His fingers are long and thin, but they're soft. Gentle. And holding them somehow makes me feel both calm and awkward.

He's quiet for so long, I start to think he's waiting on me to ask questions. So I do.

"Could you tell me if I was strangled to death in a previous life? I've always been curious. I have this awful fear of things touching my neck — I can't wear scarves or turtlenecks. Well, I don't know if fear is the right word. It just gives me, like, this gagging sens—"

"Sh," the man says. It comes out sharply, like a knife literally cutting me off. I close my mouth.

Silence envelops the room once again. Raya smacks me on the back of the head

like a mother whose petulant child can't follow the rules. To stave off boredom — and
possibly because my brain is starting to fog
from the four glasses of wine I've had — I
study the room. The walls are a beige color,
and in desperate need of a repaint, but aside
from the nicks and dings of wear over time,
they're bare. Not a tarot card poster or Bud-
dha or astrology chart to be found. Besides
the beaded curtain, this is really nothing
like *Ghost.* Where are the candles? Rita's
not even wearing any jewelry.

"How long you have gift?" Isak says, his
gruff voice drawing my attention back to
him.

It takes me a second to realize he has
spoken in English, but when I do, I'm still
not sure what he's asking. "I'm sorry, what?"

"He wants to know how long you've been
psychic," Rita says.

"Uh, I'm not," I say, chuckling.

"Yes," the man says, his eyes penetrating
mine. "You, me. Same." He thrusts his long
pointer finger at me and then himself.

"Ohhkay," I say, wondering what he's
playing at. "Well, if I was, I wouldn't have
paid you, so . . ." I'm getting a little more
irritated by the second that I let Raya talk
me into this.

The man speaks rapidly in his native language.

"He wants to know if you're creative," Rita says. "Some kind of artist?"

I notice the dried acrylic that clings to my nail beds, no matter how much I scrub. I roll my eyes and hope it's not too rude. "I paint."

He nods, as if he expected that. So perceptive, this man.

"Creatives are more open, mentally speaking, to the energy," Rita says, of her own accord.

"Energy?" I ask, looking at her.

"Spiritual, psychic, all of that," she says.

"Look, can we just get on with it?" I say. "I'm not psychic."

She stares at me for a beat and then whispers something to Isak that I can't make out.

He nods genially and closes his eyes. His grip on my hands gets a little bit tighter and I hear a low humming that sounds like it's coming from him. Finally, he opens his eyes and says something in Slovenian. I look up at Rita, impatient.

"He wants to know who the man is with dark hair," she says.

I hold in my eye roll, but just barely. I'm immediately reminded of Warner McKay and his guessing game of names that begin with a certain letter until someone in the audience yells out, "Bob! I have a Bob." I play along, so we can get out of here.

"My husband," I say. "Harrison. He has brown hair."

Isak shakes his head. "No, not him," he says. "Different man."

I get a little chill up my spine, thinking of Oliver. But obviously a million people have dark hair and there's no way this guy knows about him. I'm certainly not going to bring it up.

"There's another guy." Raya pipes up. "Oliver."

"Raya!"

"What? That's what we're here for," she whispers.

Isak slowly nods and then closes his eyes again, grips my hands. I take a deep breath and slowly exhale, trying to tamp down my irritation. It's getting stuffy down here, my head is beginning to throb from the wine and the room is so small, it starts to feel like it's closing in. How did I not notice how small it was before? When Isak opens his eyes, he says something else in his native tongue. I look to Rita.

"He's tall," Rita says.

"Mm-hm," I say, even though he's not.

Not as tall as Harrison, anyway.

"Brown eyes," she says.

"Sure," I say.

"What?" Rita asks, and Isak repeats himself. I stare at him, bored of the charade. Rita turns to me.

"You dream of him."

My eyes dart to Rita's face. "What?" But it comes out like a whisper. Raya makes a little squealing noise behind me. I glance back at Isak. He's just pleasantly staring back at me.

"How did you know that?" I ask, trying to tell myself it was just a lucky guess.

"He's good man," Isak says. "He's good to you."

"No," I stammer, as the room starts to get even smaller. There's a whooshing sound in my ears, as if I'm underwater. "I barely even . . . I don't know him —"

"Yes," Isak continues. "This man. He give you baby."

"*What?* No." This is getting ridiculous and I just want to leave. "I don't have any children."

Rita asks him something in his native tongue and Isak replies. Rita turns to me, translating: "You will."

Everything stops. The whooshing sound in my ears. The shrinking room. My beating

296

heart. I stare at her mouth. The lips that just formed the words I've always wanted to hear. Confirmation, from somebody, *anybody* — even a psychic's translator — that I will have what I've wanted for so long. I should be relieved, but everything feels wrong, somehow. There's a pit in my stomach, and I know it has to do with Oliver. I shouldn't have spent the afternoon with him. I shouldn't be here.

I stand up. I want to go home. To Harrison.

It's just after two a.m. when I pull in the driveway, and I nearly start shaking with relief at the sight of Harrison's car. I was sure he would have stayed at the hospital and almost drove there first out of my desperation to see him. Desperation that wasn't stemming from love as much as it was from guilt. I was wracked with it over my afternoon with Oliver — over the past two months I'd spent thinking about Oliver. And on the drive back to Hope Springs, it built upon itself, growing exponentially until I felt like it was going to eat me alive.

I quietly turn my key in the dead bolt and slip in the front door, eager to get to our room, to curl up beside his warm body in our bed, but what I see when I flip on the foyer light stops me in my tracks.

The worn, flattened cardboard box is gone and in its place is a table — a small, square nondescript white end table that looks like it came from some big-box chain store. But that's not what catches me off guard. Scrawled on the side of the table in hand-painted blue capital letters are the words GODDAMN ENTRY TABLE with a pitiful fleur-de-lis on either side. I stare at it, wide-eyed, and then cover my mouth with my hand, laughter bursting around my fingers, my heart swelling for Harrison.

I nearly run to our bedroom, not caring now if I wake him. Still giggling, I find my way to the bed in the dark, kicking off my shoes and lifting up the covers to crawl in beside him. He wakes up, inching his heavy, half-sleeping body over to make room. When his arms are around me and my head is rightfully tucked under his chin, he kisses the top of my hair. "Dios Mia," he whispers, his voice thick with sleep. I feel his warm breath on my scalp. "You're here."

"I'm here," I say. Harrison's hand snakes its way down my body, coming to a rest on my thigh.

"Are you wearing sweatpants?" he asks, squinting down in the dark.

"The ones you gave me."

"I thought you lost them."

"I found them."

"Mia, I don't know what's wrong with me. I'm so sorry —"

I put my hand up to his mouth, shushing him.

"The table," I whisper back. "It's perfect."

Relief rolls through me like the wave from a tsunami. I'm overcome. The world has been tilted the wrong way all day long, but now, finally, it has righted itself. Tears burn my eyes and I bury myself into Harrison's chest.

And somehow, even with my arm crushed beneath the weight of his body, my body temperature rocketing to a thousand degrees from the sweatpants, I fall asleep.

CHAPTER 19

When I was in kindergarten, a guest with a colorful gauzy scarf encircling her neck came to our classroom. The scarf triggered my gag reflex, so I focused on the stacks of rings adorning her fingers, the silver streaking her two dangling braids, the flat black loafers with gold buckles on her feet. She held a piece of paper behind her back and said it was the most beautiful painting she had ever created and was so excited to show it to us. But when she finally brought it forward and turned it around, I was imbued with disappointment. Light pink watercolor saturated the page. The gradient changed in places, but that was it. The whole painting. "Who likes this picture?" she asked. "Be honest."

We all looked at each other. One little girl half raised her hand.

"That's OK," the woman said. "I want to tell you a story: One day I was at the park with my daughter and the sun was high in the sky and it was hot. We were running around playing hide-and-seek and laughing and having so much fun. And then we saw a lemonade stand and this boy was selling cold pink lemonade. My daughter and I bought some and it tasted sweet and cool. And we were so happy. Later that night, after I had tucked her in bed, I went downstairs and I painted this picture of the cool pink lemonade. Now, every time I look at it, I'm filled with joy remembering that wonderful day with my daughter."

She looked at each of us. "What do you think? Raise your hand if you like the picture now."

Eighteen little hands shot high in the air.

And I never forgot the woman or her story.

But now, as I finish retelling it to the adults that have come to my class at Fordham Community College, I think it might be an exercise that works best on children.

I'm holding up a pink-wash painting I quickly created that afternoon, and four pairs of eyes stare back at me.

"I thought this was supposed to be an acrylic class. Isn't that watercolor?"

"Yes, but the point is —"

"I still don't like it," a gruff man with a crew cut and construction boots says.

"Looks like something a child would paint. Not a grown woman."

I look to Foster's wife, Rebecca, who is smiling politely. Perhaps this wasn't the best way to start off the class, but I wasn't as prepared as I had hoped to be. I had spent the last week trying to drown out my thoughts — my guilt over my afternoon with Oliver, the anxiety I felt at the psychic's words, my fear about Harrison not wanting a baby — by doing everything I could not to think about any of it. I gardened — clearing all the weeds that had sprouted again in the weeks since Oliver had been there. I planted beets, broccoli, carrots, spinach — everything Jules at True Value recommended — and I spent time every day watering, weeding, waiting for plants to sprout. I bought furniture. Three teal metal barstools for the kitchen from the Blue-Eyed Macaw. A leather club chair to complement the sofa. A guest bed for one of the upstairs bedrooms. A shower curtain and gray shag rug for the upstairs bathroom. I hung paintings — the chicken above the fireplace, the tomatoes (with the sticker still on) on a wall in the kitchen, Keanu Reeves in the front foyer above the Goddamn Entry Table.

Mostly to keep myself busy, but partly, too, as if it was my penance. As if I were a

302

good enough steward of the earth, a good enough keeper of the home, a good enough *wife,* Harrison would change his mind about having a baby. I knew deep down it didn't work like that — but I also didn't know what else to do.

But then a strange thing happened — somewhere in the middle of all my decorating I started to remember why I fell in love with the house when we first saw it, how it was a canvas just waiting to be filled with my ideas.

Stranger still, the more welcoming I make the home, the less time Harrison seems to want to spend in it.

He's been working later than ever — sometimes not coming home until one or two in the morning, and going in on the weekends, even when he's not on call. His morning runs have gone from three to four times a week to daily ventures — and instead of his twenty-five-minute three-milers, sometimes it's an hour or more before I hear him bang in the back door.

When he is home, it's like he's pre-occupied; his mind is somewhere else. He didn't even notice the Keanu Reeves painting until I pointed it out to him. "Huh?" he said that night in bed. "Oh yeah. Looks great."

He's avoiding me. Or maybe he's avoiding talking about babies — but then again, I am, too. Because if we talk about the elephant in the room, we'll be forced to decide what to do with it.

A woman appears in the doorway, jolting me from my thoughts. "Come in, come in." I wave to her. "We're just getting started."

"Sorry," she says, her eyes taking in the row of easels. "I'm looking for Astronomy in the Suburbs."

"Room 215," the construction-booted man says.

The lost woman holds up her hand as a thank-you, and when she turns, I look back at my four students, who are all watching me expectantly, probably wondering what jackass thing I'm going to say next.

"OK," I say, clapping my hands. "So, this is Novice Acrylic Painting — not watercolor as one of you rightfully pointed out. It is the follow-up to Beginner Acrylic Painting, which I assume you all have taken?" A few heads bob in response. "While you're getting your supplies out, maybe someone can give me a rundown of what you covered in the last class."

Rebecca starts talking about mixing colors and mentions a few different application techniques that create texture.

"And what all did you paint?"

"A still life," she says. "Of fruit."

I try to resist rolling my eyes. Of course they did.

"OK, well, we can do a still life again, of course, if you all want — but we could also try something different, maybe like a self-portrait, or a landscape, this time?"

"Ooh," a woman whose name I do not yet know says. "Like Bob Ross?"

"Mm-hm," I say, wondering what on earth I am doing in this classroom. "What's your name?"

"Marjorie," she says. I contemplate telling Marjorie that art is about cultivating your imagination, your own style, seeing a tree and painting it the way you see it. Not copying the way someone else sees it. That what Bob Ross teaches isn't art, it's imitation. But Marjorie looks so happy, and I just feel so tired.

"Yes, Marjorie," I say. "Just like Bob Ross. OK — does everyone's phone have Internet access?" They all nod at me. "Why don't you scroll through some images and look for landscapes that inspire you? And then we'll talk about how to get started."

As they do that, I walk over to the stack of my own canvases that I brought and I start sorting through them to find landscape

305

paintings that I could use as examples. There are only two that could be considered landscape-ish — a snow-covered street in Philadelphia and the huge panorama of the amusement park. It's so big I almost didn't bring it — I had to fold down the backseat so I could slide it into the trunk — but now I'm glad I did. I set them up on two empty easels in front of the classroom.

"Ooh," Marjorie says, when I turn back to the class.

"Did you find something good?" I ask her.

She points at the amusement park. "That's beautiful," she says. "I want to paint that." The other three look up from their phones.

"Well, I really only brought it as an example. It's just something I've been working on. You guys should choose something that speaks to you."

"It's happy," Rebecca says. The others murmur, nodding their heads. I thought it was dark and a little eerie — or maybe that was just how I felt when I was standing in it.

"I'd like to paint it, too," the construction-booted man says.

"Well, um, it's a rather large painting and a little detailed for what we'll have time to cover. And I was hoping you'd each have your own original artwork at the end of this class." They all stare back at me expectantly, obviously not swayed by my reasoning. "I suppose we could just take one section of it — perhaps the carousel bit — and work on that?"

The next two hours fly by as I bumble through trying to explain sketching and underpainting to form the basic structure of their work, and I learn that there's a world of difference between understanding these skills myself and trying to teach them. But then, finally, time is up, and we're cleaning up and everyone slowly drips out of the classroom.

Rebecca is the last to leave. We walk out to the warm humid air of the parking lot together.

"You're very talented," she says.

"Oh," I say, caught off guard by the compliment. I've never been able to take one well when it comes to my work. But I'm even worse with the critiques. "Thank you."

She stops when we get to my car and turns to me, concern suddenly crinkling her forehead. "How's Harrison doing?"

I tilt my head at her, momentarily confused — and then I realize she must know about the miscarriage. Maybe she knows about all of them. "Oh, he's . . . you know, we're fine. Just one day at a time."

"Yeah, that's all you can do." She offers a kind smile. "Well, see you next week." I agree that I will see her next week and then slide into my car, and before I crank the engine, I have a weird feeling in my gut that I've missed something. Something vital. And then it's gone.

It's just before ten when I walk in the front door and my phone starts ringing. Oliver's name fills the screen. My face flushes.

I had it all planned out, what I was going to say to him after the Rodin, after Isak's absurd and preposterous announcement: *He give you baby.* That I couldn't do it any longer. That I was *married,* for Christ's sake. That I didn't know why we were dreaming about each other, but it was just going to have to be one of life's little mysteries.

But I didn't hear from him for days, and when he finally texted, it was just a picture of Krynchenko's book that came in the mail, and my conjured responses suddenly seemed a little overreactionary, and a lot presumptuous. It's not like he was hitting on me. He'd never once crossed a line, and honestly didn't seem the type to do so. I responded with a thumbs-up (friendly, casual) and haven't heard from him in the week since. Until now.

Finished Krynchenko's book.

And?

It's interesting. Meet for coffee?

I stare at the words, momentarily confused. When? In Philly?

Now. Hope Springs. I'm here — just finished putting a crib together for Caroline.

Oh. I look up, around the living room, at the painting of the chicken, as if it will suddenly come to life and tell me what to do. But it's silent, as silent as the house is since Harrison's not home yet and probably won't be for hours. My mouth goes slightly dry, but I only hesitate for one more second before responding: OK.

The Coffee Bean occupies prime real estate on Waterloo, the only road downtown fronting the Delaware River. The water is calm tonight, the streetlights reflecting off it. Oliver is sitting at an iron two-top on the patio and half stands when he sees me. I take in his striped tank top that reveals his tanned arms, the Reef sandals cutting a thick fabric V over each foot, his half-sticking-up hair, and I know his hands have just been in it. I try to ignore the now-familiar electric buzz in my stomach at seeing him.

"Hey." He grins.

"Hi yourself," I say.

"They're closing in twenty minutes." He nods to the table next to us that a waitress is wiping down, and I can see through the glass door that she's already stacked chairs on the tabletops inside.

"Oh."

"If you want to grab something, we could take it to go."

So I do. I order a latte from the disgruntled teenager behind the counter, who clearly already cashed out the register. Back outside, Oliver and I start walking slowly along the river, clutching the cardboard rings hugging our paper cups.

"So. Are you keeping me in suspense on purpose?" I keep my voice light to break the tension that seems to have cropped up between us. Maybe it's the darkness of the night, the quiet of the streets or just the naturally romantic setting of the river, but the air feels more intense somehow, less buoyant.

He chuckles and gestures with his cup toward a water-facing bench beneath a bright streetlight. I sit and he digs in his back pocket with his free hand, producing a curved paperback. "Here," he says, sitting beside me.

I take it from him, rereading the title.

Psychic Psychology: The Science Behind the Supernatural. He clasps his hands together. "Do you want me to start with the far-out stuff or the really far-out stuff?"

I grin. "Ease me in. Basic far-out."

" 'K," he says. "Turn to page eighty, I think? Eighty-one, something like that."

I do. He leans closer, his shoulder touching mine. I try not to notice the solid granite feel of it, the warmth emanating from his bare skin. He draws his index finger down the page and then stops midway. "OK, this paragraph. Start here."

Recurring dreams containing historic details — horses and carriages, rotary phones, suits of armor or even people you've never met before — could be indicative of past lives. Some people who've experienced these dreams believe they're learning about important events that were formative in a former life, or people that were meaningful to them.

One of the most famous cases of this is Salvador Dalí, who believed he was St. John of the Cross, a reformer from the sixteenth century, reincarnated. Not only did Dalí claim to recall the dark nights in a prison cell and beatings St. John was subjected to in his life, he also experienced a vivid dream — a living image of Christ on the cross. Interestingly, it was the same vision that appeared to St. John at his monastery in Ávila. Dalí translated this dream into a painting, Christ of Saint John of the Cross.

I look up at Oliver. "This is the least far-out stuff?"

He grins.

"So you think we're dreaming of a past life in which we knew each other. And went to a carnival."

He laughs. "For the record, I did not say that. Krynchenko did."

"Noted," I say, and then pause. "But what do you think?"

"That it's weird. But this whole thing is weird, so what do I know?" He looks at me. "What about you? You asked me, but you never said — do you believe in all that psychic stuff?"

"Heh." My breath catches, thinking of Isak. "I actually went to see one. Recently."

I didn't plan to say it, it just came tumbling out, and I'm nearly as surprised as he looks when he says, "You did?"

I shift uncomfortably on the bench. "Yeah."

"About this?"

"Kind of. I mean, I really went more for fun, I think? But then he brought it up. Said I'd been dreaming about a man, and he described you. Well, he described a man with brown eyes and brown hair, which really could have been anybody."

Oliver sits back. "Huh."

"Yeah."

"Well, what else did he say?"

I swallow. Look at the ground, cursing myself for bringing it up in the first place. I mumble a response.

"What?" Oliver leans closer.

I clear my throat. "He said you were going to give me a baby."

"What?" He jerks his head back and chuckles nervously. And though I'm too embarrassed to look at him head-on, I can see him out of the corner of my eye stuffing his fingers through his hair. He's flustered, his patina of confidence momentarily shattered. It occurs to me he rarely is. Rattled. Embarrassed. Vulnerable. If I were a bad wife, I would find it ridiculously attractive.

I'm a bad wife.

He recovers quickly. "The plot thickens," he quips.

"Indeed."

He half chuckles again, this time bent over, elbows resting on his knees, staring

313

intently at the sidewalk that he's casually scuffing with his sandaled foot. "Suppose Harrison might have something to say about that."

I tense at the mention of my husband's name. Both at the shaming reminder that I have a husband as I sit here with another man, and at the thought that Harrison has had something to say: He doesn't want a baby. But Oliver doesn't need to know any of that. I exhale long and slow.

"Yeah. Suppose he might."

And suddenly, I'm aware more than ever of Oliver's proximity. I shift my body slightly to the left on the bench, so our shoulders are no longer touching. And I search for something else to talk about. A subject change. I find it on the side of his face, at his hairline. "Hey — how'd you get that scar?"

"Huh?" He lifts his head, reaches up, rubbing it with his index finger, as if he'd forgotten it was there.

"Oh, got in a fight with a China cabinet," he says. "We had this huge floor-to-ceiling one in the dining room. I was maybe three, four, and I got it in my head that I could scale it. I opened the drawers to climb up them like stairs, and my weight tipped it over. Whole thing completely fell over on top of me. Glass shattered, slicing up my scalp pretty good. Scared my mom something awful."

"I bet," I say. "You know, you don't have it in my dreams. Or if you do, I've never noticed it before."

"You don't have that tattoo," he says. I turn my wrist over, and we both stare at the three black characters.

"Do you think that means something?"

"Beats me," he says. And I know exactly what he means — how each new theory only sounds more far-fetched than the one before, and each new revelation only serves to muddy the water instead of making things clearer.

The muted clanging of a bell rings out into the night — the large clock on the main plaza in town. I count eleven tones. "It's late. I should probably be getting home."

"Yeah," he says. "Me, too. C'mon, I'll walk you to your car."

We stand up, and I offer the book to him. "You can keep it," he says. "It just gets crazier."

I tuck it in the crook of my elbow and we begin retracing our steps. "I was sorry to hear about your mom," I say. His mentioning her jogged my memory of Caroline saying she died. He bobs his head. "How old

315

were you?"

"Thirteen."

"That must have been hard."

He makes a soft grunting sound. "If there's a word that encompasses what it was, I have yet to find it in my life."

I don't know what to say to that — *sorry* seems utterly useless, and I've already said it, anyway — so I let the words hang in silence. We pass the coffee shop and turn onto Mechanic.

"So what's your tattoo mean?"

I think of Harrison, and when I got it — and my stomach twists with a mix of guilt and longing. "It's a long story."

"I've got time," Oliver says, catching me by the wrist, stopping me in my tracks. It's the first time he's touched me on purpose tonight and I know it because of the way it takes my breath, the way I'm fully aware of the pad of his thumb resting on the black characters of my tattoo, on my ulnar artery. I wonder if he can feel the uptick of my pulse. My eyes find his, and the way he's looking at me is the way I feel — like we're suddenly the only two people in the world.

"Ollie!"

We both start and he drops my wrist, the connection severed. I turn my head in the direction of the voice and see Caroline walking toward us, her head haloed by the bright streetlight, eyes fixed on her brother. When she sees me, she slows down. "Mia . . . hi."

"Hi," I say, my eyes drawn immediately to the bump under her shirt. Anyone else might have thought she just had one too many burritos, but I know. My heart twists.

Her attention's back on Oliver. "Hey — I figured you'd be back in Philly by now."

"I thought so, too," he says. "That hour-long crib project? Took more like seven."

She crinkles her nose. "Sorry. But thanks for doing it."

"Are you just now getting off work?"

"Yeah, this holiday parade thing has taken more effort and planning than I antici-pated." She glances my way again, her eyes betraying a touch of suspicion. "So what are you guys doing?"

I feel Oliver shift slightly beside me. "I stopped to grab a coffee for the drive back. Ran into Mia."

It's just a white lie, but it unsettles me. The fact that he feels the need to lie at all. And it brings everything into sharp focus.

"Oh, cool," she says.

"I was just headed home, actually," I say, and that's when something catches my eye, just beyond Caroline. A car. A familiar car, parked at the end of the street. A silver Infiniti. And though it could be anyone's Infiniti and Harrison is supposed to be at the hospital, something flutters in my gut. "I'm this way." I point toward the car, even though mine is parked in the complete opposite direction. "It was good seeing you both."

Without meeting Oliver's eyes, I wave, leaving them on the sidewalk, and walk to the end of the street, half wondering if I'm being crazy, but when I reach the Infiniti and see the sport coat Harrison had on this morning in the passenger seat, his orange paisley bow tie haphazardly flung across it, I know.

It's Harrison's. He's not at the hospital. The question is, where is he?

The car is parked in front of the Blue-Eyed Macaw, the inside of the store dark, the sign on the door flipped to *Closed.*

I glance up and down the street. Oliver and Caroline are gone, and though there are a few other cars parallel parked behind Harrison's, it feels like a ghost town. But then I hear the unmistakable jangle of a door opening in the distance. I turn the corner and spy a bar I've never noticed before. The Quay. I hesitate for just a second before marching forward and opening the door. The inside is dim, but there are more

people than I anticipated. They're all involved in their own conversations, their
glasses of beer or cocktails, and no one
looks up at me. I scan the half-full tables,
the soapstone bar at the back of the room,
and I spot him — the familiar curve of his
back, the straight hairline delineating his
buzz cut from his neck. I take a step forward, not to *confront* him, necessarily. So
he stopped for a drink after work without
telling me. It's not the world's worst crime.

But then he turns to his right to say
something to the person sitting next to him,
and I stop cold. I recognize her.

The perky blonde we saw at Sorelli's.
Whitney. The patient whose life Harrison
saved. The woman who is going through a
divorce.

I take a step backward and nearly crash
into a man carrying a tray of beer. "Sorry,"
I say, my face flushing red. When I glance
back up at Harrison, he's still engrossed in
conversation. He's smiling, laughing even,
and I try to remember the last time he
looked at me like that.

And then, my brain unable to process
anything else — or maybe it's my heart that
might explode — I turn and rush out into
the dark, still night.

CHAPTER 20

Harrison doesn't believe in soul mates.

I asked him once, in the early months of our relationship, on the way to that wedding in Maine, Beau and Annie's. Four hours into the eight-hour road trip, we had devoured a bag of sour gummy worms, two Pepsis, a container of cheddar cheese Pringles and a box of Mike & Ike's, the evidence littering the floorboards at my feet.

Harrison laughed.

"What?"

"That's quite a leap from asking why I don't like peanut butter."

"So, do you?" I asked.

"Believe in soul mates?"

"Yep."

"As in, two people who are destined to meet and fall in love over and over in all the past and future incarnations of their souls, forever and ever throughout the span of time?"

"Yep," I said.

"Nope." He gave his head a firm shake, keeping his eyes trained on the road. Tammi Terrell and Marvin Gaye were filling in the gaps of our conversation, singing about the world being a great big onion.

"Oh," I said. I wasn't surprised, necessarily. Harrison was more the logical one, the doctor, the science and math guy whose proofs require tangible evidence. I looked out the window. We were passing a service plaza on the Massachusetts Turnpike.

"Wait, do you?" He glanced at me.

"No, not really," I said. I thought back — I may have at one point, but when you're eleven and your mom divorces your dad and everything you think you know about love explodes, childish ideas like soul mates are collateral damage. And I learned happiness was a fleeting thing — something that's here one minute and snatched away the next, like a shooting star or a moonbeam that can't be caught or held or locked up in a cage.

"So why did you sound so disappointed that I don't?"

I thought about it. "I don't know. I guess I kind of hoped one of us did. I like the idea of it. That we were destined to be together. That some powerful universal force draws us to each other, time eternal."

"Huh," he said. "I think the opposite is actually more interesting."

"How so?"

"That in the random chaos of life, you and I met somehow. And out of everyone else in the world that we know, we choose each other. Every day."

I stared at him. "And here you're always saying you're not romantic."

"It's actually you who says that."

I laughed. "You're right."

We barreled down the highway a few more miles, passing trees, trees and more trees. Tammi and Marvin had moved on to their next greatest hit.

"You know though, the past-life thing, I could totally buy into," I said. "It's so wild to think about — being somebody else, living an entirely different life. What do you think I was? Probably something really cool, like a pirate. Or maybe I had one of those weird jobs that no longer exist today — like a bowling pin resetter. Or a lamplighter. Or an orgy planner."

"A what?"

"An orgy planner," I repeated.

"I don't think that's a thing."

"Yeah, in ancient Rome. That was a real job. Orgies didn't just happen, you know. Someone had to invite the women, organize the food, book the kithara player."

"You are so strange," Harrison said. And then, in the next breath: "Marry me." It was the second time he had asked. I would have thought he was joking the first time and this one — we hadn't been together that long and I hadn't even told him I loved him yet — but his face was so serious, not even a hint of teasing. It sent a thrill through me.

"Maybe I will," I said.

He jerked the wheel. I grabbed the Oh Shit handle. "Jesus, Harrison!"

The car came to a stop in the emergency lane. He stared at me, eyes wide. "Is that a yes?"

I shook my head, grinning. "No! You're crazy."

"Crazy for you."

I groaned, but couldn't help laughing. Couldn't stop the thrill coursing through me at his words.

He leaned over, palmed my face between his hands and kissed me. My stomach fluttered; my bones turned to rubber.

Now, as I enter our dark house, I try to remember the last time he kissed me like that. Or maybe I'm trying to remember the last time I felt that way when he kissed me. And though I know that it's only the natural progression of relationships — that it's impossible to sustain that level of fresh excitement years in — I can't help but wonder if Harrison's stopped choosing me. If we stopped choosing each other.

Without turning on a light, I pad to the living room and sit on the couch, staring at nothing, waiting for my husband to come home, so I can ask him.

But he doesn't.

In the confusion, that weird place between sleep and wake, I think the cat must be back. Every night for a week after we moved into this house, Harrison and I would hear a pitiful mewing right outside our bedroom window. But every time we'd go look — or once, offer it some milk as a peace offering in exchange for quiet — it would dart off, as if it had just been delivering a message and couldn't stay to visit. It was like some weird welcome to our new life — a reminder that we were no longer "city folk." That the late-night traffic and police sirens we had become immune to were suddenly replaced by wild animals — whining cats and crickets and the occasional owl — who don't softly hoot, I've learned, but cackle like creepy children.

But as I start to get my bearings, I realize it's not the cat. Was it me? Was I having a nightmare? Was I crying in my sleep? Groggy, I peer at the clock on Harrison's nightstand, glowing 2:36 into the dark. And then I see him, perched at the end of the bed.

"Harrison?" I whisper, my voice croaky.

He doesn't turn around and I know something's wrong from the way he's slumped over, not moving. I jerk aside the covers and crawl to the foot of the bed, put my hand on his back. And that's when I notice the trembling of his shoulders. And then the wetness on his cheeks.

Harrison is crying.

I'm stunned, like I'm watching a plane fall out of the sky right in front of me. I'm not sure what to do and I just want to make it stop.

"Harrison," I say, moving my body to sit beside him in one swift motion. This close I can smell the alcohol fumes rolling off him.

And my memory of the night comes rushing back. Harrison at the bar. With *Whitney*. My heart sinks to the bottom of my toes. Though I knew it looked bad, part of me thought there must be a logical explanation for it all. For why he was in a bar with another woman. Why he hadn't told me he was going. Besides, I had been downtown with another man, too, and I hadn't told him. Maybe that made us even. But now, he's crying and I think maybe we're not even. Not at all. "What is it?" I whisper, even though I'm not sure I want to know. That I don't think I can handle hearing the words out loud.

He doesn't respond.

"Harrison," I repeat, and he flinches as if I've burned him. "Please talk to me."

He shakes his head, but his words are muffled by his hand.

"What?"

"I killed someone," he says. The words ring out clear and sharp into the still air. I'm momentarily stunned, my brain trying to process the difference between what I expected him to say and what he said.

"What?"

But he doesn't respond, so I sit with the words, having lost all others.

Finally, I ask, "What do you mean?" Was he in a car wreck? Did he hit someone? My eyes rake over his body, scanning for injuries.

"I killed him," he chokes out between sobs.

"Who?" I say, panic gripping me afresh. "Harrison, you're scaring me."

He just shakes his head, moaning.

"*Please,* Harrison."

"I'm drunk," he says into his hands.

"Were you in a car wreck?"

He shakes his head. Clutches his mouth with his hand, squeezing his cheeks together, then moves his fingers down his chin, smoothing the wiry hairs in his unruly beard.

"Then what happened? Who died?"

He takes a deep, quivering breath. "Noah." And then he's off again, deep, heaving sobs.

"Noah," I repeat. And all at once I remember. The boy in Philadelphia. The routine appendectomy. Harrison doesn't lose patients often — especially on the table during surgery. And it's even more rare for him to lose a child, since most of his patients are adults. This one rattled him, I remember. It was the reason he wanted to get out of Dodge for the weekend. The reason we took that spontaneous road trip to Hope Springs.

"Harrison, that was months ago."

He sniffs, then lets out a slow, audible breath. "It was my fault," he says. "That he" — his voice cracks — "died."

"What?" I say. "What do you mean?"

He blows out a long breath. " 'Member Boehner?" The frat boy in scrubs. That's how I always thought of Harrison's colleague, a doctor a few years older than him. He was charming, but in a smarmy kind of way, and carried his stereotypical God complex like a badge of honor. I nod.

"Well, we had this ongoing . . . bet with appendectomies, who could do one the fastest. I mean, we did so many of them. All the time." He's slurring a little, talking low, and my mind races to understand. "Boehner was down to sixteen minutes and change and I knew I could" — he hiccups — "beat him on my next one."

"Oh, Harrison," I say, all at once seeing where the story is headed, even without fully knowing. "Noah?"

He nods. "Everything was fine — I made the incisions, got the trocar in. But when I got in there . . . he was really inflamed. Not the worst I've seen, but bad." His words are running together, over each other, as if he's talking to himself more than me, and I lean in closer to try to make them out. "I had to decide — in a blink — do I keep going or do I switch from laparoscopic to open?" He shrugs. "Got cocky. Thought I could do it and still beat Boehner's time. But —" He shakes his head and the tears are freely flowing now, silently. "I just . . . I keep replaying that moment. Why didn't I stop? And then the mom —" He swipes his palms beneath his eyes. "The way she wailed when I told her. Like this inhuman — animalistic . . ."

He shakes his head again. "It's all I can hear sometimes. All I can see."

I clutch at my heart, thinking of the mom. How horrific that would be. Both to hear those words and to have to say them. I can't even imagine. I can't imagine half of what Harrison does at work. But I know him — and even if he was thinking about that stupid bet, he never would have risked a patient's life like that if he had an inkling it would end that way. It just sounds like he had two choices, and he made the wrong one.

"Harrison," I breathe. "Why didn't you tell me?"

He jerks his head. "I *killed* him," he says, and it's so raw, so full of emotion, that it finally hits me: He's been walking around with this for months — *months* — and I had no idea. His shoulders are shaking in earnest now, his face a mix of wet tears and mucus. I put my hand on his shoulder.

He sniffs. "It's fine. I'm fine," he says. His breathing slows and he wipes his nose with the sleeve of his shirt. "I need water."

"OK." I feel grateful to have a task. My mind a jumble, I run to the kitchen barefoot in my tank top and underwear, opening the cabinet that holds our glassware in the dark. I grope for a cup, but there's nothing there.

329

Shit. I haven't emptied the dishwasher. I fling open its door and retrieve a glass, not even needing to hold it up to the moonlight climbing in the window to see that it's marred with fingerprints and lined with lip marks. Shit. I didn't run the dishwasher. I hurriedly wash it out in the sink and then fill it with tap water.

When I get back to our bedroom, Harrison's lanky body is splayed out on the bed, his hand on his still mostly buttoned shirt, his feet hanging off the bottom edge. Guttural snores rattle in steady intervals from his slack mouth.

I stand there and watch him for a minute, transfixed by this man that I have slept next to for eight years, as if I'm seeing him for the first time.

I set the glass of water on our dresser, next to a handful of loose change. The ceiling fan spins lazily over our bed as I slip Harrison's tan leather loafers off one foot and then the other. His glasses lie listlessly on the blanket next to his knee, and I pick them up, folding the temples down and setting the frames on his nightstand where he can easily reach them in the morning. I slide a hand underneath him and tug the blanket down the length of his body until it pulls free and I drape it up over him.

And then I freeze, standing over him, as suddenly something clicks into place. *This* is what's changed Harrison. It's this burden, this guilt he's been carrying around for months. It's the only thing that makes sense, that explains his sudden eagerness to move to Hope Springs, the long beard, the long hours, the long runs and — *of course* — his full change of heart about having kids. Relief floods through me, the kind that only comes with sudden clarity.

As I lie down next to my husband and turn out the light, even as I'm pained for him and all that he's enduring, for the first time in weeks, I go to sleep with a pit in my stomach that doesn't feel so much like despair, but a little bit like hope. And it's growing.

The next morning, I wake up to Harrison sitting on the foot of the bed once again. I stare at the length of his knobby spine protruding through the back of a shirt — this one baby blue instead of the white he was wearing last night — and experience a weird form of déjà vu, briefly wondering if I dreamt everything the night before.

"Harrison," I say, my voice still thick with sleep.

He turns, his face in Alfred Hitchcock

profile. "Morning," he says. "I need you to take me to my car."

I sit straight up now. Right. Harrison was drunk last night. Crying. Noah. "Where's your car?"

"I left it downtown. If it hasn't been towed."

"How'd you get home?" I ask.

"Whitney."

At the mention of her name, I prickle. "Whitney," I repeat.

"She's that patient —"

I cut him off. "I know who she is." And even though I know this is the least of our worries right now, or the least of Harrison's anyway, I can't help it. "So you went to a bar with one of your patients?"

"Not *with* her. I just ran into her there."

"Oh." Still. I think of the way he was looking at her. How the tightness of his jaw was gone, the crinkle of his forehead smooth. Like he didn't have a care in the world. The complete opposite of how he looks now. "Harrison, is there anything — should I be worried —"

"What? Mia, no. That's ridiculous." He turns to me now and I see it in his eyes — the weight of the world, yes, but also that he's telling the truth.

And then he stands up. "I'll be in the den."

"Wait!" He pauses, but doesn't turn to look at me. "Harrison, last night — Noah."

He holds up a hand. "It's nothing. I shouldn't have said anything."

"It's not nothing, Harrison. I want to be here for you. Please talk to me."

His head drops and his hands go to his waist. He sighs, lifts his chin. "I've got to get to work."

And then he turns and walks out of the room.

"OK," I say to the empty space left behind — even though nothing feels OK. Nothing at all.

CHAPTER 21
CAROLINE

At first Caroline thinks it's indigestion. She probably shouldn't have eaten three chili dogs and an order of Tater Tots for dinner, but she's been ravenous lately, and it sounded so good at the time. Two hours later, when the pain has gotten so bad she can't ignore it anymore, she calls the doctor.

Later, she calls Oliver. She hates to bother him again. Especially when he was just in Hope Springs three days ago putting together her crib, but the truth is, she has no one else. Certainly not Richard, the father of the baby, who unceremoniously dumped her and stayed with his wife after she told him. And she hasn't exactly told any of her friends about the baby yet. Maybe she's embarrassed, or maybe it hasn't completely sunk in yet that this is happening. To her. She is having a baby.

Anyway, as pathetic as it is when she really

thinks about it, she has no idea what she'd do without her big brother, annoying as he may be most of the time.

"I need you," she says, her breath hitching, when he picks up.

"What is it?" he asks.

"Cramps, I don't know. Something's not right." She grunts again.

"Did you call your doctor?"

"Answering service. Told me to go to the ER if the pains didn't stop in the next thirty minutes."

"How long ago was that?"

She pauses, glances at the television, at an old episode of *Law & Order.* She tries to remember if this is a different episode than the one that was on when she called the doctor. She decides it is. "An hour, I think?"

"Call an Uber. Go now," Oliver says, falling effortlessly into his big-brother role. "I'll meet you there."

"OK," she says. And she does.

When Oliver rushes into the ER ninety minutes later, Caroline has been there for more than an hour. She has spent the time secretly diagnosing everyone else in the waiting room. A young boy with swollen eyes and a red nose, clutching his elbow and sitting next to what appears to be his grandmother (easy: broken arm). An elderly man dozing in a wheelchair (disorientation — possible ministroke), sitting next to a younger man with the same facial structure but less wrinkles staring intently at his phone (his son, there for support). A woman in strappy heels and bright pink lipstick slumped in a chair on the far side (genital warts: is that an emergency?).

She waves Oliver over.

"You OK? Have you seen the doctor?" he says, concern all over his face.

"Still waiting. But I feel a little better. I haven't had a cramp in a few minutes."

Oliver studies her. "Are you sure it's not something you ate? Maybe just a little indigestion or something. That's supposed to get worse with pregnancy, right?"

"Oh, you're a doctor now?" she says, instantly annoyed, even though she, too, thought earlier it might be indigestion. "No, Oliver, I obviously don't think it's *a little indigestion.* I have been in a severe amount of pain. Can you try to be less condescending, please?"

He holds up his hands in deference. "Sorry. You're right. Do you need anything? What can I do?"

"Just sit down. Wait with me."

So he does. He sits, propping his elbows

336

on his knees, his heel jiggling with impatience. Caroline sniffs the air. "Is that you?"

Oliver glances down at his T-shirt. "Yeah," he says. "Been holed up in my apartment on a four-day writing jag. I panicked when you called — no time to shower."

She wrinkles a nose. "I hope I'm having a girl. Boys are so gross."

He shrugs. She picks up a magazine from the table beside her. Flips through it.

"How's work?" he asks.

"Good," she says, looking up from the page she was reading. "Busy. This parade has taken on a life of its own. Hope Springs has so much tourism money that the budget is huge. I just bought six hundred thousand Christmas lights." She grins, thinking how charming the town square is going to be after the parade, and shares more details with her brother: A real festive atmosphere, complete with hot chocolate stands and a bona fide choir singing carols and a firework display.

"Fireworks?" Oliver says. "Isn't that more of a Fourth of July thing? New Year's?"

"They're celebratory," Caroline says. "For any holiday, really."

"Well, not *any* holiday. No one sets off bottle rockets on Easter."

"Honestly, Oliver." And then: "Ouch." She

puts a hand on the left side of her burgeoning stomach.

"You OK?" he asks, sitting up straighter.

"Yeah," she says, exhaling. And then she glances at Oliver. His knee is still jiggling and he's glancing around as if he's expecting someone else to show up — and that's when it hits her, all at once.

"Ollie."

"Yeah?"

"You looking for someone?"

"What? No."

"You sure? Because if I was sleeping with Mia, I'd be awfully anxious I'd run into her husband." She'd been suspicious ever since she ran into them downtown the other night, even though Oliver said it was nothing.

His eyes shoot to hers. "What? Keep your voice down. I am not sleeping with Mia."

"Then what are you doing? I know something's going on."

Oliver holds her gaze for a beat and then drops it, along with his shoulders. "It's complicated."

"I knew it," she says. "And after you gave me all that shit, too, about Richard. What was it you said? An affair always ends like the *Titanic* — it goes down and takes everybody else with it." If she's being honest, she is experiencing a small perverse pleasure that her brother's proving to be a complete hypocrite, but mostly she's sad. Oliver isn't a choirboy by a long shot, but still, he's good, decent. He didn't even cheat at Monopoly when they were kids. And there is a dearth of good, decent men in the world — she should know.

"I just — it's driving me crazy, to be honest, Care. I can't stop thinking about her."

"Oh, Ollie," she says, and she can see that it's true. And she doesn't say it out loud, but she thinks it's probably a good thing that Oliver is going to Finland in September with that weird volunteer farming organization he loves.

Oliver remains lost in thought when Caroline is called back by the nurse, and she leaves him sitting there forlornly, wishing there was something she could do.

But in the exam room, all thoughts of her brother disappear as she stares at the grainy ultrasound screen. Dr. Leong wands her, asking her questions, but all Caroline can do is gape. She's looking at a baby. A real live baby, with a round head and a tiny nose and little fingers on each hand. It's not her first time seeing it, of course. But before, it looked a little bit like an alien creature, and for some reason her brain didn't make the connection — or chose to completely ignore — that this creature was actually in her stomach. Dr. Leong pats her leg, jolting her out of her reverie. "Everything looks just fine, Mom. Maybe a few less chili dogs next time?"

Mom.

Mom.

Caroline rips the paper gown off with more force than necessary and pulls her T-shirt on over her head. When she reenters the brightly lit waiting room, she finds Oliver. "C'mon," she says to him. "We can leave."

He glances at her. "You're done already? Everything OK?"

She mumbles something, turning around, the sudden urge to get out of there as quickly as possible overtaking her.

"What?" Oliver jumps up, following her.

She whips around. "It was just gas."

Oliver's mouth drops open and then his lips start to curl up. She raises an eyebrow and pokes a finger toward him. "Don't," she says, readjusting her bag strap on her shoulder. "Don't you dare."

It's not until later when she's resting in bed, Oliver halfway back to Philly, that the weight of everything she felt in the exam room comes crashing down on her.

She is going to be a mother.

And she's not so sure she wants to be.

CHAPTER 22

Harrison goes through the motions of his
life, waking up to his alarm, going running,
heading in to work, coming home late and
then getting up to do it all over again. I
watch him, like I'm eyeing a caged animal,
waiting — but for what, I'm not sure. It
doesn't occur to me until the third day,
when I'm staring at him and it strikes me
that I'm wondering where my husband
went, even though he's standing in the same
room I am. I haven't just been looking *at*
him; I've been looking *for* him.

The dopey-grinned Harrison clutching a
little knitted pink-and-blue-striped beanie
he had swiped from the hospital nursery the
day after my very first positive pregnancy
test.

The Harrison, lips pressed to my belly,
whispering how we met to our second,
which still would not become our first.

The Harrison, high-pitched and laughing,

as he squeals Three Little Pig voices for Finley and Griffin at bedtime.

I've been wondering for weeks, months, even: Where did that Harrison go? But now I know the answer. Noah isn't the only thing he lost that day. Harrison's brushed me off every time I've brought it up since his drunken confession, but I've latched onto it, desperate to understand what he's going through, and how to fix it. How to bring the Harrison I know back to me.

While he's been at work, I've spent hours online, researching. I Googled how doctors cope with death. A photo of a surgeon in a white coat crouched against a concrete wall, his head bowed, solemn, was the first result to pop up. It's an image that went viral — the rare sight of raw emotion from a doctor who lost a nineteen-year-old patient in the ER. I sifted through Reddit and Quora and Tumblr, reading multiple versions of the same story — surgeons dealing with the death of patients. We're not trained for this in medical school, says one. You learn how to save a life. Not how to lose one.

It lingers, says another, burns into your soul. You're never quite the same.

By Wednesday, I feel confident enough from my research to broach the topic again with Harrison.

After my art class, I wait on the couch for him to get home. The key turns in the door, he steps into the house, and before he can evade me, go to the shower, mumble that he's tired and is going to bed, I speak. "I think you have situational depression."

"Nice to see you, too," he says, standing in the archway between the foyer and the den where I'm seated.

"I'm serious," I say. "Losing a patient — the way you lost Noah — is not easy."

A puff of laughter escapes his lips, but he's not smiling.

"I mean, I'm just saying it's normal, what you're going through. Accidents happen. Doctors aren't perfect — you're human. So many surgeons struggle like this — it's like this invisible epidemic. Did you know that male doctors commit suicide at a rate seventy percent higher than other professionals?"

Harrison stares at me blankly. "I'm sorry. Is this supposed to be helpful?"

"I don't know — I'm probably not saying anything right, it's just that I thought you should know you're not alone."

"Right," he says. "OK. I think I'm going to go to bed." He takes a step toward the hallway.

"No, wait. Harrison. It takes time to get

through something like this. And I think you need to go see someone. A counselor. A therapist."

He scoffs. "Time? *Time?* Is time going to bring Noah back?"

"Well, no, but —"

"I KILLED A CHILD, MIA." His hands tighten into fists. "It's not *normal.* Please, just leave it alone."

"I can't leave it alone, Harrison! I can't. Don't you see? I get it. You're upset; you feel responsible. But you can't stop living *your* life. I know it's why you don't want to have a baby anymore. Maybe you feel like you don't deserve one or, I don't know, that you don't deserve to be happy or something. But you do —"

"*That's* what this is all about?" Harrison says. "Oh my god. I should have known."

"What's that supposed to mean?"

"NOT EVERYTHING IS ABOUT YOU!" he roars. His body is still turned toward the hallway. A vein in his neck throbs. I almost think I can hear the blood rushing through it in the silence that follows his words.

I blink, feeling the weight of those words settle in my gut. My face burns — not from embarrassment as much as shock that Harrison thinks I'm selfish. And then the raw shame that just maybe he's right.

Over the next few weeks, I vacillate between being angry at my husband and being overwhelmed with love and sorrow for him, wanting to wrap my arms around him, pull him close, suck the sadness out of him, like helium from a balloon.

The middle of the night is the worst, when he's snoring lightly beside me. Sometimes I stare at his peaceful face and offer a fervent silent wish to the darkness that he could find that same peace when he's awake. That I could wave a wand and make all of it — Noah, his guilt, his depression — just disappear.

Other times, a rage grips me so tight, every peaceful inhale and exhale of Harrison's sleeping form is an aggressive personal affront. He thinks *I'm* selfish? He's the one that's been *distracted,* consumed by this for *months,* and couldn't even bother telling me what it was. He let me believe it was only my health, the miscarriages, that concerned him. Fear of another that changed his mind about wanting a baby. And that's when the future years of my life feel both interminable and wildly short. Is this how I will spend them? In a quiet house with a long-working shell of a husband and an empty womb? It's these moments — when I'm a flailing fish on land — that I cast him as the callous fisherman, and it takes everything in me to keep from pushing his solid body off the bed and hearing it make a satisfying thud as it hits the floor.

During the day, Harrison works and runs and I water the garden and paint and teach my art class. I try to reach out to him. I ask him to play Boggle. Watch one of those superhero movies he loves. Go paddleboarding. I even attempt to cook for him one night.

"Did cows start flying?" he asks when he walks in the kitchen to the sight of me sautéing translucent shrimp in a pan.

"I thought the expression was pigs."

"My mom always said cows." He shrugs. "Must be a Cuban thing."

It's the most he's said to me in days.

I know it's the depression, but I can't help but take it personally, as if he's punishing me. And part of me feels like I deserve the punishment. Though I'd like to say all I've been doing these past weeks is focusing on my husband, on my marriage, on fixing what's broken, it's not true. I've also been talking to Oliver. It started one evening when I went out to water the garden, and I saw the first green sprouts of the seeds I had planted poking through the dirt. I was so proud of my accomplishment, I wanted to tell somebody. I snapped a picture, but instead of sending it to Harrison, to my husband, I sent it to Oliver.

Picture of thumb, too, please, he responded. Thought for sure it was black.

We've been texting ever since, and though the conversations are innocent — witty jokes, funny moments from our days — I know the action is not. I know these are the conversations I should be having with my husband and am not. But I also can't help myself. As awful as it is to admit it, texting with Oliver has become the highlight of my day, and though I know that means Harrison is right — that I am selfish — I also know that right now it's the only thing keeping me from being as depressed as my husband.

One Wednesday morning, the second week in September, instead of rolling over when Harrison's alarm goes off, I force my eyes open, force my body to sit up. I go over to the dresser and dig to the bottom of the middle drawer, where I'm pretty sure I have an old pair of athletic shorts.

"What are you doing?" Harrison asks.

He's sitting on his side of the bed, collecting his thoughts before he stuffs his feet in his sneakers.

"I'm coming with you." It was my latest idea on how to get through to him. To keep him from literally running away from me every morning. I was going to run with him.

"Running," he says.

"Yeah."

"You don't run."

"Maybe I should start."

He doesn't respond.

In the silence, my eyes drop from his face to a duffel bag on the floor, stuffed full and zipped.

"What's that for?"

"My dad's having his knee surgery? It's this week."

"Oh. Right," I say. Lost in my own world, I had forgotten about it. But then, Harrison hadn't mentioned it lately, either. And I have my art class to think about. I've never missed one and wonder if I can get a sub or will have to cancel it. My mind swirls with what I need to do to get ready. "Are we leaving today? I guess I need to shower. And pack."

He doesn't respond immediately. And then: "I actually thought I would go by myself."

"What do you mean?" Even though there's not much room for interpretation in what he said. "You don't want me to come?"

His silence is the answer.

"You don't want me to come," I repeat, a statement this time.

He clears his throat. "I just need —"

"Harrison, what you *need* is to talk to somebody. A counselor of some kind." I know I sound exactly like Vivian, but I don't care. "I don't know what else to do! You're not yourself. At all. And I get it — you're depressed. Deeply depressed. But you can't be the first doctor to deal with something like this. We can go together. We'll figure this out."

"I DON'T NEED COUNSELING," he roars, startling me. And then, softer, but firmly: "You're not listening," he says. "I *am* different. What happened with Noah, it changed me. I thought moving here, away from Philadelphia, away from what happened, that I would get over it. That I'd slowly forget. And at first, I really did start to feel better. But it's always there — *he's* there — in the back of my mind. And it's only gotten worse."

"But if you —"

"Mia," he says, a warning. And then his shoulders slump with the weight of all he's carrying, and I don't know how to lift it.

I redirect. "What about work?"

He pauses. "I'm taking a leave of absence."

"*What?* When did you decide this?"

He swallows. "I've been . . . messing up recently. I can't focus. Foster agrees it's for the best."

"Wait — you told Foster?" I suddenly feel even further removed from his life. In the dark. And then I remember Rebecca in the parking lot. *How's Harrison?* Was I the last person to know? Or maybe it's worse — maybe I was the last person to notice.

"He doesn't know . . . everything. Look, I just need to get away, for a little bit."

I stare at him, let his words sink in, what he's *really* saying. "Away from me."

His eyes flash to mine, and I know it's true.

"Say it," I say, challenging him.

"It's *that,*" he fires back. "The way you're looking at me right now — the way you've been looking at me for months. Like I'm a bigger disappointment than I already feel like I am."

I stare at him, stunned. I know I should say he's not a disappointment, that I'm not disappointed. But the truth is, I am. Devastated, really. And we both know it.

When he speaks again, his voice is softer,

sad. "I feel like we're just living in this limbo, and neither one of us wants to say it. I know you're waiting for me to change my mind. To change. And I'm not going to."

"So what are you saying?" I ask, a lump forming in my throat.

"I'm just saying," he says, then pauses. "I think we both need some time." The silence stretches between us. And then he stands up and grabs his duffel bag.

"You're leaving now?" My back stiffens. "I thought you were going running."

"I should get on the road. It's a long drive."

"OK," I say, desperation crawling up my throat. The reality of what's happening hitting me at once. I watch in disbelief as he walks toward me. He lifts my chin, kisses me lightly on the mouth. "Dios Mia," he whispers, his breath tickling the skin above my lip.

He leaves, first our bedroom and then the house, the door clicking shut behind him. I just continue to stand there, mute, numb, stunned. A Rodin sculpture of myself: *Girl Whose Husband Is Leaving Her.*

CHAPTER 23

I always thought if my marriage ended it would be an explosion — a fiery blast of fighting and screaming, a plate of spaghetti thrown against a wall. The way my parents ended things. I didn't know it could end in a trickle. A pipe under the sink dripping unnoticed until one day the entire thing crashes through the water-damaged floor.

Is that what's happening? Is my marriage ending? Did the sink already crash through the floor, or is there still time to fix the pipe?

People change, Harrison said to me months ago.

He was right this morning when he said all I've been doing is waiting for him to change back. Like he's a fifth-grade science experiment. Water that turns from a solid to a liquid — and then back to a solid. But now I think he's more like a piece of paper that's been ripped into a thousand pieces. You can tape it back together, but it will never be what it once was.

And maybe it is selfish, but if this is who Harrison is now, where does that leave us? Me?

After I pull myself from the bed, I pad around the house, going through motions — eating a yogurt, doing a load of laundry, washing dishes — anything to occupy my mind. Later, when I can think of nothing else to do, I turn on the TV, but the noise grates, so I put it on mute and just stare at the screen, where Steve Harvey silently guffaws at two feuding families. But over time, the silence becomes overwhelming. A constant reminder that my husband is gone.

It's funny — in Philadelphia, our apartment was too tiny for one person, let alone two, and whenever I found myself alone in it, I secretly cherished the solitude. The freedom to eat a cheese stick, and then a candy bar, and then a few red pepper strips with hummus, and then a bowl of leftover pasta without him gently ribbing me about my odd snacking habits. Or the ability to watch one of my game shows or blast Fleetwood Mac at full volume, without the fear that it would interrupt his intense concentration over medical journals or textbooks.

Now, here — even though he hasn't even been gone an hour — I just feel lonely.

Vivian calls at some point, my cell chiming on the trunk in front of me, but I can't bring myself to talk to her, to anyone, right now, so I flip the sound off and toss it to the floor.

I lie down, my head on the armrest of the couch, and when my eyes grow heavy I let them close, grateful for the respite of sleep.

Later I wake with a start and blink, foggy from sleep. I slowly sit up on the couch and take inventory of my surroundings. Judging by the light streaming through the window above the television, it's late morning, not even noon. And then I hear it, footsteps coming up the walk. It was a car door slamming shut — that was what woke me. I stand up now and rush to the front door. It's Harrison. I know it is. He came back. He's going to wrap me in his embrace, ask me to come with him, tell me we'll work it all out. I'm nearly crying with relief when I reach the door and throw it open.

The world around me stills.

It's not Harrison.

It's Oliver.

I blink. "Hi," I breathe, startled. But also wildly confused at the competing emotions circling each other inside me. Disappointment that it's not Harrison, yet a fluttery buzz in my stomach that, if I'm being honest, isn't just from the unexpected surprise.

"I've been trying to call you," he says, and I hear the undertone of desperation. He looks tired, as tired as I feel from my interrupted nap, my emotional morning.

I glance back inside. "Oh, I turned my ringer off."

"Do you know Beau Hartman?"

"What?" I say.

He digs his phone out of his pocket, scrolls through it and then holds the screen up to me. It's a picture of a picture. A photo of me. Wearing a seafoam dress and holding a sparkler, the orange reflecting in my eyes. I take the phone from him, the hair on the back of my neck standing up. And it dawns on me. Beau, as in *Beau and Annie.* "I was at his wedding."

"You were at his wedding."

My heart thrums. Beau and Annie. *We* were at his wedding, Harrison and I. "How did you get this?"

Oliver swipes a hand over his face and exhales as if he's not sure where to start.

"Can I come in?"

"Oh — yeah. Of course." I step aside and Oliver walks past me into the living room. He sits heavily on the new leather club chair and rubs his face again, this time with both hands. I return to my spot on the sofa and watch him, waiting.

Finally, he looks up. "Beau's my best friend. He's getting a divorce. He's been pretty messed up over it and I've just been trying to be there for him. Last night, I was over at the apartment he's been subletting on the west side. It was only five and he was already a bottle deep in gin, crying and looking through his wedding album. He was pretty incoherent and there wasn't much I could do but look through it with him. And that's when I saw you."

My eyes dart to his. It was a large wedding — more than four hundred people — but even in my alcohol-induced haze, I still feel like I would have noticed him if he'd been there. "So were you —"

"No. I was in Peru. I had a flight back for it, but there were mechanical issues and I ended up sitting on the tarmac for seven hours. By the time they canceled it and re-booked me for the next day, it was too late."

"But you were supposed to be there."

"I was supposed to be there," he agrees.

I chew my lip, trying to push the shock aside, to swallow my anxiety, to analyze this information logically, but it doesn't feel like there's anything logical about it. I stare at the floor, at my bare feet, and notice that if

I moved my left one three inches forward, it would brush up against his. I don't know why I notice this. Or why I so desperately want to move my foot forward three inches.

Focus.

Oliver.

Beau and Annie's wedding.

It feels like we've been playing that game six degrees of separation (*Surely we know each other. We must, right?*) and finally found a connection — for all the good it does us. "I mean, I don't *know* Beau," I say. "We were invited to that wedding on a whim."

Oliver nods as if he assumed as much, but he's eyeing me intensely. "Have you ever heard that saying, I think it was Yogi Berra: This is too much of a coincidence to be a coincidence?"

I haven't, but as soon as he says it, I shudder, my skin breaking out in gooseflesh. And I know exactly what he means. That's what all of this has felt like, from the first time I laid eyes on him.

"Maybe it is just a coincidence," I offer lamely, but I know it's not. Because that wouldn't explain why the same strange sensation pools in my gut, the one that gripped me in the dank basement of the psychic. *He give you baby.* It wasn't just the words that rattled me, it was the conviction with which Isak said them — as if everything was already written in stone, inevitable, a train in motion, and I didn't have access to the brakes.

I realize Oliver's still talking. "And I keep having that nightmare. The amusement park. It's worse each time and I can't get it out of my head. It's awful." I peer at him, noticing the bags under his eyes, how he doesn't look just tired, but like he hasn't slept in days. "And that book. I can't stop thinking about that book," he mumbles. And suddenly he's talking about quantum physics.

I open my mouth to tell him I've been having trouble sleeping, too. That the dreams *are* awful. To ask him why the hell he's talking about quantum physics. But what comes out instead is: "I can't do this right now."

"What?" Oliver's eyes meet mine.

"I can't do this," I repeat, but this time I leave off the "right now."

"But —" He leans toward me, confusion clouding his face. "But it feels like we're getting closer."

And I know he means *to the answer,* but it's not what he said, and that's the problem. I love my husband. I love Harrison, or I loved the Harrison he used to be? All I know for sure is that I'm hurt and raw, but mostly I'm confused, because I have feelings for Oliver, too. I don't know what they are or what it means, but I know that I'm standing on a precipice with him in this room and if I take a step — if I move my foot three inches forward to brush against his, there's no turning back.

I can't get any closer. I'm too close already. I lean back, away from him, before we do touch, before I can change my mind.

"I'm sorry," I say and stand up. "This is all . . . so much. And I need time. To think. I can't see anything clearly."

"Yeah," Oliver says slowly. "OK." I can feel his eyes on me, but I find that I can't meet his gaze. Or allow myself to wonder why it feels like I'm breaking up with him.

Or why it feels like part of me doesn't want to.

Somehow, I make it through my art class that evening with a plastered-on smile and ever-widening eyes to prevent tears from forming. It takes me longer than usual to wash out the brushes, stack the easels, recap the paints. I'm still working when a man enters the room in blue coveralls with a broom in one hand and a large black trash bag in the other. The janitor. We exchange hellos and both go about our own duties in silence. I'm too absorbed in my own thoughts to carry on a conversation with a stranger.

As promised, Harrison texted that afternoon when he arrived at his parents' house, just outside of Buffalo. I typed and deleted a thousand messages before finally settling on OK. Then I alternated between draping myself on the couch and the bed, my emotions changing by the hour. Harrison. Oliver. Dreams. Beau's wedding album. Babies. I was right about only one thing: It's all too much, and I don't know where or how to begin processing any of it.

"Nice painting."

"Huh?" I look up to see the janitor studying the amusement park that I have yet to retrieve from the easel. "Oh. Thank you."

"It's yours?"

I nod.

"Lake Cedar, eh?" says the man. "You from there?" I'm sluggish, a step behind, exhausted from the myriad events of the day, and it takes me a minute to comprehend what he's said. "What?"

"That's Lake Cedar Amusement Park in Altoona, right?" he says.

My heartbeat picks up as I come fully

back to myself, the room, his words. "You recognize it?"

"Of course. I grew up there. Went every summer."

"Are you sure?"

"That I went every summer?" He scratches the thin yellowing hair on his head. "Might have missed one or two, I guess, but for the most part —"

"No, I mean are you sure it's Lake Cedar?"

He squints at the painting. "Well yeah, it's got the giraffe and the dolphin on the carousel. Used to fight with my brother over that one. And then the lights of that ring toss game right next to it. The Tilt-A-Whirl. Threw up once on that, matter of fact. Had a belly full of Dr Pepper and funnel cake."

I stare at him, my heart hammering now.

"Wait, why are you asking why I'm sure?" He narrows his eyes at me. "Didn't you paint it?"

"Yes, I just —"

"So don't you know what you painted?"

I look from him to the painting, then back to him. "No," I say, honestly. "I didn't."

But I wonder if I do now.

CHAPTER 24

That night I lie wide awake in bed, my mind still a jumble, one thought knocking up against another, all stemming from the same three main subjects:

Harrison.

Oliver.

Lake Cedar.

I couldn't find much about the park online — no pictures — only a brief entry in Wikipedia acknowledging its distinct honor of being home to the world's oldest roller coaster, Leap-the-Dips, now a national historic landmark. I'm not sure what I was hoping to find, maybe something that would jog a memory, make me say, "Aha! Of course." But I've never been to Altoona, not that I remember, anyway.

Part of me wanted to text Oliver, but it felt like a can of worms I wasn't ready to open back up, especially considering the limbo of my marriage.

And that's when I remember the book. I sit up and turn on the light, squinting against the sudden brightness. Sliding open the drawer of my nightstand, I pick it up, rereading the title: *Psychic Psychology: The Science Behind the Supernatural.*

I flip to the table of contents, scanning until I come to a chapter titled, helpfully, "Visions, Dreams and Prophecies." Turning to the requisite page, I scan the first couple of sentences and paragraphs, not finding anything that makes sense to me. It's not until page ninety-seven that two words jump out at me: *Abraham Lincoln.*

Again, with the president? And then two more jump out: *quantum physics.*

This must be what Oliver had been talking about.

While some dreams are purely imagination, or inconsequential, precognitive dreams, like Lincoln's, are tapping into another time and space. How is that possible? Two words: quantum physics. We often think of time as an arrow, a straight line: past, present, future. But quantum physics views time as another dimension, like space. There's up, down, east, west — it's more than bidirectional. And if you think of time that way, the future already exists. It's just that our brains allow us to focus only on the here and now — just like you can see only the little patch of earth where you're standing, even though an entire world exists outside of it. Many Native American cultures understand this intuitively. They view time as a circle, where everything is happening all at once. For them it's no surprise that you can dream about the future.

I read the paragraph again. And then a third time, trying to understand. *The future already exists?* It sounds crazy, like something Raya would say. I keep reading anyway, until the lines blur together and my eyes grow heavy.

In the morning I wake up to the sunlight painting the room yellow, rather than the incessant blaring of Harrison's alarm, which in other circumstances might be pleasant, but today only underlines the fact that he's not here. I picture him, waking up next to me. His body warm against mine, his skin smelling like sleep, edged with the lingering scent of his piney deodorant. He would sit on his side of the bed, shoulders hunched, collecting himself, and then stretch, groaning lightly, his long arms reaching toward the ceiling.

Then he would stuff his feet into his sneakers and go running.

All that running. Miles and miles of running. And for what?

My cell alerts me to a text message. Raya. What time are you coming on Saturday?

My eyes feel gritty with sleep. I rub one of them and yawn. What?

Visionary Woman Awards. Did you forget?

The event at my alma mater honoring Prisha. I did forget. And I don't want to go. In college, I always thought I would one day be a recipient of Moore's distinguished Visionary Woman Award. I suppose every undergrad there thinks that. But it doesn't sink in until this moment how much I really believed it — and how my career is so far off track that it's unlikely to ever happen. Then my cell rings and I know it's Raya impatient for my response.

I slide my finger over it, without glancing at the screen.

"Geez, I was about to text you back."

"Mia?"

"Oh." It's Vivian. And at the sound of her voice, I start crying.

"Mia?" she says again, her voice now filled with alarm. "What's wrong?"

"Harrison left me," I say, and then my

tears bubble over, drowning out anything else I might say.

"What?"

When I calm down, Vivian listens patiently as I explain.

"Honey, it's just to help after his dad's surgery — it's temporary, right? He'll be back."

"I don't know," I say, unsure of anything anymore. "Do you think I'm selfish?"

"No, I think you're human. And I think you really want a baby."

"I really want a baby," I agree, through tears falling anew. And then I give voice to my other greatest fear. "What if I'm just like Mom? What if it's genetic?"

"What if what's genetic?"

Cheating, I want to say, but I haven't told Vivian anything about Oliver, and I can't bring myself to tell her now, so I go with: "Being terrible at marriage?"

"Oh, Mia," she says. "Everyone's terrible at it. Marriage is hard."

It's a platitude. One I've heard Vivian say before: when I told her I was engaged to Harrison, and even though he'd been asking me for months, she thought it was all happening too fast. But here's the thing: I didn't believe it. Not really. Or I did believe it, but I didn't believe it applied to me. To Harrison. To *us.* I thought marriage was only hard for other people. People who clearly hadn't chosen the right partner. And for the first time ever, I really consider: Am I one of those people?

What was it Dr. Hobbes said? That Harrison and I are experiencing a *mismatch.* A lump forms in my throat.

"Do you ever wonder what your life would be like if you married someone else?" I ask Vivian now.

"Yes," she says, without hesitation. "Every time I see Armie Hammer in *Us Weekly.*"

"Seriously, Viv."

"Seriously, Mia. That man is sex on a stick."

I sigh. "That's not exactly helpful."

"I know," she says. "But believe it or not, I don't have all the answers."

I sigh again. "I don't, either."

The last thing Vivian said to me before we got off the phone was: *Whatever you do, get out of the house! It won't do any good to sit there by yourself, moping.*

And I know she's right. I can't spend yet another day swapping the couch out for the bed. I scrub my plate, grab my keys and my phone and leave.

According to Google Maps, the drive to

Altoona, Pennsylvania, is a little over four hours. At first, I try to enjoy it — the leaves of the trees lining I-76 have just begun their metamorphosis from green to yellows, oranges and reds. I try to pretend it's a fun day trip, an exploration of the state, an adventure I'm embarking on to pass the time. But the closer I get, the more my stomach churns, the drier my throat becomes.

Which is ridiculous. I'm going to an amusement park.

But I can't shake this overwhelming feeling that if it's *the* amusement park, something momentous is going to happen. That Oliver's going to be there. That everything is going to play out just like in our dreams. And I'm willingly driving toward it.

The future already exists.

I roll my eyes, ignore the chill that crawls up my skin and turn up the radio.

When I finally turn left at the carved wooden placard that announces Lake Cedar Park and into the expansive tar parking lot, one thing is clear — it's completely deserted. My heart slowly sinks like the late afternoon sun hanging above the top curve of a wooden roller coaster, a crop of trees. I maneuver the car across pavement, stopping in front of a tall chain-link fence with a heavy padlock securing the gate. A yellow metal sign declares: *Under Construction.* I stare at it, and then open my door, putting one foot on the ground before standing up. As if seeing it without the intrusion of the windshield glass will change the outcome.

It doesn't. Beyond the gate lies a smattering of things one would expect to find at an amusement park: I can see four side-by-side faded blue waterslides, ending in a dry splash pond; a spider-looking ride, the red bucket seats scattered in a circle attached to a center pod by metal poles; a concession stand, a piece of plywood tacked over the open-air window. The top of a Ferris wheel looms over it all in the background.

But I don't see the carousel.

A light breeze blows a few strands of hair into my face, carrying with it the faraway sounds of metal clanging on metal. And I am suddenly possessed by self-determination. I did not drive all this way just to turn around and go home. I have to know if this is the park. Leaving my door open, I walk up to the gate, curling my fingers around the metal diamond holes in the fence. I pull on it, half hoping it will magically open despite the industrial lock, but it holds firm, offering only the tinny sound of rattling chain-link in response.

My gaze travels to the top of the fence and I'm debating if I can scale it when a movement catches the corner of my eye. It's a man — three hundred yards deep in the park, walking by a shuttered gaming booth, maybe balloon darts or water gun horse racing or knock down the milk bottles.

"Hey," I shout. "Heeeeeeeyyy!" I wave my arms.

The man stops, looks up in my direction and then — yes! — starts walking over to me. A Day-Glo orange vest pulls tight at his expansive gut, while a tool belt holds his pants on his narrow hips. His full, sun-damaged face ends in a gray goatee.

"You lost?" he asks, when he gets closer.

"No," I say. "I need to get in there."

"In here? It's closed," he says, as if that isn't obvious.

"For renovations?"

"Demolition. We're ripping everything out. Building an industrial office park."

"Oh. That's terrible," I say, thinking quickly. "I used to come here all the time as a kid."

He peers at me. "You from around here?"

"No, not anymore. Came back for old times' sake."

"Ah."

"So what happened?"

He shrugs. "Attendance has been down for years. I really thought it would come back, though, you know, like record stores, farmers' markets — people longing for a simpler time. But it's too old-fashioned, I guess. That old Leap-the-Dips isn't nearly as exciting for kids once they've been on the Superman or the Intimidator 305 or the Millennium Force."

A movie quote pops into my head and I mutter it: " 'Trips to Europe! That's what the kids want.' "

He peers at me, not following.

"It's from a movie," I say. *"Dirty Dancing."*

His eyes light up. "Oh, my wife loves that one. 'Nobody puts Baby in a corner,' am I right?"

I see an opening. "So do you think I could sneak in, just for a minute? I'd love to see it one last time, especially the carousel."

"I can't," he says.

"Oh, please? I drove four hours to get here. I'll be super quick."

He hesitates. "I don't have the keys."

"Well, how did you get in?"

"Employee entrance on the other side."

I hold his gaze.

He sighs. "Give me ten minutes. I'll meet you there."

Twelve minutes later, at the employee

372

entrance, he hands me a white construction hat identical to his. "I'm Hank," he says. "Anybody asks, you're my niece."

I follow the man's Day-Glo vest into the park, the clanging sounds of construction louder on this side, but we don't see another soul, and it strikes me how eerily similar it is to my dream — the deserted amusement park. The tiny hairs on my neck stand at attention and my heart starts competing for notice above the noise. I get that feeling again — that I'm walking toward something, but I don't know what it is, and it's the not knowing that's set my nerves on edge.

We round a corner, and suddenly there it is. The carousel. With the red top and the striped poles and the dolphin and the giraffe and the horses. I stop in my tracks to take it all in. And I wait. For what, I'm not sure. Clarity of some sort? An overwhelming aha moment? A chill of recognition?

But there's nothing. It does uncannily resemble the carousel I painted, but that's it. I don't *feel* anything else. Not that I'm meant to be here or that I have any connection with this carousel in any way.

"It's for sale."

I start, having forgotten Hank was behind me.

"What?"

"The carousel. Most of this stuff is, actually. Except the roller coaster. I think they're breaking it up and just selling pieces of it, like mementos or something. They're hoping to relocate as much as they can. Be a shame to destroy it."

He's off, talking about the old days again, and I wait patiently until I can cut in and thank him for his time, for letting me come in.

"You want me to take a picture of you with it or something?"

I consider this. "No, it's fine. Seeing it was enough." I pause and look to the right, at one of those high-in-the-air swing rides.

"Did a Tilt-A-Whirl used to be here, in this area?"

"Not that I can recall. Tilt-A-Whirl's always been on the other side of the park."

"Huh. I thought it was right here."

"Memory's a funny thing, isn't it?"

"Yeah, I guess it is."

I thank Hank, hand him back his hat at the gate and drive home, feeling a little bit foolish and a little bit relieved, and not at all quite sure why.

CHAPTER 25

Raya answers her door Saturday afternoon in a glittery army green romper with long sleeves and pants, a deep V revealing the skin between her ample breasts all the way down to her navel. Her fire-engine-red hair hangs in loose coils over her shoulders and her eyes are ringed with black kohl.

"Damn." I glance down at the T-shirt I slept in and the sweatpants Harrison gave me. "I guess I'm underdressed."

"Mia! Why *aren't* you dressed? We have to leave in twenty minutes."

"I'm not going," I say, brushing past her and throwing myself facedown on her couch.

"Yes, you are."

"No, I'm not."

"Mia, what's the point of getting out of your house only to stay in mine?"

I shrug.

"Come on. We have to celebrate."

"Prisha won't miss me."

"No — actually, we're celebrating me," she says shyly. Which is a feat in itself, because Raya doesn't do anything shyly.

"What about you?" I lift my head and peer at her.

"I got a commission," she says, her face beaming.

"You did?"

"From the Philadelphia airport."

I sit straight up now. "*What?* Since when?"

"I entered my sketches ages ago and I knew I was a finalist last month, but I didn't think for a second I was actually going to win. I just got the call this afternoon. They want four originals from my *Fish Out of Water* series."

"Oh my god. Those are my favorite." They're these huge, intricate metal sculptures of fish piloting various modes of transportation: a bicycle, an old-timey car, a hang glider. "Raya." I stand up, tears in my eyes, and give her a hug. "Let's go celebrate," I say.

"Yay!" She pauses and cocks her head at me. "But, um . . . could you shower first?"

The bare white walls in the banquet room at Wilson Hall have been draped with floor-to-ceiling gauzy white curtains lit from behind, creating an ethereal atmosphere. A girl in a white button-down carrying a tray of champagne flutes passes me and I grab two and hold one out to Raya. "Oh, I haven't finished mine," she says, so I keep both. I've already had two, and four seems like a nice round number. "Cheers," I say, tapping my glass to hers.

We're standing in a circle, with a few faculty members and women from our graduating class, discussing the twenty-two million dollars the latest Jeff Koons just sold for at Christie's.

"It's painted aluminum, but it looks exactly like Play-Doh. Incredible."

"Did you know it's twelve feet tall? They had to widen the door and use a crane to get it in the auction house."

"Can you imagine if they dropped it? Wouldn't want to be that guy, right?"

"He got the idea from his toddler in the nineties — and I just love the simplicity of that, you know?"

"Oh no, you drank the Koons Kool-Aid," tuts a professor who taught art history and curatorial studies when I was in undergrad. "Is simplicity the hallmark of good art now?"

"But it's technically complex. It took him decades to complete. It's an interesting dichotomy, don't you think?"

Normally, I would jump in with my own opinion — that the only thing interesting about Koons is how so many people worship him; call him the next Duchamp. When really, the power — and legacy — of Duchamp was his desire to challenge what art is and what it isn't. Koons doesn't challenge anything but people's bank accounts.

Instead, I down the second glass of champagne, put both on a passing tray and tug at the black lace bodysuit I now regret borrowing from Raya. It's itchy and uncomfortable and I wish I could just take it off.

As the professor's response turns into a lecture about the celebrity of art, the confluence of capitalism and culture, I let my eyes skim over the crowd of mostly strangers, peppered with a few familiar faces — some women I knew well in school or am tangentially friends with on Facebook; others I recognize, but would be hard-pressed to come up with a first name for.

And then my gaze is drawn to one guest in particular: a man with dark, floppy hair. I blink once. Twice. I stare at him, waiting for my brain to sort out all the differences between the man in front of me and the Oliver in my mind. But I can find only one: Instead of his usual T-shirt, he's wearing a tailored suit jacket.

With a jolt, all at once I realize it really is Oliver. He raises his eyebrows, his surprise mirroring mine. My heart thuds. What is he doing here?

But I don't have much time to ponder, because the emcee announces over a loud-speaker that dinner service will start in ten minutes and guests should please make their way to their tables, and the crowd beside me gently pushes forward. I allow myself to be swept up in the tide, floating toward him, realizing with sudden clarity that I couldn't swim against it if I wanted to.

Right before I reach him, a blur of a human rushes between us, throwing herself into his arms. "Ollie!"

He engulfs her tiny frame in a hug. "God, it's good to see you," he says, chin on her shoulder. But his eyes are on me. He steps back and refocuses on Prisha, while I stand frozen at the realization. He knows Prisha.

"Well, if you weren't flinging yourself off to every corner of the globe all the time, maybe I'd see you more often," she says.

"Me? OK, Miss World Traveler. How's Izzy? Is she struggling with all your new-found fame?"

379

"Ugh, you know Izzy," she says. "We were in Prague. Prague! And she complained about everything. It was too cold. The castle wasn't nearly as impressive in person. The tartare was too raw. *Too raw!* How can something that is not cooked, by design, be too raw?"

He laughs. "She's exactly the same, then?"

"Exactly," Prisha agrees. "God knows why I love her, but I do. She's floating around here somewhere; make sure you say hi. I know she'd love to see you. And Naomi — did you bring her?"

"Eh — that's done," he says, his eye catching mine.

"Again?" Her voice is deadpan, teasing.

"Yes. Thank you. Again."

That's when Prisha notices me. "Mia!" she says, as I take in the familiar thick silk of her waist-length hair, the tiny gold hoop fitted through the septum of her nose like a bull. She toggles her gaze between me and Oliver. "Wait. How do you guys know each other?"

"Oh, uh . . ." My cheeks redden as I try to determine how best to answer that.

"It's nothing scandalous, is it?" Prisha says, noting my reaction.

"No! No, no." I laugh a little too forcefully. Oliver eyes me with amusement, and I feel a flash of irritation that he's letting me flail and not jumping in to save me. "We moved to Hope Springs. Me and Harrison. And then met Caroline, Oliver's sister." I wave my hand as if the rest is self-explanatory. "Yada, yada."

"And where is that hunk of man meat?" She looks around. "Did he come tonight?"

"Ah, no — he had a family . . . thing."

"That's too bad. You know," she says, turning to Oliver, "I'm the reason Mia and Harrison are together."

He wrinkles his brow. "You are?"

"How do you two know each other?" I interject. A trip down my marriage's memory lane isn't something I'm game for right now.

"The record store," Oliver says. "Prisha used to come in when I worked there. She had the *worst* taste in music."

"But he flirted outrageously with me anyway."

"I did not."

"You did, too! It's my fault — I let him believe he might actually have a chance, so I could keep getting the employee discount."

"Anyway," Oliver continues, "she was there the day we got a first edition of Springsteen's *Ghost of Tom Joad*. She geeked out even more than I did. I was

381

shocked she was a fan." He smiles at her. "Turns out — lesbians, they're just like us."

She punches him in the shoulder.

And then Raya appears, shouting Prisha's name and engulfing her in a bear hug. She jerks back suddenly. "Wait," she says, glancing around. "Your bodyguards aren't coming for me, are they?"

Prisha rolls her eyes. "You're ridiculous." They keep talking, but I'm not listening. My gaze is locked on Oliver's, breath shallow, mind swirling.

"C'mon," Raya says, grabbing my forearm, literally jerking me out of my trance. "It's about to start."

She steers me away from Prisha and Oliver and I have no choice but to follow.

"Who was that?" Raya says as we get settled at a table on the other side of the room. As soon as I'm seated, I start searching for Oliver but can't find him in the scrum of people still milling around.

"Huh?"

"The guy. The ridiculously attractive one. I didn't even get an intro."

I look at her. "That was Oliver."

"What? *Jesus.* No wonder you dream about him."

My cell buzzes in the pocket of the ball

gown skirt Raya paired with the bodysuit. I dig it out.

Hallway? Two minutes. I scan the room again but don't see him, and I wonder if he's already out there.

"I've got to go. Bathroom."

"Mm-hm," she says, knowingly, and I don't have time to worry about what she thinks.

I slip out of the banquet room into the red-diamond-carpeted hallway. When the heavy door thuds shut behind me, everything goes still, the din of the party muffled by the thick doors. I spy a water fountain and suddenly feel parched. I walk toward it, bend over and let the cool water wet my mouth, then I splash some onto my face. As I stand up, patting my cheeks dry with my bare hands — "Mia."

I straighten my back and turn toward his voice slowly, willing my heart to slow. But if anything, it picks up when I see him steadily walking toward me. I keep my hand on the water fountain for balance.

"Hi," I say. He stops within a few feet of me and I realize I could reach out and touch him, if I wanted. We are alone, even though yards away there are hundreds of people. And something about that is intimate. Exhilarating. Terrifying. Every one of my nerve endings is on fire, alerting me to his nearness.

"What are you doing here?" he breathes.

"You just texted me," I deadpan, trying to defuse the tension. "Did you forget?"

He doesn't crack.

I relent. "I went to school here. I've known Prisha for years."

"Someone else we have in common." He levels his gaze at me, as if daring me to challenge him, to say it's a coincidence.

And I remember. "Oh my god — is that the one piece of art you own?"

He nods. "I missed opening night at one of her exhibitions. Years ago. It was hammering down rain and the record store flooded. I was stuck trying to save the records, clean up the muck. Next day, I went and bought one of her photos to make it up to her. Cost me nearly a whole paycheck."

I feel faint. "Which opening night?" I ask, even though I know. I'll never forget that rainstorm. That night.

"What do you mean?"

"Was it her very first one? That tiny gallery on Fourth Street?"

"Yes," he says, and then shakes his head as if believing but not believing: "You were there."

I nod because I can't form words. My head is blurry. I put my hand out behind me to grip the water fountain again, but it comes in contact with the wall instead. Was the wall always this close? Was Oliver? Only inches separate us.

"It's actually —" My voice cracks. "That's the night —" I stop. My heart feels as though it's beating outside of my chest. On display.

"The night what?"

I swallow. "It's the night I met my husband."

He takes a small step back, as if I've lobbed the words at him, a bowling ball that takes effort to catch. He shoves his fingers in his hair and I know what he's thinking because I'm thinking the same thing.

"Too much of a coincidence to be a coincidence," I whisper.

"Yeah," he says.

He give you baby.

It's all I can hear. That and the blood rushing through my head. And I don't know if it's how close he's standing to me or his words or the four glasses of champagne I downed in the past hour, but suddenly I'm dizzy.

"I need to sit."

When I stumble forward, Oliver grabs my

arm, sending shock waves through my body, but I don't jerk away. I let him lead me to a bench and my skirt billows out as I sink onto it.

Oliver takes off his jacket and drapes it over my shoulders. It's only then I realize I'm shivering. I stare at the floor, my mind a broken movie reel of memories, Isak's words playing over and over and over.

He give you baby.

He give you baby.

He give you baby.

"Mia," Oliver says. "Are you OK?"

I shake my head yes and then no. "I don't know," I say. Tears spring to my eyes, and then one rolls down my cheek. I don't bother wiping it away.

"You know," he says, his voice so low, I have to lean in closer to hear it. So close I can feel the heat of his breath on my ear. "I don't believe in anything. My great aunt Cici was Presbyterian. Made us go to church every Sunday. Was always saying things like, *You'll see your mom again one day.* And I always thought it was just a kind lie; a way to make it not as sad that she was dead. I don't believe in God. Not really. Or aliens. Or Bigfoot. Although — to be honest I don't think that's as far-fetched as people make it out to be. A huge, hairy man hiding out in the deep forests of Canada."

I tilt my head to look at him, trying to make sense of what he's saying. He reaches for my hand and part of me wants to snatch it back from him while the other part wants to interlace my fingers with his and never let go. I do neither, and my hand lies limp in his grip.

"I don't know why I started dreaming about you. Or why I met you. Or why our lives seem to be circling each other like water around a drain. Maybe it is quantum physics or something just too big and complicated for me to wrap my head around. But I don't think it's nothing."

My breathing is shallow.

"I know you're married. And it's messy and — God, believe me when I say this is the last thing I thought I would ever be doing, but . . . I believe that this all means *something*. That there's something here —" He gestures with his free hand, from me to him. As if it's as easy as that. A straight line that connects us. Point A to Point B. "I don't think I'm imagining it."

He drops his head and, still clutching my hand, gently rubs his thumb over my wrist, my tattoo. And I think of Harrison.

"Am I?" he asks, his voice plaintive, raw.

I want to tell him no, he's not imagining

it, that I feel it, too. But I can't bring myself to say the words.

"I'm so confused," I say instead, the tears coming in earnest now.

His thumb stills on my wrist. "Do you want me to go?" he says gently.

"No," I tell him, only because I don't think I can take anyone else leaving me just this second.

"Harrison and I —" My voice cracks. "We've been struggling."

He straightens his spine, listening.

I wipe my face and take a deep, shaky breath. "It's just — I want a baby. So bad. We've . . . lost three. And now he doesn't want to try anymore."

"Mia," he whispers. "I didn't know. I'm sorry."

I nod my head and take my hand from his, to wipe beneath both eyes with the tips of my fingers. I stare at his profile, the familiar visage, hair, ears, lips that I feel like I've inexplicably been looking at forever. He's rubbing the palms of his hands on his pants, and it tugs my heart, how vulnerable he looks. I take a deep breath.

"You're not imagining it," I say. He jerks his head up. "I feel . . . something, too."

"You do?"

"Mostly guilty and confused." I offer a

sad smile. "But . . . other things."

We stare at each other, and God help me, I imagine what it would be like to kiss him.

"I'm leaving tomorrow. For Finland."

"What?" The world shrinks, my mind focusing on that one sentence.

"My flight leaves at noon."

"Oh," I say, my breath catching in my throat.

"I don't have to go," he says. "If you want me to stay, I'll stay."

"You would?" I peer at him. "You'd stay for me." I remember our conversation in the bar, about his ex-girlfriend. How he left even when she asked him not to.

He nods. "I would." He sits up straighter, energy humming off him. "Or you could go with me. We could travel the world — didn't you say you wanted that? We could be like . . . Hemingway and Gellhorn."

I narrow my eyes. "Didn't he kill himself?"

He laughs. "Before that."

I stare at him, consider how enticing that sounds. To just drop everything and run away. Like Harrison did.

"I don't . . . This is all so . . ."

"I know," he says, slumping back over. "Sorry, that was ridiculous . . ."

"No, it's — it's nice. I just need time. I need to think."

He nods. "I'll be at Caroline's in the morning to drop off Willy, if you . . . need me. Need anything. Just to talk." He pauses, searches my eyes. I wonder if he can see the desire pooling in them. Even though I'm not saying anything, I feel like I'm laid bare — that he can see everything I'm thinking. He drops his eyes to my lips, just a glance, but I catch it, and then his eyes are back on mine. We stare at each other, my heart galloping in my chest, neither one of us moving a muscle. It feels like our entire lives are wrapped up in this one moment. Maybe they are.

"I'm gonna go," he says, not breaking our gaze.

I look away first, and bite my lip to keep from asking him to stay. And then I hear muted applause coming from the other side of the double doors and I remember where we are. "What about Prisha? The award."

He smooths his tie, one hand over the other. "She'll understand."

He hesitates and then leans over, pressing his lips to my forehead and standing up so quickly I don't even have time to register what happened, how it felt, to relish the warmth of his breath on my hairline.

"Wait," I say. "Your jacket." I move to shrug it off my shoulders, but he holds a hand up.

"Keep it," he says. "Just give it to me next time I see you."

I take it for what it is, or what I think he means it to be — a guarantee that we'll see each other again.

I watch his back as he walks down the hall, never breaking his stride, until he turns the corner and I can't see him anymore.

I exhale like I've been holding my breath for hours and collapse against the wall. I should go back in to the dinner, but I can't will myself to move. So I just sit there, as seconds tick by, minutes, hours. And then, at some point, Raya appears. "There you are," she says. And at those three words, I start to cry all over again.

"Do you really believe what you said a few weeks ago?" I ask Raya.

"Which thing? I say a lot of crazy shit." We're back on her couch, both changed out of our gala clothes. She still has a full face of makeup, and it's incongruent with her tank and boxer shorts.

"About when the universe tries to tell us something, we have to listen." I can't stop thinking about what Oliver said, that the dreams, the near misses, our lives circling each other like water down a drain, every-

391

thing points to one conclusion — that we're supposed to be together. I lean my head back on the throw pillow, grind the balls of my feet into the sofa cushion. I'm drained. Exhausted. And my brain is just as cluttered and confused as ever.

"Well, sure, I guess. I mean, I do think the universe talks to us all the time. But how we interpret what it's saying — well, there's the rub, isn't it?"

"What do you mean?"

"Just that there's a lot of room for human error." She takes a delicate sip of whiskey from the glass she's holding. "I mean, take any painting, any sculpture. Put two people in front of it and ask them what it's about, what the artist was trying to say. Nine times out of ten, they're going to tell you two different things. Everyone has their own perspective, right? Their own life experience, breadth of knowledge, emotions, whatever they happen to be going through in that moment — it all informs their responses."

I gape at her.

"What?"

"That might be one of the most intelligent things I've ever heard you say."

She tosses a pillow at me, smacking me in the head.

"Well, buckle up, this one might beat it."

I wait.

She takes another sip of her whiskey, then fixes her eyes on mine. "Look. Ever since this started, ever since you saw Oliver, you've been talking in suppositions — what all of this is *supposed* to mean, that Oliver was *supposed* to be at this place or that, who you're *supposed* to be with. But Mia, that's not you."

I tilt my head at her. "What do you mean?"

"When I met you that first week at Moore, you told me your dad didn't want you to go to art school, because you'd never make any money at it."

I scoff. "He was eerily prescient."

She doesn't crack at my joke. "But you didn't care what he thought. You went to Moore because you *wanted* to. You knew in your gut it was your path. And no one was going to veer you from it."

"But that's exactly what I'm trying to tell you! I don't know what my gut is saying or what my *path* is. I'm confused."

"I don't think you are."

"What? Of course I am."

"No. I think your brain's confused. You keep trying to figure out what you're *supposed* to do. Like life is some big game show with right and wrong answers. It doesn't work like that. You have to put all that aside and really ask yourself: What do you *want?* It's simple as that. Who do you love? Who do you want to be with? Forget everything else."

I stare at her. And then I stare at her some more. I replay her words over and over as I lie on the couch trying to sleep and then, when I can't sleep, on my drive all the way home to Hope Springs. When I walk in the front door of my house, I know exactly what I'm going to do, my mind clearer than it's been in months.

And I start to pack.

CHAPTER 26

Sunday morning, I stand on the familiar porch, holding my suitcase.

I knock, and then when minutes go by with no answer, I rap on the wooden panel again, my heart thudding in my chest. Am I too late?

Finally, the door creaks open, but instead of him, it's her, peering out at me grimly, brown curls hanging loose around her face.

Harrison's mother.

I have a sudden flash of the first time I met her, on this porch, when we came home for Thanksgiving. I had spent weeks with Rosetta Stone, wanting to speak to his mother in her native language — or at least say a few words. *"Hola, Señora Graydon. Encantada de conocerte,"* I said, when Harrison introduced me.

She appraised me with an intense gaze that was unnerving. Her face was wide, her cheeks high and full, her eyebrows drawn in with a thick brown line. And then she said: "I speak English —"

"Oh, I know," I jumped in, slightly mortified. "I was just —" She held up a hand and stopped me. "Better than you speak Spanish. So we'll speak English." Harrison didn't bother concealing his smile.

"Hi, Del," I say now.

She examines me, her penciled-in eyebrows arched in judgment, as I hold my breath, waiting. Then she grunts and mutters something in Spanish, and for a moment panic grips me. Is she going to turn me away? Does Harrison not want to see me? I've been on the road since three a.m. and can't bear the thought of coming here for nothing.

But then the stern line of her mouth turns up and she steps out onto the porch, embracing me in her thick arms. "He's in the back," she says, after leaving her mauve lipstick print on my cheek.

I walk through the house, marveling at how it hasn't changed in the eight years since I first came for Thanksgiving, though the laminate tile in the kitchen shows slightly more wear, the fashions in the family pictures hanging on the walls even more out of date. When I reach the sunporch, I see the same brown wicker furniture with pink cushions, bleached even paler by the sun. Harrison is huddled under a quilt on the longer settee, staring at a television in the corner, where Jane Pauley is welcoming viewers to *CBS This Morning.*

He turns his head, eyes registering surprise when he sees me.

"Mia," he says, sitting up. "What are you doing here?"

I think of everything I wanted to say to him — sorting through all the thoughts I had on the way here, how I did get distracted by Oliver, how sorry I am, what a terrible wife I've been — but there's time for all of that, so I lead with the most important truth, the one in my gut. "I love you."

It wasn't just the "listen to your gut" advice that struck me when Raya was talking the night before. It was the "supposition" bit. The idea that I kept circling back to — that Oliver was *supposed* to be there, at Beau's wedding, the night I met Harrison. And it was on a strip of dark highway somewhere between Philadelphia and Hope Springs early this morning that it struck me: All of the places that Oliver was *supposed* to be, he wasn't.

Oliver wasn't there.

397

Harrison was.

And then I thought of everything else Oliver wasn't there for. Every moment in the past eight years that I've shared with Harrison: the small ones, like when I have paint in my hair and on my chin and I catch Harrison staring at me, a small smile on his lips; or when someone says "intents and purposes" in conversation and we share a secret laugh, remembering the fight we got into when I swore it was "intensive purposes"; or how some mornings when he thinks I'm sleeping, he hovers over me, gently palming my face between his hands, his face inches from mine, and whispers, "I love you, Mia Graydon," and then doesn't let go right away. And the big ones, like how I walked toward him, down a trodden footpath on an old dairy farm just outside of Buffalo in front of a handful of our friends and family to the Peter Cetera and Cher song "After All"; or how his smile stretched across his face when I reached him and he mouthed, "Worst song ever"; or how he vowed to love me even when I ignore him for days in one of my manic artistic episodes and I vowed to love him even when he corrects me on my vocabulary.

And I thought of our first real date.

The night *after* we met in the art gallery

and kissed under a dry cleaner's awning —
I told Harrison what I made clear to all my
first dates: I had no desire to ever get married. As a product of divorced parents, I
didn't see the point. Most guys shrugged or
even looked relieved, anticipating an easy
fling. But not Harrison. "I bet you will," he
said, his gaze clamped on mine, over a
pitcher of sangria and a plate of patatas bra-
vas.

Caught off guard by his response, I
chirped back: "What do you want to bet?"

He could have shrugged it off as rhetori-
cal, but he didn't miss a beat. "If you get
married, you have to get a tattoo." It was a
nod to an earlier conversation in the evening, when we were swapping dumb things
we had done as teenagers: "I almost got a
tattoo once," I told him. "But fortunately I
was too drunk and the manager kicked me
out."

"Why fortunately?" he asked.

"It was going to be one of those god-awful
Chinese characters that everyone thought
made them seem so cultured and enlight-
ened, when it really only makes you look
like a fool."

"What was yours going to say?"

"I don't know. The symbol for creativity
or something equally cheesy. Although, I

don't read Chinese, so how do I know that's what it actually meant? It could have just as easily been the symbol for 'sweatpants' or something."

Harrison poured the dregs of the pitcher of sangria into our glasses and eyed me. "Do we have a deal?"

I grinned cheekily. "Only if you promise to get one, too."

He asked me to marry him for the first time two months later. Caught off guard, I laughed, and said no. Then, and the next five times, sticking to my guns. I didn't believe in marriage. But as the weeks and months passed, I became less sure of my hardline stance. Maybe it didn't work for my parents, but this was Harrison. I'd only known him a short time, but the memories of what my life had been before him had started to blur at the edges. And I knew — even though it was cliché and cringe-worthy and everything I had never believed in — I couldn't picture a day of my life without him. I didn't want to. And I knew what I needed to do.

One afternoon, ten months into our relationship, I entered the door of our apartment, breathless. "Ask me again," I said, my arms crossed behind my back, a slick of sweat on my forehead. Harrison was standing at the open refrigerator drinking orange juice from the carton. His eyes were blood-shot, having come off a twenty-four-hour shift. "Ask you what?" he said, swiping the back of his hand across his mouth.

"Just ask me," I said, grinning like mad.

He tilted his head, and I could see the dawning in his eyes. I nodded, egging him on. He set the carton back on the shelf and let the fridge door swing shut, then eyed me.

"Will you marry me?" he said. Instead of responding, I raised my left arm, slowly turning it toward him, showing him the inside of my wrist, where the skin swelled painfully red around not one, but a string of three freshly inked Chinese characters.

His mouth dropped open. "You didn't," he said.

"I did."

"What does it say?"

My eye caught the light and I smiled. "Sweatpants."

Standing in the sunporch of his mother's house now, I wait for Harrison's response to my declaration, but his eyes remain blank, and the seed of doubt blossoms in my belly. Have I made the right choice? I was being honest when I told Oliver I had

401

feelings for him. And maybe our life together would be everything — travel and adventure and babies. Or maybe we'd fight constantly. Maybe we wouldn't be able to have babies, either. It's impossible to know what the future could hold.

And so I have to live in the what-is and not in the what-could-be.

And right now, in this moment, I love Harrison. And whether he wants to admit it or not, he needs me. And I won't give up on him. Not yet.

I take a tentative step forward. "I know that I'll never understand what you're going through," I say quietly. "But you don't have to go through it alone. I won't let you. I can't."

He turns now, away from me. He stares at Jane Pauley and I wonder if this is it. If he's going to tell me to leave.

But he doesn't say anything. He just lifts up the blanket he's lying under, and I take it for the cue that it is, before he changes his mind. I slide onto the cushion, sidling up next to him, inhaling his piney deodorant, inhaling him. I lay my head on his chest and lace my fingers into his left hand, around his ring finger where I know, beneath his wedding band, he has one tiny word tattooed: MIA.

■ ■ ■ ■

When his father wakes up, Harrison helps move him to the recliner in the sunroom and I spend the afternoon letting Del order me around with household chores. She doesn't let me cook, but I am able to deliver food to the guys as they stare at golf, both dozing on and off until dinner.

That night, Harrison and I lie in the double bed in his childhood bedroom, his feet dangling off the end, his trumpet case still on the dresser where we left it years ago.

"Do you know the worst part?" Harrison whispers into the still night air.

I turn slightly toward him.

"It's not his mother's screams or the sound of the machine flatlining or anything like that. It's these little thoughts that catch me out of nowhere — these mundane every-day actions that the living perform and the dead do not. Like eating a banana or watching golf or feeling the sun's rays warm on your arms. Noah will never do any of those things. Not anymore. And it's my fault."

"Oh, Harrison," I breathe. And then we lie there in silence again, me trying to think of something, anything to say that can make him feel better, that can ease his pain. And then I remember a blog post I read, "8 Things to Say to Someone Who's Grieving," and one of them was to share a similar story of your own.

"Did I ever tell you about the salamander?" I say, my voice soft, quiet. We're both staring at the popcorn ceiling now. "We caught one once, me and Viv, in the backyard. And she told me how their tails grow back if they lose them. So I put the salamander in a shoebox and got a little plastic shovel out of the garage. And I cut its tail off. I ran back a couple hours later so excited to see its brand-new tail, but it didn't have one." I pause. "It was dead. I was so distraught, I cried for four days straight."

The story hangs in the air and telling it dredges up all the guilt and sadness I felt.

"Mia," Harrison says.

"Yeah."

"Are you trying to compare killing a lizard to killing a child?"

When he puts it like that, it sounds stupid.

"No! No, I . . ." I say. And then: "Yeah. I was."

And now that I think about it, that article might have been "8 Things NOT to Say to Someone Who's Grieving."

"Wow," he says.

We lie there, me berating myself, until I suddenly feel the bed gently shaking and then it grows stronger and I realize it's Harrison's shoulders. I look over to see that he's laughing. Hysterically.

"Harrison?"

"You know . . ." he chokes out between guffaws, "for a sensitive artist type . . . you're appallingly . . . bad at this."

And then the laughter turns into tears, and this, I understand.

I wrap myself around him, my arms and legs like octopus tentacles, trying to hold him together, while he's falling apart. Harrison tilts his head toward mine. And we sit there, connected temple to temple, until it feels like we are one — I inhale and his lungs fill up with oxygen.

Later, when he's spent and near sleep, I remember what his mom said when I showed up that morning. "Hey," I whisper, propping up on one elbow to face him.

"Hm?"

"What does *Te tomó bastante tiempo* mean?" I ask, recalling his mother's words to me on the porch.

He pauses, calculating the translation to English. "Took you long enough."

I close my eyes and tilt my head back in

understanding. I think of the babies we lost. I think of Oliver. I think of how long Harrison has been hurting. I don't know if he will ever not be hurting. If he will ever recover — if our relationship will survive. But in that moment, I do know one thing for sure. I open my eyes and look right at Harrison. "No. It took me too long."

CHAPTER 27

Harrison goes back to work the first week of October.

It took a lot of long, meandering conversations and prodding in the weeks after we returned from his parents' house, but he finally reached out to one of his professors from Emory, who has been talking to him via phone and email. He hasn't said much about their conversations, but curiosity compelled me to ask to read one.

> We all make mistakes. There is no surgeon alive that won't do something dumb that causes the loss of a life. Every procedure, by nature, is a risk. Human error is one of those risks — but should one patient's death keep you from saving other lives? You are an excellent doctor, Harrison, and this may sound like tough love, but not only do I think you should move forward in your career, you have an obliga-

tion to do so. You have the skill and potential to save many lives, and one devastating mistake doesn't absolve you of living up to that responsibility.

I think that one in particular helped, because one week he was talking about maybe quitting medicine altogether and doing something stress-free like opening a running-gear store or going to culinary school and the next he got up one morning, put on his shirt and bow tie and went in to the hospital.

He still walks heavy, shoulders hunched, the pain, though maybe a touch lighter than it once was, still weighing him down. And I catch him at times, in private moments, holding a jar of spaghetti sauce or frozen in midtie of his shoe or staring out the window at nothing. And I know he's thinking about Noah. I know he'll always think about Noah, that he'll never forget. But I so hope he can forgive.

The second week in October, I stand at the edge of the garden, staring at a row of tall green heads of romaine lettuce. I should be filled with pride at my gardening victory, but all I can think about is Oliver. I want to call him, boast to him about my accomplishment. But I won't. I think instead of the letter I left along with his suit jacket on Caroline's front porch the morning I drove to Buffalo. I try to picture him reading it — his face as understanding dawns at my words. That I didn't know what the intersection of our lives meant, but that I couldn't dwell on it any longer. That I couldn't reside in the unknown. *I love my husband,* I wrote, and though of that I was certain, of everything else, in the weeks since I left the letter, I was less so.

I still wonder; I can't help it. Every morning I wake up from a vivid dream of him. Or in the middle of a sleepless night, when the words Isak said crawl into my mind and linger like a broken record without an off switch: *He give you baby.* Or every time I pass a pregnant woman in line at the Giant or at the drugstore or walking down the streets of Hope Springs and I nearly double over from the potent mix of pain and jealousy. That little voice whispers: *Did I do the right thing?*

The third week in October, I wake one Saturday morning to find Harrison's face hovering over mine. His hands clasp my cheeks and I blink, my tongue glued to the roof of my mouth with rubber cement. The dream I'd been in the middle of comes rushing back to me in flashes. It was the carnival again, the carousel music, the flashing lights; Oliver was there.

Oliver.

I try to push the image of him from my mind. To put him back in his rightful place as an enigma, a man I knew once, like an ex-boyfriend who is not an ex-boyfriend. But I'm finding as the weeks go on, he is not so easily put away.

I focus on my husband's face, his eyelashes centimeters from mine.

"Wake up," he whispers to my nose. "Let's go paddleboarding."

"Yeah?" I say, searching his eyes.

"Yeah," he says.

We rent the boards from a tiny outfit along the Delaware and Harrison turns down the class that's being offered to teach us how to actually use them. "I've got you," he says when I balk.

And he does. He's patient and calm, and though I'm nervous, balancing on the board is much easier than I thought it would be. I catch on quickly and we start moving at a good clip, the only sound our paddles splashing in the still water. It's a beautiful morning, the air crisp with fall, the sun shining bright against the cloudless sky.

Harrison points out an egret on the bank to the right of us. I look just in time to see it spread its long wings out and silently take off in flight.

We're so busy staring at it that I don't notice my paddleboard drifting toward his until it's too late. They collide, the resulting tremor throwing both of us off balance, and there's nothing to hold on to in order to steady myself. We reach for each other out of instinct and then both go tumbling into the water, the sudden cold of it taking my breath. I come up sputtering and my eyes find Harrison, water trickling off his head, beading up in his beard.

But instead of the shock I'm feeling that I expect to see mirrored on his own face, he's smiling, an ear-to-ear grin that is so genuine it steals my breath all over again.

Because after months of searching, of looking for him, suddenly there he is. My Harrison. Who knows every lyric to Whitney Houston's "I Wanna Dance with Somebody." And thinks *Road House* is one of the greatest movies ever created. And wears bow ties daily because in med school on his gynecological rotation, he wore a regular tie and forgot to flip it over his back while examining a patient. *Let's just say I had to throw away the tie,* he said to me one night, after sex, back when we preferred whispering secrets to each other, long into the night, over sleep.

I grin back at him, and then as if he remembers himself, the smile slowly disappears and the lines return to his forehead, around his mouth. "You OK?" he asks.

"Yeah," I say. He heaves himself back up onto his board, and so I do, too, but the joy doesn't leave my face quite as quickly as his. I burn the image of him smiling into my brain, and know that I will patiently wait to see glimpses of my husband again.

And I see them. I do. Random moments throughout November — an eye twinkle here, a laugh there, a joke even — a joke! — that had Finley and Griffin in stitches at Thanksgiving. Vivian caught my eyes and smiled.

The first week of December, I am in the bathtub and hear the front door open. "In here," I call out to Harrison. It's only seven, but he's been coming home earlier recently and I'm trying not to get spoiled, while relishing the luxury of extra time spent with him.

"Hi," he says when his body fills the doorframe of our bathroom. He's flushed, grinning, and I stare up at him curiously. "I had a good day," he says.

"You had a good day," I repeat.

He nods and I can't help but return his smile, get infected by his happiness.

"Come here," I say, and when he gets close enough, I reach up for the buttons of his shirt, clutch the material in my hands and pull him toward me, his lips toward mine, and I kiss him fully, roundly. I kiss him until we're both lost, and then whether I pull him over the edge or he rolls over it is unclear, but suddenly he's in the bath with me, his shirt and pants drenched by the water. We keep kissing, both pretending it's comfortable — the slipping and knocking of knees and elbows on the hard porcelain — until we can't pretend any longer. And then he stands up, taking half the tub of water with him, and he picks me up like I'm light as air and takes me to the bed and I let him and I'm laughing and crying because I know in that moment that though my husband came home months ago, he is finally home.

CHAPTER 28

It's one of those perfect almost-winter days. The sky is a radiant blue, the sun merely a decorative ornament of yellow — it does nothing to change the cold, crisp air of the afternoon. The first snow fell two days ago, just a few inches, and pockets of it remain, hugging the bottoms of lampposts, slippery stubborn patches on the sidewalk that refuse to melt. We're standing in front of the True Value, watching our breath come out in big puffs. Harrison holds my gloved hand in his and I catch him staring at me for the third time in as many minutes. "What? Do I have something on my face?"

"No, can't a man gaze at his wife?"

"I guess. It just feels like you're laughing at me or something."

"Never. Just thinking how beautiful you are." He studies me. "Your cheeks are extra rosy."

"It's this freaking wind!" I stamp my feet

414

trying to warm up. "I don't know why I ever thought Hope Springs wasn't as cold as Philadelphia."

He wraps his arms around me. "I would go get us hot chocolate, but Gabriel would never forgive me if I missed him."

We are at the Hope Springs Christmas parade, though it's more of a festival — a holiday extravaganza — with thousands of tiny white lights and a lineup of activities after the parade: a choir performance and a Santa appearance, even fireworks. When we got the flyer in the mail, I left it on the counter. I wasn't sure if Harrison would feel up to coming, but he said he promised Gabriel at Whitney's last checkup and here we are.

We wait on the sidewalk, watching the baton twirlers and a man on stilts throwing candy to the children lined up along the route, followed by train of convertible cars, one carrying the waving mayor, one a local real estate celebrity and one a woman in a crown and lipstick, her fur shrug covering the banner across her chest, rendering it unclear what pageant she has bested.

We hear it before we see it, the marching band, enthusiastically out of tune. Four dozen ruddy cheeks peeking out from beneath the brims of their stiff hats. Harrison spots Gabriel in the back, his tongue pressed firmly between his lips as he concentrates on the rhythm of his sticks on the drum.

Harrison is smiling at the boy and he catches a glimpse of Harrison and smiles back, stumbling a bit and missing a beat. I watch them, my husband and this boy, and I am no longer cold. The hope of what could still be warms me.

After the parade, we walk around, buying a bag of spiced nuts and hot chocolate, and then when we get closer to the town square, Gabriel comes flying at us, his eyes bright with excitement. Whitney trails him, trying to keep up.

"You came!"

"I said I would."

"I messed up when I saw you."

"I thought you did great."

"Hi, there." Whitney offers a kind smile and a small wave when she reaches us.

"Hi," I reply, but Gabriel is still chattering on about the night's festivities ahead of us, Santa and the fireworks.

"And did you see?" he says. "In the town square? It's a carousel!"

CHAPTER 29
OLIVER

It doesn't matter where he's been — a mountain eco-lodge in Peru or a high-rise condo in Khartoum — Philadelphia always looks dirtier when he returns, as if an extra layer of dust has settled over the city, clinging to the buildings, the sidewalks, even the windshield of the Impala he's in — an ancient model driven by a kid that doesn't look old enough to drive, much less work for Uber.

Oliver stares out the window, at a businesswoman in a skirt suit and sneakers rushing past, a kid on a skateboard weaving in and out of pedestrians, a homeless man with matted white hair muttering to himself, and wonders, *Why do I continue living here? What's holding me to this city?* The answer is nothing, save habit, and maybe his own apathy.

When the Uber comes to a stop in front of his apartment building, he grabs his oversize duffel bag out of the trunk and heaves it onto his back. Flanked by a sushi place to the left and a palm reader to the right, the familiar glass front door to his building looks exactly as he left it months ago — a spiderweb crack in the center that maintenance has yet to fix. Rita, the palm reader, stands guard at her usual position, eyeing him and holding a Virginia Slim, as he digs his keys out of his jeans pocket and unlocks the front door. "When you coming to see your future, boy," she drawls in her indeterminate island accent, which he's fairly certain is a put-on, and then blows out a never-ending exhale of smoke.

"You should know," Oliver replies, completing their once-every-few-weeks exchange, and just like that, it feels like he hasn't been gone at all. She cuts her eyes away and he slips in the door, greeted by the familiar warm stench of dead fish that wafts over from the sushi place next door. He goes through the foyer where the mailboxes are and to the stairs, which he takes two at a time, despite the extra weight of belongings on his back — and he thinks of Mia.

He hoped the distance between here and Finland would lessen the connection he felt, but unfortunately, it traveled well. Perhaps it would have helped if he had thrown out her letter after he got it, instead of taking it with him, rereading it ad nauseam, as if the words would change on the eighth, ninth or tenth evaluation.

He unlocks the dead bolt to his apartment and drops his bag as soon as he walks in the door. He meanders over to the kitchen counter, where his neighbor has left stacks of mail — mostly bills and advertising circulars. The red dot on the base of his cordless phone is blinking wildly, alerting him to messages. He needs to listen to them. Sort the mail. Shave. Unpack.

He casts his gaze around the apartment and it falls on the open doorway to his bedroom, where he can see the corner of his bed as he left it — sheets and coverlet haphazardly pulled up toward the top. All he really wants to do is crawl in and sleep for the next four days.

But he can't do any of those things.

He promised Caroline.

He puts a pot of coffee on to brew, peels off his shirt and gets in the shower, trying not to wonder if Mia will also be at the parade.

"Your belly!" Oliver says two hours later, after he's parked and maneuvered through the hordes of people in downtown Hope Springs to finally find his sister. She looks professional in all black — pants, gloves and an overcoat that does nothing to conceal how round her stomach has grown. She clutches a walkie-talkie in one hand and is speaking into it when he approaches her. After she lets go of the button and listens to the satisfactory response, she lets it hang by her side as she throws her free hand around Oliver's neck and squeezes.

"Did you see the parade?"

"Caught the tail end of it. Very impressive," he says and he means it. "All of this, Care, really."

She beams. Then punches him in the arm. "I missed you. How was Finland?"

"Fine," Oliver says. He doesn't tell her he couldn't sleep at night for the nightmares about Mia. Or that, during the day, he saw her everywhere.

In the dog park, she was in a beige sundress and a pair of large round sunglasses calling to a droopy one-eyed beagle.

She was the dark-haired girl in tennis shoes and a flowing skirt riding a bicycle with a spray of flowers in the basket.

When he stopped at a café in Helsinki for a sweet bun, she was taking orders behind the counter, a pencil stuck behind her ear, a wad of gum tucked in her cheek.

He can't explain it — he knew it was the right thing, for her to be with her husband. But then, it felt right for them to be together, too. And he misses her, or he misses what could have been. He's not sure if there's a difference between those two sentiments. And the missing isn't an absence, as the word connotes, but a presence. A constant that he feels with his whole body. The same way he felt when his mother died. His eyes flick to the swarms of people around them, looking for her without meaning to.

"Have you been to the square yet?"

Oliver focuses back on his sister. "No, I just got here. Why, what's going on there?"

"It's the coup de grace!"

He stares at her, amused. "I don't think that means what you think it means."

She narrows her eyes. "It's, like, the main event, right?"

"No, it's more like the final blow in a fight to the death that kills someone. Like that scene in *Game of Thrones* when the Mountain stuffs his fingers into Oberyn Martell's eyes, blood gushing everywhere, crushing his skull."

Her face twists in disgust. "I do not watch that show. And no, that's not what I meant. Although the kids might die with excitement when they see it."

"Are you ever going to tell me what it is?"

"I'm telling you now! There was this amusement park in Altoona that was closing, and they were selling all of their rides and everything. So I got some of them for the town square! It will be like a real carnival! Well, for tonight, anyway. The carousel is the only thing that will permanently stay here. The bumper cars and the Tilt-A-Whirl have to go back. I just rented them."

Oliver doesn't move at first. He can't, as if he's frozen in place, as if he's in a dream. *A carousel,* he wants to say. *A Tilt-A-Whirl.* But his mouth is dry and everything has stopped or is in slow motion or isn't real. And then, just like that, he snaps out of it with an unnatural sounding yelp, panic blinding him, climbing up his throat.

He thinks of Mia.

And then he starts running.

WHITNEY

"So what do you do?" Whitney asks Harrison's wife, Mia, as they wait for Harrison and Gabriel to be done with their carousel ride. Mia seems awfully quiet and Whitney wonders if she's stuck up or just has some kind of social anxiety.

"I teach art," Mia says, never taking her eyes off the carousel a dozen yards in front of them, even though there's a crowd of people waiting in line, obscuring the view of the actual riders.

"Oh, what grade?"

"Huh?" Mia asks, her gaze flitting to Whitney. "Oh, uh — to adults. It's like a continuing education thing. At Fordham."

"Cool," Whitney says. "I'd love to get information on your next session." She's been looking for something like that — new hobbies to expand her horizons, like learning Italian or taking an improv class or a cake-decorating seminar. Things she always

423

thought about doing when she was married to Eli, but never did for one reason or another. She didn't even realize how confined she had felt until she left him and suddenly didn't have to consider his (often strong) opinions on her life.

Mia doesn't respond and the two women stand in silence, while Whitney tries to think of something else to ask her. That's when she looks up and sees him.

Eli.

He's standing near the hot chocolate stand in his beige jacket that she ordered him from the Land's End catalog. She remembers how she took it out of the mail slip and laid it on their bed, and when he saw it that evening, instead of saying "thank you," he said, *I thought I told you I wanted the blue one.* And she apologized. She hates that she apologized.

Now, she feels a mix of irritation and apprehension. That's the problem with small towns. And divorce. Every time you leave the house, there's a risk of running into the person you're running from.

But then, he looks directly at her, and she sees his eyes, blank, emotionless. And she knows. She has seen that look before. And all she can think is: *Gabriel.* The judge just awarded her custody and she knows it hurt

Eli. He cried in the courthouse, his face turning purple with rage. And she was afraid this would happen. That he would come for her son. She knows the statistics. Most children are kidnapped by someone they know — most often a disgruntled parent stemming from a custody dispute. She frantically scans the crowd in the direction Harrison walked off with her son. Are they still in line for the carousel? Did they make it on the ride already? But she doesn't see them anywhere.

"Whitney, are you OK?" Mia asks. Whitney doesn't respond.

Panicked, she looks back at Eli.

And that's when she sees the gun.

And strangely, she thinks of her sister Holly. How Holly always laughs at her when they watch crime dramas because Whitney is never able to pin the bad guy. It's always a surprise up until the very end. And suddenly she understands.

CAROLINE

Where is he going? Caroline wonders. Her brother took off so suddenly, right in the middle of their conversation, and he had the weirdest look on his face. She starts to follow him, but then a voice crackles over her walkie-talkie. She's needed at the stage. Kelvin can't remember if Santa goes on before the choir or after and the microphones aren't working properly, so maybe no one can go onstage. And Caroline sighs because she knows she planned it all, but does she really have to do *everything?*

Halfway to the town square, she hears the popping. *No!* They weren't supposed to start the fireworks this early. She looks up to the sky, but all she sees is a bright blue, the sun just starting its afternoon descent — not a star or moon to be found. And not one firework.

OLIVER

He sees Mia first. Or maybe that's not accurate. Maybe he sees everything else first, the crowds of people milling about, the carousel right next to the Tilt-A-Whirl, exactly as he's seen it before, inexplicably, in his dreams. But once he spots her, she's all he can see. But he's too far away. Then there is a loud sound like popcorn popping right next to his ear and some part of him knows it is not popcorn.

He runs as fast as he can, pushing people aside, people who are starting to understand that they have not been hearing popcorn, either, and they all start to scream and scatter in opposite directions like a frightened flock of birds. He doesn't slow down, not even when he's reached her, seeing the terror in her eyes up close. He shields her body with his, half a second before a searing pain rips into his shoulder like a white-hot metal poker, the force of it all crashing them both

427

to the ground.

And then, time passes. Whether it's thirty seconds or thirty minutes he's not sure. But the popcorn is no longer popping and the air is still. He lifts his head and sees one man in uniform and then a dozen and he can't help but think they are too late.

MIA

I knew it was the carousel the second I saw it. The one from Lakemont. And to the right was the blue Tilt-A-Whirl and I felt light-headed and terrified all at once. But Gabriel was bouncing with delight, and Harrison was beaming, and I couldn't think of a reason in the world to explain why I didn't want them to go on the ride together. So I stood there rooted to the sidewalk, listening to Whitney, and tried to come up with a reason we had to leave the instant they got back.

I'm sick. That was what I planned to say, and it wasn't even a lie because I was — nauseated with a fear, a knowing that I couldn't name.

And that was when Whitney gasped beside me and I followed her gaze to a man I vaguely recognized. It was the man from Sorelli's. Whitney's ex-husband who had made a scene.

She clutched my hand and suddenly I couldn't tell my fear from hers.

The first bullet hit Whitney in her right shoulder. And then I heard a second pop — or was it the first? Did she get hit before I heard it?

But everything was happening too quickly to react.

And then I saw Oliver. *Oliver?*

One second he wasn't there and then he was, and I was falling and people were screaming and I hit my head with a loud thud on the cement and I couldn't move and for some reason I started counting the shots as if I was going to be quizzed on it later.

Three (or is it two?).

Four.

Five.

Six.

Seven.

When I get to eight, everything goes quiet.

I look to my right and see Whitney lying on the ground beside me, a bloom of red on her shoulder, a splatter of it on her face. I close my eyes and turn to the left and that's when I see the top of a familiar head level on the ground with me. But I can't see his body.

I try to push Oliver off of me but his body

is so heavy and all I can do is scream Harrison's name. And so I do. I scream like all the words I have spoken, have shouted, have yelled my entire life were merely vocal cord practice for this one moment. I scream with everything I have. And when I finally am free, when Oliver has rolled off of me or I have somehow managed to push him off, I get to my knees and I see Harrison's red fleece and I try to stand to go to him, but my legs buckle because I remember that the fleece he put on this morning was gray.

HARRISON

Harrison wants to sit up, but there is a fire in his chest, his arm, his leg. It's a wildfire, hot and all-consuming, and it's hard to think of anything else but the urgent pain of it all. He tries to block it out, blinking at Gabriel, who is lying on the ground beneath him, whimpering. He's not immediately sure how he got there. It all happened so fast. The carousel came to a stop and they got off and were walking back to Mia and Whitney when he saw the man, and he saw the gun. Harrison stepped in front of Gabriel. Not consciously, he wasn't trying to play the hero, it was just like some innate instinct took over.

And now, he's on the ground lying on top of the boy, vaguely aware of the screaming and chaos around him and a warm wetness on his chest and he wonders briefly if Gabriel wet himself. "It's OK," Harrison says, though he isn't sure anything is OK. He

432

isn't even sure if he spoke the words out loud or just in his mind.

And then he glances down and sees the wetness is red and it's coming from the burning in his chest and he starts to feel light-headed. It reminds him of Noah. The blood that was everywhere.

He thinks of the days, weeks, months that he wanted to die for what he did. That he felt he deserved to.

But then: *Mia.*

He doesn't know if he said that out loud, either. But the word fills his mouth and then his body, the way her presence fills a room, the world.

With great effort and agony, he slowly rolls off the boy and turns his head to where he left her, with Whitney, but she's not there. And suddenly he's desperate in his need to see her. Did she run? Is she hurt? He tries again to lift himself up, but his body screams back at him, willfully disobeying his commands. He grimaces in pain and closes his eyes.

And then he hears her. Through the din of everything happening around him, he hears a keening, a primal wail that he's never heard before but still instantly recognizes as Mia. It's being carried to him like a gift on the breeze. It's his name, in her voice, drawn out, as if being played by a clarinet. A saxophone. A harmonica.

He wants to call back to her, but can't. He can't even open his eyes.

But he sees her anyway.

In a yellow wrap dress with pink barrettes in her hair. In cream lace walking to the beat of that awful Peter Cetera song. In a heap on the cement floor of her studio. And then in nothing at all, which has always been his favorite way to see her, if he's being completely honest. He sees her face, wearing a thousand different expressions, each one a contortion of her eyes and nose and mouth that is as instantly recognizable as his own name. He has a vague thought that he's hallucinating. He's lost too much blood. And then another vague thought that his life is flashing before his eyes, even as he thinks how ridiculous that is, that it's something that only happens in those terribly cheesy movies she loves, but how it also actually makes perfect sense because his life is Mia.

She is the only thing worth living for.

It's romantic, the sentiment, and it surprises him because romance has never been one of his strengths. And now he wishes he had thought it before this moment, said it to her out loud. Surely he has, though, right? He's said so many words to her over the collection of their hours, days, months, years together. But for some reason, he can't recall any of those words just now. All he can remember is the first time she told him she loved him. She didn't mean to say it. It slipped out on the way back from that wedding they went to in Maine. When they were pulled off in the emergency lane of the highway and she was hanging her head out the door, vomiting bile because she had nothing left in her stomach. He was rubbing her back and it came out in a little groan. "OhIloveyou." At first he thought she was still drunk and not sure what she was saying, but then she turned her head and looked directly at him, her face paler than usual, dark circles under her big round eyes. "I do. I love you." She said it as though it were a simple fact she was stating, but it was one that amazed him. Like learning that ninety percent of the earth's oceans haven't yet been explored. Mind-boggling. Overwhelming.

He was too shocked to say it back. But he wishes he had. He wishes he could tell her now. "I love you, too." But he's tired and just wants to sleep. When he wakes up, he'll say it. How he'd do anything for her. Give her anything she wanted. He thinks of his

Ita when he was a boy and would ask for a pastelito, and she'd sneak several onto his plate when his mother wasn't looking. That's what he'll say to Mia: *You want a baby? I'll give you ten!*

But for now he smiles at her — the Mia from today with the wind-whipped cheeks — one last time, and hopes that she knows.

CHAPTER 30

I am sitting on a hard chair in the ER waiting room. Waiting. Caroline and her large belly wait beside me and we are holding hands, but we're not speaking. The electronic doors keep sliding open, as people enter and leave, allowing gusts of cold air in. I hear snippets of conversation from other people milling around, clutching foam coffee cups, as I play a weird mind game trying to line up the number of gunshots I counted to their destinations.

One to Whitney.

One to Oliver.

Three to Harrison.

There are three unaccounted for but I don't care because *three to Harrison.*

We've been there for hours, beneath the fluorescent lights, watching the night fall outside. I try to think of the last words Harrison said to me and I can't, and that's how I know he'll be OK. Every time someone talks about a loved one dying, they repeat the last words that person said to them, and I can't do that, so they weren't the last words.

A woman in a police uniform approaches us, asking for a statement about what happened, and it's the same question I've been asking over and over. What happened? Why didn't I grab Harrison as soon as I saw the carousel? I could have said any number of things — I'm sleepy, I don't feel good, I want to go home. We could be home, right now. Watching *Wheel of Fortune* and eating ice cream out of the carton.

Finally, a doctor in mint-green scrubs walks up to us and I know his name is Leong and I know someone is dead because Leong's face is long and I think this is funny until I think it might be Harrison and then *God help me* I hope with everything in me that it's Caroline who will be getting the bad news.

And I know she's thinking the same about me, because she drops my hand. Leong comes to a stop in front of me.

"Harrison sustained gunshot wounds to the upper thigh, right arm and chest," he says. His mouth keeps moving, but I cannot hear the words coming out of it. I can't hear anything. And I wonder if I'm having a stroke.

Or no — maybe *I've* been shot.

Maybe that's where the last three bullets went. I must have been shot, but for some reason I couldn't feel it until just now. I open my mouth to tell Leong, to tell someone, but no words come out. And then I do hear something. One sentence. And then another.

We did everything we could. I'm sorry to tell you, he died.

And that's when I know the weapon that has attacked me is not a gun.

It's a cleaver, and it has split me wide open.

I am butterflied.

And everything goes silent once again.

I always thought grief was a loud, noisy affair of keening and wailing and sobbing. The way I rocked in the fetal position every time I lost a baby. But it's not. At least not always.

It's an empty stillness.

My memories of the moments, hours, days after that evening are a silent movie reel. I remember faces in the hospital, Caroline, Leong, Gabriel. But they were alive. Harrison's looked like a mannequin spackled to the dimensions of himself.

I kissed it anyway. And then I put my hand gingerly on his shoulder and realized he was cold, even though he had a blanket pulled up to his armpits. So I crawled up on the metal tray that held his body and wrapped him up, as I'd done so many times in our life together, lending him my body heat. I tucked my head under his chin, feeling the bristles of his beard on my forehead, and closed my eyes. I slipped my hand in his and lay beside him and I wouldn't leave. Not even when my sister showed up. I don't remember vomiting, but I remember the putrid scent of it filling my nose, clinging to my shirt.

And I thought of the first time I told Harrison I loved him. And I vomited again.

I remember sitting on a pew of a church I'd never been inside. The air smelled a little bit musty like a retirement home and there were men in elaborate robes and I realized it was a Catholic church, even though Harrison wasn't even Catholic anymore.

I remember seeing Oliver, his arm glued to his body by a white and navy sling. As he walked toward me outside, I thought vaguely I should say something to him for saving my life, but when he got close, all the fury I'd been saving up at myself, the world, came rushing forward and I lunged at him, screaming: "Why me? Why didn't you save *him?*" I may have punched him, or tried to. Somebody grabbed my arm.

But mostly I remember the silence. As if when Harrison left this world, he packed sound in a suitcase and took it with him, tucked under his arm. And I wish he had packed me instead.

I sleep all day and lie awake all night, and though I know there are people in my house, none of the people are Harrison and I can't be bothered to care. It occurs to me that after my outburst at the church I am probably on some kind of suicide watch and I want to tell them all it's OK. I may want to die, but I don't have the energy to kill myself.

One day I wake up, and I hear something. The pots and pans banging in the kitchen. Voices whisper-arguing. The television tuned to *Daniel Tiger.* And it's too much. I need everything to be quiet again, but I'm not sure my voice will work.

I swing my legs out of bed and stand up. I go over to the dresser and dig to the bottom of the middle drawer for my old athletic pants. I don't even know what I'm doing until I'm walking through my kitchen, ignoring the sympathetic gapes of my sister, my mother. I stop briefly when I see her. Mom? I knew she came for the funeral, but I assumed she left.

Outside, I walk past the garden and keep going, until I'm standing at the start of the dirt path in the woods, my feet tucked in a pair of Toms — the closest thing I have to athletic shoes. I peer into the canopy of naked trees, not sure what I'm looking for. And then I know.

I'm looking for my husband.

The Harrison whose feet pounded this same path over and over, running for miles but never getting anywhere.

I take off running, slowing to a trot within minutes. My foot catches on a protruding tree root and I go sprawling in the dirt, a lightning rod of pain shooting up my ankle.

I lie there for a minute, belly in the brush, trying to catch my breath. I look back at the offending tree, then up at the blue between the branches.

This is why I don't run. I want to say it out loud. To somebody. To Harrison. I want to hear him laugh the way he used to, so loud and deep that I swear I could feel the vibration of it in my bones.

I scream into the forest, at the trees, startling the squirrels and a few birds. And

I pretend he can hear me. But I know he can't.

My husband is gone.

I bang in the back door, hobbling on my left foot, gritting my teeth in pain.

"Mia? Oh my god. Are you OK?"

"Let me get you some ice."

"Are you hungry? Someone named Rebecca dropped off a hummingbird cake."

"A few people have called for you. I've been taking messages."

I hear all of these words and wish I had the silence back. I limp to my room and into my closet and I stare at Harrison's clothes. And then I start to put them on. I stuff my arms into Harrison's blue dress shirt, my legs into his trousers, and ankle still throbbing, I sink to the ground, burying my head in the stiff fabric of the shirt, soaking it with my tears.

"Heard you could use this," a familiar voice says from the doorway. I lift my head to see Raya holding a bag of frozen peas. She walks over and lowers herself down beside me, gently pressing the cold against my foot.

"Wrong one." I take the bag and lay it on my injured ankle and then I lay my head down in her lap and she strokes my hair. I notice my phone in her other hand and a piece of paper and I realize it was her voice that said I had messages.

My eyes are drawn back to my cell phone again and my heart thumps an extra beat. I grab it from Raya and sit up, the drumbeat in my chest picking up its pace. I thumb through the screen, ignoring all my missed calls and text messages and going straight to my voice mails. I scroll through, my eyes intently searching for Harrison's name. When it doesn't appear, I click on the deleted messages. He rarely called — we communicated either in person or via text — but surely, *surely* I have an old voice mail in here somewhere. Telling me to grab more granola bars at the store or that he'll be three hours late coming home or even a *Saw that you called; trying you back.* All I want in that moment is to hear his voice, saying something banal, something to keep him here. With me. In one last halfhearted attempt, I call his number. It rings four times and, clutching the phone to my ear, I listen, holding my breath in the empty beat before the familiar robotic intonation states: *Your call has been forwarded to an automated voice message system.*

I resist the urge to chuck it across the room, and thrust it back at Raya instead.

She palms it, and as if by magic, the phone comes alive in her hand. For half a second, I allow myself to believe the impossible — that it's Harrison calling me back. I glance at the screen and see a number I don't recognize.

"Do you want me to get it?" she asks.

"Please," I say, closing my eyes, swallowing the bile creeping up my throat at the realization that Harrison's voice is gone. As gone as he is. "Just pretend to be me."

So she does. I hold Harrison's sleeve up to my nose again, only realizing now that it smells too much like detergent and I should have picked one from the dirty clothes basket. I sit up in a panic — what if someone did the laundry? I crawl over to the hamper in the corner of the room on my knees, leaving the ice pack behind, my right ankle throbbing with each movement. When I reach it, I turn the entire thing upside down, dumping all the contents out. The first few articles of clothing I paw through are mine, and my panic ratchets up to a ten.

"Mia?" Raya says.

"Yeah?" I'm throwing clothes over my shoulder.

"Did you give blood at the hospital?"

"Huh?" And then I spy it, a white undershirt with dark stains at the armpits from him wearing it so much. Relief floods my limbs as I hold it up to my nose and inhale my husband. I consider Raya's question. "Yeah, I guess I did." I remember it was Caroline's idea. That we should do something while we waited. Something to help. But then, she couldn't even give blood and it was just me, with a futile needle in my arm, not helping anything.

"That was the blood bank."

"Mm-hm," I say, and I lie down on the hardwood floor and ball up the shirt so I can tuck it under my head and pretend I'm lying on his chest.

"Apparently they run some tests to make sure your blood is safe to use."

" 'K," I say. I'm too tired to say I don't care if they use it or not because it can't save Harrison, so what's it matter? I just want her to leave, and then think maybe if I ask her a question, it will speed up the conversation and she will do just that. And then it occurs to me, belatedly, that they must have found something in the blood, or they wouldn't be calling. "What — do I have AIDS or something? Hepatitis?" And I laugh a little, when I realize that I wouldn't care even a little bit if I did.

She's silent for a few beats.

"You're pregnant."

CHAPTER 31

Everyone makes a fuss about the pregnancy.

Vivian comes up for the first appointment and watches the grainy heartbeat on the screen when I cannot.

"Don't get attached," I say. "It's not going to stay."

One afternoon, Del shows up on my front stoop, though I can't remember agreeing to her visit, and she spends three days cooking and filling my freezer with ropa vieja and picadillo and a lentil stew that was Harrison's favorite. "You don't have to do this," I repeat for the third time, as she stands at the stove, wooden spoon in one hand, the other on her hip. She cuts her eyes to me and raises one eyebrow. "What's this baby going to eat? You going to cook?"

I don't have the heart to tell her what I told Vivian.

Then, in February, two people show up at once — a man in a florist van with a spray of hydrangeas and Rebecca, Foster's wife, carrying a cardboard box of Harrison's things from his office. "I thought you'd want these," she says. She puts the flowers on the kitchen island and makes a pot of tea — I didn't even know I had tea — and we sit on the teal barstools while she talks. I don't think I say one word, but she doesn't let that stop her. She tells me about her grandbaby's first tooth and about Foster retiring soon and about the fashion show she's helping produce for the Junior League.

"Caroline had her baby," she says.

"Oh, I didn't realize you knew her."

"Small town." She shrugs. I realize even if she didn't know Caroline before, she'd know her now. Everyone probably knows of us all by virtue of what happened.

I know I should reach out to her. To Oliver. I still haven't apologized. Or thanked him.

"Do you know if her brother —"

"He stayed on for a little bit. To help. And then left. Somewhere out of the country, I think?"

"Oh," I say.

When Rebecca stands up later, she puts her hand over mine. "I do hope you'll come back to teach the class soon," she says. "The substitute has us painting a bowl of fruit."

I look at her, considering. "I'll be there on Wednesday," I say. Not because of the fruit, but because I need to get out of my house.

When Rebecca leaves, I take the box to the den and start pulling things from it: Harrison's Gollum bobblehead; the coffee mug I bought him for his birthday one year that says IT'S GOING TIBIA GREAT DAY; the Eagles Super Bowl Champs helmet paperweight he won in a bet against a colleague, a lifelong Patriots fan. I take my time, holding each item in my palm as if weighing its worth. And then — *then* — I spy it. Tucked in the bottom of the box, against the side, the slim beige rectangular device that was sometimes tossed along with his keys and wallet on the upturned cardboard box in the entryway or on the kitchen island or tucked in the side pocket of his laptop bag.

Harrison's Dictaphone.

I stare at it, my breath catching in my throat. It's a gift worth more than all of the others combined. Hurriedly, I gather the bobblehead and the cup and the paperweight and I go lie on our bed and curl around all of my husband's belongings. I take a deep breath and press play. Harrison's deep voice fills the room. *December third, two thousand eighteen. Carotid endarterectomy.* A mix of joy, grief and relief well up,

449

pricking the corners of my eyes. I close them and listen to my husband methodically describe every step of his final surgery. And then I listen to it again.

And again.

And again.

And at some point, I fall asleep wrapped in the cocoon of Harrison's steady voice.

The next day, I read the card that came with the flowers and learn they're from Whitney.

He saved my son. I will forever be in debt.

I stare at it, trying not to be alarmed at my brief but fervent wish that Gabriel had died instead of my husband.

I go out to my studio. Instead of painting, I draw. On the floor. Next to the tiny hand, I add a big hand and then a face and then another one. And then another one. Every face is Harrison's.

I think about moving. Back to Philadelphia. Maybe to Maryland, to be near Vivian and my dad. But then I'm back teaching my class every Wednesday and Rebecca starts showing up every week for tea and Raya drives up on her days off and Vivian keeps booking the next doctor appointments and coming in for them. In March, when the ground begins to thaw, I plant more greens in the garden. Swiss chard, this time, and broccoli, along with the spinach and lettuce.

And I tell myself it just feels like too much to change everything, but really, this is the last place I lived with Harrison and, ironically, it's now the only place that feels like home. And so I stay.

In April, I feel the baby kick, like the faint flapping of a wing, but it was there and I sit, stunned. But still, I hold my breath.

One day, the sun is a ball of fire in the sky, scorching the earth. My class has been out of session for weeks; the start of fall semester is closer than the end of spring. I can't get down on the floor in my studio anymore because my belly is too big, so I'm half perched on a stool — standing every few minutes to stretch my aching back — drawing on a sketchpad propped on an easel.

And that's when I hear it, the crunch of tires on the gravel in the driveway. At first I think it's probably a lost driver, or maybe a cable salesman trying to convince me to switch my provider.

I wait to see if whoever it is will just leave,

but I hear the car engine cut off and a door slam shut. Footfalls crunch the gravel now, instead of tires.

And somehow, I know.

Slowly, I wipe the charcoal off my hands on a rag and walk toward the studio's door, peering out the glass pane. The hood of the Prius gleams in the sun, confirming my prescience. I'm suddenly overwhelmed in my embarrassment that I haven't reached out before now. I thought about it — a few times. But something always stopped me. I hesitate now, only for a second, and then I turn the handle and step out into the day, squinting against the rays of bright sun.

"Oliver." His back is to me as he walks to the path toward the front door. He pauses, then twists his body toward the sound of my voice.

"Hi," he says. He's wearing a striped tank top with a pocket, army green pants, his Reef sandals. His hair is scruffier, his eyes still intense. And only then do I consider what I must look like. I'm wearing what I slept in — one of Harrison's undershirts, stretched tight across my belly, and leggings. My hair, a messy topknot at the crown of my head. If the roundness of my belly surprises him, it doesn't register on his face.

"I'm sorry," I say. "About the . . ." I'm

452

experiencing every emotion at once and they cloud my brain, make forming words an impossible task. A trickle of sweat crawls between my breasts. A plane flies far overhead, the distant hum of the engines the only sound in the air.

"I know," he says. "It's nothing."

"I heard you were out of the country."

"Costa Rica."

"Coffee farm?"

"Banana plantation."

And then we look at each other and I know I don't have to say anything else. I don't have to say how strange it is, the way the paths of our lives intersected. How neither of us could have ever guessed how it would have all turned out. How no one would ever believe us if we told them.

I don't have to say that sometimes I get confused. That because my nightmare about Oliver became reality, I start to wonder if Harrison was the dream. Not in the romantic way that people usually say that, but in that way when you wake up from a really good one and try so hard to capture the feeling you had while you were in it, to hold it. Like a moonbeam, a bolt of lightning. But it's fleeting; it dances in your peripheral, teasing you, and then it's gone. I can't remember what my husband feels like anymore. What he smells like. The timbre of his laugh. And sometimes I go to sleep hoping he is a dream, if only so that I can see him again.

The plane is gone now and Oliver is still here. "I won't stay long," he says. "I just wanted to make sure you were . . . OK."

I don't have to tell him that I am both OK and not sure I'll ever be OK again. So I just nod. "And you?"

He wiggles all the fingers on his right hand. "Almost good as new."

"I'm glad," I say. And then I ask after Caroline and find out she named her son Lewis. And I tell him I started taking a class, that I've decided to get my master's in education. And he tells me he's going back to Australia for his next trip. I ask him if he's just trying to break up with someone and he laughs.

"No. But the gun laws are quite a draw."

"Ah," I say. "Right."

We stare at each other another beat. And I think of the months we spent together trying to understand the how and why of it all. And how, strangely, I still don't have any of the answers. Why was Oliver in my life? I could say it was to save me, but then that begs the question: Why was Whitney in Harrison's life? One life was saved, only for another to be lost. And that's when I think maybe Harrison was right — maybe there's no rhyme or reason to it all. Maybe instead of wondering why we're all connected, what's important — the only thing that's important — is to know that we are.

"I'm working on a book. A novel," he says. "Another one. Figure it doesn't hurt to try again."

"Based on true events?"

"No," he says, chuckling. "You know that saying — truth is stranger than fiction."

"Yeah," I say, smiling. "Well, congratulations."

He shrugs. "We'll see if it goes anywhere."

I open my mouth to respond, to assure him it will, but a pain grips my belly. I clutch my stomach and grimace.

"What is it?" Oliver asks.

"The baby," I say, and the next pain almost brings me to my knees. "It's too early."

When we get to the ER, I'm in so much pain I can't even stand up. Oliver rushes in to get help and an orderly comes out pushing a wheelchair and somehow between the two of them they get me into it and the next thing I know I'm in a bright room with my feet in stirrups and a woman with a mask has her hand between my legs and is screaming for me not to push yet.

But I do anyway, because I can't not. Oliver squeezes my hand.

Another woman enters and the nurse holds out rubber gloves and she shoves her hands into them and I realize it's the doctor as she takes the nurse's place between my legs.

"It's too soon," I tell her.

"This baby doesn't seem to think so. How far along are you?" I try to think. To do math. It's the first week of August. How is it the first week of August already?

"Thirty-two weeks," I say.

She nods, but the wrinkles in her forehead deepen and I know she's concerned. And then I remember. That's how long Harrison's been gone.

"No, wait. I'm thirty-six weeks," I say. But still, I had a plan. Or Vivian did. She was going to come up, a week before my due date. Stay with me until I went into labor, drive me to the hospital. "It's not supposed to be like this."

Oliver squeezes my hand again and all I want is for it to be Harrison's hand. *It's not supposed to be like this.*

The doctor's expression relaxes as she peers between my legs. "There's the head," she says. "Keep pushing."

Fire rips through my groin and I feel the pressure build like a bottle of champagne that needs to be uncorked.

"I can't do this," I say. "I can't do this without him."

"You can," Oliver says. "Look at me." I do. "You can do this."

"Deep breath," the doctor says. "One more big push."

I follow her instructions and Oliver squeezes my shoulder. But it's not one more big push, as the doctor promised. And it's not two or three or four. During the eighth excruciatingly painful push, just when I start to think that it's never going to end — that I will be in labor, my stomach contracting, my groin a hot ring of fire, until the end of days, the pressure in my abdomen suddenly lifts and I feel something flop out like a slippery fish from between my legs and into the doctor's waiting hands.

"It's a girl," she announces, holding up a squiggling spaghetti squash covered in goo, with arms and legs and a tuft of curly brown hair, like an offering.

I stare at its scrunched face in disbelief. Stunned awe. It's a moment I've conjured a million times in my head, but sometime after the third miscarriage never truly believed would materialize. It's my baby. Harrison's eyes peer back at me from her tiny head.

Our baby.

I lamely lift my tired arms, reaching for her, but a nurse whisks her away to a plastic incubator tray. I listen to her whimpers turn into full-on wails and think how unfortunate that all she seems to have inherited from me is my predilection to cry.

"Is she OK?" I say to no one in particular.

"She's perfect," the nurse responds, swaddling the baby in a white cloth rimmed with blue and red stripes. She hands the baby to Oliver, who brings her directly to me.

And just like that, I'm holding my daughter. She's tiny, I can barely feel the heft of her beneath the swaddle, but when she looks at me, my breath catches. And I'm overwhelmed by how wonderful and miraculous and unfair it all is.

I think of that banal platitude: *Love isn't supposed to hurt.* But really, if you're doing it right, love hurts all the time. I look down into my daughter's eyes and I see my husband. And my heart is so full it feels like it's going to burst and so empty it feels like I could float away into nothing.

That's love. For all the great mysteries in the world, perhaps it's the most mysterious

458

of them all.

Or maybe not the most mysterious. I think of the psychic. And the realization slams into me like a freight train.

I look up at Oliver through wide wonder and tears.

"You gave me a baby," I say.

"I gave you a baby," he repeats slowly, as if he's just now realizing it, too. Then he tilts his head, considering, the corner of his mouth turning up. "Not quite the way I was hoping to."

Laughter bursts out from deep within me. I look back down at my daughter, taking in her tiny ears and fingers and perfect wisps of eyelashes, and think how wonderful and awful it is that nothing in life happens quite the way we expect.

I'm standing at the base of the Rocky statue, peering up at the bronze metal glinting green in the afternoon sunlight. The sky is a brilliant blue, one of those rare times it actually matches the color of the crayon by the same name. People pass by in a blur.

I spot a man running up the stairs, his forehead slick with sweat, jaw clenched in effort. I don't recognize him, yet he's familiar. I know that I know him.

Then, just like that, he's next to me. Close

enough that I can almost feel the heat radiating off his skin.

"Hi," he says, slipping his hand in mine.

"Hi," I say.

And then we're in the middle of the Philadelphia museum, one scene fading into the next. One setting morphing into another in the way only dreams can do. I'm staring at a framed tattoo — three Chinese characters. My tattoo. I glance down at my wrist and see that it's no longer there. It's now in this museum. I look to the left and there's a life-size rendering of David Bowie's face looking back at me. I've seen it before.

"It's funny," the man says, still holding my hand. "The things people leave behind."

A bird squawks above and I look up.

I look back at him then. Really look at him. And I know. "Harrison," I say.

He smiles. "Dios Mia."

I am overcome with relief. And the inexplicable urge to laugh.

"Why don't you look like you?"

"I don't know. It's your dream."

"Have you seen her?"

"She's perfect."

"She is."

I stare at him. This man that isn't Harrison, but is. "I don't want to wake up."

"But you have to," he says. "She needs you."

And that's when I hear it, the birdcalls, which have now melded into faint baby cries. Harrison starts to fade away. "Wait! Don't go!" I say.

But he does.

I wake up, the baby's cries crackling loud and tinny over the monitor. I blink, long and slow, trying to straddle the gap between dream and reality. Between what I want to believe is true and what is.

Maybe the future already exists.

Maybe I will see my husband again one day.

Maybe time is a circle.

Or maybe not.

Maybe all that matters is that love is a circle. Infinite. Eternal. Present, even when the person you want to be there most is absent.

I think of Oliver. What he said when he left the hospital, right before Vivian got there.

"Mia," he started, and I cut him off before he could voice the words I saw in his eyes.

"I'll always love him," I said, quietly. "It's always been him."

"I know," he said, nodding. "But maybe one day while you're doing that, you could let me love you."

Maybe one day I will.

But not today.

I close my eyes and try to return to sleep, to the dream, to Harrison — to allow the ache in my chest to lift for the briefest of moments — but another squawk from the monitor on my nightstand reminds me that life beckons.

I slip out of bed and go to our daughter.

ACKNOWLEDGMENTS

First, a heartfelt thank-you to my readers and all of the talented bloggers, booksellers and librarians I've met over the years. Without you, I'd have to actually put on pants and get a real job. Thank you for your support and for making the world a better place.

And many thanks to the following people, without whom this book would most certainly still be a tangle of incomprehensible words hidden away on my laptop:

My extraordinary agent, Emma Sweeney, and her supportive and hardworking team, Margaret Sutherland Brown and Hannah Brattesani. Kira Watson, you have since moved on, but I'd be remiss not to thank you as well.

My editor, Kerry Donovan, for her unparalleled enthusiasm and sharp insights — and for giving me a wonderful new publishing home at Berkley.

The rest of the Berkley team, including Diana Franco, Tara O'Connor, Fareeda Bullert and Sarah Blumenstock.

Dr. David Rice, who kindly spent hours upon hours (upon hours!) explaining medical terminology and minute details of his profession.

Dr. Brent Stephens, for answering all of my very strange and personal questions, and for decades of enduring friendship.

Dr. Jane Greer, for her insights into relationship therapy and psychic dreams.

C. Noel, for sharing her knowledge of art, past lives and talking to the dead. That was a weird afternoon. And yes, the light flickered.

Any mistakes or inaccuracies regarding these professions and/or topics are mine alone.

The books *The ESP Enigma: The Scientific Case for Psychic Phenomena* by Diane Hennacy Powell, MD, and *The Mind at Night: The New Science of How and Why We Dream* by Andrea Rock, both of which filled in the gaps of my knowledge about dreams and psychic phenomena, and gave a sound scientific base to my outlandish plotline.

While writing is a solitary activity, editing and revising often takes a village. Thank you to my village, who all read various drafts of this book, often many times more than once, and all had valuable insights that helped shape it into its current form: Caley Bowman, Karma Brown, Brooke Hight, Kelly Marages, Kirsten Palladino, Amy Reichert, Renée Rosen, Jaime Sarrio and Barbara Khan, for the gas station pizza anecdote. With special thanks to Aimee Molloy and Pam Cope for their incredible writers' retreat where I finally found the threads of this story and began reweaving them together.

Thank you to my sister, Megan Oakley, who has never once yelled at me for pestering her to "Read this!" and then, "No, wait, read this one instead!"

My brother, Jason Oakley, for traveling far and wide for my book events, even if he is just there for the vodka.

My mom and dad, Kathy and Bill Oakley, for their unwavering support, but especially my mom for reading this book at least forty-seven times, and somehow maintaining the same level of enthusiasm for the material.

My grandmother, Marion Oakley; my grandparents, Jack and Penny Wyman; and the rest of my Tull, Wyman and Oakley families for their ridiculous amount of support. It's an embarrassment of riches.

Henry, Sorella, Olivia and Everett, my

four children whose creativity wildly outpaces mine and who make each day an utterly chaotic joy to live. I hope I make you at least half as proud as you make me.

And last, but never least, my eternally patient, logical, supportive, loving husband, Fred: If our life is but a dream, may we never wake up.

■ ■ ■ ■

READERS
GUIDE

YOU WERE THERE TOO
COLLEEN OAKLEY

■ ■ ■ ■

QUESTIONS FOR DISCUSSION

1. Near the beginning of the book, Mia admits she's been dreaming about a man on and off for most of her adult life. Have you ever had any recurring dreams? What do they mean to you?

2. When we meet Mia, she tells her sister, "It doesn't feel like this is where I'm supposed to be." Why do you think she feels that way?

3. Mia and Harrison suffer a third miscarriage. What does the way they handle it tell you about their relationship? Do you think they have a strong marriage?

4. When Mia runs into Oliver a second time, he offers to help her with her garden, and after spending the day with him, she realizes she feels like she's known him forever. Have you ever felt that way when

you first met somebody? What, if anything, do you think it means?

5. After Harrison misses Mia's first appointment with the fertility specialist, she thinks, "The downside of being a surgeon's wife isn't just the long hours, but that strangers' misfortunes can impact you so greatly." Do you think there are any circumstances where the demands of one partner's job should be more important than the marriage?

6. When Mia and Harrison have dinner with Caroline and Oliver, she inevitably compares Oliver with her husband. Did you note any similarities between the two men? What are the biggest differences between them?

7. Mia decides not to tell her husband right away when Oliver confesses to dreaming about her, too. Do you think it's a betrayal? Should spouses tell each other *everything,* or is it sometimes understandable to keep something to yourself?

8. Even though Harrison says he needs time, Mia continues to seek out information about IVF. Do you think she's being

too pushy, or is Harrison not being supportive enough?

9. On their mini getaway in New Jersey, Mia describes marriage as being like her television from childhood: "The connection gets loose sometimes — even to the point where you think it might not work anymore — but then something jars it and the wires slip back into place, exactly where they belong, lighting up the screen and bringing back the sound; everything working as it should." Did that strike you as an accurate description of a marriage?

10. After Mia spies Harrison with Whitney downtown, she remembers that Harrison doesn't believe in soul mates. What does "soul mate" mean to you?

11. In a drunken moment, Harrison finally reveals the burden he's been carrying for months — that he feels responsible for the death of a young patient. Why do you think he kept this from Mia?

12. When Oliver shows up at Mia's house, bewildered at the realization that Mia was at his best friend's wedding years earlier, he repeats a Yogi Berra quote: "This is too

much of a coincidence to be a co-incidence." What do you think that means?

13. What qualities do you think Mia needed in a partner? Who do you think was a better match for her?

14. After talking to Raya, Mia drives back to Hope Springs and makes her decision about who she wants to be with. Were you surprised by her choice?

15. Have you ever had a dream that came true before? Do you believe people can truly dream about the future?

16. At the end, when Oliver stops by Mia's to see how she's doing, she wonders why Oliver was in her life, and that "maybe Harrison was right — maybe there's no rhyme or reason to it all." Why do you think people come into our lives? Do you think it's all haphazard or is there a greater design for the people we meet?

ABOUT THE AUTHOR

Colleen Oakley is the author of two previous novels, *Close Enough to Touch* and *Before I Go,* which were named best books by *People, Us Weekly, Library Journal* and *Real Simple,* and both were long-listed for the Southern Book Prize. Oakley is also a former senior editor of *Marie Claire* and editor in chief of *Women's Health & Fitness.* Her articles, essays and interviews have been featured in the *New York Times, Ladies' Home Journal, Marie Claire, Women's Health, Redbook, Parade* and *Martha Stewart Weddings.* She lives in Georgia with her husband, four kids and the world's biggest lapdog.

CONNECT ONLINE
colleenoakley.com
facebook.com/writercolleenoakley
twitter.com/OakleyColleen
instagram.com/writercolleenoakley